preservation

THE WALSH FAMILY

KATE CANTERBARY

VESPER PRESS

about preservation

Riley Walsh doesn't want a fake girlfriend but he needs one.

It's the only thing he can do to deal with an ex who doesn't believe it's over and years of pining for the most off-limits woman in his world—his sister-in-law.

Alexandra Emmerling can't catch a break.

She's left picking up the pieces of her ex's humiliating lies and manipulations, rendering her reputation in her ultra-competitive surgical residency program seems beyond repair.

A simple arrangement.

Two months. Four dates. Five at the most. But possibly six. Definitely no more than six. Only the appearance of a romantic relationship is required. No other *benefits* involved in this agreement.

One weekend to unravel the entire plan.

After waking up in bed together—very naked, very hungover—the terms and conditions of their arrangement no longer apply. But that doesn't mean they're finished with each other.

CW: *History of emotional and physical abuse by a parent (not on-page); parent illness; parent loss; main character experiences with sexism at work.*

Editing provided by Julia Ganis of JuliaEdits. www.juliaedits.com

Proofreading provided by Marla Esposito of Proofing Style. www.proofingstyle.com

To second choices.
They wouldn't exist if the first had been meant to be.

prologue

RISD.
Pronounced riz-dee.

One

RILEY

"RILEY, PLEASE," she begged, her legs hooked around my waist and her lips on my neck. "I *need* you."

If there were more satisfying words to hear from my brother's wife while her bare body was beneath mine, I didn't know them.

"Anything," I whispered, the words muffled as I spoke straight to the glory that was her breasts. "Anything, I'll give it to you."

"I just *want* you," she said. Her hands fisted in my hair as I thrust into her, and the primitive, seed-spreading part of my brain kicked into gear. I wanted to fuck her until she was filled with proof of my possession, and then fuck her again for good measure.

This woman is mine. Mine.

That was the only thought in my head, the only word on my lips as I wrapped my arm around her lower back. I needed her closer, as close as possible until there was nothing we didn't share. I was holding on tight, my finger-tips pressing into the tender skin at her hip without mercy. I wanted to leave her with a memory of me, a mark that would take days to fade, something to remind her that she belonged to me.

Mine, mine, mine.

This night knew neither masterful technique nor finesse. There'd been no seduction, no foreplay, nothing more than trembling need. Every touch was desperate, packed with the knowledge that our time was limited. But it was always like this—stolen moments, secret rendezvous, nights that no one else knew about.

And it was indefensibly wrong.

"Lauren," I groaned, that single word rolling up everything I wanted her to know right now. That I adored her, that I craved her, that I'd do *anything* for her. That I'd forgotten how to function without her at the center of my solar system.

But there was no time for words. Not tonight, not ever. We had right now, and it wasn't to be squandered. It had been this way for months—covert meet ups where the fire between us turned explosive—and there was no end in sight. I hated it. Fucking *hated* it. I loved it, too. She was mine, even if we were the only two who held that truth.

Lauren came with a shudder and a scream, and then whispered, "It should've been you. I should've chosen you. I love you more than—"

She didn't need to finish that sentence. I didn't let her, instead capturing her lips. Regardless of the lengths that making time together demanded, my brother wasn't far. It never escaped my consciousness that she slipped her wedding rings into her purse before shedding her clothes, or switched off her phone—and her husband's endless stream of text messages—around me. I required no reminder that her affections were divided between me and Matt, or that he was the one she'd fall asleep with tonight and tomorrow and all the nights after that unless something changed.

And what could possibly change? I couldn't force my siblings to choose sides and tear my family apart by stealing my brother's wife out from underneath him. I couldn't force Lauren to leave Matt and lose the friendships she'd formed with my sisters. I couldn't do anything but love her while I had her, and thank the stars that I got that much.

Unless there was some kind of accident.

"I know you love me," I said, angling her body to take me deeper.

Every time she opened herself to me like this, I wondered whether he gave her as much as I did.

He doesn't.

Whether he knew how to make her purr and beg and shake.

He can't.

Whether he could possibly love her as much as I did.

He couldn't.

With both hands locked around her hips, I stared at the place where we were joined. She was beautiful, all dusky pink and bare, and the only thing better than burying myself inside her was licking her to another orgasm afterward. Her flesh clamped down around me, drawing me in and demanding more, and my cock was slick with her arousal.

For me.

"I love you m-m-more than anything," I said, the words stuttering out in a panting rush as the knots holding my orgasm in place unfurled. I hooked her knees over my shoulders and thrust with abandon, concerned only with drowning her in my release. I wanted to give her everything inside me, every last drop.

I wanted an *accident* all our own. It was really fucking wrong—all of this was wrong—but it was the only way I could find a path to right. That, or pushing my brother into oncoming traffic. I was a pond-scum-sucking bastard but I wasn't ready to do that.

"I have to get home. I can't stay," she whispered. Her fingers brushed over my temples and down the back of my neck, but she made no move to leave.

"A few more minutes," I murmured, nuzzling the crook of her shoulder. "You always smell so good here. Like birthday cakes."

"It's cocoa butter," she said, laughing.

I nodded and pressed a kiss to her birthday cake skin. "Promise me this isn't the last time," I said. I was growing tired, my body loose and eyelids too heavy to lift. "Please, Lauren."

She didn't respond. She never did. She never committed to more than these moments because we couldn't know what waited for us on the other side. But I always asked.

The weight of my exhaustion got the better of me, but before I drifted off a shiver rattled through my bones. I bolted up, and found myself drenched in an icy sweat and panting like I'd been running four-minute miles.

I was cold, breathless, and alone. Just as I'd been since falling asleep after watching the Red Sox clean some Los Angeles clocks at Dodger Stadium.

My loneliest days on this planet always followed those dreams. Or were they nightmares? I didn't know.

But those fleeting, diaphanous moments were nothing more than the collusion of my wants and needs and unconscious mind. I was allowed to touch and taste everything I'd been craving, only to wake up and discover none of it was real.

I flopped onto my back and blinked up at the same bricks-and-beams ceiling I'd been staring at for the past four years. Light was brightening the centuries-old bricks, and I turned my head in the direction of the dawn. Summer sunrises were always preferable to acknowledging guilt-ridden erections.

It wasn't like I could minister to my cock's needs, not when fucking my sister-in-law was this morning's reason to rise. Oh, I'd indulged in plenty of Lauren-inspired self-love sessions over the years. *Plenty*. But the trouble was that it only made this situation worse. It left me feeling empty and traitorous, and wondering whether love was an experience I was to admire from a short distance, and never, ever keep past sunrise. I couldn't deal with that kind of shambles this morning.

So I didn't jerk it, not even when my brain was crowded with thoughts of a woman who would never be mine. Instead, I counted the bricks on the ceiling—again—and thought about wood rot. Dry, destructive wood rot.

Not unlike me, that shit could cause some real problems.

THE SEVEN THIRTY Monday morning meeting was as much a part of Walsh Associates—my family's third-generation sustainable preservation architecture firm—as bricks and cobblestones. It was the one time when we crowded into one place and ran through our current and upcoming projects, and everything else worthy of discussion. Although we lived in the same town and shared a Beacon Hill office, we often moved past each other like ships in the night.

Despite the fact a very large portion of me wanted to challenge my brother to a duel for his wife's affections, my family was everything to me. These people were all that I had in this world, and I didn't know where I'd go or who I'd be without them.

Shannon had bailed me out of several regrettable situations over the years, and paved the way for me to attend Rhode Island School of Design instead of Cornell like my brothers.

Erin, the baby of the family and the only one who didn't

work at the firm, had schooled me in the ways of not giving a fuck—while actually giving *all* the fucks—from an early age.

Sam had invited me to share the restored firehouse he called home after I'd finished grad school, and he'd trained me on how to drink and dress like a grown-ass adult. He thought he'd educated me on the ways of women, and though that couldn't be further from the truth, I let him keep on believing.

Patrick had taught me, in his grouchy, impatient way, that this work was about families, those before us and those yet to come, and it was always worth taking seriously.

And Matt, he was the best of them all. While I was fantasizing about Lauren, he was coaching me through my first years at the firm and making up for everything I should've learned in school. I was kind enough to repay him with a running mental montage of his wife in every perverted position I could imagine.

So I climbed the stone staircase to our office's attic conference room steeped in shame that I wanted someone who didn't belong to me and resentment that my world was all rocks and hard places.

"Oh my god," Shannon said, groaning when I set the foil-wrapped tacos beside her laptop. "*Thank you.*"

She was pregnant with baby number two and liable to turn into a fire-breathing honey badger when hungry. It was still amusing that my older sister, the most notoriously picky eater in North America, could consume mass quantities of nameless food truck tacos but only while growing another human.

"No sweat," I said. It was easier to bring her breakfast

than have mine ripped from my hands. I'd learned my lesson after she'd commandeered my burrito when she'd been pregnant with Abby.

I dropped into my seat, careful not to bump her chair or jostle her in the process. Jostling was a known instigator of her morning sickness, and her morning sickness was a known instigator of my sympathetic vomiting. Shannon and I had cleared this room on more than a few occasions. For everyone involved, caution was necessary.

It was cozy up here these days. I could still remember when adding a fifth chair—four years ago, after I'd finished school and joined the firm—required a major reorganization of the world according to Walsh Associates. But then Patrick took on Andy Asani as his apprentice. Another ripple, another chair. Now she was his fiancée. Tom, Shannon's deputy in all things finance and management, had found his way into the Monday morning meeting about a year ago. We were gradually outgrowing this attic conference room.

"It's quiet this morning," Matt said. "I didn't realize how much noise three summer interns generated."

He shook his iced coffee, and it annoyed the fuck right out of me. I wanted to knock the cup out of his hand. Just to *take* something—however insignificant—of his.

I considered it for a moment, and then hated myself for giving life to the thought. What kind of bastard did that?

Oh, yeah. This kind. I was *that* kind of bastard.

Patrick dropped his elbows on the table and rubbed his brows. "I never want to see another intern as long as I live," he said. "Children are not allowed in this office ever again."

"Okay, let me update the list," Andy murmured, flipping open her notebook. "Is it children in general, or only extensively vetted interns whom you consider children?"

A lot of people gave my oldest brother shit. He deserved it. But no one gave it with Andy's unflinching ease. It was beautiful.

"Asani," Patrick warned. "Not in the mood."

"It's worth noting that you did not have an intern with you this summer as you've been objecting to this venture for eleven months," she continued. She was right about that. Shannon was always scouting new talent, and had cooked up a plan to bring on interns for the summer. To say the experiment had met with mixed results would be too generous. "Your aggravation is tangential at best, Patrick."

"Enough with that bullshit. We're getting more interns, and you'll just need to deal," Shannon said as she unwrapped her tacos. She glanced at me. "Hot sauce?"

I dug in my messenger bag for the small bottle of sriracha I kept handy. "Here you go, boss," I said, passing it to her.

Her taste for spice was new with this pregnancy, but I wasn't complaining. As long as she wasn't eating yogurt next to me, I'd share all of my snacks with her. I fucking detested yogurt. I mean, what exactly was that shit?

"While I don't often agree with Patrick, I do think we should steer clear of undergrad interns in the future," Sam said. "It was a fascinating endeavor, although I would've appreciated someone a little less green."

Matt rapped his knuckles on the tabletop and pointed at Sam. "Precisely," he said. I was still a bastard, and as such, required great restraint to eat my breakfast burrito without glowering at my brother. "They all learned a lot, but they weren't ready for this level of practical application. For purely selfish reasons, I'd rather see a more advanced pool and I don't have an issue with spending more to acquire one."

Shannon plucked cilantro from her taco—not cured of the picky eating in full—and shot a glance at me. "You haven't weighed in," she said.

I laughed into my burrito. That I'd been gifted an intern for the past ten weeks was equal parts awesome and odd. Awesome because I had someone to organize everything in my office, unjam the printer, and run out for coffee whenever I needed a refill. And she baked cookies. Odd because I couldn't help thinking it was a mistake to give me an intern. Most days, I was certain that I didn't know enough about what I was doing to explain any of it to anyone else.

"Bergman was, uh," I started, shrugging. "She was fine. Asked good questions. Did some…useful stuff." I reached for the sriracha. I didn't want to criticize my intern for not knowing what was going on around her when I rarely knew what was going on. "Although Sam has valid points."

"Bergman left a DVD in the laptop we issued her," Tom said. "I wiped the devices on Saturday morning and came across it then."

"Why were you working Saturday morning?" Shannon asked him. "Balance. We've talked about it."

"Torsion," Matt added. If anyone else had registered his wonky engineering quip, it didn't show.

"I wasn't going to be able to enjoy the weekend until I got it done," he replied with a hint of defensiveness. "Not that it matters but it was porn. The DVD. In Bergman's laptop. She left porn in her laptop."

"Didn't expect *that*," Shannon said.

"All right. I'm done," Patrick said. He pointed at Andy. "Put that on your goddamn list. We're finished with interns. All of them."

"People still watch porn on DVD?" I asked. "Why? Why would you do that when the internet exists?"

"What kind?" Shannon asked. She wiggled her fingers at me for the sriracha. This baby *really* liked the heat. Pre-pregnancy, my sister was known to complain about gingersnaps being too spicy.

"There was planning involved," Sam murmured. "DVD porn is only necessary when it's a set piece. She was probably watching it with Edwards or Pierson. Or both. Maybe they had an intern threesome thing going on. With visual aids."

"You're the worst," Shannon said to him. "The actual worst."

"Let's not shame her," Patrick said. "We have enough issues in the water this morning, and we don't need her suing us for…whatever we're doing right now. She's probably going to die of embarrassment when she realizes it."

"Or not," Shannon replied. "Women don't have to be embarrassed by enjoying sex."

"She probably left it for you to find, RISD," Matt said, pointing that goddamn iced coffee at me. I took no issue with my alma mater nickname, but he couldn't breathe without drawing my ire this morning. "She had a thing for you."

"Erroneous," I said, sparing him a brief glance. I couldn't look at him without seeing his wife naked. Or, what I imagined her to look like without the constraints of clothing.

"Oh, come on," Matt continued. "You couldn't have missed it."

I shook my head, avoiding his gaze.

"We do have an agenda," Patrick said. "This discussion is not on it."

Shannon dropped her hand on Patrick's forearm. "Intern threesomes and porn isn't on our agenda, no," she said. "But *that*"—she gestured to something on his laptop screen—"is."

"Yes, but it's the seventh item on my list," he argued. "We can visit it after hitting one through six."

Shannon held up her hands and shook her head. "It's your meeting, Optimus."

"You make it sound like he needs the reminder," Sam muttered.

"First item on the agenda," Patrick started, "is current properties. Matt, let's talk about Mount Vernon and why the fuck it's exceeding cost projections."

Patrick loved his lists. Order, structure, precision. His desk looked like a whirling dervish lived there, but he held tight to his systems everywhere else. I didn't know whether it was a first-born thing or a CEO thing, but it was certainly a Patrick thing.

"I told you those projections were weak," Shannon said around a taco. "There's no way to marry twin brownstones and restore twenty thousand square feet without spending some money. If we do this right, we're going to make a fuck-ton more than we'll spend."

Patrick shifted in his seat to stare at her and his eyes cut to her screen pointedly. It was his not-so-subtle way of telling her to keep her dissent contained to their private chat. That they messaged throughout the meeting was the worst-kept secret at this table, especially now that we were packed in like the Red Line at rush hour. The only one who'd failed to notice was Sam, and I could forgive him that because he always sat directly opposite Shannon.

Under her breath, Shannon murmured, "You can suck my dick."

"Matt," Patrick said, still staring at Shannon, "talk to me about Mount Vernon."

I flipped open my notebook to the page with my most recent project notes. Bergman had been good for a few things, some of which being her oatmeal raisin cookies and notebook magic. She had this nifty trick where she marked the current page with a paper clip, and never had to shuffle through to figure out where she'd left off. It was amazing.

I was managing five properties right now, the most I'd ever had on the board at once. Berkeley, Commonwealth, Joy, Marlborough, Pinckney. It was a handful, and one I was sweating hard. I wanted to get this right, and I wanted to do it without anyone stepping in to lend a hand. It wasn't that I didn't appreciate their help—I'd really fucking needed it— but I also wanted to prove I could hold my own.

I hadn't always known—or embraced—my place in the family business, but now…now I got it. I understood how my style and vision could exist alongside those of my brothers. I didn't have to spend my days struggling to fill their molds, not when I could make my own.

But none of that knowledge erased the anxious tremors that took up residence in my chest when I knew I was due to present on my work. Even surrounded by my siblings, I had to plan everything I intended to say and listen to those words in my head twice before speaking. It was the only way to keep from stuttering or stumbling over my words.

It was easier to speak when it didn't seem like anyone was listening to what I had to say.

"Riley," Patrick said, his focus trained on his screen as he typed the last of his notes on Matt's properties. "What the hell is going on with Marlborough Street? It was supposed to be down to punch list items last week."

The only problem with planning my words was that Patrick's questions never followed the order I'd mentally constructed. "Uh, yeah, about that," I said. "During the last walk-through, the client requested we convert one of the garage basement closets to a half bath."

"Which was on your original design," he said. "Off the mudroom."

"Correct," I replied. "But they didn't want the expense of rerouting the plumbing."

"And now they do?" he asked.

"Evidently," I said.

"That shouldn't take long," he started. "You should be—"

"Down to punch list items later this week," I interrupted. "Yeah. That's why I'm staying in the city. To get it wrapped up."

That was mostly true.

"Is it not possible for us to agree on anything?" Shannon asked. "Is it really that difficult? We close down for two weeks over the holidays and two weeks in the summer. That shit is no secret. What *is* a mystery is why we can't seem to enforce vacations."

"Look," Patrick started, gesturing toward me. "That kind of work doesn't require a close eye."

"No," I conceded. "But while that's underway, I can work on the punch list. If I wrap it up early, I'll join you guys on the Cape." I nodded at Shannon.

That was mostly false.

The last thing I was going to do was crash the coupled-up summer getaway. No, I didn't need to spend two weeks with Patrick and Andy, Matt and Lauren, and Sam, his wife Tiel, and their infant son. Getting slapped in the face with coupledom's dick wasn't my idea of a good time.

"Or Montauk," Shannon added. "Will's business partner will be there. They tell all manner of Navy SEAL stories after a few drinks. That's always entertaining."

Patrick frowned. "You could always check in with your trades later this week, and take off next week. You need a break, Riley."

I nodded. "I'll keep that in mind and see how it goes," I said easily, hoping my tone turned down the volume on the no-vacation outrage.

They didn't know that it *was* a vacation, and one I needed more than they could ever understand. For me, a week at the beach with my siblings wasn't *getting away from it all*. Not when I'd spend the entire time clawing the scowl from my face as Matt and Lauren loved all over each other.

"Moving on," Patrick said.

Amen to that.

Talk of our summer break was abandoned as he dove into my other projects. He spoke quickly—typed faster—and kept one eye glued to the clock as he barked questions. Soon he was shifting gears to Sam and Andy's work, and then transitioned to Tom and Shannon's updates on properties they were considering for investment purposes.

"All right," Patrick said with a heavy exhale. "Shannon. Number seven."

She reached for her water, nodding. "RISD Weekend is coming up," she said, smiling at me. "I want you to go and find some interns."

"Oh my fucking god," Patrick murmured.

"I can't go to RISD Weekend," I replied automatically.

"Yes, you can," Shannon replied.

"Was I somehow unclear about my stance on interns?" Patrick asked.

"You're passing on a trip to Rhode Island?" Matt asked, shaking the ice in that motherfucking coffee cup again. "Are you feeling okay?"

"I'm fine," I snapped. "But I can't go to RISD Weekend. Send someone else if you're determined to snare some interns."

The Rhode Island School of Design wasn't like most colleges and universities. Our mascot was a scrotum—no lie. Marijuana appreciation was a general education requirement —slight exaggeration. *Slight.* Rather than a traditional home-coming weekend loaded up with football and parties, we had a left-of-center iteration: part gallery opening, part art critique symposium, part street fair. It was weird and different to the point of distraction, but I loved everything about it.

I just couldn't go.

"Why the hell not?" Shannon asked.

"Is this about the cat?" Sam asked.

"A cat?" Andy asked.

"A woman," Sam explained. "But she's more of—uh—"

"An outdoor cat," I supplied.

As if I didn't have enough problems with dreaming about knocking up my sister-in-law, I had numerous stream-of-consciousness emails and texts from my college girlfriend. Even a few babbling brook voicemails. She was like that, always ejecting every single thought in her mind without concern for logic or structure. Somehow it worked for her.

"Oh," Patrick said with a knowing groan. "Her."

"Right," Sam said, adjusting his cuffs. "If she's going to be there, you're in trouble. You just don't know how to say no to her. You can't face that chick without protection." He brushed a hand down his tie. "And I don't mean condoms."

"It's not that I can't say no to her," I protested but there was no conviction behind it. I was capable of saying no. She wasn't capable of comprehending the word.

"How have I never heard about the outdoor cat woman?" Andy asked. She leaned forward to catch Tom's eye. "Do you know?"

He smirked. "I know all about Miss Kacie-call-me-Dorrance Strawbridge and her"—he cleared his throat—"antics."

Antics. That was the right term for it.

Dorrance's favorite expression was "on the prowl." She was always *prowling* for something. Parties—raves when we were in college. Mind-altering substances—it used to be Adderall and MDMA, but now her tastes ran to weed and Xanax. Inspiration—for art and life and food and literally everything. Podcasts. Sex. Frozen yogurt. Music. More sex. Prowl, prowl, prowl. All day, all night. That was how she came to be known as an outdoor cat. It wasn't my best work as it pertained to nicknames but it spread like ironic humor at art school—quickly.

"I thought she didn't go to RISD Weekend, or any of the alumni events," Shannon said.

I held up my hands. "She's going to this one," I said.

Dorrance called New York home now. She was living in a Tribeca loft and working at a studio space-slash-second home in Brooklyn. Both purchased by her parents. I knew that much from the email I'd opened and then promptly closed. I figured it was easy to play the part of the bohemian artist when your parents were willing to foot the bill.

She'd been a lot of fun in college, and we'd had a good time together. Some really good times. So good that I had a tramp stamp, permanently disfigured nipples, and a police record as souvenirs. Shannon had *actually* bailed me out of more than one Dorrance adventure gone bad. She'd forbidden me from seeing Dorrance again after my license had been suspended. I'd only been able to comply with that edict because Dorrance had graduated and moved to Manhattan a few weeks later. But that didn't stop Dorrance from prowling.

"Then don't go alone," Matt suggested.

"Is Miss Honey free that weekend?" I asked, the words out of my mouth before I could stop myself.

"She's *my* Miss Honey," he replied, laughing. And that was the only response. He passed it off as a joke. A little more of that *Riley's trying to steal my wife and isn't that hilarious* humor.

Yeah. It was so fucking funny.

"Lauren just hired a new second grade teacher," Matt continued. In addition to being the star of my subconscious and the most perfect woman on the planet, Lauren was the principal of an elementary school. "Audrey with the gluten-free cupcake blog. She's from around here, and moving back home after living down south for a couple of years. I think she's about your age. Recently divorced."

A grin tugged at my lips for the first time this morning. "Did Lauren hire her because she's a decent teacher, or for the cupcakes?" I asked him. Lauren had quite the sweet tooth.

He held out his hands. "A little more of one and some of the other," he said, laughing. "Can't be sure how the ratios shook out." He pointed to his mobile phone. "You want me to set something up? I'm sure she'd love to introduce you."

"No," I said, snatching the sriracha back from Shannon. "That won't be necessary."

"Magnolia would go with you," Sam added, referring to my favorite landscape architect. "I've seen her chase away raccoons and actual feral cats. She can handle Dorrance."

"Yes," Shannon said, slapping her palm on the table for emphasis. "Do that. She'll keep you in line."

"She does have a life and business," I said. "Accompanying me to Providence might not be on her list of priorities, you know."

"That's fair. But we do have some time until RISD Weekend," Shannon said. She drummed her fingertips on the tabletop. "Enough for you to convince Magnolia or Audrey to go with you." She shrugged and pointed her pen to the side. "Or Tom."

He glanced at me. "Would we be sharing a bed?"

"Without a doubt, sugar." I studied him for a beat. "But you look like a cover hog."

"I am," he replied, a teasing smirk on his lips. "Among other things."

I shook my head. "Another time, Mr. Esbeck," I said, winking.

"Then Magnolia or Audrey," Shannon said, waving away the flirty banter. "I'll reserve two rooms for you, and you'll come back with some interesting résumés. Deal?"

I doused the last chunk of my burrito in sauce and bobbed my head. "Sure," I said, still holding tight to the sriracha bottle. "What's the worst thing that could happen?"

"Are we speaking statistically?" Matt asked. "If so, there's obviously—"

"Shut the fuck up about your fucking statistics, Matthew." I pointed the bottle in his direction, *this close* to squeezing hard enough to paint his starched white dress shirt in puréed pepper.

"Right," Patrick said, running a hand over his jaw. "And this is where we adjourn."

Three

RILEY

IT WAS a great day for baseball and beer. But then again, my threshold for greatness was low. I didn't require much from the teams or the beverages, and the weather was never a major factor. All I needed was a game on the field and a drink in my hand, and it was good.

But today was one of the best days. It was sunny without being sweltering, the Red Sox were in top form, the majority of my family had vacated the city, and I was balancing four frigid beers as I trundled down the ballpark steps. We were seated behind home plate, in season ticket seats Magnolia's aunt had held for more than forty *years* before passing them to her niece and nephews. One of the best perks of hanging out with Magnolia Santillian—aside from her being a legitimately good friend—was reliable access to local sporting events.

"Take one," I ordered when I reached our row, the diamond of plastic cups pinched between my fingers.

Certain things could only be enjoyed to their fullest in certain situations: sandwiches on the beach, popcorn at the movies, and beer at the ballpark. For this moment, everything was right in my world. Life was easy. Or it would be easy until I had to ask my friend whether she was willing to spend a weekend babysitting me in Rhode Island. Maybe scare off a hyper hipster trust fund baby, too.

She relieved me of two cups but shot an arched eyebrow at my shorts. "Are you open for business or pleasure?" she asked.

I glanced down and found my fly unzipped. That damn thing. It was always getting away from me.

"For you, baby," I started, "I can pull off both." Setting the remaining beers on the ground, I handled my business with an apologetic wink to the family behind us.

Magnolia—I called her Gigi, a perversion of her nickname around the Walsh Associates offices, Roof Garden Girl, or RGG—snorted out a laugh. "That would require you seeing me as a woman, don't you think?"

With my drinks in hand, I wedged in beside her and surveyed the field. There was a sticky situation brewing on third base, but it was only the bottom of the second. There'd be time to recover before this game was finished, presuming the shortstop found some speed. I dropped my arm to the back of her seat and squeezed her shoulder.

"I know you're a woman," I said, sipping my beer. "You're a woman just like my sisters are women."

"Yep, and you're a man, just like my brothers are men," she said, laughing. "It's funny how I have no desire to fuck any of you."

"Hilarious," I said, giving her another squeeze.

Nope, there was nothing there. We were close, me and Gigi. She worked on the majority of my properties, adding roof gardens and other sustainable landscape features, and she had a good brain for wrangling architectural snags, too. And we were intimate in the sense that I always celebrated the Feast of St. Anthony with her family, and I'd kicked the snot out of her shit-stain of an ex-boyfriend when he stole her dog, and we'd cried real tears of joy together when the Patriots pulled another Super Bowl victory out of the fire.

But that was where it ended. There was nothing amorous, no sexual tension, no sparks. With almost three years of working and playing together under our belts, we were living proof that men and women could be friends without getting naked.

"Hey," I said, tapping my cup against hers in an overdue toast. Better late than never was my philosophy. "Want to come to Providence with me for a weekend in October?"

"All *right*," she called, clapping as the catcher tagged out that problem from third base. She glanced at me. "What are we doing in Providence?"

"What aren't we doing?" I asked, holding open my arms. "There are now *two* artisan donut shops, a restaurant dedicated entirely to sausage, and the PawSox. What more could you want?"

She shook her head, laughing. "You know I'm no fan of minor league ball," she said, gesturing to the field. "It's fun and all, but why would I choose that when I could have this?" She shook her head again. "And I gave up donuts for Lent."

I shot her an unimpressed frown. "Easter was almost five months ago," I said. "You're relieved of your sacrificial bonds."

"I'm getting a jumpstart on next year," she said, but then her eyes narrowed and the shits-and-giggles portion of this conversation was winding down. "Really. What's happening in Providence?"

I tipped back my beer and drank for a few moments before replying. "It's RISD's form of homecoming weekend," I said. "I've been tasked with scouting a new crop of interns."

Gigi snorted again. "You guys like the beatings, don't you?" she asked. She'd met all our summer interns. She knew we'd had a rough run of it.

"Something like that," I murmured. "So. Come with?"

She pulled at the frayed hem of her jean shorts. "Why do you need an accomplice for this crime? Aren't you the king of Rhode Island? Don't you have royal subjects awaiting your return?"

I offered a vague grunt of disagreement. I'd been known to wax ecstatic about the Ocean State, but that was merely a product of living there for eight years and enjoying the fuck out of it. I'd taken the long way through college, and for a period of time seriously considered dumping it all for a career in bartending. And why not? Bartending was awesome. The hours were good, the people were amusing, and the work was fun.

But then, after ducking out of a year of grad school to pour drinks, I found that I was bored. I missed being in the business that was as much a part of my family as yelling unnecessarily, struggling to articulate emotions without sprinkling on some insults, and solving problems with whiskey. And I missed the art.

Most people didn't see architecture as art, not in the way that painting and sculpture and symphonies were art. But that was what it was for me. I didn't see it as precise systems or structures the way my brothers did. The discipline and mathematics of it all were secondary to me because architecture was art that you lived in, and I fucking loved it in my wonky way.

I studied the field for several minutes, watching some weak pitches and antsy runners on base while I sipped my beer. "Are we betting on this game?" I asked.

"Sure," she replied. "Loser buys afternoon coffee all week?"

"Deal," I said. "I'm taking the Sox by four runs."

"Oh, so you came with your balls today," she scoffed, tipping her chin toward the scoreboard. The home team was trailing by two runs. "I don't see them putting this one in the win column, but I won't turn down free coffee delivery."

I held out my hand to her to settle the agreement. I could count on Gigi for several things, and good-spirited wagers was one of them. I'd wound up wearing a kilt to Sam's wedding when the Sox didn't make it to the World Series a couple of seasons ago, and then cutting my so-called hipster hair and beard when the Bruins lost the Stanley Cup this past spring.

"Now start from the beginning with your Providence situation," Gigi said. "And give me the real story. Not the one you've sent through the spin cycle."

I drained one beer and moved onto the next. "My crazy ex-girlfriend is going to be at RISD Weekend," I said. "I'm trying to avoid her."

"Come on, man," she said with a groan. "The crazy ex-girlfriend shit is ridiculous. Don't be that guy."

"What guy?" I snapped, immediately annoyed. She knew I wasn't *that guy.*

"The guy who acts like it's a problem when a woman wants a relationship," she said as if it was painted across the Green Monster and I was too dim to see it for myself. "The guy who calls a woman's advances clingy and needy and annoying, but has no problem fucking her as often as he can. The one who calls an ex-girlfriend crazy because she didn't see it coming when he broke it off, and she took it hard."

Ah. I got it now. For the middle triplet flanked by two brothers, her experiences with men were alarmingly bad. It was like she just couldn't see the red flags.

"That's not the situation here, Gigi," I said evenly. "Remember when I told you about this scar?" I tapped the faded line running the length of my palm. "She's the one who insisted on blood oaths."

"*Ah ha*," she said. "That one." She sipped her beer, nodding as if my request suddenly made sense. "Right. Okay. Sorry about the sermon."

I waved her off. "It's all good," I said, and I meant it. There was no reason to stay pissed at Gigi. "What d'you say? There's a bakery on Smith Street that has some of the best zeppoles."

"That's just another form of donut, Walsh," she yelled. "My ass doesn't need donuts."

"All right, so I'll eat the donuts and you'll watch," I said. The words weren't out and she was socking me in the shoulder.

"Bastard," she murmured.

Before I could reply, she was shooting out of her seat and shouting at the umpire to get the dirt out of his eyes and make a decent call for once in his life. She peppered it with enough profanity to make the first baseman turn and stare at her, open-mouthed.

"Well done, bro," I said as she sat down.

"So listen," she started, gesturing toward me with her cup. "I'd love nothing more than a tour of Providence guided by the king himself, but I don't think that's a good idea. For us. Right now."

"Would it be a good idea at a different time?" I asked, confused. "Or was 'for us' the operative clause?"

She fidgeted—tugging at her ball cap, twisting her ponytail, shifting in her seat, crossing and then uncrossing her legs, passing her drink from hand to hand, chewing a fingernail—and waited a short, awkward eternity to respond.

Finally, after the better part of an inning had passed, she said, "I'm seeing someone."

I lifted an eyebrow. "Who?" I demanded. "Since when? From where?"

I hated to say it, but Gigi would've benefitted from an arranged marriage. Or the convent. Anything to keep her from finding the biggest scumbag in every room and falling ass-over-tea kettle in love with him. Again.

She pursed her lips and shook her head. "I don't want to get into it."

"I swear to god and John Malkovich, Gigi," I said, jabbing a finger in her direction. "If it's that jackass who took Gronk the Dog, we're going to have words. You and me, we'll have words and they won't be good ones."

"No, it's not him," she said.

Thank you, Peter, Paul, and Mary. I didn't intend to be a paternalistic son of a bitch, but really. With Magnolia, it was necessary. Someone had to do it, and her fucking brothers had this bizarre minding-their-own-business thing going on that I couldn't begin to comprehend. And she'd gone back to that dog-snatching dickhead too many times and ignored all offers of common sense when it came to bad news boys.

"But I don't think it's a good idea for me to go away for a weekend with you. Obviously"—she waved between us as a grimace crossed her face—"nothing's happening here. But things are still new with Peter, and I don't want to make him uncomfortable."

"Peter," I repeated, and my back was all the way up now. She'd obviously been seeing him for a bit, and it wasn't like she made a habit of keeping her dating activities to herself. She'd chosen to withhold that information. "And where did we meet Peter?"

She sighed and stared into her beer. "On my penthouse project," she said.

"Okay, so he's a general contractor? Trades? Designer?" I asked. She offered no response, and squinted at the field. "Architect? Are you dating my competition, Magnolia?"

"Not an architect," she said, laughing.

That only left one other possibility. "Client?"

Gigi lifted a shoulder and I let out a low whistle. The last thing Gigi needed was to hook up with a goddamn client. Sure, it wasn't scandalous or particularly unethical, but it wasn't a wise idea. If there was one life lesson I'd learned from bartending, it was that it wasn't smart to mix sex with the exchange of goods and services. It always got weird, and never in the *let's drink all the tequila and get weird* way.

And I still didn't want to be a paternalistic son of a bitch. I truly didn't. But I'd stood by while this woman wandered into the forest with wolves who didn't even bother with the sheep's clothing. Getting involved with a client—one paying major money for a penthouse roof garden—was no different.

"Before you lecture me, just know that I declined about ninety-three invitations before I accepted one," she said. "My work on his project is almost finished, too."

"Great, so he doesn't know how to take no for answer," I

said under my breath. I yanked my hat off and ran my fingers through my hair. "Fantastic."

"No, no, no," she argued. "You're reading it all wrong. He's funny and sweet, and he understood when I said I didn't date clients." She shrugged. "Okay, maybe he didn't *understand* but he backed off. Then he asked one last time, and…and I like him, Walsh. We've been out a couple of times, and I like this one. He's different. Or, different than what I'm used to."

I rubbed my forehead. "All right, Gigi," I said. "All right. But I expect to hear about it if things go sideways. No, don't wait for sideways. Tell me if things get a little strange. Even if it seems like nothing, I want to hear about it. I expect to hear in a timely manner, too. None of these *we've been out a couple of times but that seemed like superfluous information until you asked me to go away for a weekend* shenanigans."

"About that," she said, pointing to home plate as two runners blew past it, one after another. Sox were down by four. "I'll update you when you deliver my coffee. You remember how I like it, right?"

"Just wait," I said, draining the rest of my second beer. "The air's changing. This game isn't over yet."

Four

RILEY

THE TROUBLE with early afternoon games and day drinking was that I was thirty fucking years old and my body wasn't capable of sustaining twelve hours of drunkenness anymore. Yeah, I could *technically* achieve that feat but it would require two days of recuperation. I didn't have that kind of time on my hands. It wasn't like I was resentful of this universal midlife truth either. I'd partied my ass off in college, and my oats were long since sown.

But now it was five o'clock, the Sox had lost, and I was one or two beers past the point of strictly sober. I could've hit up the pubs to watch another game or the Lawn on D for some playground-for-adults fun, but I wasn't in the mood. With Gigi off meeting Penthouse Peter, I wasn't about to be the lonely, broody guy at the bar.

Lonely and broody pulled down far too much of the wrong kind of attention. Women could smell lonely and broody from fifteen miles away, and their vaginas always held the secret remedy. It was like they'd all beckon me closer and say, "Here. Here's the magical pussy elixir. It will chase off all those bad feelings right quick. Have a taste."

Believe me, I'd tried to fuck away that which ailed me. I'd taken every short, curvy blonde in Boston to bed with the halfhearted hope it would purge the Lauren lust from my system. It succeeded only in honing my skills with the "it's not you, it's me" conversation.

That, and dodging an assortment of flying objects. Shoes, purses, phones, open-handed slaps, glasses of water.

Instead of parking myself on a barstool and turning up my *leave me the fuck alone* glare, I went to work. My Pinckney Street project required some tedious masonry restoration in the cellar, and I could manage that task with the remnants of my beer buzz. No problem.

This project was the tits. It was old as fuck (built in the 1790s), tiny (nine hundred and ninety-one square feet), and in my favorite neighborhood (on the corner of Joy Street, behind the State House). As if that wasn't good enough, the Federal-style property was remarkably well-preserved. It needed only light strokes to bring it into this century and restore some of the original features.

One of those features was the old stone wall on the eastern side of the basement. It was in better condition than most of the stone walls I encountered, but needed a bit of mortar around the joints and some replacement rocks to compensate for the ones that'd gone missing over the years.

With my ear buds in place and A Tribe Called Quest streaming on my phone, I sat down with a bucket of mortar and sculpting tools. Most people would've used their fingers or trowels to apply the mortar, but I wanted it to look like it'd been there for centuries.

This method took longer, but what else was I going to do tonight? Listen to the greatest hits of Sarah McLachlan while cocooned in my nephew's baby blanket? Eat cereal in my underwear? Watch the latest from the LPGA tour? Concoct another plan to steal my brother's wife?

Okay, I'd probably do most of that. Those lady golfers had legs worth admiring.

Once I'd worked my way through ATCQ's latest album three times and had the patchwork completed, I took stock of the missing stones. I really didn't know how a goddamn rock got up and wandered off, or how someone could look at an element of the foundation and say, "Yeah, throw those out the window. We'll be fine without them."

That left me on the path of cannibalism. I poked around the dark edges of the cellar until I spotted a few rocks butting up against the ceiling at the top corner. The joists had been cut to accommodate them, even though they weren't serving any structural purpose up there. That was the way of old homes. They weren't built to precise, manufactured specifications, but the natural contours of the readily available materials.

With an awl and mallet in hand, I climbed a ladder and started chipping away at the mortar holding the stone in place. My back was flat against the ceiling as I balanced as best I could with tools in both hands, but that position fucked me right in the ass.

I yelped and cried out as a nail punctured the skin on my lower back, invoking the names of god and Jay-Z and everyone else who deserved to be called out over this disaster, but I didn't move for a second. Moving required getting off the spike of Satan.

"Why the fuck was that necessary?" I yelled at the cool, empty room. "I thought we were motherfucking friends. I was restoring your foundation, not selling you off for salvage, and this is how you repay me? Stabbing me in the fucking spine?" With a hand braced in front of me, I eased away while skin tore and tears burned in my eyes. "Just for that, I'm gonna paint your front door hot pink, you fucker. You take your pound of flesh, and I take mine."

I set the stone down—I wasn't dropping that thing after it cost me my spleen—and covered the bucket of mortar before touching my fingers to the wound.

"Sarah McLachlan and lady golfers," I said, shuddering at the sight of blood on my hand. "They never would've done this to me."

THERE WAS ONLY one place to go when blood was gushing out of my back and it felt like my internal organs were shutting down: Nick and Erin's place in Cambridge.

Come on. Why would I bother with a busy emergency room when my brother-in-law was a surgeon?

I would not. Also, I fucking hated hospitals. Avoided them the way most people avoided venomous snakes and clowns. I'd sooner die of gangrene from a centuries-old rusty nail than drag my ass to a hospital. And my sister and her husband still owed me a few favors for keeping the lid on that secret marriage of theirs.

The uphill trek from the Pinckney property to the Walsh Associates office—where my SUV was parked—was short, but walking there in a blood-soaked shirt certainly raised some eyebrows. There were a few "Sir, are you all *right*?" and "Hey man, I think you're bleeding" moments but I tipped my hat to those Good Samaritans and kept moving.

A long-forgotten beach towel saved me from staining the leather seat, but it was teeth-clenching will that saved me from screaming in pain as every bump on the Harvard Bridge rattled my body. That wasn't even the most efficient route to their house, but fuck me if I could manage driving around the TD Garden or Museum of Science without mowing down some pedestrians in the process.

I didn't bother knocking when I reached their front door. Nope, no time for that shit. I barreled—or stumbled, same difference—right in with the towel wrapped around my torso and the shredded remains of my t-shirt in hand.

"Nicholas," I yelled down the hallway. "I require your services."

Erin came around the corner, wiping her hands on a checkered blue dishtowel. "What in the hell happened to you, kid?" Keeping an eye on me, she pivoted and called, "You might want to come out here, Nick."

"I've got my hands in carne asada, darlin'," he yelled back. "What do you need?"

I gestured to the floor. "Should I stay here and bleed, or can I go into the kitchen?" I asked. "I'm woozy, Erin. Can't you let a man sit down before he drops dead?"

She waved me forward. "I don't understand your life at all," she murmured.

I followed her into the bright, open kitchen at the back of the house. I'd designed this space and the adjoining dining room, and always felt a pulse of satisfaction when seeing it used as I'd intended. I wasn't one to dictate how people lived, but it made my brain itchy when their interactions with the room missed the entire point of the design. That pulse was quickly followed by lightheadedness, and I steadied myself with a bloodstained hand on Erin's shoulder.

Nick looked up from the butcher block and his easy smile immediately fell into a serious line. He nudged the faucet on with his forearms and started washing his hands as he tipped his chin toward me. "What's the situation here?"

I looked around, taking in the plates and utensils stacked on the farmhouse table, and mason jars filled with flowers. "You're making carne asada? Is that rice on the stove? Are you guys having people over? Am I crashing?" I asked.

"Buddy, you've left a trail of blood from the front door and have yet to offer an explanation," Erin said. "Let's talk about dinner later. What the hell happened?"

She propelled me toward a seat at the island and immediately unwrapped the towel. I reached into my pocket while she hissed at the carnage.

"This fucker is to blame," I said, slapping the blacksmith-forged nail on the countertop. If I hadn't been so pissed about this, I would've admired the craftsmanship. "It stabbed me because I was trying to take a stone."

Nick nodded toward Erin. "Would you grab the kit out of my car?"

She murmured in agreement and marched out of the kitchen. Nick came around the island with that stoic, professional expression in place. I felt his fingers on my back and flank, and gave into the desire to put my head down on the cool marble. I needed a minute. Just a minute before I turned to complete shambles.

There weren't too many things that I truly hated but blood was on that list. Specifically, large volumes of blood spilling out of bodies. No psychoanalysis was needed to find the origins, either. It was a straight shot back to my childhood. The one vivid memory I had of my mother was from the day she bled to death.

And where else could you find large volumes of blood spilling out of bodies? Hospitals.

"I was gonna patch it up with some duct tape but it wouldn't stop fucking bleeding," I said, my words muffled. "Do you have some doctor grade of duct tape? Or medical super glue?"

"Duct tape really isn't one of our options. Here's what we're going to do," Nick said after a thorough inspection. "You need thirty or so sutures and a tetanus shot. I'll take you over to the—"

"Nope," I interrupted, sitting up quickly. Too quickly. Everything was fuzzy, even my ears. "Don't say it. You stitched up Patrick after that thing with the nail gun."

"That was *two* sutures, and they were in his *finger*," Nick argued. He dropped his hand to the back of my head and guided me to the countertop. "And that gun wasn't shooting eight centimeter nails from"—he picked up the square black spike—"1920?"

"1790, son," I corrected.

"Holy shit," he said. His gaze zipped to the nail. "That's like American Revolution era." He shifted to study the wound again, and then blew out a long breath. "Listen. I'll patch this up, but I'd rather do it in the ER. I don't have the best tools here."

"It's good to want, Nicholas," I grumbled. "You've accomplished more in worse settings than this."

That much was true. Nick had spent months in Africa and Central America on tours with Doctors Without Borders. He could handle a kitchen stitch-up, even if I was half convinced that I was meeting my death any minute now.

"Yeah, you know that medicine isn't a parlor trick, right?" he asked. "Just because I can perform a craniotomy in a tent doesn't mean it's my go-to approach."

A door shut on the other side of the house, and I heard footsteps approaching. In my sideways vision, I saw Erin carrying a red backpack.

"Are we going to get the real story about this injury?" she asked. "Or is this going down with the rest of Batman's secrets?"

I kept my cheek on the countertop while Nick unzipped the bag and laid out his supplies. "I was working on the masonry at my Pinckney Street project—"

"You were *working*?" she interrupted. "It's Saturday night. Why aren't you out with Magnolia? Better yet, why are you even in the city this weekend? You should be at the beach with everyone else."

"Okay, so you don't want to hear the story," I said.

"Darlin', could you handle the meat?" Nick asked as he snapped on a pair of gloves.

"You know I can," she replied. I snickered at that but I wasn't going any further. I couldn't step up for a round of dick jokes with my sister and the resident penis in her life. Too squicky. "Get back to the story, and then explain why you're not at the beach."

"I'm going to start by cleaning the wound," Nick said, his tone calm and doctorly. Like that was supposed to make me feel better. He was a good friend, one of the best, but I hated the doctor stuff. I didn't like hearing about it, seeing it, or even thinking about it. The worst experiences of my life had occurred in hospitals, and I couldn't think of those events without an icy finger of foreboding dragging along my spine.

"Anyway," I started, "I was at my Pinckney Street project. I was shoring up the masonry in the basement, but then one thing led to another and this nail stabbed the shit out of me."

"Three inches higher and a little to the left, and it would've stabbed the shit out of your kidney," Nick said under his breath.

"Good thing you've got two," Erin said. "And the beach?"

"I couldn't. I just couldn't." I blew out a pathetic breath and knocked my head against the countertop, and she nodded.

"Okay. I get it," she said.

And she did. She got it, all of it. Erin and Nick were the only two people on this planet who knew about my affections for Lauren. They'd kept me from objecting during the wedding, and for the past few years steadied me whenever it seemed that I was about to do something unforgiveable. They allowed me to vent and rage and whine, and they understood as best they could.

"You should stay for dinner," Erin said. "As you might've heard, we have carne asada."

"And that rice you like," Nick added. "My grandmother's recipe."

I waved my hand in the direction of their table. "You're obviously having people over," I said. I didn't want a pity invite.

"Yeah, but it's just friends from the hospital," Nick said. "Gastro Girl and the Heartbreaker."

"I really admire your efforts in superhero-inspired nicknaming," I said. "That's some solid work right there. I could write a comic book based on that. *The Adventures of Gastro Girl and the Heartbreaker.* A superhero duo that goes around saving the world from stomach ulcers and falling in love with your sister-in-law and shit like that. People would go crazy for it."

I could see it already. The Heartbreaker would be a big, burly guy who ripped off his shirt to activate his powers. A shield was mandatory. Something almost anatomically correct, blood red, and covered in welded patch marks. He'd possess the strength to crack skulls like they were walnuts, but underneath the raw force would be a tender soul in search of someone to mend *him*.

Gastro Girl would wear a skintight bodysuit in emerald green—had to be green—and a long cape. Something that was always rippling in the breeze and showing off a whole lot of ass. She'd need thigh-high boots, a gunmetal tiara, and some kind of bright, shiny amulet right between her breasts. Nothing delicate for this chick.

Fuck, I wanted to draw this *right now*. Some people did yoga, others gardened, some read books. I drew. There wasn't much order to it, and I hadn't shared my work with anyone since my days at RISD. But every so often, ideas flooded my mind and demanded presence on the page. Usually it was a quick burst and nothing more, but certain ideas lingered long enough for me to revisit them for days and weeks on end. I liked that. I liked having something stewing on my mind's back burners.

"How much longer there, Doc?"

He released an impatient sigh. "I'm gonna need some time," he said. "Unless you'd rather we drive over to the hospital and find someone who sews up wounds like this all day, every day."

"Thank you, no," I replied.

Erin was busy on the opposite end of the kitchen but I heard her ask, "Do they know about these nicknames? Do you call them that around the hospital?"

"I fucking hope not. The art of the nickname comes from using it sparingly, *Rogue*," I said to her. "One doesn't simply toss out a nickname in every exchange. It needs to serve a purpose. Make a point. Highlight a trait."

"No, not really," Nick replied. "I think you've met Cal once or twice, Riley. They live in my old apartment building off Cambridge Street."

Erin shut the refrigerator door and came up beside me. "You make it sound like she and Cal live *together*," she said. "They don't, by the way. I don't think they'd hook up if they were the last two humans on the planet."

"That might be a little extreme," Nick said. "But you're right. She isn't Cal's speed at all."

"What does that mean?" I asked.

"You're going to feel a few pinches while I numb the wound," he said. "You should stay for dinner. You'll see what I mean about Gastro Girl when she gets here. I'm warning you right now, she's a little intense."

For the record, it was not a few *pinches*. I knew all about pinches. These were white-hot jabs into my flesh. And I was no shrieking pussy. I'd spent three months dating—nah, that wasn't the right word *at all*—a dominatrix who had a taste for spiked heels, canes, and double-tailed whips. I could handle my shit.

"Intense? You're warning me about intense? Are you kidding?" I asked through a groan. "I know all about intense.

Between my sisters and Andy—the woman who speaks primarily via raised eyebrows—how much more do I need to know about intense?"

"There are levels to this shit, man," Nick murmured. "Levels."

THE FRONT DOOR slammed shut and then—

"You are *never* going to believe the conversation I just had with Chapelton. I've fucking *had it* with this guy, and he's gonna miss me when I'm gone."

"Levels," Nick repeated.

I couldn't see much from my head-down perch at the kitchen island, but I heard the thwack of sandals as they slapped against the hardwood floors.

"Oh, for Christ's sake. This is how malpractice suits start, Acevedo," Stompy Sandals said.

My off-kilter view landed on her red flip flops first. Her legs came next, and what a pair they were.

So this is Gastro Girl.

She was all strength and sinew, and thick thighs that looked prime for biting. Ah, I loved thick thighs. I didn't know what it was men—or women—found attractive about skinny bird legs. I liked something to hold onto. Skin to squeeze.

"Trust me, Alex. I know it," Nick murmured. "But this

guy's family, and my wife would pummel him with rocks if he tried."

"True story," I replied, angling for an above-the-waist look at Nick's guest. Her red shorts were loose enough to allow a hand under them, and now I was thinking about panties. Mmmm, *panties*. Fuckin' loved panties. "Greetings. Riley Walsh." I extended my hand in her general direction, though given my angle, it looked like I was trying to grab her crotch. She took a gigantic step back, and I didn't blame her. "My bad, my bad."

She plunked a bottle of wine down on the countertop and moved from my line of sight.

"What the hell kind of technique is this, Doctor Acevedo?" she asked, ignoring me entirely. "It looks like you're maximizing epidermal puncture points. Is scarring the objective of your suturing?"

Add to Gastro Girl's defining characteristics: the ability to morph into a fire-breathing lady-dragon.

"Of course not, Doctor Emmerling," he said. "Given that the wound moves along the external oblique and lumbar triangle, my preference is for a closure that will hold up against frequent flexing even if that comes with some slight scarring."

I couldn't decide whether to be concerned or irritated. I didn't know anything about this chick or her slamming-doors-and-stomping-around routine, and I wasn't thrilled about her rolling in and hollering at Nick. He was a smart guy. He wasn't going to fuck this up. *Of course not.* He had a long history of treating assorted Walsh injuries, and we were all still standing.

Or sprawled out on an island. Either way, we were good.

"Don't listen to them," Erin said. She brought me a glass

of water with a long straw, and I drank while she watched them over my shoulder. "They play hospital all the time, and by *play* I mean argue about every little thing."

"Right, yeah," I said, trying to sneak a glance at the surgeon battle going down behind me. "Hey. Nick. I'm not going to die while you debate this, am I? Internal bleeding or my guts spilling out or something like that?"

"Your fascia is undisturbed so no worries about disemboweling," Stompy Sandals replied as her frigid hands came to my flank and belly. "Any pain here?"

I tried and failed to suppress a giggle at her touch. It didn't matter that she wasn't attempting to tickle me. It still felt that way. "All good."

"No immediate signs of internal bleeding," she said, and it almost sounded like she was disappointed. About my lack of organ failure. "If we wanted to be really certain, we'd go to the—"

"Don't say it," I interrupted. "Don't even try because the answer is no."

Nick cleared his throat. "Can I finish this now?"

"No, no. Look at the dermal tension," Alex continued. Her tone was a cross between condescending and aggressive as fuck. "We're starting over. You're going to leave him with an uncomfortable wound, and that's going to lead to an ass-ugly scar. We're doing a running subcuticular closure, and that's the end of it. Where are the sterile gloves?"

Oh my fucking god. I hadn't even gotten face to face with this chick yet, and all I could think was *Is there anything you don't know?* She was straight out of the Tracy Flick and Hermione Granger School for Smarty Pantsing.

"Under the sink," he replied.

I got my first real look at her when she rounded the island and started washing her hands.

Alex Emmerling was disarming. Even her hand washing was terrifyingly competent. I had to admit she was pretty hot—especially when she wasn't busy reminding everyone that she was the brightest bulb *and* sharpest tack in the room —but no less terrifying.

She was long on that salty attitude, her presence punching far above her weight class. It made up for every- thing she lacked in height. She was a pixie, not much taller than Erin. She probably had to take those lovely legs up a stepladder to reach the top shelves. I figured she had a year or two on me, but not much more than that.

Her hair refused categorization. It was too dark to be blonde, too light to be brunette, and lacked the flame to be red. It existed at the intersection of all three, like an aged whiskey. Those rich, wavy strands came in sharp contrast to the severe line of her frown and the hard, determined glint of her green eyes. It didn't seem that she made a habit of smiling, but just as the Mojave Desert was known to find itself awash in wildflowers on a single spring day, those rare instances were probably worth months of inhospitable conditions.

"Where's Hartshorn?" Nick asked. "I thought he was coming with you."

She tilted her head to the side, her eyebrows lifting while she patted her hands dry. Then she snapped on a pair of gloves with brutal efficiency. There wasn't a man alive who didn't experience some asshole puckering from that sound.

"I'd just finished a bowel obstruction when I saw him running into an OR," she replied. "We'll save him a plate.

He'll catch up with us later." She moved behind me and said to Nick, "I'll take it from here."

"By all means," he said, stepping aside. "I'm going out to fire up the grill, Emmerling. You're in charge."

I stifled a groan. Sarah McLachlan and cereal were looking pretty good right now. And those lady golfers. I had no trouble muting them.

"What's the nature of this injury?" she asked when Erin, Nick, and the tray of meat stepped outside. It was a whole new voice. Still abrupt, but it was as though she'd decided this moment wasn't entirely about her legendary skills but me—the guy with the blood and gaping wound and all the shambles.

"Rusty nail, old basement," I said.

Full sentences didn't come easily to me when faced with someone I didn't know well. Without Nick or Erin nearby, I was right back to saying words in my head before they passed my lips. I hadn't yet hammered out the damage from my father beating my ass over my speech impediments as a kid.

"That's no fun," she murmured. "See the time over there?" She set her gloved hand on my shoulder and pointed at the wrought iron clock in the adjoining room with her other hand. It was an upcycled salvage job Lauren discovered at a flea market in Connecticut. She was miraculous like that. "Focus on the second hand. I'll be finished in five minutes."

She hummed while she worked, and when she told me to anticipate a few pinches, they actually felt like pinches. Score one for Gastro Girl.

"Don't people around here call them cellars?" Alex asked.

"They do," I replied.

"But you called it a basement," she said.

"I did."

"So it's obvious to you that I'm not from around here?" she asked.

"No," I said, swallowing a laugh. This pixie really did believe *everything* was about her.

"Then why—"

"Because, by strict definition, cellars are below-grade rooms in residential properties used for storing coal or wine. I don't believe this particular space was used for either. Yes, in my Bostonian mind, underground spaces are 'down cellar' but my architect's mind reaches for the technical terms first," I said. "That's why I said basement. It had nothing to do with you."

Honest to god, I didn't know how all of those words came out of me without a single stutter. It was like one of those freak incidents where a skydiver's parachute didn't open but he managed to tuck and roll when hitting the ground, and walked away without a scrape.

"Oh. I see," she said. "You're an architect, then."

Two minutes down, three to go.

"Yes."

"What was Chapelton on your case about now?" Nick asked as he and Erin returned to the kitchen.

Alex exhaled heavily and her breath tickled my spine. "Like I said, I was working on a bowel obstruction. It was situation normal, no need for the Chief of Surgery to scrub in and watch over my shoulder, but he did it anyway. He doesn't say a single word during the entire procedure. Asked no questions. Probably didn't even blink. Just watched and scowled."

"What a bastard," Nick said under his breath as he popped the top off a bottle of beer.

She exhaled again, and tossed a growl in with it. I liked a girl who growled. "He observes the whole damn procedure and then—in front of my goddamn residents and the OR nurses and basically everyone in the entire hospital—he launches into a tirade about my *surgical posture*. Surgical fucking posture."

Nick shrugged. "Yeah, that's obnoxious." He pointed at her with his beer bottle. "But don't blow it off entirely. You *are* hunching."

Two more minutes.

"Shut the fuck up," Alex snapped. "If anyone else had been running that procedure today, Chapelton would still be going on about the surgeon's clean, efficient work and low incidence for complications. He'd be throwing down bonuses and cushy schedules before wheeling the patient into post-op."

"I don't disagree," he said.

"There's literally nothing I can do to break even here," she said. She wasn't working so hard at being right anymore, and the brassy beat of intimidation was gone from her tone. Now she just sounded sad. Defeated. "He's not going to fire me because I'm the best gastrointestinal surgery attending he has, and he knows it. But he's not allowing me to advance at all, and he's not giving me a drop of credit for my performance. I'd quit right now, but I can't leave without a decent recommendation from the guy. We all know I'm not going to get that."

"Not until you correct that surgical posture," Nick quipped.

"Thanks for that," she said. "I just need to prove that I'm not the same—I don't know, slut? floozy? idiot?—who hooked up with one of her interns."

Erin shook her head. "Women are always getting punished for having sex. It's the worst."

"It wasn't even *good* sex," Alex groused.

"Now *that's* the worst," Erin replied.

"The Chief will come around," Nick said, but it didn't sound like he truly believed it. "Keep on keeping on. Soon enough, your reputation—"

"My *reputation*," she interrupted, "is based on being the resident who slept with her intern, and not realizing that he was using me to get access to additional OR time and better procedures before going back to his girlfriend in Minneapolis. That's my reputation, Acevedo. Every time we get a new cohort of interns or residents, everyone starts wondering which one I'll take to bed. Which one will get the preferential treatment this time around? They whisper about whether I like them young, or just love the power trip of it all. I could drop a stomach on the operating room floor or remove the wrong duct and people would still think of me as that one bitch who didn't know better."

"Well," Erin said as she opened a bottle of wine, "if you ever want to get drunk and complain about the patriarchy, a bunch of us go out for pedicures on Thursday evenings. I don't always make it since I travel for work a fair amount, but it's a good time. We go to this cool spot where they serve margaritas, heavy on the tequila."

"Thanks for the invite. I'll think about it." She brought her hand to my shoulder. "All done and"—she pointed to the clock—"thirty-five seconds to spare." I sat up and reached back to touch it but she slapped my hand away. "No. We have enough issues with the rusty nail wound, and it wasn't a pretty one. Don't add irritation to infection by touching it. Wash your hands, and I'll write you a course of antibiotics."

"Not so fast." Nick set his beer on the countertop and dug through the backpack. "I think I have a vial of tetanus in here somewhere. I stocked up after that nail gun incident. Yeah, here it is." He glanced at me while drawing the fluid into a syringe. "You ready for this?"

I stood and unbuckled my belt, and my shorts hit the floor. "I guess so."

Alex studied me while she peeled off her gloves. Her brows were furrowed and that frown was firmly in place, but her eyes were all over my chest. I pushed my boxer briefs down just enough for another stab wound, and her lips parted with a sigh that sounded too delicate to be real.

And she was staring at my ass, her mouth open and her hand pressed to her throat like she was trying to clutch a strand of pearls or something.

Nick looked from the syringe to me, to my bare ass, to Alex, and then back to me. "Dude," he said. "Pull your damn pants up." He pointed to his upper arm. "Deltoid, not gluteal."

I tipped my chin toward Alex. "Only if Gastro Girl can do it."

NO ONE HAD any business with an ass like that.

Or abs…

…or arms…

…or face.

It was obnoxious, really. The whole perfectly built picture. No one needed that *much*.

And yet, I was still studying his exposed backside as if there was an anatomy quiz in my future.

But no, there wouldn't be anything anatomical going on with this guy. No, not *at all*. He was gangly, all long limbs and broad, tanned shoulders and hands like bear paws. Dark hair, thick and wavy. Bright, expressive eyes that weren't simply blue but sapphire. He was a young one, too. He was still growing into that body. And what a body it was. But he had a Batman tramp stamp, for fuck's sake. There was no quicker way of announcing one's man-child status than that.

I'd put money on him being a player. Oh, but he'd play hard. He'd play to *win*. I couldn't explain how I knew that but I *knew*. He was the kind of guy—with his lower back tattoo and forceful statement about cellars and objectively awful laceration—who'd throw down in a seedy bar because someone looked at a woman the wrong way. But he'd have to be trained. He probably ate pussy like a dog drank water, all unmeasured tongue flapping and a soggy mess.

Then he opened his mouth. "Only if Gastro Girl can do it."

"Don't fucking call me that," I snapped, balling my non-latex gloves and depositing them in the trash with more force than necessary. I was in a slammy-bangy-yelly mood. There were a lot of people on my short list for a throat punch today.

"Okay," he said, smiling at me like *All you had to do was ask so why get all worked up*? "It's Alex, right?"

I jerked my head in some semblance of a nod. "Yeah," I said.

I crossed my arms over my chest but then my boobs were popping out of my sleeveless shirt like it was time for the annual melon festival. I resorted to my default pose, the one my male colleagues could pull off all damn day but screamed "raging bitch" on me—hands on the hips.

If the broomstick fits, ride it.

I glanced at him briefly, not one hundred percent certain I could deal with the entirety of his tall-broad-rippled-tanned-gorgeous. That kind of smile with those kinds of abs? It was like staring straight at the sun. There was no way I could deal with this much *man* without resenting him for existing. They weren't supposed to be this perfect. "I'm sorry, I don't think I caught your name."

"Riley," he said.

"Listen, people," Nick said, waving a hand between us. "Let's speed this along, shall we? There's meat on the grill and I'm more concerned with that than who jabs Walsh with a tetanus."

I held my hand out for the syringe. "You invite me to dinner," I said to Nick, steering Riley back to the stool so I could reach his damn delt without getting on my tiptoes. His shorts were still around his ankles and his boxers nudged down enough for a girl to dream, but I wasn't getting lost in those details. "And the second I get here, you put me to work. What kind of dinner party is this?"

"You're getting off easy," Riley said. There was no exaggeration about the rough, intentional way *getting off* sounded, or how it went straight to my nipples. Stupid nipples. Those damn things didn't know when to stand down. "The last time I was here, these two had me repaving the driveway."

"That isn't what happened at all," Erin said, wagging a large spoon at him while I wiped an antiseptic swab over his arm. "You tripped on a crack, and then announced you were getting a jackhammer and pouring concrete. That was all you, kid."

I tapped his shoulder. It was finely sculpted granite. "Relax your arm." With the syringe cap between my teeth, I said, "Quick pinch, a little burn, then we're done."

He dropped his chin to his chest. "I'm painting that door so fucking pink," he murmured.

"What are you babbling about now?" Erin asked.

She was busy filling small bowls with tomatoes, cheese, and lettuce. My stomach growled at the sight of avocado. I could exist on avocado alone. Well, avocado and eggs. And chocolate. And toast. Okay, so not *just* avocado but close enough.

"Nothing important," Riley said, turning his head to

glance back at me. Those cheekbones. They didn't even look real. "Someone's hungry."

I pressed a small square of gauze to the injection site. "Yeah, well, I haven't had a minute to eat since six this morning," I said.

The deck door slid open, and Nick appeared with a long pair of stainless steel tongs and a platter loaded with the carne asada he'd promised for this shindig. My stomach rumbled again.

Nick's gaze pinged between me and the arm I was *still* rubbing, and he did a poor job of stifling his amusement. "Tetanus shots hurt," I snapped. *Nope. Not at all defensive.*

"Right," Nick said with a snicker. He pointed at the owner of that arm. "You're sitting in my kitchen with your ass hanging out, dude. I think it's time to pull up those pants. Maybe get you a shirt, too. What do you think?"

Riley tossed up his hands. "We're all friends here," he replied as he stood and yanked up his shorts.

The pale skin of his backside disappeared beneath black boxer briefs, but not before I snapped enough mental pictures to keep me warm at night. Those pictures were going to have to do it for me because I was on a strict man-free diet. It'd started out as a thirty-day cleanse and now, fifteen months later, it was a lifestyle choice.

Honestly, it was better this way. Men were distractions. Men were drama. I didn't have room for any of that in my life right now, and there was nothing men could give me that I couldn't give myself. Orgasms included.

"Yeah," Nick called as he headed toward the staircase. "And friends tell friends to pull up their damn pants."

Erin pressed her fingertips to her lips as she shook her head and laughed silently. "All right," she said. "This is not how I expected this evening to go. I hadn't planned on any kitchen surgeries or bare asses at my dinner party." She glanced from me to Riley. "I guess I should have."

DINNER WAS GOOD. Great, really. The food was amazing, the wine never stopped flowing, and the conversation elevated me—slightly—out of the Chapelton-criticizes-everything-I-do funk.

But I couldn't tell you what was on my plate or in my glass, and I couldn't be sure what we talked about because that Riley had to sit across the table from me in the tightest-fitting t-shirt on the planet. The University of Texas-Austin's logo was stretched to the point that it resembled a squiggly line rather than the Longhorn.

His arms were testing the limits of the shirt's seams. They looked uncomfortably constricted with the way his muscles popped every time he reached for his beer bottle or built another taco. It was troubling. *Medically*, of course. The sleeves of that t-shirt were putting a lot of pressure on his brachial arteries.

But I was thankful he was sitting. I didn't need another look at his abs courtesy of the belly-baring shirt. I couldn't decide whether Nick was just that small or Riley was just that big. Not that it mattered. It didn't. Even though I was pretty sure it was the latter.

Yeah, no. I didn't need to spend another second contemplating his precise degree of physical perfection. That wouldn't feed the bulldog.

"Like I said," he continued. "She's an outdoor cat."

A player. Total player. Completely misogynistic. I knew it.

"Do you talk about all women as if they're animals?" I asked.

Erin gestured toward me with her wine glass. "While I'd tend to agree with you," she started, "it's apropos in this case. He's magnificent like that"—now pointing her glass at Riley—"with the nicknames. It's one of his many strange gifts and talents."

He had the decency to offer a small smile and glance away. Like he wasn't used to a pig pile of praise.

"You know," Nick called from the kitchen, where he was collecting another round of beers for him and the model of masculine perfection. "You two have a lot of the same problems. You could help each other out."

"Wait. What?" I said, and at the same time, Riley said, "No. I don't think so, dude."

Then we shared a *you could do a lot worse than helping me out* look.

"You"—Nick dropped a beer bottle in front of Riley—"just spent the past forty minutes complaining about RISD Weekend and all of the issues with being near the outdoor cat, as you put it." He dropped into his seat and pointed at me. "You've been complaining for weeks about the Chief's cocktail party and how you'll be bribing residents to get an ER shift that night." He waved toward us both and then brought his hands together. "You could help each other out."

Riley picked up his beer bottle and studied the label, but didn't respond.

Nick was right about me doing anything to avoid this cocktail party. It was an annual event for attending surgeons, and it was only a few weeks away now. It would've been fine if I hadn't been the problem child of the hospital's faculty for no reason other than my poor choice of bedfellows. That, and the Chief's parties were aggressively coupled. It was the land of significant others, as if completing residency came with a signing bonus, relocation package, *and* life partner. Anyone who rode solo was damned to Mrs. Chapelton's relationship interrogation and matchmaking services.

"What is it you're suggesting?" I demanded. "We can't really plan for his appendix to rupture that night."

"Let me spell it out." Nick reached for the bowls of cheese and tomatoes, and positioned them like toy soldiers. "Alex, no one is going to talk about whether you're hooking up with an intern if you take Riley to the Chief's cocktail party. That shit will end," he said. "And Riley, you can take Alex to RISD Weekend. She might not be Magnolia, but she can throw down just as good." Nick waved between us again, as if he could whip some logic from the evening air. "Both of you are putting a lot of effort into being miserable. Be miserable together."

Riley went on staring at his beer, registering no other reaction.

"Just for appearances," Erin added. "No one is suggesting you move in together or get married or anything."

Nick gave her an impatient frown. "You and your low expectations, woman. What am I going to do with you?"

That caught Riley's attention. "Don't start," he said to Nick while snagging a tortilla chip from a dish. "As if your damn housewarming-slash-marriage-celebration didn't do enough." He popped the chip in his mouth and then folded his arms on the table. He leaned forward and caught my eye. "These two had a very ad hoc wedding reception last month, and—"

"I know," I said apologetically. "I tried to be there. I was tied up with surgeries that night."

That was one time when I hadn't been trying to evade social situations due to the inevitable chatter that started whenever folks from the hospital were around. I was happy for Nick and Erin. I'd actually wanted to celebrate them making a home together and finally living on the same continent. I'd watched him suffer through his separation from her, and that they found a way to make it work was nothing short of amazing. It was like all the stars and planets aligned for them.

Riley nodded, and continued. "It was a complete and total trauma. Everyone wanted to know when I was going to find a nice girl, move out of my brother's house, settle down. Every-fucking-one had a friend they wanted to fix me up with."

"At least they don't start tapping their watches and telling you biological clocks won't snooze forever," I said, laughing.

He shook his head and dug in the dish. "Nah," he said, piling meat on his chip. "They say that to me, too. You know, I'm just a big kid so I'll be great with children." He rolled his eyes and ate his deconstructed taco creation. "I did a lot of smiling and nodding that night."

"You also drank a *bit* of whiskey," Erin said.

"A wee bit." He rubbed the back of his neck and—*my god, that forearm*—said, "Sleeping in your bathtub was a good idea until I woke up and couldn't turn my head. Or remember anything that happened after midnight."

There was a sigh waiting to unfurl in my throat. A breathy noise that could only serve as an offering to the stone-carved man—the one being hounded to find a wife—

across the table from me. But there was also a snarl. A snap of annoyance that I should be forced to select a faux beau if I wanted to get out from under the shame cloud of having sex with someone from work.

"I don't think I can—" I started, but then the front door banged open.

"I love aortas," Hartshorn said when he appeared in the dining room. If we were comparing big guys, Cal Hartshorn, cardiothoracic surgeon extraordinaire, he was a hunk of granite. Riley was what happened after the sculptor got his hands on the granite.

"I love temporal lobes," Nick said.

"I love pancreatic ducts," I said.

Nick motioned to the empty seat beside me and retreated into the kitchen. He returned with a wine bottle tucked under his arm and three beers cradled against his chest. He handed one to Cal—who was already loading his plate with meat, rice, and vegetables—and Riley.

"Thank you for joining us," Erin said with a laugh as she refilled her wine glass and then mine. "Even if you are two hours late."

"I caught this one right before it dissected," Cal said. "Just in time. Love aortas."

Erin caught Riley's eye and shrugged. "They do this a lot," she said. "Sometimes it gets detailed. They used the chalkboard wall in the pantry to sort out something with a liver a few weeks ago. Occasionally, there are videos. There are even some interesting Instagram accounts with some really involved photos."

"That's adorable," he replied. I tried to draw my gaze away when he patted his hand over his belly. Failed. "And not unexpected. Those two did argue about the proper way to sew me up while I was sitting *right there*."

"It's the same as when you, Matt, Patrick, and Sam argue about houses," Erin said. "Instead of blood you have bricks, but the philosophies and personal styles are just as robust."

Despite my definite lack of interest in this guy, I found myself saying, "So, you're an architect?"

Nick stood and reached for the wine. "Okay, you two. Take the bottle," he said, pushing it into my hands. "Go outside. Get to know each other. If that doesn't work, drink and hate the world together."

Riley stared at the table for a moment, his easy smile now turned down as if he'd heard it was time to leave the dog park. I was halfway out of my seat but stuck there, stalled, because I wasn't about to take the lead. I was only going out on that deck if I was following Riley. I wasn't dragging any man anywhere.

I wanted him dragging me.

"If I'm being exiled, I'm taking the chips," Riley said with a confrontational tip to his chin. "And the guac."

RILEY WAS quiet for several minutes after we settled in cushy chairs under the dark night sky, and I was certain we were taking the path of drinking and misery. That was the best option available. It wasn't like we were going to hatch a plan like Nick had suggested. We didn't have anything in common, clearly. He was young—maybe twenty-five or twenty-six—but I didn't think he'd appreciate me bringing that up, not the way he bristled at being called a big kid. And he was dealing with some issues. I wasn't sure which issues those were as I'd been preoccupied with imagining how small my hands would look on his shoulders while he talked through that story at dinner.

Me and my man-lust. Forever causing problems.

This wasn't a trick we could pull off. No one would believe we were together. He wasn't my type, and I doubted I was his. He was funny and a little silly, and I was serious and seriouser. He was alarmingly handsome, and I was doing okay but not alarmingly anything.

"Where would you go?" he asked. His voice was low and deep, and the words didn't resemble words at all. They were growls and sighs, and…and I reminded myself that he was a player man-child who passed out drunk in bathtubs. Just a gorgeous, growly player man-child.

"What?" I replied.

"You said you wanted to leave the hospital," he said. I folded my arms on my thighs and leaned forward to hear him better. To his credit, his eyes didn't drop to my cleavage once. Yup, not his type. "Where would you go?"

"Oh, right," I replied, tucking my hair over my ear. "Probably somewhere out west. California. Maybe Oregon. Hartshorn's from Oregon, and he makes it sound like the greatest place in the world."

"The land of the ducks," he said.

Again, I was left replying, "What?"

The two of us, we didn't speak the same language. And it wasn't like I needed him to talk. He could just sit there and look pretty, and my night would be better for it.

"The University of Oregon Ducks," he said. "Their football program is a big deal. You'd probably need some mallard green and yellow in your wardrobe. You gotta root for the home team."

Even if I landed in Oregon, I wasn't going to be stocking up on mallard green or yellow. I wasn't friends with football. I'd had my fill in high school.

"So, this guy. The intern," Riley said, sitting up. "It sounds like he really fucked you over."

I stared into my wine for a second, considering this. "He used me," I said eventually, hating—*hating*—the sound of those words. It was fine to admit them to myself in the quiet of my mind but they were so much worse out loud.

Riley allowed his gaze to fall and nodded, as if he understood.

"We weren't official. We didn't announce that we were seeing each other outside of the hospital. But people knew," I said. "A lot of them also knew that he—Steve—had a girl-friend who was doing her internship at the University of Minnesota. I didn't know any of that until I overheard some people talking about how he was going to propose to her."

Riley scooped some guacamole onto a chip, but a chunk of it landed on his shorts. It was in an awkward location. If I pointed it out, he'd assume I'd been staring at his crotch. I was already confessing enough truths tonight. I didn't want to add that one to the list.

"And that got your spidey sense tingling?"

Such a man-child. "Enough that I kept eavesdropping," I said. "They said he was waiting for Match Day—the day in March where doctors are matched with internships and resi-dency programs—because he was hoping they matched in the same area." I paused for a gulp of wine. "I wasn't in the Match. I was finishing my fellowship, and I'd already accepted an offer to stay here in Boston."

"How did it end?"

"Quietly, at first," I said. "It was like he was slowly

sneaking away. Then, when he and his girlfriend both matched at Hopkins, it got loud. And why not? He had a spot in a top program. He could run his mouth to residents and attendings all he wanted. Tell them about the *close, personal* learning experiences he'd gotten. Or joke with his fellow interns about *working the system* to his advantage, and warn incoming interns that I'd make one of them my pet."

"What a douche waffle," Riley murmured. The guacamole was still on his shorts. "Did you kick his ass? I bet you've got a hell of a roundhouse."

I decided against asking him to explain any part of that. "No, of course not. I didn't want to call any more attention to the situation," I said. "And the only things that should matter are my surgical outcomes."

He stared at me for a long beat, the corner of his mouth tipped up in a wan grin. "Doesn't sound like that approach is working too well for you, Honeybee."

With a pathetic sigh, I dumped the remainder of the wine into my glass. Thank god I had tomorrow off. I could pay for these indulgences by lazing in bed all morning and then wander the aisles of the grocery store, all while planning the amazing meals I'd prepare this week. If I knew anything about cooking, of course. But I really enjoyed thumbing through the pages of *Food & Wine* and *Everyday Food*.

"This cocktail party?" Riley asked, scraping the bowl for the last of the guacamole. "Let's do it. We're gonna show those fuckers something."

"What?" I asked.

Goddamn it, I had to stop sputtering over everything this guy said. He wasn't *that* pretty.

Okay, yes, he definitely was.

"I will go to this cocktail party with you," he said, careful to enunciate every word slowly.

I was *this close* to telling him he didn't have to offer because I didn't want his help or pity or misplaced sense of chivalry. That was his motivation, I knew it. He was a player and a man-child and St. Bernard of a boy, but something about him was so fucking loyal that it hurt. He didn't even know me but he wanted to save me the lingering effects of a douche waffle.

But before I could reconsider, I was saying, "It's two weeks from tonight."

"I'll be there," he said. "Any other events on your calendar?"

"Yes—no—I mean, wait," I said, holding up my hands. "This is ridiculous. You're not even my type."

"You're not my type either, Honeybee." Riley scooted to the edge of his chair and leaned forward, dropping his palms to my knees. Now the guacamole was irrevocably smooshed. "You don't want to attend this cocktail party alone. I don't want to attend RISD Weekend alone," he said. "It would be a mutually beneficial arrangement, and nothing else."

"It's never going to work," I said. I could already hear Mrs. Chapelton's questions about our *courtship*. She always knew when someone brought a second cousin along, and she didn't take kindly to fraudulent relationships. Someone really needed to have a conversation with her about the arrival of this century and all its social conventions. "We don't even know each other, and, and—"

"I'll buy you dinner sometime this week," Riley said. "We can cover the basics."

I dragged my eyes away from his big hands on my legs

and the way his thumbs were pressed against the backside of my knees. I didn't even have the presence of mind to snap back about buying my own damn dinner. "Why don't you want to go to this weekend thing alone?" I asked.

He tipped his head from one side to another, and his brows wrinkled in a way that had my fingers itching to smooth out the lines. "My ex-girlfriend will probably try to eat my soul, or at least trap it in a jar," he said. "I need a little distance from that, but I have to attend the event. It's home-coming, basically, for Rhode Island School of Design."

"I've never been to Rhode Island," I said. "Actually, I've never been anywhere else in New England."

His brows furrowed harder. "That's a tragedy," he said. "But I can cross Rhody off your list, if you're up for it."

He shrugged and squeezed my legs. It was probably intended to be friendly or comforting, like a pat on the back. I couldn't imagine that he was trying to remind me that I'd eliminated men—and flirting and sex and intimacy—from my life.

"What else can I do for you?" Riley asked. "This cocktail party is only a couple of hours but you're giving me two, maybe two and a half days for RISD Weekend. What else do you need?"

A whole lot of filthy streamed through my mind. "Um," I said, just praying that I didn't let *your scruffy chin between my legs* slip out. "There's a ball."

Without missing a goddamn beat, he said, "Usually two."

I fell back in my seat as a laugh rolled through me. "Thankfully for us, this is a single ball situation," I said. "It's the hospital's annual black tie fundraising gala. It's usually in the spring, but for some reason, they're gala-ing twice this year."

"Like I said, there's usually two." He gripped my legs again. I tucked my bottom lip between my teeth to hold in the giggly grin that my body was trying to force. Silly senses. They were letting some strong hands override my brain. "Add something to your list. While I'm probably doing you a favor by introducing you to Rhode Island, I want this to be equal and fair."

There was one more event that could benefit from the presence of a man in my life, but... "It's a bridge-crosser," I said. "Going to hospital events together is one thing, but adding this last item to my list would—"

"It would cross a bridge," he finished. "A bridge you're not sure you want to cross?"

"My parents," I said with a sigh. "They're really excited about the whole New England foliage thing, and they're planning a stop in Boston at the end of their trip. I don't want to lie to them, but I could really use a break from marriage-and-babies talk."

"We won't have to lie," he replied. "We're friends, and we'll show them a good time in the city. If they want to draw their inferences, we can't stop them."

"All right," I said slowly. "Four dates. We can—"

"Five," he interrupted. "Five. I'm taking you out to dinner this week because the only things I know about you are that you're a doctor, your ex is the human version of recurrent foot fungus, and your regional education is lacking."

"Five," I repeated.

In my head, I'd already downgraded that dinner to a quick coffee date. No sense spending more time around this guy. It was too dangerous, especially since I was already high off the pressure of his skin against mine. His fingers, my knees, and all kinds of chemical reactions inside my body.

Men are drama. Men are manipulators. Men are not my priority.

"After those five engagements, we'll part ways amicably and no one ever needs to know the real story. Can you promise me that?" I asked.

That ass, though. That ass should be someone's priority.

And that was all it took to remove Riley's hands from my legs. He grabbed his beer and leaned back in his chair, drinking deeply for several silent moments.

"Like you pointed out, I'm not your type. You're a nice lady, you know, once you've been fed and wined, but you're not my type either. We're just people in really fucked-up situations, and we need some help dealing with those situations," he said. "What we're talking about here, Alex, it's preservation. I need it as much as you do."

Riley: When do you want to get dinner this week? My schedule is open.

Alex: How do you feel about coffee?

Riley: I enjoy coffee.

Alex: Okay. Let's do that. Thursday works best for me. Starbucks near the hospital?

Riley: Slow your roll, Shortstop.

Alex: Are you one of those devout Bostonians who only acknowledge the existence of Dunkin' Donuts?

Riley: What happened to dinner?

Alex: Does it have to be dinner?

Riley: Yeah it has to be dinner. I'm a growing boy and you get real moody when you're hungry.

Alex: You aren't still growing. You haven't been growing for years.

Alex: Not unless you're 24. Or on growth hormones. Or both.

Riley: I'm 30 and all natural, thank you.

Alex: How are you 30? Where is your fountain of youth?

Riley: Rhode Island.

Alex: Ha.

Riley: If you're nice, I'll show it to you.

Alex: I'm not nice.

Riley: I've noticed. I don't mind.

Alex: Thank you? I think? I don't know what the appropriate response is to that.

Riley: It's you meeting me for dinner without trying to talk me down to coffee.

Riley: The Seven Ales House. Thursday. 830 p.m. Get your life story down to bullet points.

I STARED at my sparkly red clogs and then back at my watch. I was due to meet Riley in fifteen minutes, and was still sitting in the attending surgeons' locker room, outfitted in scrubs, clogs, and my doctor's coat. It was my inside-the-hospital garb, and since the first days of internship, I'd made a practice of always leaving the hospital in street clothes. It had started at my mother's neurotic insistence that if I didn't, I'd be bringing all the communicable diseases home with me. It also saved me from walking straight back into the hospital when I saw an ambulance roll up at the end of my shift, or assessing every little old lady's strange bump or barky cough in the cereal aisle of the grocery store.

But right now, I was thinking hard about breaking this tradition.

It wasn't a date if I was wearing scrubs, right? I wouldn't fixate on Riley's square, scruff-covered jaw if firmly in doctor-mode, right?

I shot another glance at my shoes, and caught sight of

some blood splatter. Even if I didn't have a thing for ruby slippers and *The Wizard of Oz*, I'd still wear red clogs. They were the best at hiding all matter of bodily fluids. Kicking them off while I slipped out of my coat, I kept telling myself it wasn't a date. It couldn't be a date, not when it was an arrangement. If anything, it was a contractual obligation.

Nothing sexy or square-jawed and scruffy about contracts.

After depositing my scrubs in the hamper, I stepped into white jeans, a summery shirt, and sandals. Red flippies, of course. I had seven different pairs and no, it wasn't a problem.

If *Town & Country* or *Vanity Fair* had a special summer feature about what to wear on midweek ale house non-dates in late August, this look would be their top recommendation. They'd add a straw bag or a watercolor-painted scarf, but I had the basics. I was feeling good and ready to roll when the toiletry kit on the top shelf of my locker started taunting me.

You'd be pretty if you'd put on a little mascara, Alex. A touch of lip color, too. Maybe some bronzer so you're not so washed out from all that time indoors.

My toiletry kit had an uncanny ability to sound exactly like my mother. She was well-intentioned to the max, but had the habit of starting too many sentences with "You'd be pretty *if*." I knew now, after hearing some iteration of her critiques for thirty-three years, that she wasn't telling me I wasn't good enough in my raw form. It was that my mother worshipped at the altar of Miss Cover Girl. She didn't believe in stepping out of the house without a full face of makeup. Women who didn't put their faces on were as befuddling to my mother as suicide bombers.

"Maybe I don't want to look pretty tonight," I muttered to the empty room. I said this, but I unzipped the pouch and dug inside for the mascara. I swept some on but scowled at the lip colors and other products. I was sticking with untinted lip balm, even if I could hear my mother's fraught protests with every swipe of Burt's Bees.

She'd have something to say about these jeans, too. I wasn't breaking the *no white after Labor Day* rule, but that rule only applied to people who should wear white. According to Betty Mackay Emmerling, women with fuller hips weren't to accentuate those queen-sized curves. She'd throw herself out a window while wailing about her failings as a mother if she could see me now.

But I didn't live to contradict my mother. There was nothing wonderful about gradually discovering that we had little in common, and then struggling through years of trying to bend each other to different angles. It was even harder to swallow when it was painfully obvious that my father and brother were the picture of bosom buddies. They shared the same interests, motivations, mannerisms. Adam was my father's Mini-Me. There were moments when I still had to force myself to appreciate what they had instead of resenting what I didn't.

"Okay," I said to my toiletry kit. "A little lip color won't kill me."

I made it out of the hospital without incident—an accomplishment, considering I couldn't usually walk out at this hour without getting roped into a consult or being slammed with questions from my residents—but I spent the walk down Charles Street ordering my hormones to behave. It was amazing that we'd come this far in human evolution but one grin from a virile man could still crank my ovaries into overdrive.

At the tavern door, I took a deep breath and reminded myself this was necessary to pulling off a decent fauxmance, and that was necessary to getting out of this city.

I spotted him immediately. He was kicked back in a booth with a half-empty pilsner glass in front of him, scowling at his phone. Perhaps *scowling* was the wrong sentiment. He didn't look angry so much as contemptuous, almost resentful.

"Hi," I said as I pulled the chair from the table. He hadn't noticed me approaching. "How's it going?"

Riley blinked up at me and set the phone on the table, face down. "I wasn't sure you were going to go through with this," he said, gesturing to me. "Do you like red in general, or is there something special about red shoes?"

I quirked an eyebrow. "What?"

He shook his head once and cleared his throat. "Both times I've seen you, you were wearing red shoes," he said, his words measured. "Last weekend you were wearing red shorts, too."

I pointed over my shoulder at the door. "When did you notice my shoes? You were looking at your phone when I came in."

Riley rested his head against the booth and laughed. "You get really bogged down in the process, don't you, Short-stop?" He brought his hand to his open collar and dragged his fingers over his sternum. "I noticed your shoes, even if you didn't catch me looking."

The waiter saved me from responding when he appeared with a plate of small pretzels and an interest in my drink order. Riley watched while I asked about the beers and wines available, and then nodded in approval when I requested a Harpoon summer brew.

"Last weekend was wine, tonight's beer. You're an equal opportunity drinker," he said with a smile. "Good to know. These days, I stick to wine and beer, too." He pointed at the plate between us. "These are my favorite pretzel bites in the city. Try some."

I shot him a sharp look. "Are you just trying to get me in a good mood?" I asked. "I *did* eat lunch today."

"Oh yeah?" he asked, dipping two pretzels in the accompanying sauce. "What did you have? Based on you yelling at me about noticing your shoes, I'd say it was an iced venti skinny latte."

"Almonds," I replied. And an iced venti skinny latte but I wasn't copping to that just yet.

Riley tried to fight a laugh, failed. "Almonds?" he repeated.

"Chocolate-covered almonds, yes." I folded my arms across my chest. "It was an appropriate amount of calories, fat, protein, and carbs."

He shook his head and ate another pretzel. "I don't want to live in a world where a few almonds—chocolate or otherwise—are lunch." He pointed to the plate and pushed his beer toward me. "Eat. Drink. Please."

I glared at the pilsner and pretzels. I hated being told what to do. Just fucking hated it. But then my stomach growled—goddamn digestive muscles—and Riley shot me a pointed glance.

"People think that a rumbling stomach is the sign of hunger," I said, reaching for his glass. I drained the beer and then selected a pretzel for dipping. "It is not. The muscles of the stomach and small intestines are always contracting, and those contractions make more noise when the organs are empty."

Riley gazed at me, his expression flat. It gave me a moment to study him while choosing another pretzel. He was wearing jeans, a tailored shirt with the cuffs rolled up to his elbows, and a pinstriped vest, and his hair was a wreck. It looked like he'd been tugging the dark strands in every conceivable direction. His eyes were rimmed with a bit of red and his lids heavy, as if he'd been rubbing them or hadn't gotten much sleep. Perhaps both. There was a small notebook beside his phone, and a mechanical pencil tucked into the spiral binding.

And he was still more attractive than I knew how to handle. Even tired and irritable, and ordering me to eat his pretzels and drink his beer, he was hot as fuck. I bit into another pretzel and offered him a small smile.

"Would you say the chip on your shoulder is massive or epic?" he asked. There was no hint of amusement in his tone, and he was staring at me with more ice than I'd believed he could muster. It didn't feel like we were sniping at each other anymore. "It might be semantics to you but I'm trying to get a feel for what I'm dealing with here."

But then one of his big hands found my leg under the table. He squeezed and rubbed his thumb along the hollow of my knee, and I started to believe I'd been all wrong about this man. There was the player and there was the overgrown kid, but there was so much more than that.

"LET'S DO THIS LIGHTNING-ROUND STYLE," Riley said when he'd inhaled half of his burger.

"Just the basics," I said, wiping my mouth. "We don't need to go crazy here."

"Crazy, meaning tattoo origin stories?" he asked, pointing to the ink on the inside of my left bicep.

I glanced at the ultra-fine lines and shook my head. "Yeah, we're not going there tonight," I said. I waved at him with a french fry. "I take it you're from Boston?"

He tipped to his head to the side. "I grew up in Welles-ley," he said. "It's a suburb just west of the city. You?"

"Nevada," I said. I barreled on, and didn't give him a second to offer a sideways comment about the Silver State. Everyone had something to say about Vegas and brothels and Area 51. "Obviously, I've met Erin. Other family?"

"My parents are dead and I'm the fifth of six kids in my family," he said.

It was the dual impact of the deceased parents and enormous family that had me cocking my head and blinking in surprise. Even by aggressive estimates, he wasn't old enough to have lost both parents unless there'd been an accident. Or two hits in the genetic disorder lottery. I withheld the barrage of questions that I had about the cause of their deaths because the only time it was appropriate to ask those questions was in a clinical setting, and this tavern wasn't that.

"But everyone thinks I'm the youngest," he continued. "Either I'm that immature or they stopped counting Erin. Their low expectations certainly offered me the leeway to live my twenties to their fullest."

I wanted to hear his misshapen stories but I didn't want to find myself liking him. If we were attending events together and going away for a weekend, liking him meant that I'd start believing the ruse and we couldn't have that.

I didn't have any man-free manifesto on living my truth or being my best self to support this argument, but I was still taking the hits from my barely-there relationship with Steve. I wasn't ready to let myself feel things yet.

Feeling things was fucking scary.

"Just the basics," I repeated. "We're going for cocktail party passable here. We're not writing Wikipedia entries."

"My bad, my bad," he said. He flattened his hand on his breastbone. "Forgive me for asking, but what is it you do? I know you're a doctor but—"

"Surgeon," I interrupted. "I'm a general surgeon specializing in gastrointestinal surgery. I repair hernias, perform solid organ removal and colectomies, and whatever else needs cutting."

Riley swallowed thickly and set his beer down. He looked a little green. "Do you enjoy it? The cutting?"

I laughed self-consciously. It was hard to explain surgery to those outside the medical community. Most people thought of it as a dire, dreaded situation. While I wasn't one to cut without a damn good reason, surgery excited me. I loved exploring new cases and fixing things that only a surgeon could fix.

"I do," I said carefully. "It might sound weird, but I enjoy my work, and I'm very good at it."

I clasped my hands under my chin and shrugged. I'd learned over the years that men who announced their competence were viewed as confident but women who did the same were arrogant. Bitches, every last one of them. I'd also learned that I didn't give a fuck what people thought of me. That had worked remarkably well and never stopped me from rising to the top of my field until I'd found myself in this "But you slept with your intern!" quagmire.

Riley yanked his shirttails from his jeans and twisted to glance at the wound on his back. It was healing nicely. "I'd say so," he murmured. "Thanks for that, by the way."

"No problem," I said. "And you're an architect?"

"Yeah, but not in the way most people think of architects," he said. "Instead of building new structures, I work on the old ones." He pointed to the thick wooden beams overhead. "And the things inside them. My family has been restoring historic homes for three generations. I work with my brothers, Matt, Sam, and Patrick, and my sister Shannon."

I volleyed his earlier question back to him. "Do you enjoy it? The restoration?"

He traced the edge of his notebook and offered a quick nod. "More than I thought I would," he replied. "I'm, uh"— he held his hands in front of him like he was reaching for something—"I'm good at my work, too. But my good is different from my brothers' good, if that makes any sense."

I ran my fingers over my lips to repress the sigh attempting to break free. I really didn't want to like him this much.

Nodding, I said, "It does make sense."

"Right, so," he started. "Any siblings?"

"One brother. Adam is the oldest," I said carefully.

No need to put a finer point on that fact by mentioning my brother was only four *minutes* older. Twin stuff was a novelty to most people, but we were terrible at being twins. He'd once asked our mother why we had the same birthday, and seemed genuinely irritated that we had to share the twentieth of April. Eventually, they'd allowed him to celebrate on the twentieth and bumped me to the following day.

If that didn't sum up my place the family, I didn't know what did.

"We've covered the superficial stuff. Now I want you to answer a real question. Why aren't you on any one of the ninety-six dating apps out there and using all the guys in this town for some good old rebound sex? Why haven't you moved on yet?" he asked. "From the douche waffle."

I wrapped my hands around my glass and chewed on my lower lip. I wasn't ready for this level of real tonight. Instead of answering, I punted the question back to Riley. "Why are you still clinging to the soul-sucking ex from college? If we're weighing baggage, I'd say yours is heavier."

He opened his mouth to speak but then stopped himself. Lifting his hand, he gestured to the bartender in the universal signal for another round. He didn't wait for a server to bring the drinks, instead trotting to the bar to collect them himself.

Riley returned with two pilsner glasses and spared me a quick glance as he settled into the booth. "These are both for me," he said, drawing a circle around them with his finger. "And it's complicated in a way that will always fuck me over, and I'm going to drink these beers because I don't want to talk about it."

"How long has it been complicated?"

I wasn't sure why I asked. I didn't want to know him and I didn't want to like him, but I felt compelled to heal him. And that wasn't the doctor talking. Medicine hadn't made me a nurturer. But here I was, wanting to gather up his torn edges and bring them back together in a way that would erase all memory of the pain that had put them there.

He tipped back his glass and drank deeply. "It's been a couple of years, Alex," he said after a pause. "Is that your real name? Or is it your way of distracting people from the fact you're a woman?"

"It's Alexandra," I said tightly. "But I've only ever been called Alex. It's not a ploy to blend in with the boys."

"That's good," he replied, mostly to himself. Then his gaze shifted from the amber liquid in his glass to my chest. My skin heated under his watch, and though I fought like hell to think warm, flat-nippled thoughts, I sensed them hardening against my bra. "It's not like you could blend in anyway. Not with your"—he took another sip, eyes still mapping my cleavage—"little red shoes."

"My parents were expecting a boy," I said, eager to turn his attention in a different direction. Much more of that staring and I couldn't be held responsible for my actions, which would include rubbing his chest, ordering him to snuggle with me, and nakedness. So much nakedness. "It's understandable that the sonogram was wrong. My balls are pretty big."

He snickered into his beer. He was still working on the first and didn't object when I plucked the second for myself. "So they called you Alex," he said.

"They did," I said. "But don't worry. They weren't disappointed. Just surprised. It all evened out, but they'd taken to calling me Alex before I was born, so it stuck. They adjusted course soon enough, and made sure to slap big bows on my head every day."

That was close enough to the truth for now. The reality was that my parents were great but they had this head-tilting, eyes-squinting way of looking at me that clearly said they forgot about me until my existence intersected with Adam's.

Riley's lips turned down in a sharp frown as he eyed my

hair. "I can't imagine why you've abandoned that practice," he said with a chuckle. Then he folded his forearms on the table and leaned toward me. "What d'you say? Are we ready for next weekend?"

Wiping my hands on a paper napkin, I shrugged. "That really depends on how far you're looking to take these shenanigans."

"Shenanigans," he repeated. He stared at me, his eyes twinkling like I'd spoken a secret incantation. A smile pulled at his lips, and power surged through me. I'd put that smile on his face, even if I didn't understand its origin. I wanted to do it again, regardless of whether I didn't want to know him or like him or any other lie I'd sold myself. "I'm ready for anything, Shortstop."

I reached into my purse. "Let's get out of here," I said. "I can't do work-week hangovers."

"Why am I not surprised?" Riley mused, his eyes trained on the red wallet in my hands.

"I happen to like red," I said. It came out as a challenge, and his answering smirk told me he'd accepted.

He gestured over my shoulder toward the bar, and then turned his attention to my lips. It was then that we were both leaning forward, and only a breath apart. It was almost as if we'd forgotten, just for this second, that it was all pretend.

"If we were really—uh—whatever," he said, jerking his shoulder to discard the nuances contained in *whatever*, "I'd probably know all about how you liked your red. Whether it was all for show, or also for your secrets." His eyes shifted down, and he tilted his head as if he was trying to see beneath my shirt. "I'd know how you liked everything."

"Here you go. Thanks for stopping in tonight."

My heart pounding, I jolted back into my chair when the server dropped the bill—and Riley's credit card—on the table. My cheeks were burning and my mouth was dry, and I wanted to rewind time by about thirty seconds so I could punch the server in the balls before he could interrupt the single most sensual moment of my entire life.

That was either a comment on Riley's ability to make the mundane memorable, or the pathetic state of my sensual encounters. I wasn't interested in proving either of those hypotheses.

I watched while he signed the receipt and tucked his card away. "You've already paid," I snapped. I did that often. The snapping, but also the yelling, slamming, and stomping. It wasn't intentional. It was just how I operated, and I'd stopped worrying about whether people took offense at my sharp edges.

"I'd said I would. You can get the next one, dude," he said.

Dude. That was quite the fall from where we were only a breath ago. But this was the deal. The mutually beneficial arrangement that looked real and felt hollow.

"Yeah. Thanks, *dude,*" I said, working hard to put as much icy cold indifference into my voice as I could find. All that came out was fire. Needy, resentful fire.

"Sure. Whatever," he murmured. From under the table, he produced a worn leather messenger bag. He slipped his notebook and phone inside, and swung it across his chest as he stood. "Shall we?"

We made our way through the narrow tavern and out onto the sidewalk. We stood there, shooting glimpses at each other while we watched the traffic and pedestrians near the Public Garden.

"Where do you live?" I asked.

"Fort Point," he replied, dipping his hands into his pockets. "My brother Sam bought an old waterfront firehouse from the city a couple of years ago. It'd been condemned and was one hiccup away from collapsing in on itself, but we restored it." He lifted his shoulders and then let them drop. "It's a big place, so we both have our own sides. His wife makes amazing meatballs." Another shrug, another opportunity to drool over the mountain range known as his shoulders. "I stick around for the meatballs."

"Is that far from here?"

The way he was peering at me indicated we were probably in Fort Point right now and I'd somehow missed that information in the years since moving to this region.

"Do you know anything about Boston?" he asked. "Anything at all?"

"This is my fourth city in fifteen years, not including the summers I bounced all over the country for various programs and internships. And even then, I wasn't there to see the sights or meet the locals. During my sub-internship, I had every fifteenth day off."

"That's insane," he murmured.

"Pretty much, but it's getting better. My training is finished and my schedule isn't as terrible these days. Nick and Cal and I went hiking once, and we've hit up the bars and restaurants around the hospital," I said. "But to answer your question, no. I don't know much about Boston."

He nodded down the street, in the direction of my apartment. "We're going to fix that," he said. "I'll tell you about the north slope of Beacon Hill—that's where you live—while I walk you home. You probably didn't know that this side of the neighborhood used to be known as Mount Whoredom during the Revolutionary War. Beacon Street was a lane for cow grazing."

"You're not walking me to my apartment," I said, ignoring that helping of trivia. "That's not necessary. I got here just fine. I can get home without issue."

Slowly, he dragged his gaze from the street and leveled it at me. It was hot and demanding and not even close to friendly. "I'm sure you can, Alex. I'm going to do it anyway."

This time, I couldn't hold back the sigh. It was lost in the city noise and light summer breeze, but it was a bridge-crosser.

Alex: How are those sutures doing?

Riley: Fine.

Alex: Itchy?

Riley: Now that you mention it…

Alex: Time for them to come out. I have a break this afternoon if you want to swing by the hospital. It won't take long.

Riley: I can't do that.

Alex: Maybe later?

Riley: Maybe not at all?

Alex: They need to come out. I don't want them getting any more uncomfortable.

Riley: You're being unexpectedly tolerable today. Did you go for a squirt of sugar-free vanilla in that iced skinny venti?

Riley: Maybe an extra almond?

Alex: As a matter of fact, I had an avocado for breakfast.

Riley: An avocado? Like…all by itself?

Alex: Yes.

Riley: Do you eat it like an apple, or do you scoop it out and put it in a bowl?

Alex: In a bowl, with a little bit of salt and pepper.

Riley: You are some sort of strange.

Alex: Again, I'm not sure how to take these comments from you.

Alex: If you don't want to come to the hospital, you can drop by my apartment tomorrow morning. Someone should check out that wound.

Riley: Don't worry about it.

Alex: Well, I am. That's the basis of this conversation.

Riley: Don't. Nick still owes me a few favors. I'll head over to his place tonight.

Alex: Have him send me a picture when he's done.

Riley: So. Fucking. Strange.

Alex: I want to see how my work turned out. Don't you look at your houses when they're finished?

Riley: That's not the same.

Alex: It's EXACTLY the same!

Alex: If I hadn't been busy arguing with Nick about the proper closure, I would've gotten a picture beforehand.

Riley: That solves it. I'm never swiping left or right when I look at pictures on your phone.

Alex: That's probably smart.

Alex: I have a picture from a surgery last week where I removed a 10 pound trichobezoar from this guy's duodenum.

Riley: I'm going to regret asking this but…what the fuck is that?

Alex: Trichobezoar or duodenum?

Riley: Let's start with the first one, and if I don't find myself in the fetal position after, we can move onto the other one.

Alex: A hairball. It tends to appear in people with trichotillomania, which is compulsive hair pulling, and trichophagia, which is eating the hair you pull out.

Riley: Oh my fucking god.

Riley: No. I don't want to hear about the other thing.

Alex: It's just the first part of the small intestine.

Riley: Now you tell me?

Riley: Okay, Shortstop. Listen. You could've mentioned that one of those things was really fucking horrible and the other was basically not a big deal. I need some context on the horrors waiting behind your doors.

Alex: My apologies.

Alex: But obviously, by comparison, a picture of your wound shouldn't be a big deal.

Riley: All right but if my back ends up on some scar fetish Instagram feed, we're going to have words.

Alex: What if I crop out that cute tramp stamp of yours?

Riley: Words, Alexandra.

Riley: What's your mixed drink of choice? We talked about beer and wine, but nothing else.

Alex: It's six thirty in the fucking morning and you want to talk about mixed drinks?

Riley: I want to talk about anything other than the shit that's been on my mind for the past four hours.

Riley: Drinks say a lot about a person.

Alex: What does a lemon drop say about a person?

Riley: It says she thinks she's a vodka girl but should stick with rum.

Alex: You're sure about that?

Riley: I bartended through college and grad school.

Alex: What about sangria?

Riley: She can't handle rough sex or her cabernet without the fruit.

Alex: Dirty martini?

Riley: She swallows every time and likes it.

Alex: Rum and Diet Coke?

Riley: Sister of Pi Beta Phi who speaks via screaming and will definitely be crying twice before the night is over.

Alex: Those mixed shots with weird names like Hot Buttered Rimjob?

Riley: She's never ordered a salad without the dressing on the side even though she uses all the dressing. Every time.

Alex: Tequila on the rocks, no salt?

Riley: Woman of my dreams.

Alex: I guess it's a good thing that I stick with white wine.

Riley: Yeah. Definitely.

Alex: What's yours?

Riley: Whiskey on the rocks, but I rarely drink it.

Alex: Any reason, aside from sleeping in bathtubs?

Riley: I get a little too honest for my own good.

Alex: That's funny. I'm always too honest for my own good. I've never needed liquor for that.

Riley: Quick question for you, Shortstop.

Alex: If I'm the shortstop, what does that make you?

Riley: Not in the mood to extend a metaphor.

Riley: Sorry. Didn't sleep last night. Long day. Bad mood. Didn't mean to aim it at you.

Alex: I know why I didn't sleep last night but what's your excuse?

Riley: Your story first.

Alex: Why are you so demanding?

Riley: The penis, mostly.

Riley: It really gets in the way.

Alex: Mmhmm. My balls do that all the time.

Riley: You know…whenever you mention your balls, a small part of me believes you're being serious.

Alex: You'll get a good look at them when they're on your chin.

Riley: Well. We know what my nightmares will be about tonight.

Alex: You'll get some sleep between them though.

Alex: I'll be night float sleeping, which isn't really sleeping.

Riley: Explain.

Alex: I'm the attending covering the overnight general surgery floor for the rest of the week…on top of my regular hours. It's one of those last-minute perks the Chief likes to drop on me.

Alex: So what kept you up?

Riley: The penis, mostly.

Alex: Ha.

Riley: What's the dress code for Saturday night?

Alex: I don't know. I haven't really thought about that yet.

Riley: Are we talking black tie? Diddy's white party? Luau? Backyard barbeque?

Riley: Ballpark it.

Alex: I asked Hartshorn. He's wearing a suit. Five bucks says he rolls in twenty minutes before closing time.

Alex: If he shows. He's the one person who can get away with missing this party.

Riley: And why is that?

Alex: He's amazing. Really, truly amazing. Some people go to the theater or the ballet. I watch Hartshorn from the gallery.

Riley: Wait…do you have a thing for him?

Alex: Cal? Cal Hartshorn? No. Hell no. He's in brother/uncle territory. Same with Acevedo.

Riley: Just checking.

Alex: Jealous?

Riley: Is it an issue if I am?

Alex: Sounds like a personal problem.

Riley: This attitude of yours…

Alex: It's a handful.

Riley: Good thing I have two hands.

"THAT'S BUMBLEBEE," I said, pointing at the screen. "He's an Autobot, and a loyal soldier. He's very protective."

Dave kicked his feet up and waved his arms, a wet gurgle accompanying his movements on the round mat. He was just over four months old now, and the cutest little dude I'd ever met. I liked Shannon's kid, Abby, too, but it was different with Dave. I got to see him every day, and the two of us had a gentlemen's gathering whenever Sam and Tiel needed some time together. Or sleep, as was often the case.

"And that's Optimus Prime," I continued. "That's what we call your Uncle Patrick. I'm not sure whether he's always been this serious or he grew up to resemble the reluctant leader of the Autobots. It's a chicken and egg situation."

He gurgled again and went to work at cramming his entire hand into his mouth. It didn't appear he was interested in a primer on *Transformers*, not when he had hands to explore.

"That's cool, bro," I said. "We've got plenty of time."

I eyed the row of bookshelves beside my bed. Dave wasn't mobile yet, but I'd moved my comic book collection to the top shelves the day he'd rolled over on that mat. I loved my nephew to pieces but a small part of me would shatter if he decided to use one of my early edition *X-Men* as a chew toy.

It was somewhat unusual that I lived with my brother and his wife, but I liked being around people. Specifically, *my* people. I enjoyed seeing them in the kitchen each morning and coming home to them each night, and all the times in between.

My sister-in-law Tiel was an incredible friend, and the one person in my family who never defaulted to comments about me being slow or immature. She'd never suggested that I'd overstayed my welcome at the firehouse either, and I couldn't articulate how much I appreciated that.

I hadn't known what to expect when Sam and Tiel announced they were having a baby. I was thrilled for them, of course, but we had a nice little ecosystem here. I'd worried about things changing, or finding myself in the way of the new family. That hadn't been the case, and I'd only confused the squat bottle of breast milk in the refrigerator for cream once.

And I didn't mind having an infant for a roommate. Especially since I got to introduce him to the world of super-heroes and villains while Sam caught up on designs and Tiel worked in her studio on Saturday mornings. She was a classically trained musician, but didn't get much time with her instruments these days.

Over dinner last night, she'd mentioned being anxious about teaching second graders how to play the violin when school started up in a few weeks, as she'd barely practiced since Dave's arrival. Tiel's lack of rehearsal time was only one of her worries. She and Sam still hadn't found a nanny or daycare solution for Dave, not one that met their many requirements. Since they weren't willing to settle and their careers offered some degree of flexibility, they were patching together a schedule that allowed one of them to be with Dave at all times. Sam was convinced it would work and was already building a small crib for his office. Tiel wasn't as confident.

Dave caught his feet in his chubby fingers and cried out in celebration. His face and fingers were shiny with baby slobber but he was too pleased with himself to care.

"Nice job, Simba," I said, shaking the dog-shaped rattle he enjoyed so much.

"He's obsessed with his toes," Tiel murmured from the doorway. "How's he been? Fussy much?"

"No, he's been a cool kid," I said, shaking my head. "We've just been watching *Transformers* and chewing our hands."

"We have tasty hands, don't we?" she asked, kneeling beside him on the other side of the mat. "And how's Uncle Riley? Fussy much?"

I paused the film and stretched my legs out in front of me. "No more than usual," I replied. "I have plans tonight, though. I won't be here for dinner."

She glanced at me while running her finger down the baby's cheek. "Ohh, *plans*," she said.

"It's nothing," I said, laughing. "Just a cocktail party with a friend."

"A cocktail party," she repeated, sending a purposeful glance at the freshly pressed suit and dress shirt hanging from my closet door. She didn't try to conceal her smug smile. "You're wearing a suit for a friend." She said that as if it explained the secrets of the universe. "Who is this friend?"

Dave pitched the rattle across the mat, and I handed it back to him. "No one you know," I said, and her smile fell into a confused scowl.

"This friend isn't Magnolia?" she asked. "What do you mean? I was over here with my Team Gigi shirt all ready to go. I was going to arm wrestle Patrick until he declared his love of roof gardens and force Sam to play nice with some dinner parties and double dates." She held up her hands and let them fall into her lap, as if I'd dashed all of her hopes. Every last one of them. "Are you sure it's not Gigi?"

"Positive," I said, laughing. When it came to her people, Tiel was fierce. I loved that about her. "But thanks for being ready to go to bat for me."

"I don't know what I'm going to do with that Team Gigi shirt," she said. "I might wear it anyway, just to get Sam fired up." She tapped her chin as she considered this. "If not Gigi, who's gotten you into a suit on a Saturday?"

I hated misleading Tiel. Not only because she deserved better but because she could see right through me. It wasn't the cover story I was worried about her seeing. It was the fucked-up state of my head. Lauren continued to monopolize that territory, but now Alex was fighting her way in, too.

An Alex-and-Lauren mashup would've been sensational, but my brain couldn't do us all a favor and take the easy route into girl-on-girl. Instead, I'd emerge from another torturous Lauren dream and—on top of all the issues I already had—I couldn't shake the feeling that I was now deceiving Alex, too. Sure, we were pretend-dating and this arrangement had a clear termination date, but it felt wrong.

Or I'd text with Alex about balls or liquor or something inconsequential like that, and I'd walk away in awe because she managed to be sexy while spitting nails. Talking with her felt easy, which probably had something to do with us both sailing the high seas of shambles. She was pretty, too. It was the kind of pretty that was subtle and slow to sneak up on you, but when it did, it struck hard.

Every time I'd think about Alex's lips or wonder whether she was as aggressive in bed as she was everywhere else, I was reminded that I *loved* Lauren. It wasn't an outcropping of overdue mommy issues or a childish crush. It was one-sided and ill-fated and the most emotionally disastrous thing I'd ever experienced, but it was real.

In a weird, not-entirely-grounded-in-reality way, my growing attraction to Alex was a betrayal to Lauren. Those morning erections were now made of shame and guilt *and* a bone-shaking quantity of lust for two completely different women.

"Her name is Alex, and we're just hanging out," I said. That much was accurate. No cloudy half-truths to be seen. "Just friends. That's it."

Not as accurate. Not when I'd dreamed of my hand on her throat and my cock in her mouth last night.

"Did this start while we were away on vacation?" Tiel asked.

She watched as Dave worked hard at rolling onto his belly. He'd only succeeded twice, and that seemed to infuriate him. This boy wanted to roll and creep and explore, and he wasn't stopping until he could. Her hand hovered an inch from the baby's back while he struggled to complete the turn. He'd made it to his side, but wasn't happy about having his arm trapped under him.

"Or did you have a summer romance that I completely missed because I've been busy being a milk maid?"

"You didn't miss anything," I said with a shrug. If I kept it low-key now, it wouldn't be a big deal when things ended. "I met her at Nick and Erin's place a couple of weeks ago. She works with Nick. She's a surgeon."

"That's handy," Tiel replied.

"Yeah," I said. "She was there for dinner. Actually, I crashed their get-together." I scratched my chin. "Do you think I need to apologize for that? Or go mow their lawn, or something?"

"I'm sure it was fine." Tiel turned back to Dave. "You did it! Look at you, my amazing little man!" she cried, clapping her hands as he landed on his belly.

He held his head up and offered a slobbery grin to acknowledge his accomplishment. He burped loudly—it was shocking how much noise that small body could produce—and Tiel patted his back. She cut a glance across the mat and motioned for me to continue.

"Like I said, we're hanging out," I said.

"You're keeping it casual? The *just friends* routine?"

I murmured in agreement. "Totally casual."

If casual involves a detailed dream of biting the soft part of her inner thigh.

"Let me offer a tiny bit of advice from someone who's been there," she said with a smirk. She'd noticed the filthy stop my mind had taken. "Don't assume she's cool with friends-only when things get a little more than *friendly*. And don't assume it has to stay casual if you're ready for more."

"You know me, Punky Brewster," I replied. "I don't mince words."

"You don't," she conceded, bringing Dave to her shoulder.

"But you don't always talk about the things that are bothering you either. Even when those things have been bothering you for a long time."

She pinned me with a sharp look that had me wondering what else she'd noticed.

"Did we not have a fully unpleasant conversation about the necessity of wearing pants around the house?" I asked with a clear intent to reroute this conversation.

She stared at me a beat longer but then blinked away as she looped Dave's blanket around the crook of her elbow and pushed to her feet. The thing that people missed about Tiel—or, one of the *many* things they missed—was that she never pushed anyone further than they could handle. How she knew where the line landed was beyond me but she knew it, and she never crossed it.

And I fucking adored her for it. She was the closest thing to the mother I'd never known, and I couldn't help but vault off the floor and wrap my arms around her shoulders.

"Thank you," I said, my words muffled against her dark hair.

"Anytime," she replied. Dave let out a primal roar and beat his little fists against my shoulder. "You know I'm always going to be here for you, right?"

"Would it be wrong for me to call you Alfred?" I asked. "Because you're the closest thing I have to him."

"That's a Batman reference, right?" she asked.

"Of course it is," I said, giving her another squeeze. "Batman would've been nothing without Alfred."

Tiel stepped back and ran her hand over Dave's mostly bald head. "I'm sure Batman would've been fine," she said. "But it never hurts to have a boost from someone who loves you."

Nine

ALEXANDRA

SHIT, *he cleans up good.*

That was my only thought as I watched Riley from across Chief Chapelton's patio. He was standing in profile while he talked with Nick and Erin at the bar, one hand in his pocket and the other holding a bottle of beer. It gave me a delicious view of his long, lean torso wrapped in the crispest white shirt I'd ever seen. And those trousers. *God.* I couldn't decide whether the fabric was draped with the intention of high-lighting his tree-trunk thighs or his pinch-worthy backside. I resisted every urge to twine my fingers around the silver necklaces at my throat. It was too early for full-on pearl clutching.

I still couldn't believe that one man had been blessed with so many gifts. That body, that face. It was overwhelming. He was gorgeous in a fresh, arresting way that made all the other pretty boys out there look airbrushed beyond belief. But I figured perfection came at a price, and he was probably paying for it with a small dick or lack of post-coital decency.

I couldn't even think that with a straight face. Aside from the fact those trousers were quite *illustrative*, Riley wasn't the type to fuck and flee. Or so I presumed.

As he turned away from the bar, a drink in both hands, I worked hard at keeping my eyes above his belt. I wasn't even smooth about it. Nope, I was just staring at his face and scowling to the extent that his easy smile had morphed into a concerned frown when he reached my side.

"What's wrong?" he asked, glancing around.

"Nothing," I said, reaching for the martini glass he was holding. The handoff was rocky, and I ended up with cranberry-tinged vodka dripping from my fingers.

"My bad," he murmured, offering the soggy napkin that had been wrapped around the base of his beer bottle.

"Don't worry about it." I wiped my hand on the side of my dress. Dark blue was good for minimizing hips and hiding wet spots in a pinch.

Once dry, I looked up and studied the crowd. The Chief was seated on the near side of the patio, and from the gestures he was making, he was telling surgery stories. There were a half dozen doctors sitting or standing nearby, hanging on every word. I would've been hanging, too—I loved me some surgery stories—but my purpose was to be seen with my hot-as-sin new man. That was why we were parked in this spot, right where everyone could see us.

I was still bitter about resorting to the fake boyfriend strategy of getting ahead, but after the Chief's earlier welcome address and toasts, it was definitely necessary. It was his standard "woohoo, we're good at surgery" but he also highlighted the accomplishments of several surgeons. Acevedo was on the list, along with Hartshorn—who'd found another dissecting aorta this evening—and several other truly deserving doctors. Despite the fact I'd logged more hours, had better outcomes, published more frequently, *and* had the lowest mortality rate of any surgeon in my department, I didn't make the cut tonight.

I shouldn't have expected to be on the short list—not with my surgical posture issues, of course—but the disappointment was getting old. It was like being a kid all over again. I'd always been secondary to Adam. I was convinced that my parents didn't start out with a shady plan to favor one child over another, but that was how it had shaken out. Adam's interests were the ones we'd pursued, and that was how I ended up running for eighth grade class secretary when he ran for president. Or how I'd found myself on the sidelines as a cheerleader when he got into high school football. That I'd made it to med school—and not working with Adam at one of the car dealerships our father owned in Reno —was the greatest trick I'd ever pulled off.

"This property was meant for entertaining," Riley said. He leaned closer, and his breath tickled against my neck. "And I know I'm not supposed to tell you, or any other woman, to smile, but do it. You look like you're being held against your will, and I'm not in the mood to get arrested tonight."

I'd missed everything he said because I was busy suppressing a whole-body shiver. He was so close and smelled so good and it had been so long since anyone's anything had stirred a systemic reaction from me, and I almost wanted it. The shiver. The closeness. Him.

"What did you say?" I asked.

"Smile," he said, brushing my hair over my shoulder. "Pretend you want to be here."

"I don't," I replied automatically.

"Trust me, I know," he said with a laugh. "But we'll do what we have to do, and then we'll get out of here and have some nachos."

"Nachos?" I repeated. "Thank you for the invitation, but I don't really think I want nachos tonight. I've had a long week and—"

And then his *hand* was on my *ass*.

"Look alive, Gastro Girl," he whispered. He was way, *way* too close for me to hold back the shiver this time. And that hand. Well. It did things to me. "It's show time."

By the time I'd recovered from the feel of his long fingers pressing against my backside, it was too late to school my dazed expression when Mrs. Chapelton spotted us from across the patio. She was headed straight in this direction, all curious, smiling eyes and relieved glances, as if it was a real weight off her shoulders to see me with a man.

"Shit, what am I supposed to call you?" I whispered.

"Riley would be fine," he replied.

"That's not what I meant," I hissed, bumping his side with my elbow for emphasis. "What are we? Are you my, uh—"

He replied with a sharp slap to my ass.

"Doctor Emmerling, I'm tickled to see you this evening," she said. She shifted toward Riley of the Ass-Grabbers, who didn't limit himself to grabbing. Not when he could pat and squeeze. "Vivianne Chapelton. Welcome to our home."

"Riley Walsh. Thank you for having me," he replied.

Her white hair glittering in the evening light, she was holding the cut crystal tumbler with both hands and pressing the glass to her chest as if she was worried someone would snatch the precious away. "Are you also a physician?" she asked him.

Another squeeze, another shiver. "No, ma'am," he replied. "I'm an architect—"

"An architect!" she cooed. "That's fascinating. Have you designed anything I'd know?"

The hand on my ass urged me closer, and the position forced my arm around his waist. I didn't need to reach under his suit coat to do it, but that was how it went with slippery slopes. Inch by inch until it was simple enough to rationalize falling for a man who wanted another woman.

He pointed over the thick line of shrubs bordering the yard to the neighboring house. "I believe my partners worked on that home for several years," he said. "Do the Castavechias still live there?"

This extricated one hand from the glass as she waved at Riley. "Yes! I had lunch with Rosemary just last week and she was telling me about wanting to hire the team who handled her remodel to work on her new cottage on the Cape." Mrs. Chapelton turned to me, her eyes twinkling. "Where did you and Mr. Walsh meet? You must tell me everything, dear."

"I—uh—I mean, we—"

"We met at a dinner party," he replied. "Mutual friends were hosting a small gathering, and that's where I had the pleasure of making Alexandra's acquaintance."

I would've been fine with Riley's hand on my rear end. Really. I would've gotten through this exchange without too much trouble. But then he decided to turn his face and kiss my temple, and I was done. Down for the count. Finished.

Mrs. Chapelton gave him a deep, appreciative smile. "Aren't you a delight," she said, glancing at me for confirmation.

"He is," I said through gritted teeth. I couldn't relax while he explored the terrain of my ass. Not unless I wanted to dissolve into a moany-needy-swoony puddle. And I wasn't interested in that. *Not here.* If he wanted to get me behind closed doors, he could *explore* to his heart's content. "Such a delight."

"And will you be able to join us for this autumn's gala?" she asked him. "I do hope so. Handsome young men like you make tuxedos worth wearing."

Riley laughed and took the compliment like a champ. Bashful enough to be humble, but smart enough to know he wasn't to contradict this woman. "Yes, ma'am," he said. "I'm looking forward to it, but for entirely different reasons."

"Oh?" she replied. "Now you have me curious, Mr. Walsh."

"Yeah, he does that," I murmured.

His hand shifted to my waist, and that would've been well and good if it hadn't tugged me even closer. My cheek was pressed to his chest and I was drowning in the scent of him.

"Any evening I get with my Alexandra is special," he said.

Despite the fact I hadn't been drinking anything, I choked on the words *my Alexandra.* I'd never been referred to that way before. It didn't even sound like my name, and I didn't know how to file it away with the rest of this ass-grabbing charmer.

"But there's something extraordinary about escorting a beautiful woman to a ball." He glanced down at me, smiling. "And then escorting her home."

Mrs. Chapelton leaned toward me with a conspiratorial wink. "Hold onto this one," she said. "Hold on tight." Her gaze pinged between us and she offered a warm smile. "I'd stay and chat but I just spotted Doctor Gupta and Doctor

Garritty. They look terribly lonely. What will I do with all of these bachelors?" She pointed at us. "I'll be expecting you both at the gala."

Neither of us moved as she stepped away, her gauzy white sundress floating around her legs as she traversed the yard in search of single men to harangue. Riley turned his head, and his lips were on my temple again.

"I think we passed, as far as she's concerned," he whispered, the words spoken into my skin. "But there's an audience over your shoulder." His hold on me tightened when I shifted. "Give it a minute, would you? If you run away from me now, the jig will be up, Honeybee."

"At least tell me who's in that audience," I demanded.

"That crew you've been watching," Riley answered. "The one from the patio."

Nodding, I traced the line of his suit coat from shoulder to wrist. "This is fitted within an inch of your life," I murmured. "How can you even move?"

"I'm a little bulkier than I was when I had it tailored," he replied with a shrug. That shrug tucked me closer to his chest, and now I was stifling sighs. "I've been lifting more than usual."

"Any particular reason?" I asked. My hand was on Riley's forearm, and the pretense of inspecting his suit had long since dropped. Based on his smirk, he knew it, too.

"Needed to funnel some pent-up energy. Working out keeps me from doing irresponsible things," he said, his breath ghosting over my ear. "Speaking of irresponsible things, what would that douche waffle intern of yours have to say now?"

I figured he was squeezing my ass for some expressive purpose but I couldn't think beyond a screaming desire to have his hands all over me, everywhere. "I don't know," I admitted.

"Give me your phone," Riley ordered. There was an authority in his voice that had me reaching into my wristlet without thinking better of it.

"Are you planning to call him up?" I asked, handing over the device. "Have a chat?"

"Definitely not, no." He tapped the camera icon and switched it to selfie mode. Holding the phone out, he snapped several photos of us. "Smile like you want him to know he didn't win," he whispered. "Smile like you mean it."

And I did. I meant it.

"Now post one of those on your social media. Wherever you have lots of mutual friends and you know he'll see it," Riley said, handing the phone back. "Or just text it to the fucker, and tell him my dick wins for length *and* girth."

I slapped a hand over my mouth to contain a burst of hysterical laughter.

"I don't know what you're laughing about," Riley murmured. "We're discussing empirical facts."

"Can't be sure about that," I said as I posted the best image to Instagram and Facebook. "Haven't examined all the evidence."

"You just tell me when you'd like to get your hands on the evidence. It'll be available to you, Alex." He shifted, his hold on my backside loosening. "They went inside," he said.

"Mmhmm," I murmured, stowing my phone. "Time to show off the Chief's model boats. Or yachts, or whatever."

Riley nodded and patted my ass one last time. "All right, Honeybee. Mission accomplished. Fall back."

It should've been easier to disentangle myself from Riley but it quickly turned complicated when one of the decorative buttons on the waist of my dress caught on his suit coat. "You're stuck on me," I said. "Don't move. I don't want to rip your suit."

"There are lot of things I want to say about that right now," he murmured. "Gonna keep it all to myself."

"Wise," I replied. "Here, you go that direction. I've almost got it."

"You stay there," he argued. "I have a better angle. I'll get it."

We bent to free the button at the same moment, and in the process, Riley's elbow upended my drink. The pink liquid splashed down over my legs and doused my shoes.

"Oh, shit." He shucked his coat—still hooked on my dress—and draped it over my arm. "Hold this and stay right there. And do as you're told this time, Alexandra."

He dropped to the grass, set his beer bottle down and mopped vodka from my legs with the same soggy napkin he'd offered earlier. It was indecent, really, watching this man tend to me from his knees.

I didn't want him to stop.

"It's fine," I said, reaching for his shoulder. "I don't even like those shoes. Obviously. They're beige."

He went right on hunting for stray vodka, with one big palm curled around my calf to hold me in place. Or maybe he was trying to steady himself? I wasn't sure, but I did know this had to stop. I crouched down, hoping to get him off the ground, and that was the exact moment his head snapped up…and connected with my face.

"Oh *shit*," he said as my hand flew to my wounded lip.

The quick burst of pain sent tears prickling my eyes, and I fought to blink them away. I wasn't crying in front of this guy, and definitely not with my colleagues and boss nearby.

Didn't need to add Emotional Woman to my list of professional faults.

Riley's eyes were wide and panicked, and he shot to his feet. He brought both hands to my face. "I'm so sorry. Are you all right?"

I nodded. "Just a fat lip," I said from behind my fingers.

"Oh my fucking god, you can't take me anywhere." With a sigh, he turned his attention to freeing my dress from his coat. It took only a moment, and he blew out another breath when it was fixed. Dragging his knuckles down my chin, he said, "I want to see. Show me what I did."

I pulled my fingers away, wiping the spots of blood on my skirt. "It's fine. A little ice and it will go right down."

Riley stared at me, his brows pinched together as he traced the swollen line of my lower lip with the pad of his thumb. "Let's get out of here," he whispered. "Are you still up for nachos?"

No. I want to go home, take off my soaked shoes, and sleep for days.

I almost said that. The words were right there on my tongue, ready to jump off and shut down this evening. But his forehead was crinkled with concern and his palms were cupping my cheeks and I didn't want to stop pretending yet.

"Only if they come with plenty of beer," I said. I shifted toward the side yard that led to the driveway, and promptly knocked over Riley's forgotten beer. Groaning as the frothy liquid splashed on my skin and trickled down to my toes, I shook my head. "Stupid beige shoes."

"I'm guessing you'd rather drink the beer than wear it," he said, hooking his arm around my shoulders. "That can be arranged, you know. I'm familiar with many establishments that specialize in delivering beer in glasses *and* bottles. Would you like that?"

Again, Riley was holding me close, my cheek on his chest and his scent going to work on my hormones, and I was sliding down that slope. I didn't know how many inches I'd slip before this arrangement ended or I slid all the way down.

"Yeah," I said. "I'd like that."

His expression was tight as he studied my lips, but he dragged his gaze up to my eyes and smiled. "That's convenient," he said. "I want more Alex time. You haven't insulted me nearly enough tonight."

All the way down. I was going to find the bottom of this slope, and if Riley had a mind to continue smelling like such a—a *man*—I was finding it soon.

Ten

RILEY

"AND YOU KNEW THE NEIGHBORS," Alex said, slapping her free hand on the table. The other hand was occupied holding a towel-wrapped chunk of ice to her bottom lip. "You knew the damn neighbors and you'd remodeled their damn kitchen, too."

I shook a tortilla chip at her. "Someone had to carry that conversation," I said.

"Because *someone* was groping someone else's ass," she cried.

"And I'd do it again." I shrugged as I piled chicken atop my chip. There were buffalo nachos for me, the good, old-fashioned chili version for her, and a collection of empty beer bottles between us. "It's a fabulous ass."

Fabulous was inadequate. Alex's ass was meant to be squeezed, spanked, licked, bitten. Fucked. That I'd managed to speak to a white-haired lady who seemed irrationally protective of her gin and tonic while touching that ass was proof of the higher powers. And that I'd refrained from touching that ass in the past hour was proof that I was, at heart, a hero with superhuman qualities.

"Thank you for…everything," Alex said carefully. "You were amazing with Mrs. Chapelton. I'm surprised she didn't drag you inside and get your professional advice on a few things." She looked away, frowning. "Nevermind. That didn't sound right."

I laughed and raised my glass in salute. "I knew what you meant."

"It went really well," she said.

It sounded like a concession, but I wasn't sure which one of us she'd doubted more. Given the spectacular way we'd concluded our performance of Happy Couple, I was deserving of that doubt.

"Except for that," I said, nodding at her swollen lip.

"And these," she said, pointing to the heels drying on the bench beside her.

I shot a grimace at them. "Two questions," I said, holding up two fingers. "First, when did you get non-red shoes?"

She used a broken chip to scrape guacamole from the bowl. "Believe it or not, I've had those shoes since high school. That's probably an indication of how infrequently I wear them. But," she continued, "my mother feels very strongly that beige heels—she calls them *nude*—are absolutely essential to, and I quote, lengthen the leg."

Leaning back in my chair for a better angle, I peered at Alex's legs. Her bare feet were crossed at the ankles and propped up on the booth beside me, and all I could see was smooth, glorious skin until it disappeared beneath the skirt of her blue dress. "And why do you need to do that?"

"Because I'm short," she said. "Short girls always need to lengthen the leg."

"You don't need to change a thing," I said. I wrapped my hand around her ankle because I wanted to touch her again. Just one more time. "Stick with the red shoes. They're spunky, and I like a little spunk on you."

She opened her mouth to respond and then promptly closed it, instead staring at the decimated trays before us. Then reached for another chip without meeting my eyes.

Good. She'd heard it exactly as I'd intended.

"I'll take it under consideration," she said. It looked like she was blushing, but sports bars weren't known for their lighting, and The Fours was no exception. "And your second question?"

I glanced down at her toes and the chipped ruby nail polish there, and couldn't help admitting that I liked this girl. Every salty ounce of her. And I didn't like her because we needed to help each other survive a rocky patch of life. I liked her because I couldn't know her and *not* like her. She was fierce as fuck and had more balls than any man I knew, but there was a quietly adorable side to her, too. Adorable like bright, bright eyes and tattoos I didn't understand and (ass) cheeks that required squeezing.

I blinked up at her, suddenly disoriented. I didn't have a place for these reactions, and I wasn't sure I wanted to make room. Wasn't sure I knew how.

"I'm—I'm sorry," I said, catching myself before losing control of my words and pelting her with rapid-fire stutters. "I didn't catch that. What did you say again?"

If Alex had noticed me stumbling, she hid it well as she rifled through her wallet-purse-thingy. Upon discovering a rubber band, she twisted her hair into a knot atop her head. "You said you had two questions for me," she replied, the band snared between her teeth. "What was the second one?"

"What's the story with the red?" I asked.

Alex lifted a shoulder and waved away the question. "I like red," she replied. "No story."

I squeezed her ankle. It wasn't right to continue touching her when I wasn't capable of processing the recognition that I liked her without an emotional spasm, but here I was. "I don't think I buy that," I said.

She shrugged as if my rejection of her non-explanation didn't matter, and she went back to picking through the plates of nachos between us. "I wasn't selling it."

I shifted toward the bar to catch the highlights from tonight's games. It was a welcomed distraction from collating the competing thoughts in my head. In recent years, I'd always been able to lose myself in something long enough to forget that I adored my brother's wife. Whether it was work or sporting events or a weekend spent filling in behind the bar in Rhode Island, I knew how to get lost.

But I didn't know how to be lost in a woman who wasn't Lauren. I'd never found myself in quicksand but I had to imagine the heart-thumping confusion that came from working like hell to get out but only sinking farther down was something like this.

"I'm astounded, actually," Alex mused. "I'd expected Mrs. Chapelton to properly harass you. You know, demand your résumé and family tree."

I dragged my attention away from the screens and back to Alex. "Have you figured it out yet?"

She offered a quick glance in my direction as she hunted for the chip of her dreams. "Figured out what?"

"You wanted to know how to introduce me. Now that you've had some time to consider it, I'm curious whether you've determined what we are." She paused, her hand frozen over the plate. "You know, we could have some fun with it," I continued. "We could say we're the product of a modern-day arranged pairing because we're too fucked up to meet other humans."

"No exaggeration there," she said with a hearty laugh. "Better yet, we're too hip and sophisticated for titles. Fuck anyone who asks. They don't deserve to know our lives."

"That's right," I said. It was good to laugh, and even better to remember this was fully contrived. "Fuck those fuckers."

"All of them," she said. "Or, we're in wild, hot love. Romeo and Juliet but less death. Much less death."

"Yeah, let's skip the suicide," I said, laughing. "And we're neither teenagers nor stirring up the village gangs by getting together."

"Why not say we're lovers?" Alex asked. "Tell people that it's purely carnal, and you just fucked me in the coat closet."

My beer was halfway to my mouth when those words tumbled from Alex's lips, and I froze. "Yeah," I said, setting the glass down. "That one works."

My brain was busy rewinding and replaying the moment when *you just fucked me in the coat closet* slipped past her battered lips. It left my skin feeling hot and tight, and my pulse racing to catch up with these notions of *Alex, naked, sex, now*. My cock shook off its slumber and glanced around for some indication that it was time to get up and go to work.

"Or," she started, gesturing toward me like there wasn't an ongoing discussion of fucking her in a semi-public loca-tion, "we're dating, casually. It was a fix-up by mutual friends, and we're taking it slow. Casual." She nodded and held up her finger. "I like that one. It sounds plausible, and it's safe for mixed company."

"That's important," I said, dropping my free hand under the table. This wasn't the right time to be inadvertently unzipped. "When I fuck you in a closet, you'll be the only one who needs to know about it."

I went back to my beer because what else was there to say? That I was thinking about flipping that cute little skirt up over her ass and making this night even more interesting? That I was debating whether I'd have to keep her quiet so that no one outside this hypothetical closet could hear me owning her body? That I was acutely aware our arrangement involved none of that and I was a handsy motherfucker who couldn't stop touching her? That I couldn't manage the competing desires of my heart—of *Lauren*—and my cock?

Beer. Soul food for sad fools.

"It's good of you to clarify that," she said. "We never did finalize the *sex in small spaces* portion of our agreement."

With my thumb, I drew circles on her ankle as I watched her dig into the nachos again. This woman was a bottomless pit. "Have you ever been to a Red Sox game, Alex?" I asked.

"I was supposed to go to a game with Hartshorn and Acevedo last summer, but it didn't work out," she said. "I think they went, but I was tied up with a patient. The next time we were all free on the same day, the season had ended."

"You're tight with those guys," I said.

She laughed at that, deep and loud like a woman was supposed to laugh. "Hartshorn is on the floor beneath me, and he's lived in that building since the dawn of time, or so he'd like us to believe," she said. "Acevedo was on the floor above me until he moved out a couple of months ago, and he's a hoarder."

It was my turn to bark out a laugh. "Is he now?"

Alex reached for her glass and sipped. "Not the way we typically think about hoarding," she said. "He hoards people. The oddities and strays and lost causes." She motioned between us with her drink. "I hope this doesn't come as a shock to you, but we're part of his collection."

I glanced around the tavern, studying the assortment of games on the televisions and patrons seated at the bar before looking back to Alex. "I hadn't thought of Nick that way, but you might be right."

"He's a good guy," she said. She selected a chip and took a dainty bite from the corner before meeting my gaze. "Hartshorn, too. Good surgeons, good friends, good neighbors. But we can't manage to get our shit in line to do much more than grab lunch or dinner together. Not often. We're a little too scattered to plan for baseball games. To make matters worse, Acevedo's only interested in cutesy married shit now, like dinner parties and wine tastings."

"I'm going to fix that. The Red Sox part, not the cutesey married shit," I said. Without releasing her ankle, I swiped my phone to life and called up my ESPN Sports app. "Plenty more games in the regular season, and then there's the playoffs. Obviously, we're looking toward the World Series, too, but let's not jinx things."

Alex tilted her head as she took tiny bites from her chip. Long moments passed with nothing more than quiet crunching. Finally, she said, "Are we adding another date?"

I brought my hand to my chest. "I cannot abide you living in this city without a proper introduction to Fenway Park," I said. "It's necessary, Alexandra."

She brushed some crumbs from her skirt but kept her eyes averted. I was certain that she was blushing this time, but I wasn't sure whether it was my request for more time with her or the use of her full name that brought color to her cheeks. Regardless of the source, those blushes always struck me with the sense that no one had ever done right by this girl.

None of that made sense. Alex was pretty and funny and interesting, and there should've been several non-douche-waffley guys lined up for her attention.

"While we're at it," I continued, "you need to visit the Hatch Shell and the Waterfront. A ride on the Swan Boats, too. Don't worry about keeping track of all this. I'll make you a bucket list."

"That's an interesting idea," she said, a yawn swallowing up her words. "Sorry. I slept this morning but I'm still underwater from my schedule this past week."

"I should get home, too," I said as I stood and slipped some bills under my half-empty beer glass. "If I stay out much later, I'll turn back into a pumpkin."

"I have a hard time seeing that," she said, dragging her gaze up and down my body. It felt nice, her appraisal. I wouldn't mind feeling it more often. I wouldn't mind another conversation about sex in closets—or any other room—either. "Short and round, sure. But not orange. I can't see you orange."

She set her wet shoes on the floor, her face pulling into a grimace as she stepped into them. Her bottom lip was swollen and purple. All of those offenses, courtesy of me. *Oh my fucking god.* I had a thrilling history filled with tales of spilled beverages, ever-present yet mysterious stains on my clothes, and tripping over my own feet, but tonight's series of events was vying for the top spot.

"Ah, well," I said, rubbing the back of my neck. I motioned for Alex to lead the way through the tavern, not out of some throwback chivalry but an authentic concern that I'd assault her again. "I'm one of those bizarre white pumpkins. The kind that no one wants because they're suspect."

"They really are," she said as we reached the sidewalk. "Suspect, that is. People probably prefer those warty gourds to the ghost pumpkins."

The air was a thick, clingy contrast to the chilled tavern. My shirtsleeves were rolled to my elbows and my tie was long banished to my car's cup holder, but that did little to combat the humidity. The evening had taken a sharp turn from the pleasant breeziness we'd enjoyed in the Chapeltons' backyard, and a heavy sky was pushing down on us as a summer storm gathered.

We walked up Causeway Street slowly, neither of us heeding the warning of the occasional crack of thunder or lightning strike in the distance.

"The pumpkin prejudice is unfortunate," I said. "Now you understand why I need to get home before midnight."

"Evidently," Alex murmured. She pointed to the side street where I'd parked. "Go on. I can manage the rest of the way on my own."

Of course she could. I could also walk her to the door, and she could deal with it. "I'm good," I said. "Gotta get my steps in for the day."

Alex scoffed at this while we crossed to Cambridge Street. The sidewalk was narrow, forcing her to walk slightly in front of me. We were close enough that her shoulder bumped my chest every few steps, but neither of us sought to change that. Fine hairs curled at the nape of her neck, and before I could recognize that I was the owner of the limb extending toward her, my palm was on her shoulder and my thumb was stroking her neck.

She shot a fleeting glance at me over her shoulder, her lips parted, and pink dotting her cheeks, and said, "I still can't believe you know the Chief's neighbors, *and* your firm worked on their house."

"This is a big city," I said as dueling cabbies laid on their horns in the intersection ahead. "But it's also a small town."

We stopped at her building, a classic brownstone with a bay window on each floor, and I was still touching her neck. I'd missed every opportunity for a clean break, and now she'd have to wiggle out from under my hold or I'd have to back away and pretend I knew what to do with my hands.

"But what are the odds?" she mused, her attention on locating her keys. "And now they have a beach cottage. How cute is that?"

This hand, it was operating of its own volition. I couldn't tear myself away.

"Those people were nightmare clients. My brother and his fiancée worked on that property for several *long* years," I said. "They went away to Vermont for an extended weekend to celebrate when it was finally finished." Instead of seizing this moment to gesticulate or even shove my paws in my fucking pockets, I steered Alex closer. *Closer.* "I don't think they'd take on that project for any amount of money."

She flattened her hand on my chest and nodded. "Thank them for me," she said.

Lowering my chin, I gazed down at her, fascinated and

confused and compelled to do something—*anything*. A snap of lightning and the quick roar of thunder crashed nearby, and it was like the universe was ordering me to make a fucking decision already.

Take her or leave her, but do it now.

Alex tipped her head back, toward the building. "It's going to start raining soon. Do you want to come upstairs?"

Yes. Right now. Upstairs. You and me. Fuck *yes.*

Like reaching for her, it was a decision I'd made without thought, and one that I didn't regret. But a fat raindrop hit my neck before I could reply, and then another, and I flinched at the chilly sting. Alex's eyes widened and her cheeks colored. She thought I was recoiling from *her*.

"No," I said, immediately frustrated that I'd confirmed her inference when trying to correct it. "Alex, I mean—"

"You know what?" she asked in a high, snappy tone that was working hard at diffusing the greatest sequence of mixed signals two people had ever thrown at each other. "Maybe not tonight."

But that was our shitty reality. She was fucked up from the douche waffle and I was fucked up from loving my sister-in-law, and I was sure we both had some extra helpings of fucked up from parts as yet unexplored. Combined, that was a lot of fucked up in one place. Mixed signals were par for the course.

She took a step back and wrapped an arm around her torso. The other arm was used for some aggressive gesturing that was effective in redefining the space between us. "It has been such a long day"—a clean slice through the air to mark the end of touching for this evening—"and I really do need to get back into my regular sleep schedule." A rapid wave between us to remind me to stay where I was rather than follow her inside. "Another time, okay?"

Shoving my hands in my pockets, I blinked at the sidewalk. "Yeah," I said. "I'll text you about getting to a game. The Sox are at home next weekend, so—"

"So, we'll do this again next weekend," Alex said as she backed up the stone stairs. She stopped on the stoop and leaned against the door, her keys dangling from her index finger. "Or some version of this."

I rocked back on my heels, nodding. The sky was the color of a bruise, the clouds dipping low and churning fast as the storm settled over the city. "Maybe you could grab my ass next time," I said.

"I'm all about returning the favor," Alex replied. She smiled, and dropped her hand to the doorknob. "You should head home. It can't be good for pumpkins to get caught in the rain."

"Terrible," I said, raising my hand to wave goodbye. "Again, I'm sorry about your lip, and the shoes."

"Forget about it. I needed a reason to get rid of these shoes." She was inside now, her spine pressed to the jamb as she held the door open. "Text me when you get home, okay?"

I waited until the door closed behind her and the second floor lights illuminated the street-side window before jogging in the direction of my car. It wasn't the easiest undertaking, running downhill in the rain. In dress shoes. While every muddled, contradictory urge waged war in my head. But I made it there, and managed to get home without turning around, driving back to Beacon Hill, banging on Alex's door, and then demanding that she explain to me what the fuck was going with us.

It wasn't that I required confirmation as to her mixed

signals. No, I'd understood her conflict. What I didn't understand was whether part of that conflict was a desire to purge the memory of her douche waffle ex with *some*one or her *any*one.

As the garage door closed behind me at the firehouse, I realized that I didn't know whether I wanted to be Alex's someone or anyone. At one point, I could've been that anonymous anyone. I could've given her some fun times and hot nights, and then forget her.

But now, with the silk of her skin still warming my fingertips, I wasn't convinced I *could* forget her. Between her hunger-induced mood swings and big, brass balls, my memory would require a power washing to get rid of her.

That left me being Alex's someone, and I couldn't do that either. Not when Lauren was my someone. I wasn't Lauren's, but—but the affection I had for her wasn't one I could pick up and put down on a whim. If I'd been able to get over it, I would've done that by now. A bright-eyed surgeon in ruby slippers didn't erase years of adoration.

"Fuck, that's it," I said to the empty garage. "Ruby slippers. *The Wizard of Oz*."

I slipped into the silent firehouse, careful to tread lightly and not disturb my roommates. When I reached my room, I stripped out of my damp shirt and trousers, and pulled on a pair of athletic shorts. My phone in hand, I settled on the edge of the bed and fired off the message I owed Alex.

Riley: Home.
Riley: Or, as some prefer to say, there's no place like home.
Alex: You're right. Some do say that.

Riley: You stole the Wicked Witch of the East's shoes, Dorothy.

Alex: And your point?

Riley: I told you I didn't buy that story about "just liking red."

Alex: Would you stop?

Riley: Definitely not, no.

Alex: I was going to apologize for making it weird tonight but you're winning at the weird game now.

Riley: You didn't make it weird, Shortstop. Don't think that.

Riley: So is it a full-blown Dorothy thing or what? Are you off to see the Wizard? Are you angling for some kind of polyamorous relationship with three dudes?

Riley: Okay, okay. Wait a hot second. Are you into furries?

Alex: Oh my god.

Riley: Not judging. Hell, I've seen far stranger than three dudes in cosplay worshipping their goddess. And that was just a Tuesday night.

Alex: Well. Let's hear about that.

Riley: Not until you get real about the Dorothy complex.

Alex: I do NOT have a Dorothy complex!

Alex: I just love that movie. Sometimes a girl needs a sparkly pair of shoes.

Riley: You do you, Honeybee. Now come on. You can tell me the real story. If it helps, I'm known for my secret-keeping skills.

Alex: This is going to sound so lame.

Riley: Probably not, but I'll let you know if it does.

Alex: I really identified with Dorothy when I was younger. I always wanted to run away to somewhere my brother couldn't follow and I'd pretend I was an only child.

Riley: He's older, right?

Alex: Technically, yes.

Riley: What the hell does that mean? Technically?

Alex: He's a couple of minutes older. We're twins but we're not close.

Alex: I don't want to talk about the twin thing, okay?

Riley: Sure. But hurry up and get to the lame part, would you?

Alex: That's it. I loved Dorothy because she ran away from home and started over somewhere new and wonderful, and she did it in kickass shoes.

Riley: Still waiting for this to get lame. Are you sure you're not interested in some Yellow Brick Road group sex?

Alex: Sorry. No polyamorous or furry interests.

Riley: Hmmm.

Alex: What?

Riley: Can't decide whether I'm disappointed or relieved.

Alex: Okay, spill it. I want to hear about your far stranger experiences.

Riley: I knew a chick. She kept a dungeon.

Alex: A dungeon?

Riley: Yeah. I'd go on but you've had a long week.

Alex: Not too long that I don't want to hear about a fucking dungeon.

Riley: I've already won the weird game. Must save the dungeon for another night.

Riley: And…common misconception…dungeons are not always for fucking.

Alex: Whoa. I did not know that.

Riley: Yeah, true story. Goodnight.

I FLOPPED BACK against the mattress and stared at the ceiling. My phone went on humming with the arrival of new messages, and a huge part of me—the *someone* part—wanted to respond. I wanted to talk with Alex all night, and that was why I couldn't.

Not yet.

Eleven

RILEY

ALL CONVERSATION STOPPED when I stepped into the attic conference room on Monday morning. I was arriving a couple of minutes past seven thirty, but I didn't imagine that level of tardiness required silence and six pairs of eyes glaring at me.

"Hey," I said, holding up the bag of tacos I'd procured for Shannon. "The taco truck had some generator issues this morning." I gestured to the gear grease on my trousers, hoping it served as adequate evidence of my delay. Of course I jumped in there and fixed the thing. It wasn't like I could show up *without* food for the mother-to-be. Now *that* was grounds for some glaring. "Sorry, guys. We can get started."

My ass hadn't hit the seat before Shannon chirped, "Let's hear about the cocktail party first. The work cocktail party. The one you attended with a woman."

Ah. Fuck.

I snatched the bag away from her. "No tacos for you," I said. "Interrogators don't get tacos."

I should've expected this. I really should have. My siblings were creatures of many habits, and our favorite habit was pouncing whenever someone had a new relationship. That would've been peachy and keen if I hadn't historically been the one to initiate the pouncing, and thus was due for an inspection that redefined *thorough*.

I probably would've expected it if I'd slotted my relationship with Alex into the *Real* and *Not Temporary* categories.

"I can wait," Shannon replied.

"I doubt that," I said. With my messenger bag on my lap, I sifted through the contents as if I had the entire Library of Congress stored in there and where oh where could my laptop be? "I'm starting to miss the days when you and Erin didn't talk about everything. Or ever."

It was only a hunch that Shannon had heard about this from Erin. A hunch and an opportunity to rattle her cage about her born-again relationship with the baby of the family. Tiel could've outed me, although if it had been her, I knew she'd kept the details to a minimum.

"Is this woman the same one from the pool table?" Matt asked.

Still searching for that laptop. My fingers landed on a pen, one of those nice fine-tipped Sharpies that always went missing, and I studied it for an entire minute before shaking my head.

"No, not the woman from the pool table," I said to Matt. Uncapped it, inspected the point, recapped it. "That was...no one."

Just someone I used to forget about your wife.

"Okay, not the pool table girl," Matt murmured. "Do we even know who that was? My money's on one of Patrick's assistants. Seems fitting."

"Oh, *please* tell me that's not the case," Patrick said. "And it is *not* fitting. Leave my assistants alone."

"It's the great mystery of our time," Sam mused. "Who did Riley fuck on my pool table? And when? And should I light it on fire?"

"Can we please get back to cocktail party girl?" Andy asked. She gave a mason jar filled with dark orange liquid a vigorous shake, and then unscrewed the cap. I couldn't tell whether this morning's cold-pressed creation was a blend of carrot or beet juice, and I wasn't asking. That shit horrified me. It was right up there with yogurt. "I want some pertinent details on this lady."

"I'll have you know Erin didn't tell me," Shannon continued. "Tiel did. She said you got all spiffed up. Suit *and* tie, and that you cleaned out your car before leaving the house."

"And I thought that girl was my Alfred," I muttered into my bag.

I opened my notebook, paging through it in search of something else to divert my attention. Between dashed-off designs and checklists for each day were my first attempts at *The Adventures of Gastro Girl*. She existed as disembodied parts—hands, face, ass for days—and aggregate swag—boots, tiara, amulet—but I could see where it was going, how it would fit together.

"Have you *ever* cleaned out your car?" Patrick asked.

"Have *you*?" Tom asked Patrick.

Andy shook her head. "RISD's car is always clean," she said. "Patrick's, too. It's Matt who collects coffee cups by the dozen. It's like he's building an altar to Starbucks in his backseat."

Matt glowered at her. "It was one time," he said, holding up a finger to demonstrate. "And it was *two* empty cups."

"And a thousand napkins," Andy said.

"Shut up right now," Shannon yelled. "Hush, all of you. Not another word." She shifted in her chair, one hand on her rounded belly, and faced me. She offered a quick smile, and then her gaze darted to the tacos. "We'd love to hear about her, Riley."

That was the thing about Shannon. She didn't fuck around, especially when pregnant-hungry. What little time I'd had to prepare myself for the full-court press of my siblings was over. I plucked my laptop from my bag, nodding.

"Her name's Alex and she's from Nevada. She's a gastrointestinal surgeon and has pictures of truly disgusting things on her phone. She has green eyes and many pairs of red shoes and a twin brother, and she loves avocados. That's all I have to say to you jackals."

I set my laptop on the table and my bag on the floor, and silence yawned around me like the quiet before a wave crashed down on the shore. And then everyone talked at once.

Patrick: Well, that's great. Let's get back to work.

Andy: How old is she?

Tom: Where'd you meet her?

Matt: Patrick, when are you going to understand this? We can't get back to work until we reach the bottom of the important shit, and in our world, the *important shit* is never business-related.

Shannon: When do we get to meet her?

Sam: Is anyone else astounded we're not talking about Magnolia right now?

Matt: Is this the gastro surgeon from Nick's building?

Sam: Am I the only one who was convinced he was hooking up with Magnolia?

Tom: Was this a Nick-and-Erin fix-up?

Matt: If we're talking about the same person, I've met her. I mean, maybe not *met* but I've seen her in the stairwell. Nick introduced me, too.

Andy: Oh, I like the idea of Nick-and-Erin fix-ups. That should be a thing.

Shannon: She should come to the farmers' market this weekend. We'll have lunch and get to know each other.

Patrick: Of course he wasn't hooking up with Magnolia.

Tom: Can Nick and Erin fix me up with someone? I'm not picky. Doesn't have to be a doctor.

Andy: I need more details than green eyes. Height, hair color, ethnic origins. More, please.

Matt: Short-ish, right?

Shannon: This is not about you, Thomas. Your time will come, my dear, but this is not it.

Patrick: I mean, she's nice but…*roof gardens.*

Matt: If memory serves, she's taller than Erin but not much. Right?

Tom: When my time comes, can it come with Tom Hardy? Can someone pass that along to Nick and Erin, please? We'll be The Toms and it will be precious.

Andy: We need more to work with than this. Where've you been? When are you seeing her again?

Patrick: What would you even talk about? Moss?

Shannon: Should I interpret this to mean you're not taking Magnolia to RISD Weekend?

Matt: She's a little thing but she's not much of a smiler, huh?

That did it. That was all it took for me to look up from

my notebook and spear Matt with a sharp gaze. "Shut the fuck up when you talk about my girlfriend," I snapped.

My reaction was over the top and irrational, and more ridiculously ironic than I cared to admit. But I wasn't open to commentary from Matt. He already had *everything*. He wasn't entitled to peck away at the little I could call my own.

"Well then," Sam murmured.

He held up his hands in surrender. "No, no. I just meant that she seemed serious," he said. "I wasn't trying to imply—"

"Shut the fuck up," I said, each word broken off with more edge than the one before. It didn't matter to me whether this response was proportional or even appropriate.

Matt folded his forearms over the closed lid of his laptop and fiddled with the wedding band on his ring finger. "You're not understanding me, Riley. I wasn't trying to say that she—"

"Stop talking, Matt," Shannon said. She gave him a quick head shake before glancing at me. "I can't wait to meet Alex. I know I'm going to love her even if we don't share a fondness for avocados."

"It's fine," Andy said, waving off Shannon's comment. "I love avocados enough for both of us, and if you like her, Riley, I know I'll like her, too."

Patrick rubbed his palms together and bobbed his head. "Am I allowed to talk about business yet?" he asked.

"That depends," Shannon replied. "Am I allowed to eat these tacos yet?"

MAGNOLIA PACED the length of the Marlborough Street brownstone's roof deck twice, alternating between tapping and clicking her pen as she walked. "You're not giving me much to work with," she said as she started a third turn. "With the budget you're offering, I could give them a potted Japanese maple. Maybe a gnome."

"The roof garden was a last-minute add," I said, shrugging. "That, and several other last-minute adds."

Half bath off the garage. Copper gutters. Extra master bedroom closet. And now, a roof garden.

She shot me a pointed glance over her shoulder. "Get a handle on your client," she said.

I rolled my head from side to side, struggling to relieve some of the tension gathered in my neck and shoulders. "Thank you for that suggestion, Gigi," I called. "I can't imagine why I hadn't thought of that yet."

She walked back and stopped beside me. "I can give you a roof garden proposal for the budget you indicated but it will be light on the garden," she said, waving at the deck's splintered floor and rickety railing.

"That's fine," I said. "And throw in a secondary proposal, too. One with—"

"All the bells and whistles," she finished. "I figured as much, with those fancy new gutters. Are we doing that now? Copper gutters?"

"They saw it on a home design show. They were damn expensive," I replied. "Cost more than the marble countertops."

"What you're saying is that they can afford a decent roof deck."

"That's what I'm saying," I replied.

Magnolia proceeded to measure and photograph the roof

deck while I scrolled through my emails and text messages. I hadn't heard from Alex since Saturday night, and that left me with a pinch of longing. I'd meant to message her about getting to a Red Sox game, but avoiding a post-meeting chitchat with Matt and getting the fuck out of the office had been my main priorities this morning. Thankfully, the owners of this property had called with an urgent request for a roof garden.

"Are you up for some Monday Night Football?" Her iPad was cradled in one arm and her attention focused on the screen. "If you feel like it, we could grab a beer after I put together this proposal." Then she added, "Peter's out of town."

"Ah, Peter," I said. "How is that old chap?"

She glanced at me, jerking a shoulder in response. "He's fine," she murmured. Her tone was one of reassurance, but it wasn't clear which of us she was attempting to soothe. "Busy. He's usually on the road about ten days each month, but this month is really busy. He has some personal issues going on, too."

I ran a hand through my hair and looked out over the city. "Personal issues," I said eventually. And then, because even if you disliked someone on principle, you asked after their well-being, "Is everything okay?"

Giving a shit about people. It was the only way to stay a step above the douche waffles of the world.

"I'm not sure. I don't know all the details," she said quickly. I stifled a groan. That wasn't a good sign. "But he's really sweet. *So sweet*." She wagged a finger at me. "And *mature*. I didn't realize how much I wanted to be with someone who's lived a little and sorted out his priorities."

"Yeah, that's important," I said but there was no conviction behind it. *Personal issues* and *on the road* sounded a whole hell of a lot like *wife or girlfriend in another city*. "I hope everything works out."

"Peter's really responsible. I'm sure it will be fine," she said. Again, it wasn't clear which of us required the convincing. "Did you ever find anyone to go to the RISD event with you?"

"Uh, yeah," I replied. "A friend of Nick's. She works at the hospital with him." My head snapped up. "And she's a twin."

Magnolia shot me an unimpressed glance. "That's great," she said. "I'll be sure to say hello to her at the next meeting of the Multiple Births Club."

"I didn't mean that all twins or triplets know each other," I said. "But you and Alex are the only ones *I* know."

She shook her head as she laughed. "I have two more appointments this afternoon," she said, glancing at her phone. "Just text me if you're free tonight, and I'll meet you somewhere to watch the game."

"I have another few hours at this site," I said, following her through the brownstone and down to the curb where her truck was parked. "If I can get this day back on track, I'll catch you later." I dipped my hands into my pockets. "I might also be busy with a few other things."

Nodding as she set her bag in the passenger seat, Magnolia said, "Don't worry about it. I can watch football alone or with people. It's one of my many talents."

"Impressive," I said. "Thanks for dropping by at such short notice."

I waved goodbye when she hopped in her truck, and then retreated to the home. There were crews on every floor and not a single room without the noise of nail guns, saws, or sanders. It was fucking ridiculous. I'd never had clients who kept changing their damn minds—not to this extent— and it was teasing at the threads of my patience.

I hated redoing good work and wasting the time and efforts of my tradespeople. Sure, it all went on the clients' tab but this sort of inefficiency was driving me nuts. It was particularly annoying because I'd proposed all of these upgrades and options back when I'd designed this restoration. The roof garden, the extra closet, everything.

I was beginning to understand Patrick's brand of anal retentive. If it was possible, I was embracing some of it, too.

Instead of attacking my checklist for this property, I pulled out my phone and scrolled through my exchanges with Alex. Being around her was like my favorite flannel pajama pants—easy and comfortable, and roomy enough for unexpected erections. I liked her, even if we couldn't decide whether we were running toward each other or away.

And when I was with Alex, I wasn't aching for Lauren. I didn't want to ache all the time. I didn't want to verbally backhand my brother in status meetings, and I didn't want to be miserable.

I wasn't miserable when I was with Alex. Maybe it was time to capitalize on that.

Riley: Saturday night. You, me, Fenway Park.
Riley: First pitch at 7 p.m.
Riley: Do you want to see batting practice? It starts about an hour before the game.
Alex: I don't know…do I?
Riley: We'll skip it this time and get dinner instead.

Riley: I'd rather lose some of the experience if it means not having to deal with your food moods.

Alex: I don't have food moods.

Riley: It's one of those things you can't notice about yourself. Kind of like how you can only see the Great Wall of China from space.

Alex: That doesn't make sense.

Riley: Probably because you only had four almonds for lunch.

Alex: Sometimes you're an asshole.

Riley: Sometimes? Often.

Riley: But at least I don't get into food moods.

Alex: That's great. I have to prep for surgery.

Riley: Have a few more almonds. I don't want you to stab some poor guy in the heart while you're in there.

Alex: This would be an awesome time for you to choke on my balls.

Riley: I'm good on balls for today, thanks.

Riley: I don't want any pictures or anything, but text me when you're done. I want to go over your Boston Bucket List.

Alex: Are you serious about the Swan Boats? I googled that and I'm pretty sure it's not my style. I don't like bird-shaped boats on little ponds. Seems juvenile and bizarre. Like I should be wearing a fairy princess dress and drinking pink tea.

Riley: Of course I'm serious! Non-negotiable!

Alex: Then you're getting a picture of a necrotic bile duct before the day is done.

Riley: Everything is negotiable!

WITH A SMILE, I tucked my phone in my back pocket and opened my notebook. The rough sketches of Gastro Girl greeted me, and I indulged in several minutes of sketching. She was different than I'd first thought, a little sharper but also softer in certain ways, and those boots had to be red. No question about it.

Riley: I'm guessing the answer to this question will be no, but I'm asking anyway…

Riley: Have you been to the aquarium?

Riley: It's a cool spot. There's a really old sea turtle there.

Riley: The Museum of Science is also fun. They have one of those giant IMAX screens that stretch around a concave wall so it feels like you're right there in the Galapagos Islands.

Riley: Actually, it's kind of a trip.

Riley: My friend, Gigi, she's a landscape architect, loves the Isabella Stewart Gardner museum. They have a special installation in the spring. Something with hanging flowers, I think.

Riley: True story—there was a full-on art heist there about 30 years ago.

Riley: Some real *Thomas Crown Affair* and *Oceans Twelve* shit.

Riley: *Oceans Twelve* is almost unwatchable. It's the crazy acrobatic scene with the lasers that saves it.

Riley: But that Brad Pitt. He's one fine motherfucker, am I right?

Riley: Okay, well, now that I've shared my celebrity man crush, let's pick which museum is going on your bucket list.

Riley: For what it's worth, I'm not embarrassed to admit that

I think a dude is hot. If Brad Pitt ever wanted to take a run at me, I'd let him.

Riley: I'd let him and I'd like it, and I'm 99% certain I'm as straight as a saint.

Riley: But as my brother Patrick likes to say, it's important to account for all scenarios, regardless of likelihood.

Riley: You think about that and get back to me.

Riley: The museums. Not whether Brad Pitt would give me a toss.

Riley: I do believe I've won the weird game AGAIN.

Alex: Hey, sorry. I was in a 13 hour surgery.

Riley: What the hell kind of surgery takes 13 hours?

Riley: Wait. I don't want to know. Don't tell me.

Alex: You'd rather see pics?

Riley: You're the strangest girl I've ever met and I'll remind you that I know a dungeon mistress.

Alex: Can I hear about that now?

Riley: No. We're talking about museums.

Riley: Don't tell me any details but what do you do for 13 hours? Is that 13 hours of standing at an operating table or do you tag in and out? Are there bathroom breaks? What about snacks?

Riley: I really hope there are snacks.

Alex: This surgery was about 13 hours of hands-on time for me. Sometimes I tag in. It all depends on the patient and the issue.

Alex: Bathroom breaks mean scrubbing in all over again, so those are at a minimum. No snacks. I can't really eat a granola bar over an open abdominal cavity.

Riley: On a scale of Hawkeye to the Hulk, how hungry are you right now?

Alex: I'm not going to destroy New York City, but I could go for 30 tacos and a back rub.

Riley: The best part is that you're not even exaggerating. Which do you want first?

Riley: Nevermind, I know the answer to that.

Alex: Food.

Riley: Yeah, of course. Are you up for a quick drive to East Boston? Angela's has the best tacos.

Alex: Yes, please.

Alex: You can tell me all about your man crush.

Riley: You can tell me how hard you like it.

Riley: The back rub, that is.

Alex: About Rhode Island...

Riley: I will cry actual tears from my eyes if you tell me you can't go to RISD Weekend.

Alex: Don't cry. Everything is fine.

Alex: What's the game plan? When do we leave? I need to make sure I'm not scheduled for any coverage or on-calls.

Riley: We'll leave on Friday. Whatever time works for you. It all depends on how much of the Ocean State you're prepared to experience.

Alex: I don't know how to respond to that.

Riley: I think you can take the full Rhody experience.

Alex: Um...great?

Riley: It's definitely great. There's a lot to see just in Providence.

Alex: Aren't you also supposed to be finding some interns?

Riley: We're going there for the art, the food, the city, and then—after we've had enough of those things—we'll talk to some students.

Riley: It's not like we're really hiring interns for next summer. My sister says she wants to, but my firm doesn't know what to do with them.

Riley: They're either disasters or my next sister-in-law.

Alex: Yeah. You don't need to remind me about disaster interns.

Riley: How do you feel about football?

Alex: Ambivalent.

Riley: That's a terrible way to feel about football.

Alex: Would you rather I hate it?

Riley: Anything is better than ambivalence.

Alex: I don't hate it.

Riley: Thank god. You really had me worried there.

Riley: My landscape architect friend has some tickets to tomorrow night's Patriots game. You really haven't experienced the city of Boston until you've left it and made the pilgrimage down south to Foxborough. Interested?

Alex: I'm on call but if I can find someone to trade with, a pilgrimage sounds good.

Riley: Awesome. You're going to love this.

Alex: This landscape architect. Is she a "friend" or a friend?

Riley: I'm not aware of the difference between "friend" and friend.

Alex: Truer words…

Riley: Does it bother you that I have friends who are women?

Alex: Actually, no. I don't have a problem with anyone having friends of the opposite sex. My best friends are Acevedo and Hartshorn.

Riley: But...?

Alex: But nothing. She must be a really good friend to give you her tickets.

Riley: She is a really good friend. She's the best people and she's always on the struggle bus.

Riley: Some family event came up, so I was the only one left to take the tickets.

Alex: Thank your landscape architect friend for me.

Riley: I will. She's a triplet. Two brothers.

Alex: That's wonderful. I do try to meet all the products of multiple births when I move to a new town.

Riley: She basically said the same thing when I told her you're a twin. Is that a twin/triplet thing or is it that easy to bust my balls?

Alex: You told her about me?

Riley: Yeah...

Alex: What did you say?

Riley: I don't know. It was more than a week ago. I forget things.

Alex: No, you don't. You rattled off a million baseball statistics at the game last weekend.

Alex: And you know how to get everywhere without ever looking at maps. You know the beers that every bar in the city has on tap from memory. You don't forget a fucking thing.

Riley: I just said that you work with Nick and you're going to RISD Weekend with me, and your hair is like whiskey and your ass was made for spanking.

Riley: And you're a twin.

Alex: WHAT?

Riley: Just the basics.

Alex: WHAT?

Riley: Which part don't you understand?

Alex: Tell me you didn't actually say my ass was "made for spanking."

Riley: Is that not appropriate for people who are dating casually? That's what we agreed on, right? Dating casually?

Riley: What does that even mean, dating casually? I assume khakis and jazz are involved.

Alex: Just tell me what you said. Please.

Riley: Did I talk about spanking your ass out loud? No.

Riley: The thought crosses my mind with some frequency. Would there be an issue with me sharing that with people? We are "dating."

Alex: What kind of response would you like from me?

Riley: That's just it, Shortstop. You don't have to say anything. I know what you need, and I'll do all of the work.

Alex: This discussion is quite the detour from football. This was a sharp left turn.

Riley: I got a sharp lefty for you.

Alex: Now you're just being ridiculous.

Riley: No. I am not. You know how I feel about your ass. It's delicious.

Alex: Okay, so…

Riley: Great. Let me know if tomorrow night works out for football. I'll pick you up.

Alex: Do you really think my hair is like whiskey?

Riley: Yes. I do.

Riley: I have to ask you something.

Alex: Shoot. I'm hanging out in post-op for about twenty more minutes.

Riley: Bear with me. I can't believe that we haven't discussed this yet so I'm a little nervous.

Alex: Now I'm nervous.

Riley: You have nothing to worry about. Your life will continue just fine. It's mine that might come crashing down here.

Riley: How do you feel about comics and superheroes?

Alex: DC or Marvel?

Alex: Nevermind, that's a terrible question. I'd never want to choose. I love the ensembles. The Avengers, the X-Men, the Justice League.

Alex: But I haven't read any in 20 years. I've caught up with the movies as they've been released, though. Most of them have been really good.

Alex: Are you still with me?

Riley: Yes. Sorry. I just spontaneously orgasmed.

Alex: What?

Riley: Nothing. But I'll talk to you later. Something just popped up.

"THIS WASN'T the worst idea in the world," I said, licking the powdered sugar from my fingertips as we exited the bakery. This degree of indulgence would've had my mother tsking "A moment on the lips, forever on the hips." The only indulgence she allowed herself was fat-free yogurt that claimed to be cherry cheesecake flavored but tasted like a scented marker.

Riley snorted beside me. "Happy to hook you up with cannoli anytime you need it," he said, tugging me closer. It was Friday evening, and the kind of late September night that brought everyone in Boston outside, and the sidewalks were jammed. "Especially if it means you're going to smile like that."

My ponytail was trapped under his arm, and in my quest to loosen it, I jabbed him in the chest. "Sorry, sorry," I said, running my fingers through my hair.

"No worries," he said with a wince. He rubbed a hand over his breastbone. "I'm getting used to your attacks."

There was a gravity associated with Riley. A pull. I

couldn't be near him without being drawn closer, and he never failed to take it a step further. A hand on my waist. An arm around my shoulders. A leg pressed to mine.

But that gravity was never smooth. There were bumps and fumbles, and no one was safe from errant elbows. It was awkward, but an iteration of awkward for which we were uniquely suited. Gravity was where it stopped, too. The flirty texts with talk of—*my god*—spanking were nothing more than suggestion. I hadn't invited him back to my apartment since the night of the Chief's cocktail party, and he hadn't stared at my lips like he meant to taste them since then either.

We were affectionate like an intramural softball team. Sloppy and a little silly, and with no real purpose beyond our own amusement. And I took no issue with this. I wasn't on a mission to figure out what it meant or where it was going because it wasn't going anywhere. It was good times and cannoli, and not much more.

This arrangement, the fake-boyfriend-but-also-touchy-feely-friend thing, it wasn't the worst idea in the world either. I was getting a guided tour of Boston—including stops at all the best restaurants, bars, and bakeries—and as if the first domino had fallen, life at the hospital gradually stopped feeling like a scene from *The Scarlet Letter*. Within a few days of the Chief's cocktail party, things started feeling...normal? Or what my dusty old memories of normal resembled.

The Chief had refrained from dumping extra shifts and on-calls on me, and even nodded in vague approval after I'd led a group of residents through a complex technique in the skills lab last week. I was still annoyed that fabricating a relationship was the key to getting my career back in gear, but that annoyance didn't outstrip my relief.

All I needed now was for the gala to go well, and then I could start looking for new jobs. In all likelihood, I wasn't busting out of Boston before the new year or even next spring, but I was finally taking steps in the right direction. That was all that mattered.

"This was fun," I said. I stared off into the distance as we walked along Hanover Street in the North End. "We should do it again. I usually prefer salty—"

"Imagine that," Riley murmured.

"To sweet, but bakery crawls should be a thing," I continued.

Fallen leaves crunched under my shoes and one thing was certain: summer was long gone. Somewhere in the past few weeks, long, sunny days had been replaced with early evenings, and the chill in the air promised that autumn was here to stay.

Another thing was certain: I enjoyed every minute I got with Riley Walsh. I enjoyed him more than I could manage, more than was appropriate for this arrangement. More than any one person should enjoy another without the influence of sex. I liked him, and I loved when he noticed my shoes and smiles. Even when he noticed my so-called food moods.

"Authentic cannoli from the best bakeries in the North End. Another item successfully crossed off your bucket list," he said, squeezing my shoulder. "Now we can move onto more complex offerings. Boston cream pies. Lobster rolls. Frappes. Clam chowder. But not in that order." He glanced at the time on his phone. "Or, we could head downtown for tacos."

"Let's not get carried away," I said. "I won't be hungry again for hours."

"More like forty-five minutes," he murmured. "An hour, tops."

"That sounds like an insult," I mused.

Riley shook his head. "Hardly," he said. "You're a marvel, Shortstop. A bottomless pit, but a marvel as far as pits go."

We walked in silence as we wandered from the North End to the Waterfront and Financial District and then back toward my apartment on Beacon Hill. For all of our awkward exchanges, we could always manage the quiet without resorting to idle chatter.

Riley jerked his chin toward a narrow, cobblestone side street. "Sam has a new project around the corner. We picked it up as an investment property, so there's no client or home-owner, and we found a ton of random stuff in the basement," he said. "Old trunks and armoires. Windows from a million years ago. More doors than could've ever been in that house. A ping-pong table that we decided to keep at the office."

"Does that happen often?" I asked. "Finding strange things like that?"

He murmured in agreement, nodding. "More than you'd think. Everything is saved for a reason. I'm sure of it. But no one ever plans to die suddenly and leave a home's secrets and stories for distant relatives or estate sales."

I continued walking but turned to face Riley. His words were laced with a whip of emotion that I'd never before heard from him. I started to respond, but he suddenly jerked me closer. With my chest plastered to his and an arm tight around my waist, the words dissolved on my tongue.

"Watch it, Alex," he said, coming to a stop on the side-walk. "Were you trying to plow into that fire hydrant?"

The hydrant was right there, just over his shoulder, all red and obvious. "No," I said as casually as I could manage with his heart thumping against my palm. Which was not casually at all. "I was just going to ask whether you wanted to get a drink and tell me about the things you find in old houses."

Riley loosened his hold on my waist and stepped back. "How about a game of ping-pong first?" he asked. "Winner buys the drinks?"

RILEY BOUNCED the ball on his paddle and regarded me from across the table. We were at the Walsh Associates office, in a basement room that was home to ten metal filing cabinets and an ancient ping-pong table.

This place was *nice*. To start, the foyer was bigger than my entire apartment, and the chandelier hanging there looked like its life story could fill volumes. Everything was clean but it was also remarkably lovely, like a fancy furniture showroom or a feature from *Architectural Digest*. Even the garage and basement were pristine.

There was no rational reason why any of this was surprising to me. I knew from Nick that the firm was highly regarded, and though Riley never talked up his work, it was clear that his services were in demand. But seeing his office when we'd gone up there to retrieve some balls from his desk, filled with books and diplomas, and framed magazine articles featuring his designs, solidified it for me.

"I assume that standard strip ping-pong rules apply. Right?" he asked.

I reached for the paddle and examined it. "Define standard," I said. "Wait a minute. What the hell are you talking about, strip ping-pong?"

He gestured to the table like *That's how the game is played in these parts, missy.* "It's quite simple, Alexandra. You score, I drop some clothes," he said. "I score, you drop some clothes."

"Oh, *hell* no," I said, suddenly shaken by the idea of getting naked with this guy. I wasn't worried that I'd lose—that wasn't happening—but I *was* worried about how I'd handle seeing him in nothing more than his skin. Again. I couldn't do that without molesting him with my eyes. The fake-boyfriend-but-also-touchy-feely-friend thing only worked so long as everyone remained clothed. "I'm not playing strip pong."

He smiled with one of those *you don't have to get so worked up, Honeybee* grins. "I get it," he replied. "You're worried that I'm going to beat you, and you'll be stripped down to your nakeds before you know it."

I laughed at that, hard. It had been years since I'd played this game, but it was the one thing Adam and I had done together with any regularity. We'd gotten a ping-pong table as a joint birthday gift from some aunt or uncle who thought children were inherently good at sharing. We weren't, and we were especially bad at sharing with each other. But the only way to determine the true and rightful master of the table was through playing for it. Over time, we'd resorted to resolving our issues by whacking little hollow balls at each other.

I wagged the paddle in his direction. "I'm not worried about that at all," I snapped. "I'm worried that *I'm* going to beat *you*, and it's a little chilly in here."

Riley glanced around the room and then back at me,

nodding pointedly at my chest. "You're right. It is a tit bit nipply in here."

"Hilarious." I tapped the paddle against the edge of the table, rolling my eyes. "What's wrong with the original plan? Winner buys the drinks?"

"Here's a compromise," he said. "For every point, we'll undress or answer a question."

"Like, trivia?"

"No," he said with an exaggerated head shake. "Personal questions, but you have to choose clothes or questions before anything is asked and you can't change your mind after. Either way, we're stripping."

"*You'll* be stripping," I said, beckoning for the ball.

My plan held together for a few minutes. Riley soon realized that I was a more capable opponent than he'd expected, and he upped the level of play in response. We were diving and lunging to return each shot, and grunting like it was Wimbledon down here.

"You could've mentioned you were a ringer," he said as he fired the ball across the table.

"Are you kidding?" I asked. "I'll have you out of those pants before you know it."

That did it. His concentration faltered for half a second, and the ball sailed past his outstretched paddle. "Motherfuck," he seethed, flattening his palms on the table. "You play dirty."

I twisted my hair into a bun on the top of my head. "I play to win," I corrected.

He hooked his thumb around his waistband, his fingers resting just above his zipper. I swallowed thickly. *Please don't take your pants off, please don't take your pants off, please.*

"Ask your question, Shortstop," he said.

"Have you always been perfect?" The words tripped out of my mouth before I considered whether they deserved oxygen. "Pause. Rewind. Pretend I never said that. It's not what I meant. It's just that you seem to have a lot going for you, and I want to know whether that's always been the case. Did you even have a gawky adolescent phase?"

Riley started to respond but stopped himself, laughing. "I didn't speak until I was four, and when I did, I had major speech impediments," he said. "I stutter almost every day. I've never been anywhere near perfect."

"Oh," I said, shocked and a little mortified with myself. "Oh, wow. I had no idea. I never would've guessed."

Stop babbling. Stop it right now.

"You might not notice it, but it's there. I'm better at controlling it now," Riley said. "And just so you know, it only *looks* like I have a lot going for me. I've got a lot of shambles here too."

I was about to keep on babbling, but he moved into serve position. The ball came at me hard and high. He was capitalizing on my height—or lack thereof—and it wasn't long before I was struggling to return each shot. My paddle scraped the underside of the ball, but it wasn't enough to send it across the table.

"What will it be?" Riley asked, eyeing me with his arms crossed over his chest.

In addition to a bra and panties, I was wearing jeans, a sweater, and flats. No socks, no jewelry, nothing. It wasn't much to work with. "Question," I said.

He spun the handle of the paddle between his palms. "Tattoos," he said. "What's the story there?"

The ink on my left bicep was covered by my sweater, but I rolled the sleeve up enough to explain. "That's Nevada," I said. Riley circled the table and narrowed his eyes. "Then, South Dakota. That's where I went to undergrad. Next, Wisconsin, where I went to med school."

He tilted his head to get a better look. "Oh, yeah. I see it now. I've been staring at those lines for a month. How did I not figure that out?" he asked. "And where's Massachusetts?"

You've been staring at my arm for a month? I had no idea he'd been that interested. "I haven't added Massachusetts yet," I said with a shrug. I wasn't convinced I wanted a permanent reminder of my time here.

Riley reached for me, his fingers curling around my arm and his thumb sweeping over the ink. "You should," he said.

His voice was soft yet husky, the way I would expect to him to speak in bed. It made me lightheaded. "We should finish the game," I said.

He met my eyes and nodded, but didn't release my arm. "Your story is much better than mine," he said. "My college girlfriend—"

"The soul catcher?" I asked. "The one we're hoping to avoid next weekend?"

Riley cut his eyes to the side as he exhaled, but he still didn't let me go. "Her name is Dorrance, and she's just a little *spirited*," he said diplomatically, his thumb tracing the southern triangle of Nevada's border. "And when we were both young and stupid, she drew the tattoo on my back." He offered me a smirk, and for a second, his eyes dropped to my lips. "I'm sure you noticed it the night you stitched me up."

"I did," I admitted. "It's not that bad."

"You're right. It's not." His hand was still on my arm and his eyes on my lips, and he offered a vague murmur of dissent despite his words. "Let's finish this game," he said.

After another beat, Riley released me and returned to his

side. Heat was pumping through my body and I found myself leaning toward him, wanting more of that studious gaze and unrelenting touch. I couldn't resist it, and that was why those pants could not hit the floor tonight. But it wasn't like I could hide behind the questions, either. Those were equally revealing, and we'd only put two points on the board.

And then he won another two, and I surrendered my shoes.

I came back strong and claimed three points. Riley gave up one shoe, a Super Mario Brothers sock, and his belt. I had to press my fingers to my lips to suppress a moan when the leather whooshed out of his belt loops. It sounded like the dirtiest type of promise.

Then it happened. He scored *another* point.

"I've got a good question ready," Riley said.

That sealed it. I couldn't take any more emotional moments or deep, dark stories. I had to take off my sweater.

"Oh, my Jesus," he murmured as I reached for the hem. "I didn't think I'd live to see the...*damn*."

I tossed my sweater to the pile of shoes, and reached for the ball. I felt his eyes on my skin like a warm caress, and there was nothing better. Nothing at all. And I didn't care whether it was a good idea to get semi-naked with a fully gorgeous man. I just didn't want to care about that right now.

"Grab your paddle, Walsh," I ordered. My bra was basic black, and didn't do anything special for my cleavage, but Riley was staring at my tits like they were the juiciest peaches in town.

"Yes, ma'am," he murmured.

I took three more points off him, and with them, his

remaining shoe and sock, and button-down shirt. It shouldn't have been so disarming to see his bare chest, but everything had changed since that night at Nick and Erin's house. He wasn't an obnoxiously perfect player man-child anymore. He was a man I cared for now, and he was neither player nor child.

I lifted my paddle to serve but found my attention on his chest. Specifically, his nipples. Stabbing the paddle in his direction, I asked, "What the fuck is that about?"

He glanced down and then brought a self-conscious arm across his pecs. "More of my youthful stupidity," he said. "Don't worry about it."

"No, no, no," I said, rounding the table. There was something about a bare chest—*this* bare chest—that called to me. I pulled his arm away and studied the thin scars. "Okay, seriously. How the hell did this happen?"

Riley stared at me for a beat before his gaze dropped to my breasts. His shoulders lifted as he sucked in a breath, and he turned his eyes to the ceiling as he blew it out.

"All right, Shortstop," he murmured, his big hands landing on my waist. He set me on the table and stepped closer, until my breasts were pressed against him. He just picked me up and put me where he wanted me, and I liked it. Too much. Oh, *way* too much. "Me and Dorrance, we were partying one night—there was probably some Ecstasy involved—and she decided she wanted to get her nipples pierced. For reasons that I still don't understand, I decided I wanted to get mine pierced, too."

"This isn't going to end well," I said, covering his scarred areolas with my palms.

"Nope," he said. "The guy who did it—Dorrance said he

was a famous tattoo artist and body piercer, but I'm almost certain he was just a guy at a rave—used fish hooks—"

"Oh, my god," I said, cringing at the thought. No one brought clean fish hooks to a rave.

"—and left them there. Or I liked the hook look. I don't know. But when I woke up the next day, I didn't know what the hell had happened and the world was hazy, so I just yanked them out—"

"*Oh, my god*," I repeated, dropping my forehead to his breastbone. "I've seen a lot of heinous things, but that's awful."

He brought his hands to my shoulders and dragged his fingers up and down the skin beside my bra straps. "It's all good," he said. "I survived. My nipples looked like tuna tartare for a while, but I survived."

"I'm beginning to understand why you need me around next weekend," I said.

It was long past the time when I should've pulled away from Riley's chest and shaken out of his hold, but I couldn't bring myself to do it. We stayed there, slightly undressed and silent, as the minutes ticked by and I got high off his masculine scent.

"What are we doing?" I finally asked.

"You're rubbing my chest and feeling sorry for my nipples, and among other things, I'm trying to figure out what your hair smells like," Riley murmured into my scalp.

"Purple," I whispered.

He laughed, and the warmth of him curled around me. "Your hair smells like purple? You mean grape?"

"Not grape," I said. "Purple. Just smell it again, and you'll get it."

He inhaled deeply and then hummed, and I felt those

vibrations in my hands and behind my eyes and every-where, all at once. "I can't believe this, but I think you're right."

I murmured in agreement and shifted just enough to bring my cheek to his chest. I'd been in this position before, but always with a layer of clothing between us. Now it was skin on skin, and all of those promises I'd made myself? The ones about keeping it casual and sticking to the arrangement and the man-free diet? Poof. Gone. *Long gone.*

"I know I'm right," I replied. "I've been using this shampoo since I was fifteen. It's a basic drugstore variety and it smells like purple, and I love it."

"I love it, too," he whispered.

"Should we keep going?"

It was a question that could be interpreted however he wanted, and I needed it that way. I didn't trust myself to take the first step here, not when I knew I'd order him to get his cock out. And I wanted him to do the ordering.

"With this game?" he asked. "I think you've won."

"Are you forfeiting? I can go a few more rounds and get you out of those pants," I replied. I'd meant it as a joke, and as with most things I said, my words came out sharp and serious.

"I'm sure you can," he said. A noise rattled in his throat, something between a rough sigh and a growl, and he stepped away from me. I wanted that sound in my ear again. I wanted it in my bed, and I wanted it for always. "Get dressed, Shortstop. You're buying."

"I WANT TO HEAR ABOUT NEVADA," Riley said when we were settled into a booth at The Red Hat, a tavern around the corner from the Walsh Associates office. "No place like home?"

I frowned into my beer. "That's two different topics," I said. "I can tell you about Nevada, which is always pronounced Nev-*add*-uh, never Nev-*ah*-duh. Or I can tell you about why it's not home, not anymore."

"Do both," he ordered.

There was a hard glint in his eyes, something I hadn't noticed earlier tonight. He'd also kept a safe distance from me on the short walk to the tavern, and his head down and hands tucked in his pockets until we were seated on opposite sides of this booth. Clearly he'd gotten his fill of me back in the basement.

It never escaped my notice that Riley was dealing with some shit. He wanted the world to believe he was all easy smiles and goofy commentary, but those were the layers he used to gain distance. No one stopped to look under the surface when he was recapping sports highlights with his wonky brand of wit, or diffusing situations with self-deprecating humor.

But it was all there, right under the radar.

I knew he was hung up on someone. While I'd originally assumed it was the ex-girlfriend from college—of scarred nipples and tramp stamp fame—I wasn't completely convinced. He never bashed her or blamed her for things without taking some of the responsibility himself, and that left me wondering whether he still held a torch for her. But those pieces didn't fall into place. If he wanted to start things up with her, it sounded like she'd jump for joy and find some other perfect part of him to maim.

Whoever it was, she was occupying a whole hell of a lot of his mind and probably all of his heart. And I hated her just a tiny bit.

"Nevada is great," I started. "I'm from the Washoe Valley, which is in northern Nevada. Reno, to be specific. There are casinos and some legalized prostitution, sure, but there's so much more than that. When you live there, all of that fades into the background and you're left with mountains and lakes and more sky and sunshine than you've ever seen in your entire life."

"You grew up there?"

I nodded as I sipped my beer. "Yeah, Adam and I were born there," I said. "My mother's family has been in northern Nevada since silver was discovered in the mountains near Virginia City almost two hundred years ago. She knows *all* the old Bonanza King families from the Comstock Lode, and can tell you generations upon generations of gossip. It's like the West's version of the Daughters of the American Revolution."

Riley studied the menu for a moment before glancing back to me. He was smiling now, the hard glint fading. "So you're *real* Nevada people," he said.

"Pretty much," I said, laughing. "Kind of like how you're real Boston people."

Scratching his chin, he said, "And here I was, telling you how my family had been restoring homes in Boston since the Great Depression when you have stories about the freaking Comstock."

"See, that's what I love about Nevada," I said. "Everyone thinks it's this dusty old place with some casinos and maybe a few aliens, but it actually has this amazing history and weird little mining towns and people who still tell stories about what really went down back then. It's more than you'd ever expect."

A waiter appeared at our table, and Riley ordered half of the appetizers on the menu before swinging a glance in my direction. "Does that work for you?" he asked, but he didn't wait for my response. "Let's get another order of potato skins."

I handed my menu to the waiter. "Okay," I said, laughing. "Not interested in sharing?"

Riley leveled a hot glare in my direction, as if I was still half-clothed. Or maybe he was remembering me half-clothed and that wasn't a problem in the least. Quite the opposite.

"I do believe it's you who doesn't share," he said. "Now, back to my original question. Would it be fair to say you're a big fan of Nevada and Reno?"

I brought my fingers to my chest, right over my heart, tapping as I pulled together the right words. "I am. I really am. It's special to me in the way that certain memories can make everything better," I said. "My Reno is a Keep Tahoe Blue sticker on every car. It's ditching class to drive up Mount Rose. It's juniper bushes and ice skating on the Truckee River. It's Deux Gros Nez Café and Pneumatic Diner. It's getting lost in Zephyr Books and watching divorcées throw their rings off the Virginia Street Bridge. It's lying in the grass at Idlewild Park, surrounded by roses and bearded irises and lilacs every spring. It's the high school known as the Big Bathroom on Booth Street, and painting the boulder near the football field. It's jokes about Pyramid Lake and Sparks, and the boys of Sigma Nu making a rock formation with their letters on UNR's hillside. Before they lost their charter, of course." I paused to take a drink. I needed it to swallow down the surge of emotions. "It's not like anywhere else in the world."

"It sounds like Nevada is delightful. Why isn't it home?"

I didn't want to talk about this. It wasn't something I could explain to others without coming off as petulant and bitchy, and I was too off-kilter from everything that had happened over ping-pong to speak with much sense.

"It's still home in the sense that it's where my parents and brother live, and I'll always go back and enjoy my time there. But it's changed," I said simply. "The pieces that made it strange and special, many of them are completely gone now. Others have drifted away." I traced the edge of the table, letting my fingers glide back and forth over the well-worn wood. "I can't go home without wanting it to be something it isn't, and I don't want to walk around with that much longing. I want to love something, someplace, for what it is. And I don't ever want to force myself to love anything, or force anyone to love me."

"I don't think you could. Force anyone to love you, that is," he said, scratching his chin. "The way you feel about your hometown, that's how I feel about Rhode Island. It hasn't changed, but it's not the same place it was when I was in college."

"Yeah, exactly." I patted my chest again, feeling the absence not of the places but the moments and memories. "And I've changed, too. I'm not the same person I was back then."

Riley scratched his neck, frowning. "Clearly you need to explain that," he said. "No one appreciates a cliffhanger."

I was getting antsy. I wasn't accustomed to having this volume of attention trained on me, and I didn't enjoy the feeling of careful inspection. Much more of this, and I'd admit that my parents preferred Adam, always had, and that I was the one who didn't belong in Reno. And that was far more truth than I was willing to part with tonight.

"Why can't you keep your pants zipped?" I snapped, gesturing in the general direction of his crotch. I'd never met a man with such prevalent zipper issues. "Answer me that."

He examined his fly and dutifully tugged the zipper into place before responding. "I don't think you're going to like the answer," he said.

I rolled my eyes. "You're feasting on all of my personal information tonight," I said. "It only seems fair."

He braced his arms on the table, his fingertips on his forehead. "Sometimes I forget," he conceded. "But other times, my cock doesn't fit in my pants."

I'd picked up enough shifts in the Emergency Department that nothing shocked me anymore. Spoon in the rectum? No problem. Accidentally drank a cup of hydrogen peroxide? Handled. Glued your eyelids shut in the name of fake lashes? Got it. But the too-big-for-trousers penis yielded a different variety of shock. "What—what do you mean?" I asked.

Pointing at his crotch helplessly, he said, "It doesn't fit comfortably in most pants. The zippers don't stay up." At my incredulous expression, he continued. "Come over here and see for yourself."

Circling my hand around my side of the table, I said, "I am staying right here. I will not be seeing anything for myself, thank you very much."

We stared at each other, him with his giant penis and me with my thinning shreds of restraint. I'd said I was staying over here but if he asked even one more time, I was vaulting over this table and breaking every land-speed record known to woman.

Even though this was an *arrangement*.

Even though I didn't know where it would go.

Even though he couldn't belong to me until he stopped belonging to *her*.

All I wanted was to curl up beside Riley and chase away the demons of whoever left him in this heartsick state. If the situation warranted, I was also willing to evaluate the anatomy. For *medical purposes*, of course.

Riley held his palm out and tilted his head to the side. "Alex," he said, all rough and insistent, and the only way I ever wanted to hear my name again.

"Be careful," the waiter interrupted as he set plates of every shape and size between us. "This one is very hot."

Oh, you have no idea.

Thirteen

RILEY

IT HAD BEEN the type of week where Friday couldn't come soon enough. Surviving Monday had required heroic efforts, and it'd been all downhill from there.

Matt kicked off the weekly status meeting by detailing each of the open houses he and Lauren had attended over the weekend. They couldn't find anything quite right because—*oh my fucking god*—she wanted five kids and at least two dogs, and everything was too small for their big-family needs. I'd already heard some version of that before —*fuck me*—but hearing it again before I'd consumed an adequate amount of coffee was a smack in the face I didn't need.

This came on the heels of a weekend where I hadn't thought about Lauren once. Not a single time. She hadn't dominated my days and nights, and that absence had slipped my notice until the reality of her making babies with Matt slammed into my consciousness. But there I'd been, squeezing the shit out of my burrito and trying to light Matt on fire with my glare, as jealous and bitter as I'd always been.

And I hated it. I hated everything about my reaction and the energy I was dedicating to that bitterness and jealousy. But the problem with feelings like these was that they didn't die with a single game of strip pong. My feelings for Lauren were deep and complex, and tangled around history and family and everything I associated with goodness. They were losing their poignancy, that was definite, and I wasn't fighting to get it back. Allowing them to fade away was the best option around, but that didn't make it any easier.

From there, things turned even more Mondayish with a lengthy discussion of Andy's work on the property on Eastern Pond in Wellesley. By itself, the project was standard and she was handling it well. But there was a hitch, and not a small one. Wellesley wasn't just another old house under our care; it was our childhood home and a giant, haunted disaster.

The biggest problem was that, nearly three years after my father's death, we were still dealing with that house. He'd asked us to spruce up the place because of course he left us a list of chores in his motherfucking will. Rather than burning the inspiration for *American Horror Story* to the ground, we'd delegated it to Andy. Why not? She didn't have any skin in the game. She hadn't watched while her mother died on the master bedroom floor. She'd never been molested, beaten, or emotionally tortured there.

Because Andy was physically incapable of doing the bare minimum, she'd taken care to restore the property and trick it out with all the hottest sustainability features. She'd approached it with precision, and since none of us wanted to think about the Nightmare on Eastern Pond, she'd had free rein and no one hurrying her along. That meant she'd perfected every corner and crevice of the 1880s Arts and Crafts.

And now she was done.

Since Andy wouldn't allow a bonfire, we had to make decisions about the next steps. We weren't keeping it—*hell* no—but we didn't know much else.

When she'd raised this question, we'd looked around the table at each other with blurry eyes and sour grimaces, as if we'd awakened after a long night of liquor and questionable decisions, and were now expected to explain quantum physics. The response had been an assortment of head shaking and brow rubbing, and broken statements like "I don't think we can, um, or should—" and "Are we? Or, does it? I mean, when?" and "Well…"

Tom—sweet, precious Tom—stepped up to the plate, and promised to minimize the details that came our way. He and Andy probably didn't see their roles on that project as critical to the health and well-being of me and my siblings, but it was the truth. We'd all dealt with the past—our mother's death, our father's vicious abuse in the name of grief, our gradual emergence from the goddamn horror of that childhood—in different ways. But the one thing we shared was an inability to deal with that house. Much like our father, it hit us in different ways, but it always hit us.

After a morning packed with those dueling dick slaps, it had to get better, right? Wrong.

Then there were permit issues on one of my projects, and all work had to stop. My meatball sub had failed to arrive with the lunch order. Another project had a slow, steady basement leak but no obvious water source. The Red Sox lost two exceptionally winnable games on the road, and one of the Patriots' key players was out with a season-ending injury. A project set to start in two weeks was pulled when the homeowners called to announce they were getting divorced and would not be needing their farmhouse renovated. Alex was busy all day and on call most nights, and she barely had time to return texts. The clients from my Marlborough Street project requested a meeting to discuss "a couple changes" which basically meant they wanted to redo the entire house. I doused myself with coffee every day, and twice on Thursday.

Something about this one-punch-after-another week reminded me of those loyalty club cards where you get a stamp every time you bought a sandwich. But instead of getting delicious sandwiches, I got a week's worth of bullshit and douche water, and I was looking forward to the added bonus of weekend weirdness with my ex-girlfriend.

So when Alex asked from the passenger seat of my SUV while we cruised down the highway on Friday afternoon, "What's the schedule for our time in Rhode Island?" I didn't have a good answer.

I'd barely managed to get out of the office, and I had no clue what I'd packed. I wasn't even certain where we were staying, and was hoping to find those details in one of the emails I'd ignored from Shannon. *Shambles.* I'd spent the entire morning on the phone, wrangling one issue or another, and greeted Alex with ten minutes of incoherent ranting about people who never returned voicemails.

It was worth noting that until a year or two ago, I was one of those people who never returned voicemails. Hell, I didn't even listen to them. Wasn't that the whole point of text messaging?

But I was hypocritically bitter about those damn voicemails today.

"There's a lot to see," I said, bouncing my fist against the gear shift. "What are you in the mood for?"

My eyes were on the road but I still noticed her twist in her seat to face me. "What?" she asked around a yawn. She'd been in and out of surgery since—apparently—Columbus had arrived in the New World and she was feeling the sleep deprivation today. "You've been talking about Rhode Island for weeks. You made it sound like you had every minute planned out."

I held open my palm and let it fall to my leg. "Yeah, I have some ideas," I said, the hesitation heavy in my voice. "But the week got away from me, and I didn't get a chance to sort it out."

"Okay, then. What do you want to do? You'd mentioned a bunch of restaurants and sights to see, and something about bakeries," Alex started. "One with great breads, one with great cakes."

"Seven Stars and Pastiche," I replied automatically.

"You also mentioned two donut shops, but I don't know whether I can do two bakeries and two donut shops in the same weekend," she said.

"I don't share that concern." I shot her a glance, smiling. It hadn't registered until now, but she was all kinds of sexy-cute today. Jeans, a gauzy shirt-type-thing, cardigan, and red sequined shoes. The clothes helped but the sexy-cute was all Alex. "And you can always bring a doggie bag back home with you."

"Snacks for days," she quipped, pushing her sunglasses to the top of her head and pressing her fingertips to her eyelids.

She was tired, and who wouldn't be after the week she'd

put in? I didn't understand how she functioned on so little sleep.

"We don't have to do much," I said. "Maybe drop by the event at the Providence Art Club tonight, and then get dinner on Federal Hill, or somewhere over on the East Side? It'll be quick. I'll have you in bed by nine."

"Is that a promise?" she asked, her fingers still on her eyelids.

I was about to joke about taking her to bed anytime she wanted, but I stopped myself. Knowing the state of my mind right now, I was liable to say that without an ounce of humor and reveal that, yes, I'd thought about sleeping with Alex.

More than once. A lot more than once.

I'd thought about it when I'd texted her late at night and early in the morning, and every time we'd hung out together this month. I'd thought about it in detail while she kicked my ass at ping-pong last weekend, and I'd debated whether the table would hold us.

But that wasn't part of this arrangement. I wasn't going to fuck it all up by fucking Alex.

"Unless you'd rather get food first," I said, skirting the bed topic entirely. "Nevermind. You probably need food before and after the event."

"I'm not that hungry," she said, stifling another yawn. "I got a smoothie with Hartshorn before rounds this morning. He said there was extra protein powder in there. He's all about the protein. Macros or something. I don't know. I don't pay attention to that shit."

"We'll do whatever you want," I said, my words tight and clipped. "Or nothing at all."

"No, no, no," Alex said, blinking. The city was giving way to long stretches of green. "I know you've had a difficult day and you're rocking one hell of a salty mood, but we're going all the way to Rhode Island—"

"It's not that far," I said under my breath.

"—and you've promised me the full Rhode Island experience. I'm not going all this way—"

"It really isn't that far. The states are smaller in New England than out west."

"—to take a nap," she said. "We're doing this, and we're doing the full Rhody."

I resumed tapping my fist against the gear shift, and jerked a shoulder in acknowledgement. After this hot mess of a week, I would've preferred to stay at home with a big bowl of cereal, pajamas, and a Marvel movie marathon. I didn't want to deal with people—or pants—this weekend.

But Alex was right. I'd talked up the wonders of the Ocean State, and I couldn't abandon it because I'd been reminded that Lauren was having frequent, purposeful sex with my brother. And this was where I went to get away from it all. For years, I'd been able to find a new home for myself on College Hill or lose myself to good times in Newport. This was where I went to shake it off.

"We have another half hour to go," I said, gesturing to the navigation system. Then I dropped my hand to her thigh and squeezed. I needed an anchor, something that would prevent me from floating back into the rapids. "Take that nap now. I need some more time with this salty mood."

ACCORDING to the email I'd dug up from Shannon, we were staying at an 1800s courthouse-turned-inn on Benefit Street, just three minutes from College Hill and RISD. It was a lovely, wonky place that hadn't decided which time period to embrace. There was old-fashioned wallpaper and wide plank pine floors, and art and furniture that drew from every major style in the past two hundred years.

It would've given Patrick hives. I was halfway to hives myself, but for entirely different reasons.

The handful of rooms were named in accordance with their themes, and the husband-and-wife proprietors had charming stories about each. What they did not have was our reservation. Or, more precisely, both of our reservations.

"I think I know what happened," the owner said as she tapped at her keyboard. "It looks like we set aside the Roger Williams room, which has two beds, instead of two *separate* rooms." She glanced up at me. "I wish I could fix this for you, but we're booked up. It's RISD Weekend, you know."

"I *do* know," I said, fighting to keep the edge out of my voice. Knocking my knuckles against the front desk, I pivoted to face Alex. She'd taken a call from the hospital when we'd first arrived, and I wasn't sure whether she'd heard the continuing saga of my shit-ass week. "We have a small issue here."

She was busy typing out a message on her phone and only spared me a quick glance. "Yeah? What's wrong?"

"There was a misunderstanding," I started, offering the owner a tight smile, "with the reservations. Instead of two separate *rooms*, we have two separate *beds* in one room."

Her fingers froze and she slowly lifted her head to meet my gaze. "Oh," she replied. "Okay."

"Since everyone's in town for RISD Weekend," I continued, "there are no other rooms here. I'm sure we can book something else. There are plenty of big hotels in Providence.

Either you can take the room here and I'll go downtown, or—"

"No," she interrupted, slashing a hand through the air as she spoke. "No, that's crazy. We're already here, and you gave me a lecture about how great it was to stay in this neighborhood ten minutes ago."

I stared at her, waiting for the realization to hit that we'd be *sharing a bedroom*. A bedroom. The type with *beds*. Which, when mixed with consenting adults, were intended for *sex*. And *we* were those adults.

When a minute had passed without a single flicker of wariness or alarm in her eyes, I asked, "Are you sure about this?"

She bobbed her head and held out her hands as if to say *What's the big deal, dude?*

The big deal, I wanted to shout, *is that you had your tits in my face a week ago and I only walked away because I didn't trust the ping-pong table to stay standing while I fucked you. How do you expect me to walk away when there are* beds *involved?*

Or, *I've never perfected the art of jerking off in silence, and that's what I'm going to need to do with you asleep four feet away from me.*

Or, *What happens when I start talking in my sleep about wanting your mouth on my cock?*

Or, *You've seen yourself, right? You're a walking wet dream.*

"I just want to be—" I paused, scratching the back of my neck while I searched for the right sentiment. What did I want to be right now? Part of me was convinced that the only choice was another hotel room, and the other part needed to know what Alex wore to bed. *What if she doesn't wear anything?* "I want to be respectful of your-your-your privacy."

"I sleep in on-call rooms all the time. This will be fine," she said. To her credit, she didn't even blink at my stutter. She never did. "There's no sense splitting up and making it more difficult." She held up her phone as she backed away. "I have a patient with some post-op complications. Give me a few minutes to handle this. Okay?"

Alex wandered into the adjoining dining room, her head bent and her fingers flying over the screen. If she was uncomfortable about this, it didn't show. And maybe she wasn't uncomfortable because she had no problem sleeping naked—a guy could dream—in the same room with me because she was a cool, self-possessed chick who didn't let strange situations ruffle her feathers.

But it wasn't that this attraction was one-sided. It wasn't part of the plan and it wasn't what either of us needed considering the baggage we dragged along with us. But it was there. And two nights in a bedroom—one named for the founding father of this state—wasn't going to do anything to minimize it.

It was a hardscrabble time back then, with people crossing the Atlantic just to get the fuck away from England and the second King Charles. Roger Williams was too liberal for Massachusetts and fled to the south in search of freedom of conscience—the right to believe whatever the fuck he wanted to believe without any state-run religious body breathing down his neck—and settled the Providence Plantations about four hundred years ago. This was before the colonies declared independence, before the Brown brothers founded a college, before Rochambeau docked in Narragansett Harbor to aid the revolution, before this place was even called Rhode Island. Williams went hard at the notion of a separated church and state, and to many, he was a heretic. The crazy old cooter trusted men and women to get on their knees and pray the way that suited them. To colonial sensibilities, that meant this region was a hotbed of unchecked, unprincipled living.

I glanced back at Alex, swallowing roughly as my eyes mapped her thick thighs. I didn't want to make this complicated, and I didn't want to want her.

But right now, my state was real interested in getting into her church.

I turned back to the owner. "The Roger Williams room it is," I said.

Fourteen

RILEY

AFTER SETTLING into the coziest room in the entire universe and learning the close quarters waltz, we hit up the Providence Art Club to kick off the weekend's festivities. The Club wasn't a single location but rather a string of four homes on Thomas Street, deeded over time to the cause of showing off art and sustaining artists.

I couldn't help looking over my shoulder during the toast from the college president. Dorrance was in town, and she was drawn to open bars and art critique like a moth to a flame. But I didn't see her, and wasn't interested in looking too hard. Alex and I wandered through the student exhibitions in each of the four homes, lukewarm wine served in plastic stemware in hand.

The work was impressive, and without putting forth much effort, I'd met several talented architecture students. It was the best blend of stoic academic types wearing bowties and green-haired fringe types with neck tattoos. There was reminiscing about the professor who was still bonkers and that other one who was determined to die at the lectern, and I handed out several business cards.

With that task completed, I had a mind to pack up this party, cancel the sleepover, and drive back to Boston tonight. But Alex asked for the walking tour of the area, and I couldn't say no. Not when I could stroll along South Main Street with my arm around her shoulders and drop every random bit of historical and architectural knowledge in my arsenal.

We'd stopped to take photos with the city as our backdrop, though I wasn't sure whether we were still sticking it to her douche waffle intern or now preserving memories of our time together. It didn't matter that much. I was taking whichever sliver of her life she was offering.

Instead of staying on College Hill for dinner—the place was mobbed with students and alumni and most likely Dorrance, and Alex couldn't survive an hours-long wait to be seated—we settled into a tiny bistro on Hope Street. The server was quick to deliver a charcuterie board, and I sipped an Ithaca Flower Power IPA while Alex sampled the assortment of meats and cheeses.

"Tell me something terrible," I said. "I've had a terrible week, and I'll feel better knowing that someone else experienced some of the same shit."

"Let me think about that," she said, tapping her fingertips against her bottom lip. She didn't do it to draw my attention to her mouth, but my cock didn't know that. "Well, my mother did send me a set of bracelets. Those thin silver bangle-y bracelets with the charms?"

"Oh, the horror," I said, reaching for a slice of salami. "Not *bracelets*."

Alex laughed and leaned closer. We were slotted into a

narrow table, and though the bistro was small, it was loud enough that we had to bow our heads toward each other to hear. I was inches away from her mouth, and intently focused there because I couldn't look away. That forced proximity hadn't been part of my plan when selecting this location, but just like the Roger Williams room, it was what I got.

"My mother loves all kinds of jewelry. *Loves* it. And she's generous about it, too. She can't just buy a bracelet for herself. She has to get one for me and my sister-in-law. But I can't wear bracelets," she explained, holding up her hands as if it was self-explanatory. "Not when I'm in surgery all day. Rings, bracelets, none of it." She pointed at the blueberry-sized pearl studs in each earlobe. "This is all I can manage, actually. And I never take them out. Some doctors can pull off the *put it on, take it off* routine, but I'm not one of them. I take it off and never it put it back on."

She was talking about jewelry, but again, my cock didn't know that. He wasn't the sort of fellow who understood nuance.

I cleared my throat and took a pull from my beer. "So, these bracelets," I said. "You think they qualify as terrible?"

"Probably not, but it's difficult when she sends me something like that because she ignores me when I tell her that I prefer earrings or necklaces. But then I feel guilty because it's a freaking gift. But then I remember I won't wear it, which means the gift is going to waste. And then I feel guilty about that," she said. "That's a lot of guilt, but I don't know what rises to the level of terrible for you."

With a groan that had more to do with my needy dick than this week, I said, "Terrible is having every step of a project lined up, all of my tradespeople and materials scheduled, and getting slapped with a stop-work because an inspector doesn't understand how solar energy feeds into a home's power supply."

Alex winced as she reached for her wine. "That does sound terrible."

"On certain occasions," I continued, "terrible is working with your family. There's none of the professional boundaries or distance that comes with a typical office, and there are days when I wish my coworkers didn't have stories about the ridiculous shit I did when I was fourteen." I grabbed my beer but paused before it reached my lips. "Or twenty-four. There's never a time when everything isn't personal."

"I can't imagine working with my brother," Alex said. "I don't even know what that would look like. A one-stop shop for all your oil change and gastric bypass needs?"

"I'm sure there's a market for that," I said, laughing. "Your brother, he works with cars?"

"My father owns a bunch of car dealerships back in Reno, and Adam's been working with him for as long as I can remember," Alex replied. "Washing windows, answering phones, sweeping the service bays. He started at the bottom, for sure, but that didn't matter. He just liked being involved in the business."

"But you didn't?"

She shook her head once. "Not really," she said. "I didn't have any major objections or issues with it, but it wasn't for me."

"That's how I felt about Cornell," I said. "My brothers all went there. My father and his brother, and their father, too. I would've been fine there, but it didn't give me any warm fuzzies." I plucked some almonds from the tray and munched on them before continuing. "Cornell was our tradition, but it wasn't too much of a problem for me to choose RISD. My family had its hands full with other issues when I was going off to college."

"I hear you on the tradition." Alex set her wine down and smiled at me, her eyes bright. "My entire family, all the way back to the pioneer days, went to the University of Nevada in Reno. My grandfather called it Nevada State University even though the name had changed before he was born. We never corrected him because he was a sweet old man, but that should tell you something about how long my family has been part of the Wolf Pack."

"And yet you went to the University of South Dakota," I said.

"And you went to RISD," she replied. "I guess that makes us a couple of rebels."

That forced a laugh out of me. "I'm not sure that's how my family would tell the story. How did your people handle it when you broke with the custom?"

"They were really cool about it. I mean, that's how I view their reactions now," she said. "At the time, I viewed it as them meddling and being controlling and not respecting my wishes, and all that bullshit. It actually took me a really long time to understand that it was none of those things." She reached for her wine, bobbing her head as she drank. "They pushed me to consider UNR and doubted whether I truly wanted to go out of state."

I tapped my inner arm, in the corresponding location of her tattoos. "They wanted you to pick one state?"

"I think they expected me to change my mind at the last minute, especially since it was the first time that Adam and I were attending different schools." She brushed her hair over her shoulder and *fuck*, I loved it when she wore it loose like that. "Hell, we'd been in all the same classes right up until the last year or two of high school."

Alex was one big web of contradictions, and I liked wandering down the bumpy roads of her stories. Within the same instances, she was bold and self-assured but also guilt-ridden. She knew exactly what she wanted and where she was going but she had a revisionist's view of the past. She was sweet, and more than a little salty.

Just like Dorothy and her sparkly red shoes.

"Was it difficult?" I asked. "Being away from your brother?"

She stared at the table for a minute, her chin propped on her fist. I watched as her lashes fluttered against her cheeks and her teeth sank into her bottom lip, and I thought about brushing my thumb over the dusting of freckles on her nose. She was lovely, just lovely.

My cock wasn't the most disciplined creature in existence. There were times when it would stir to life with every warm breeze and short skirt, and others when it would perk up for no discernible reason. It was an attention whore like that.

And now, with the knowledge that it would be sleeping an arm's length away from the pretty girl who kept saying and doing things that brought to mind sex, my cock was like Lassie. All hopped up on adrenaline and bouncing again because *this is go time!* There was trouble in the pretty girl's dark, wet cave and we had to save the damn day.

"It was different because I was accustomed to considering his opinion on everything, and I didn't have to do that anymore. But no, it wasn't difficult. Actually, we're the worst twins," Alex said. "There were two other sets of boy-girl twins in our graduating class, and we were the worst by far. It's like we spent nine months together and then determined we needed to go our separate ways."

"I didn't realize there was a ranking system for the best twins," I replied. "Is there a prize, too?"

Alex laughed at that, and dragged a hand through her hair. "There's no prize, but there's an expectation that twins have a connection unlike any other," she said. "The sixth senses, the kinship, the bond. Adam and I aren't like that. We've never had any of it."

"So what?" I asked. "I don't say that to be flippant. But… so what? Why does it matter? Why hold onto that as a ding against yourself or your brother? And don't tell me you're not because I can hear it in your voice."

Alex paused, her lips pursed and her brow wrinkled. I wanted to smooth out those wrinkles. Kiss them away. There were all these things I wanted to do to her—spank her, fuck her, lick her, all of it—but perhaps my greatest desire was to touch her without reason or restriction. And not like I was permitted to touch her now with the casual arm around her shoulder, the easy leg squeezes, the friendly hugs. But touch her with meaning and intention.

"During my third year of residency, I was on a pediatric surgery rotation. A set of boy-girl twins were born, and one of them had required surgical intervention because he was born with his intestines outside his body," she said.

"Please don't continue," I begged, a shudder moving through my shoulders at the thought.

"The worst is over," she said, reaching across the table to pat my forearm. I layered my hand over hers, keeping her there. "Gastroschisis isn't uncommon, but this case was rather severe and even after the surgery, he wasn't getting stronger. The parents wanted the babies to spend as much time together as possible because it seemed like he wouldn't survive. He was in the incubator with his twin a matter of hours and his heart rate was up. That night, a few of us watched while they wiggled out of their swaddles to hold hands, and the next morning, he was eating. He was fighting, and the only explanation was that he'd been with his twin."

I stared at her for a moment, studying the way the light hit her hair and waiting for her to acknowledge that saving her brother's life wasn't the primary marker of good sibling relationships. It never came.

Eventually, I said, "You know, you expect a lot of yourself."

With the hand that wasn't trapped under mine, Alex reached for a chunk of cheese and popped it in her mouth. Her eyes sparkled as her lips turned up in a sharp, devious grin.

"I expect a lot of everyone."

THE THING about Rhode Island was that I was free to be whomever I wanted here. When I came here for college, it was a rebirth. No one had known anything about me, and no one had known my siblings, my obnoxious father, or anything about my mother's tragic death. They definitely didn't know I'd been banned from my high school's athletic and extracurricular programs after getting caught smoking weed—in only my underwear—on the football field, ditched more classes than I'd attended, or graduated mostly because the school couldn't handle another year of me.

The only thing that had accompanied me to Rhode Island was a plastic box filled with my loose drawings and sketchbooks. And that was why I'd embraced Dorrance and all the freedom she'd represented. Instead of trying to figure out who I was when I wasn't standing in the long shadows of my siblings, she'd given me permission to have fun in the name of exploring the art of living. There were absolutely no restrictions in the Kingdom of Dorrance, population: anyone who was down for a wild ride. And I'd needed that.

To a point.

Looking back on it now, I wasn't sure whether that point had been the fish hook nipple piercings or the getting arrested after waking up naked in a pumpkin patch in northeastern Connecticut or losing my license after driving while tripping balls. To be fair, I hadn't actually been *driving*. It was more like inching along an empty rural highway because I'd been convinced there were colonial people trying to cross the road.

Perhaps it had been the accumulation of points. Or perhaps it had been Shannon screaming at me in a country police station. Probably a bit of both.

Let me be clear about one thing: Dorrance was great. She was a fun-time girl and we made a lot of memories together. It was probably the perfect match when it came to distilling people down to their most basic attributes, considering I didn't talk much and she never stopped. But we weren't right for each other, not by a long shot. I might've been the hell-raiser in my family, but Dorrance was the hell-raiser for all of RISD and now New York.

And she wasn't especially loyal. People were interchangeable in her world, whereas they were permanent in mine. I didn't believe in swapping out friends when it was convenient or blowing off siblings because they weren't adequately entertaining. That, and Dorrance was blind to most social cues. There was no breaking it off easily with her. She required direct, forceful words, and even then, refused to hear exactly what I was saying. In her mind, we were still on some kind of years-long break.

I wasn't worried that seeing her again would result in me getting swept under her spell. I wasn't popping any Molly and I wasn't letting her use my dick like a rubber stamp for another one of her designs. *Fuck no.* I'd pissed blue paint for days the last time I'd agreed to that.

The more I thought about it—what else was there for me to do while Alex slept an arm's length from me?—the more I regretted the suggestion that I needed protection from Dorrance in the first place. That I couldn't face her without also violating a gourd or altering my body, and required a woman at my side to block and defend.

I could've come to this event by myself, and I should've. Then I wouldn't be staring at the exposed beam ceiling at five in the fucking morning while my cock pitched a tent that could comfortably sleep a family of four. I wouldn't be fantasizing about slipping my hand under Alex's t-shirt or pushing her little shorts down, which I'd decided she wore to simultaneously comfort and torture me.

I'd only caught a quick glimpse at her sleepwear when she'd emerged from the en suite hours ago. Her t-shirt read *Buy Me Brunch*, and I'd promised I would before shutting myself up in the bathroom. I'd made a production of turning the water on and off several times, even though I was only gaping at myself in the mirror while hoping divine wisdom made an appearance.

I didn't know what to wear, what to say, how to play it,

anything. It was alarming, actually. Never in my life had one woman robbed me of my game. Before Alex—and Lauren, technically, but those were some extenuating circumstances —I'd said what I thought and gone for what I wanted.

But I couldn't do that with Alex, not all the way. I couldn't explain why her opinions and reactions mattered to me as much as they did, and I couldn't shake the feeling that we'd long outgrown the confines of our arrangement.

Where that left us was a mystery, but I'd known hiding out in a bathroom wasn't the answer. So, dressed in nothing more than my boxers, because I hadn't planned a pajama strategy for this journey, I'd stepped back into the room with the intention of saying something. Anything, even an oblique reference to the words stretched across her tits.

But Alex was asleep. I'd stared at her for a bit, just watching the gentle rise and fall of her chest and the way her hair was fanned out over the pillow.

Ripping my attention away from the ceiling, I shifted to face her. She was on her side, one arm curled under the pillow and the other tucked against her chest, and her pouty lips were pursed as if she was in deep thought.

My cock was aching, and terribly confused as to why we weren't rescuing the pretty girl when the dark, wet cave was *right fucking there*. I'd thought about visiting the bathroom to relieve that situation, but I couldn't do it quietly. The idea also made me feel dirty, and not the good-and-fun type of dirty, but the smarmy-skeezy type of dirty.

"Sorry, buddy," I whispered to the sheets. "Not tonight."

"IT'S INTERESTING," Alex mused as she glanced around the Chace Center at RISD Museum.

We were parked between a display of reimagined historical clothing and abstract paintings, but I wasn't admiring any of it because I couldn't tear my eyes away from Alex. She was wearing a dark blue dress, something that most people would categorize as simple, but I was hypnotized. Those red heels should've come with a warning label because they were equal parts Maneater and Come Fuck Me. But I didn't mind the added height they gave her. It brought her closer to me. Her hair was loose, hanging just past her shoulders, and with every movement, the scent of purple dug into my awareness.

That purple, it was much like the ticking of a clock. It'd always been there, but now that I was listening, it was the only thing I could hear.

"What's interesting?" I asked.

I was working hard at keeping my gaze easy because this was a classy event and I didn't want the RISD alumni and student body watching while I eye-fucked her. That was my present level of operation. DEFCON Eye-Fucking.

And who could blame me? We'd spent the day browsing the outdoor art sale, wandering along Blackstone Boulevard, and talking about a million things. We loved old-school rap and coffee frappes, but not necessarily at the same time. We couldn't cook but did a decent job of eating. She was lakes, I was oceans. I'd climbed Mount Washington, she'd hiked the Grand Canyon. Our politics weren't fully aligned but we agreed on the important things.

It was possible that I knew Alex—and her residents and interns, her colleagues, her best friends from college and medical school—as well as I knew anyone.

But I wanted to *know her* a little better.

"It's a diverse bunch here," she remarked. She subtly gestured with her wine glass. "You've got the tweeded-up academics, but then you've also got the blue hair and septum piercings."

I ducked my head, laughing. "I thought the same thing last night," I confessed. "The exact same thing."

"And somehow they seem to coexist peacefully."

"Yep, that's art school for you," I said, nodding as I scanned the crowd. "Lots of incongruous elements that work despite all logic."

Alex tapped her glass against my empty beer bottle. "I need to find the ladies' room. Can I get you another on the way back?"

Before I could answer, a young man appeared at my side. "Mr. Walsh? One of your designs was featured in last month's edition of *New England Homesteads*. Could you tell me about your ideation process?" He wiped his hand on his pant leg and then held it out to me. *Charming*. And a move I was certain I'd pulled in the past. "Sorry. Trevor Quinsberry. I'm a fourth year in the architecture program."

Alex plucked the bottle from my hand. "You two talk," she said. "I'll be back."

Even as she walked away from me, I couldn't stop staring at her. I watched her hips sway as she picked her way through the crowd, her hair fading from view like a sunset. And I was left with a blowjob-on-Christmas-morning smile plastered on my face.

I have a serious problem. A don't-ever-leave-me-again problem.

"Your work is fascinating, Mr. Walsh," the kid continued. "How do you find the inspiration when working within the bounds of preserving historical structures?"

My gaze swung back to him. I deserved a cookie for keeping my expression neutral considering that the only thing I wanted in this life had just left my side so I could talk *inspiration*. As if I could wrap that up in a tidy package and hand it over.

When had it happened? When had Alex stolen all the warm, tender places inside me for herself? And the rough, barbaric ones, too? It was as though she'd wandered into my life, all tiptoes and whispers, and reached in and rearranged my entire existence until it started and stopped with her.

I didn't know, but I was thankful for it. Hungry to explore it, too.

"First of all, it's Riley," I said, cutting my hand through the air. "Mr. Walsh is my, uh, he's other people. I'm Riley."

"Okay," the kid—what the fuck was his name again?—said with an eager nod. "Riley, I'm so excited to meet you. My roommate said you were at PAC last night, but I had to work so—"

"No sweat, brother," I said. "Second, we're going to head out into the main hall because I don't want my lady friend hiking all over creation." I hooked my thumb over my shoulder and motioned for him to follow me. "Now, what is it you want to know?"

The short answer to that question: everything. He wanted to know *everything*. If I could've opened my skull and invited him inside, he would've been down for the ride. But somewhere along the way I stopped being annoyed at the undergrad's steady stream of questions and started enjoying the discussion. I liked talking shop, even if I was doing it while scanning the crowd for Alex.

Speaking of which, was she fetching that beer from Montreal?

"Thank you for taking the time to talk to me, Mr. Walsh," the kid said. He slapped a hand over his eyes when the formal name registered. "Sorry. *Riley*."

"Yeah, no problem," I said, sweeping my gaze around the exhibit hall again. With a frustrated shake of my head, I reached into my pocket for a business card. "Look, my firm probably isn't hiring many—if any—interns next summer. But shoot me an email with your résumé and one of the best pieces from your portfolio." I handed it to him. "What was your name again?"

"Trevor Quinsberry," he said. "And I'll send everything tonight. I'll go back to my apartment right away. You'll have it within an hour. Thank you so much."

I waved him off. "You can do that, but I'm not opening my email until Monday morning."

"Thank you again," Trevor said. "I'm really digging preservation design and—"

I had to find Alex *right fucking now*. "Save it for the email," I said, shifting away from him.

She was probably queued up at the bar. That had to be it. There were never enough bartenders at events like these, and Alex wasn't the type of woman who'd go on a beer run and then turn up empty-handed.

Busy scouting the fastest route to the main reception area, I didn't notice the woman approaching me.

"Look what the beagle found in the foxhole," Dorrance said. "Riley Walsh, it's been a lifetime. Almost two."

Swallowing a groan, I smiled at her. She was still pretty, still pulsing with an energy that registered well above normal. And then there was the rainbow ribbon-and-tulle skirt that was definitely an original Dorrance design. Somehow, it worked. Everything just worked for her.

"Hi, Dorrance," I said. "It's good to see you."

She bounced on her toes, her eyes and smile brimming as her head bobbed. "How are you? What's new? Where are you staying? Nevermind that. Here's what we'll do. Let's go to Red Fez, sit at our old table, and catch up on everything. Oh! And I have a boat here. We'll go out on the water."

I dipped my hands into my pockets and resisted the urge to react in any way. A murmur, a nod, anything, and she'd have me trimming the jib while we set sail for Bermuda.

"I can't. I'm here with someone, and we have plans for the weekend."

"Then bring her along," Dorrance hollered, shimmying her hips. "Or him. Whatever. I love everyone." I started to protest, but her fingers snapped in my face like firecrackers. "I need a full update from you. It's not like you answer my texts or emails or social media messages."

Goddamn, where are the chatty undergrads when I need them?

"I've been experimenting a lot recently," she continued, oblivious to my disinterest, "and trying to find beauty in everyday things. Apple cores, subway stations, coffee mugs. I'm channeling it into sculpture, painting, textile work. I have to tell you all about it. And—I can't believe I didn't mention this sooner!—I'm sketching nudes again. I feel like it's my form of digestion. They're not for anyone else to see, but if I don't do it frequently, I get creatively constipated."

The artist's temperament. That finicky bitch.

"But you're still my favorite nude," Dorrance went on. "Please, Riley. I know I'll get through some of the blocks I've encountered if you'll sit for me. Oh! You'll love this. I have a new blend from my organic cannabis guy, too. So good you don't even have to chase it with Ecstasy to really get into the right headspace."

Oh my fucking god.

I brought my hand to my forehead. "Dorrance, I really—"

"There you are." An arm curled around my waist, and then I caught a hit of purple as Alex tucked herself into my side. "Sorry that took so long," she purred.

I braced myself for the inevitable series of minor injuries that followed nearly all of our embraces, but it never came. That left me blinking down at Alex, my shoulders bunched and jaw tight, while her thumb stroked my lower back over my shirt.

"I've been right here this whole time," I said. "Right here. Just waiting for you, Honeybee."

Alex swallowed thickly as she ran her palm down the length of my tie. She stopped at my belt buckle, and there was real comedy in the way Dorrance's gaze widened when she noticed Alex's hand a couple of inches from my cock. I didn't believe I'd been on the receiving end of such an overt show of possession in my entire life.

It made me want to reciprocate. Kiss her, hold her, mark her, club her over the head and drag her back to my cave. Anything. Anything that would scream *This one is for me and I'm for her.*

In the back of my brain, a tiny voice was busy reminding me that we were only playing. This performance was some well-timed theater bolstered by friendship and an undercurrent of attraction, and this scene wouldn't outlast the weekend.

But that voice was an asshole and it was time to stop listening to him.

Stop thinking.

Stop waiting.

Start taking.

I brought my hand to Alex's cheek, tipping up her face as I leaned down, and our lips met for a brief, electric moment that stole my breath. Sucking in a lungful of air, I lashed my arm around her waist and forced a squeak from her throat.

"Not done," I growled.

"Neither am I," she replied, her palm flat on the small of my back and urging me closer.

Yes. *Yes.* That was exactly the reaction I wanted.

I kissed her the way I'd been wanting to kiss her for weeks. She tasted of wine and her lips felt like they belonged on my skin. Lips crushed against each other, rough and demanding. Frustrated to the point of desperation. Promises spoken in sighs and sealed with tiny bites.

Then I kissed her as if I'd been doing it for months and already knew her body, her desires. In a way, I did. I knew so much of Alex that kissing her was simple. Simple, and hot enough to sear my skin.

I dug my fingers though her hair, wanting to gain some degree of control, and dragged her bottom lip between my teeth. She hummed, the noise vibrating between us, and it rattled away all sense of time and place. It didn't matter where we were or who was watching. The only things worth minding were the way she melted into me and begged for more with her urgent hands.

I was on fire, just burning up for her. All it took was her lips on mine, and one by one, my fuses blew. I could almost hear them popping and fizzling out in my head, and I welcomed the single-minded darkness that followed. All the restraint I'd exercised, it was gone. The arrangement, the good intentions, the better judgment—none of it could compete with the mandate to fuck this make-believe relationship straight into reality.

It was different—Alex was different—than all the times we'd embraced in the past. Even if those moments weren't completely platonic, they weren't more than flirtatious. But this, with her hair between my fingers and my shirt fisted in her hands, was nothing like anything that came before.

And now, that asshole voice in my head was telling me I'd never have anything like this again.

I ran my hands over her shoulders and down her back, and then palmed the supple globes of her ass. Her belly met the hard ridge of my cock, and her nails dug into my lower back.

"Not even close to finished," I whispered against her lips.

Alex broke away but made no move to step out of my arms. *Fucking right.* I wasn't prepared to let her go, nor was I convinced I could continue standing without her as an anchor. She touched her fingertips to her lips and blew out a shaky breath. "Neither am I," she replied.

The asshole was right. I'd never have anyone like this again.

"Let's get out of here," I said, brushing her hair over her ears. I cut quick glances around us, and found the spot where Dorrance once stood vacant. *Thank fuck.* I didn't need another conversation about creative constipation or an invitation to board her nudes-and-weed boat. "I want to take you on an adventure."

Fifteen

ALEXANDRA

A FEW MINUTES. That was all I needed. Just needed a few minutes alone with my thoughts and my waffles because *whoa*.

I couldn't stand without my legs wobbling beneath me.

The simple act of sitting wasn't even that simple because my thighs were still *quivering*. I'd never had occasion to properly quiver before, and I had to say it was pleasantly uncomfortable.

I was aching in ways I hadn't thought possible, but much like the quivering, it wasn't the worst thing I'd ever experienced.

Oh, and then there were the bite marks. Bite. Marks. *On my body.*

How I'd managed to scavenge for some clothes in the wreckage that was our room and make it downstairs in one piece was still a mystery. Apparently orgasms from Riley came with a collection of superpowers.

The only thing he hadn't fucked out of me was the hangover. I had a headache that throbbed in five different spots, one for each form of alcohol I'd consumed last night. Wine, beer, vodka, champagne—*where the fuck did I leave my good decision making?*—and whiskey. Who told me that I could drink whiskey? So much whiskey.

And now I needed some time and several waffles to get myself in order. Although noon didn't technically qualify as morning. *Goddamn it.* When had we finally fallen asleep? After the time against the door, or after the time bent over the footboard? *Ahh.* Last night, it was all hazy.

When I'd woken up beside all six-and-a-half naked feet of him, I knew I needed to get the fuck out of that bed. Not because I was embarrassed or regretful or couldn't deal, but because I'd desperately needed to pee. Once I was behind the closed door of the bathroom and the mirror revealed the wreath of faint bruises around my breasts and belly, I knew I required some time to put my world back in order.

This wasn't the kind of sex that I had…ever. And there'd been a lot of it, too. More sex than I'd believed any two people could have in one night. I was going to be limping this week.

But the specifics of last night, I couldn't reach them. It was like everything from that kiss in the museum to this morning—err, afternoon—was hiding under a thick layer of burlap, all indistinguishable lumps and bumps and boob bites. There were places and moments and words—*oh,* those words—but the double trouble of liquor and orgasms pushed everything else into a fuzzy blur.

So here I was, demolishing a few Belgian waffles and driving myself crazy with questions about last night.

Where did we go? What happened between us? What did we do? What didn't *we do? Were there condoms? I don't remember any condoms. What happens now?*

It was a full hour before Riley ambled down the stairs and into the dining room. He was freshly showered and wearing an expression somewhere between deer-in-headlights and hand-caught-in-the-cookie-jar.

"Hey," he said, running his fingers through his damp hair without meeting my eyes. "Good morning."

I was no better with my eyes glued to the bacon-syrup-waffle-more-waffle carnage on my plate, but it still stung that he wouldn't look at me. "Yeah, good morning," I said. "How are you doing?"

Riley laughed, dropping into the chair across from me. With the heels of his palms pressed to his eyes, he groaned. "Uh, okay, I guess. I've been better."

If there was a list of the wrong things to say after drunkenly having sex with your maybe-fake-but-maybe-real girlfriend, that response would be on it. My stomach dropped right to the floor, and I could almost hear the slippery *thunk* as it rolled around under the table.

Shit. Just…shit.

Maybe *I* wasn't embarrassed or regretful or having troubling dealing with this, but Riley was. And I fucking hated that.

Here I was, thinking he'd been serious about wanting me —and wanting me for more than one wild night—but that wasn't the case. Nope, he'd wanted to get drunk and fuck away his weird Dorrance hang-up, and I'd been in the right place at the right time.

Once again, I was the fool. The one with the willful blindness and the undying desire to be wanted. That was it, all I needed. Just to be the girl someone chose. The one wanted more than any other.

And once again, I wasn't that girl. Every time I'd wound

up in this spot, I promised myself that I'd stop trying so hard. Stop begging for scraps. Stop looking for affection, validation, love. I was going to let it all come to me because I knew I couldn't force anyone. I knew because I'd tried countless times before. My parents, my brother, every one of my previous boyfriends.

And I'd tried. I'd really tried with Riley. Despite it all, I was sitting across from a man who'd said some of the filthiest, naughtiest, most amazing words ever uttered between the sheets a handful of hours ago, and *he's been better*. That wasn't the kind of statement associated with being wanted.

An eternity passed before Riley unfolded himself from his chair and shuffled over to the buffet. He returned with a plate piled high with every remaining item—eggs, bacon, waffles, fruit, all of it—and promptly submerged it in maple syrup.

There was a quip ready on my tongue, but I held it, not trusting this new version of us with our vintage banter. Instead, I snuck glances at him while he inhaled his breakfast. All told, it wasn't more than ten minutes, but it dragged on like an unending hour.

"Hey. So…" Riley set his fork down and propped his chin on his clasped hands, and turned his full attention toward me for the first time. "Would you mind heading home early? I have—uh—a client who is waiting on an updated proposal from me, and I n-n-n-need Matt to look over the structural elements before I can send it out."

His voice was hoarse, each word a low snarl, and it had me squeezing my thighs together without thought. It was automatic, after one night. Same with the curl of desire in my belly, the heat between my legs. That was the power of Riley Walsh's growls: immediate, undeniable lust.

Too bad lust was a fucking idiot who didn't know what was good for her.

"Fine," I replied, meeting his gaze with an arched eyebrow because fuck him. Fuck his hang-ups, fuck his issues, fuck his blow-off attitude.

He blinked away, deflating as if he'd heard my thoughts. "Okay, so—"

"I'll be ready in half an hour." I dropped my fork to the plate with a clang and pushed away from the table. I marched past him but stopped once I'd cleared his chair. Speaking over my shoulder, I said to his back, "And I want to be alone."

I went right on stomping until I reached our room, and then stumbled inside with my quivery-shaky-lusty legs. Sliding down the door, I covered my flushed cheeks with my hands and wondered how the hell I'd gotten here. Not here, the floor of this inn, but here, this inside out and back again disaster. But then I blinked, suddenly concerned I was in the wrong room.

Our room had been a mess of pillows, bed linens, and clothes. An overturned chair, a curtain hanging askew, all the tchotchkes out of place.

This room was pristine.

But it was our room. My red wristlet sat on the desk, and Riley's messenger bag lay beside it. Gulping, I gazed at the crisply made beds, the precise order of the framed artwork and draperies. No longer abandoned beside the bed, last evening's dress now hung in the closet with my shoes seated on the floor directly beneath it. Riley's things were packed, his luggage standing tall beside the door.

I knew housekeeping hadn't been through because I'd left the Do Not Disturb sign on the door when I'd gone in search of breakfast and it was still there now. This was Riley's handiwork. He'd put the room back to rights and—

—are—

—those—

—my—

—panties?

He'd folded my panties. The ones he'd peeled off my body last night. Folded like he'd taken a professional lingerie-handling class at Victoria's Secret, and left on the corner of the bed alongside my bra.

I couldn't decide whether he was a decent guy who simply couldn't handle the awkward morning-after shit or a straight-up psychopath. Instead of getting to the bottom of that conundrum, I scrambled off the floor and into the bath-room. There was dried semen on my thighs—and probably everywhere else—and I needed it gone.

With the hot water cranked all the way up, I stripped out of my clothes. I caught sight of a dark patch on my upper thigh, and shifted to get a better look at it in the mirror. It was ink, almost the size of my fist. There was a shape there, maybe some lines, but it was smudged beyond recognition. Right now, I didn't want to know what it was or how it had gotten there. I wanted to get all of it—all of him—off me.

This arrangement couldn't continue. We couldn't pretend to be dating anymore, and we couldn't actually be dating either. That was out of the question because…because it was.

Because he didn't want me this morning. *Give him another chance, maybe he will.*

Because he was stuck on his ex-girlfriend. *He wasn't last night.*

Because he was a man-child who hadn't outgrown his clumsy. *Except in bed.*

Because he wasn't my type. *Like that stopped anything.*

Because I didn't need a reason.

I didn't take long to wash and dress, and then throw my things into my overnight bag. There was neither mascara nor lip color in the cards today, and I was happier without them.

Riley was waiting in the lobby when I emerged, and offered only a nod as he rushed past me. I assumed he was heading upstairs to collect his luggage, but one of the many things missing from this day was open communication.

I didn't understand how this had happened. How we'd gone from friends—*good* friends—to people who couldn't choke out more than a few syllables at a time. Even if he didn't want anything to come of this weekend, he wasn't required to be an asshole about it. He could've said *Hey, Alex. That's not what I want from you* and I would've been fine. My pride and what was left of my heart would still be wounded, but at least I'd have something to work with. Anything was better than the shifty-eyed brush-off.

When Riley returned with his bag in tow, he headed straight for the door and held it open. Again, I was forced to assume that he meant for me to follow. "I take it we're leaving now," I said, stepping out onto the sidewalk.

He nodded in response, and we walked the two blocks to the parking lot in silence. If the entire trip home was going to be this awkward and tense, I was in trouble.

"Would you mind if we made one stop?" Riley asked as he opened the back gate of his SUV.

"Whatever you want," I murmured.

I moved to toss my tote in the trunk, but he yanked it out of my hands. "I've got it," he said quietly. He took care to stow our things, perhaps more care than two clothing-filled bags necessitated. "My sister Shannon," he continued, his attention still fixed on securing the luggage, "asked me to bring her some bread from one of the local bakeries. I'd forgotten about it until now, but if it's an issue—"

"It's fine," I snapped.

Riley emerged from the depths of the trunk and turned to face me. But instead of the quick glimpses and avoidance he'd treated me to earlier, he was studying my jeans and sweater, my face, my still-damp hair. He was looking at me the way he had last night, and I didn't know what to do with that.

"Shannon's pregnant," he started, "and I don't want to be the person who doesn't deliver the bread she's requested. That's an invitation to my funeral. She'd put my head on a spike in the middle of the office, and leave it there as a warning to all those who dare deprive her." He rubbed the back of his neck and nodded to himself. "I could also go for some coffee. This bakery has great coffee. And I'm sure you'll need a snack for the road."

He seemed like Riley again. Sweet. Funny. Grumpy without his daily ration of coffee. Preternaturally concerned with food. Where'd the shifty-eyed brush-off guy gone? Not that I wanted him back but I damned well wanted to know what was going on.

He drove through the city with ease, and led the way to a low-slung building with blue awnings, where the aroma of bread and yeast hung heavy in the air. It was busy inside the bakery, and the line was moving too quickly for me to get a good look at the offerings.

"You'd like the almond croissant," Riley said from beside me.

He was staring straight ahead again, his eyes averted.

Boys. Women always got a bad rap for being clingy and emotional after sex, but it was boys who couldn't hang.

Did I want last night to mean something? Yes. Would I survive if it didn't? Of course.

When we reached the counter, I started to order but he silenced me with an abrupt wave. "Two almond croissants, an iced coffee with room for milk, an iced nonfat latte, and three durum sticks."

As the cashier read back Riley's order to him, I pulled some bills from my wallet and moved to set them on the counter.

"Oh my fucking god, would you stop?" he hissed, slapping my hand away. "I've got it, okay?"

What the fuck is going on?

WHAT THE FUCK *is going on?*

That was the only question in my head. Over and over, an endless loop of those words until I started doubting everything and wanting to sneak another glance at the bruise. *On my thigh.* Just to confirm I wasn't losing my fucking mind.

It certainly seemed like I was. I mean, was there a different explanation? I'd woken up naked and alone, our room trashed and a giant fucking hickey sucked into my leg. Because I was a goddamn fucking idiot, I couldn't remember much after kissing her in a dark booth at The Magdalenae Room in the Dean Hotel. The broken condom that I'd found under a pillow certainly corroborated...something.

And Alex had been no help. Instead of recapping the events between last call and waking up with the burn of well-used muscles, Little Miss Thigh Sucker had no use for me. She'd gone about breakfast as if nothing had changed.

I was never drinking again. I said that every time I woke up from a night of whiskey but I was serious this time. I couldn't handle that shit. It didn't matter whether it was a lot or a little. It fucked me over and hung me out to dry. Or more precisely, it left me choking back vomit in the middle of a busy bakery, all while staring at a woman I'd slept with and wondering how to ask her for the key details.

That right there was shambles.

I'd kissed her—hell, I'd fucked her, more than once, if the sated state of my balls was a worthy barometer—and now she was trying to buy her own coffee. Even if whiskey had pissed all over my brain and this relationship was a work of artifice, I'd been *inside* her just a few hours ago.

I was buying her fucking coffee. The croissant, too.

"Oh my fucking god, would you stop?" I snapped, batting away her hand. "I've got it, okay?"

"Sorry," Alex muttered, though there was no apology in her tone. "I must've misunderstood. *Again.*"

She grabbed her coffee and pushed past me, and I had no idea how to make this right. How could I? If I'd had my way, she'd still be underneath me right now. We wouldn't have left that room all day.

But I didn't know what had sent her scrambling out of our room or why she wanted nothing to do with me today. I'd done something or said something, or maybe I'd been bad in bed, and what intimacy we'd had was now hostility.

I didn't say anything as we walked back to the car. Nothing was going to come out right. I couldn't grab her by the neck and kiss her until she turned molten in my hands. I couldn't tell her I wanted her lips stretched around my cock. I couldn't even drag my fingers through her hair. I couldn't have any of it until I figured out where I'd gone wrong.

The drive to Boston was quiet. We shared little more than basic conversation about the weather, radio stations, traffic.

We'd never experienced an awkward silence like this before, and it made me fucking crazy. I was torn between putting it all on the table and talking about last night and pulling over to vomit on the side of the road.

I rolled up to Alex's street, a narrow cobblestone lane just off Cambridge. I needed more time to get myself in order but I couldn't let her go yet. I wrapped my hand around her wrist, ready to slather her in the apologies I'd been mentally rehearsing since hitting the Massachusetts border, but she shook me off. "Alex, I have to—"

"It's obvious that you don't care but I have an IUD," she interrupted. I gazed at her dumbly, blinking as those words registered. "Thanks for asking, asshole."

"I care," I replied. "I definitely care."

She bolted from the car and I followed, beating her to the trunk. "Could you let me know whether I need to be tested for Hep B? Or should I just order a full blood panel and cross my fingers?"

Opening the trunk gate, I curled my hand around her bag's handles and pulled it close to me. She wasn't going anywhere yet. "Alex, would you wait a fucking—"

"You don't get to call me *Alex* today," she interrupted, and it certainly seemed like I was meant to understand her meaning. "Not after what you called me last night."

Oh, fuck me sideways, what did I call her last night?

"I'm so s-s-s-sorry. I didn't mean it."

She glared at me, disgusted. "Of course you didn't," she said. It was clear I was missing the pertinents here. I rubbed a hand down my face, trying and failing to call up the hours I'd lost. "Look, Riley. This arrangement isn't going to work out."

Alex yanked her bag from my hands and stomped into

her building, the door slamming hard behind her. I watched her go, and I didn't try to stop her. She didn't want to hear anything I had to say, and it was just as well. I didn't have the right words.

I would've stood there longer, staring up at her windows, but I was blocking traffic and the cabbies had some choice words for me. I thought about going home, where I could stare at my bruised thigh and wonder how a pixie like Alex could leave a mark like that without leaving behind a treasure chest of filthy memories. But I didn't want to explain to Sam and Tiel why I was back early or how the weekend had gone.

With one last glance at Alex's windows, I hopped in the car. I circled the city for an hour, aimless. I ended up in Wellesley, near a deli I'd frequented as a teenager. The institution of family dinners had held up after my mother's death, but only when Shannon was in the house. Once my father had kicked her out and most of my siblings were off to college, this red brick shop had become a second home to me.

I parked and made my way inside, and studied the menu board with glazed eyes. Several waves of customers passed while I read the items, my fingers itching to text Alex and ask what interested her. I figured I could also order a little of everything and let her decide.

But I didn't believe any quantity of cured meats was going to turn things around for us.

Eventually, I ordered an Isabella—prosciutto, mozzarella, tomatoes, and basil—because that sandwich had been by my side for many youthful run-ins with bottom-shelf liquor. I knew it would see me through the worst of last night's whiskey.

With my lunch and three cans of ginger ale in hand, I drove back to Beacon Hill. I wasn't banging on Alex's door—not today anyway—but I was right around the corner, at my Pinckney Street project. There was a glass tile fireplace in need of delicate restoration, and I could only do that type of work when no one was around to bother me.

It also offered me hours of uninterrupted solitude where I could focus on *one tiny thing* and leave the rest of my brain to work on everything else. I'd finished the sandwich and a decent amount of tile work when it dawned on me: I hadn't pined for Lauren all week. Not even once. I couldn't remember the last time I'd dreamt of her.

And somehow, my life was still in shambles.

Riley: I know it's totally inadequate but I am sorry.
Riley: I want to make things right.
Riley: Alex, please…
Alex: Go away, fuck boy.

***

EITHER MY WEEKEND fuckery was stalking me or Mercury was in cuntrograde because this Monday wasn't off to a great start.

I'd overslept and that was laughable considering I hadn't fallen asleep until after three in the morning.

The breakfast taco and burrito food truck was on va-fuck-ing-cation. I didn't know who decided that taco trucks were allowed to take vacations, but I sure as shit hadn't signed off on that. My backup taco truck was on the second string for a reason.

My notebook was missing, and I'd had to bumble through my status reports.

And everything with Alex was still fucked all the way up.

But if I hadn't been driving the struggle bus, I probably would've derived some strange pleasure from this meeting. Sam and Matt were yelling at each other about structure versus style. Patrick was muttering to himself like an old man feeding ducks at the park. Tom and Shannon were embroiled in a debate about lines of credit which exceeded my interest and pay grade. Andy kept needling me for details about my weekend; I kept devising subtle ways to ignore her.

This was the type of chaos I'd come to expect from working with my family. We knocked the *fun* right into dysfunctional.

I was gazing into my coffee and debating whether I had time to get a replacement for my backup burrito when one of the overhead lights went out. At first, I didn't register it, but Patrick made sure everyone noticed.

"What the hell?" he asked, pushing out of his chair. He stood beside the table, his hands fisted on his hips and his irritated glare pointed at the chandelier.

"Are we adding this to your agenda?" Shannon asked dryly.

"Those bulbs were changed out in June for high efficiency ones," Patrick said. "They shouldn't be burning out within five months, Shan."

"That might be the case but—what the fuck are you doing?" Shannon cried as Patrick boosted himself onto the table. At once, everyone reached for their beverages and laptops.

"I just want to check something out," he said.

"I do love watching people use my handcrafted furniture

as jungle gyms," Sam said. "Really validates all the time I put into each piece."

Patrick moved to the middle of the table, reaching for the dimmed bulb. "Would you rather we spend the next ten minutes moving the table and getting a ladder up here?" he asked.

"Yeah, let's turn the light *off* before we start playing with electricity." Andy crossed the room and flipped the switch, and murmured, "Hello darkness, my old friend."

I had a Rage Against the Machine lyric ready in response but it took a backseat to the dim memories that were quick to emerge. They descended all at once, disjointed and shocky.

The shadowy booth flanked by erotic murals at The Magdalenae Room where I'd touched Alex and kissed her and whispered all the ways I wanted her.

The taste of whiskey on her lips.

The heat of her perfect body.

The feel of her dainty hands tangled in mine.

The knowledge that we'd wanted the same things and we'd—*finally*—wanted to make them reality.

"Get the fuck down," Shannon yelled.

Her words snapped me back to the attic conference room and out of my memories with a startle. I still didn't know how we'd gotten to the swishy cocktail lounge at the Dean Hotel in downtown Providence or why we'd gone there when the simplest, most logical destination would've been the inn. Looking back, I wanted to slap myself upside the head for continuing the great tour of Rhode Island when I should've been worshipping Alex behind closed doors.

"I mean it, Patrick. Get the fuck down," Shannon repeated. "We don't repair the fixtures during meetings."

"Just calm down and give me a minute to figure out what's wrong," he replied.

"Ohhh," Sam said. "Did you just invoke the calm down clause?"

"That does trigger the articles of ass-kicking," Tom added.

"Listen, buddy. I don't think you know anything about electrical engineering," Matt said, rising from his seat. He climbed onto the table. "Let me take a look."

"You don't know anything about electrical engineering either," Shannon roared. "I'm not asking anymore. Get down right now before you crack your fool heads open."

"I'm never building you people another piece of furniture as long as I live," Sam muttered. "Not when you're using it for fucking box jumps."

"Andy," Patrick called. "Grab me some needle nose pliers."

"No. Not unless we're cutting the power at the breaker," she replied.

"Then cut the fucking power," Patrick said.

"No," Shannon yelled. "We're not doing any of that."

The debate raged on—in the goddamn dark—while I struggled to put the pieces of last weekend in order. There'd been a logic to it all, but I couldn't find it. What had I said, what had I done that turned a perfect night into a disastrous morning?

"All right, all right," Patrick said as he returned to his seat. "Back to the agenda. Let's talk through investment projects."

It wasn't clear whether he'd solved the mysteries of the chandelier, and I tuned out the rest of the discussion. Investment projects—properties bought by the firm with the purpose of restoring and selling for a tidy profit—didn't interest me today. I needed to handle things with Alex, and I needed to do that before the hospital's fundraising gala on Friday.

"That needs to be delegated and that's the fucking end of it," Patrick said, his tone sharp enough to cut through my thoughts of long-stemmed red roses and groveling.

"I'm in charge here," Shannon said, stabbing her finger at a purple file folder in front of her. "You presented this property to me. I took it. It's mine. I'll determine when and if delegation is necessary."

My mind flashed to our room at the inn and I saw my hand circling Alex's neck. I heard myself saying, "I'm in charge here. Understand?"

And then I remembered it *all*.

Her hand on my leg under the table at Magdalenae.

The devious sparkle in her eyes when she ordered the best bottle of whiskey in the house and told me she wanted us to get a little too honest.

My mouth on her neck, jaw, cheeks, lips, everywhere.

The backseat of the hired car where she was straddling my lap.

Stumbling into the inn and barely making it to our room because I couldn't wait another breath to taste her and feel her heat around me.

Stowing away my strength to keep from tearing the door off its hinges or slamming it shut, and then unleashing it all on Alex.

The scent of her skin and how it tasted just below her ear, and the way goosebumps rippled over her breasts when I pushed inside and called her Aly. *Aly.*

Fucking her while her pulse thrummed against my fingers.

Watching her shake off everything, and showing me a softer, hungrier side, one that had her eyes widening and brows lifting as if to say *Don't you think you can fuck me a little harder than that?*

Sliding my palm between her legs while I moved inside her, and saying, "I'm going to serve you like a queen and fuck you like a whore."

I sucked in a breath as I saw my hands all over her. Twisting in her hair, pinching her nipples, wrapping around her throat, slapping her ass, digging into her skin, sliding between her lips. *Everywhere.*

And I should've done everything differently. Not the fucking or the spanking or the choking, but the entire morning. I should've gone down to that dining room, thrown her over my shoulder, and carried her sweet ass back to bed.

And that was what I needed to do now. That, with some slight modifications.

I stood up then, fumbling everything within reach. My laptop flipped over, my coffee went flying into my lap, my phone bounced off the hardwood floor. It was a tiny tornado, an entire weather system of my own creation.

"I have an emergency," I said, running a hand over the soggy patch on my leg. "I have to step out. Now. Right now. I have to go."

Patrick was immediately concerned, and that was reasonable considering immediate concern was his dominant reaction to most things. "What's wrong? Is it Berkeley Street? Comm Ave? Pinckney? Joy Street? Marlborough Street?"

I rubbed the face of my phone down my chest and answered, "Yes."

Not waiting for Patrick's response, I darted down the stairs and back to my office. I shoved my things into my messenger bag and then headed for the door. If I was fast and Alex was running late, I could still catch her before she left for the hospital.

I sprinted down Derne Street, toward Cambridge Street and Alex's apartment. I knew her mornings were usually tied up with rounds, but it was possible her schedule was different today. Unlikely, but possible. It could be one of those days when she went in later because she was picking up the night floats or on-calls or whatever that was all about.

When I reached her door, I pressed her buzzer over and over, until I couldn't feel my fingertip. No answer. Then I rang Hartshorn's apartment. Nick's too. He hadn't lived there in months but it would always be Nick's apartment to me.

Still nothing.

Dejected, I dropped down on the top step and hugged my bag to my chest. The passing traffic sang an erratic lullaby of blared horns, roaring engines, and shouted cursing. I sat there for a long time.

When I was younger, I used to crawl out the attic window and onto the roof. Weed had often been involved. I'd watch the clouds, the stars, the flights taking off and landing at Logan. I'd stare up at the sky for hours and hours, not really seeing anything but granting my troubles the space to wander away from me.

These days, people would call it self-care. Treating myself kindly to compensate for living with an abusive demon father. Back then I'd seen it as a reprieve from everything. A secret corner of the universe where I hadn't been required to talk or think or confront any of the issues teeming under that roof.

I'd been free to let everything *be* up there. That wasn't the same as letting it go, but leaving it to the side while I went on with the business of surviving. My mind—maybe it had been the weed—had a way of working things out and pointing me in the right direction.

So, I did that now, here on Alex's stoop. I let all the things I'd fucked up in the past forty-eight hours be—I sure as shit wasn't letting any of it go—and I stared off into the distance. The sky and clouds and rooftops sucked me in, the cold granite beneath me numbed my ass, and an hour passed between eye blinks.

But I knew. I knew what I had to do, and I was dialing as I crossed the street toward the hospital. I could take charge all I wanted but Alex was the one in control. As much as it betrayed my sense of what was necessary right now, I had to submit to her terms and conditions. I had to respect the arrangement.

"Riley," Nick said when he answered. "I just saw Alex. What the fuck did you do?"

"About that," I replied. "I need your help."

Eighteen
ALEXANDRA

"THIS IS ALL YOUR FAULT," I said, stabbing at my salad.

Nick tore open a bag of chips, chuckling. "I don't see how that's the case," he replied.

I dragged my gaze away from the salad I was abusing and across the picnic table we'd commandeered for lunch at Lederman Park. It was the type of sunny autumn day I'd long for once the gray of winter had set in, but I was struggling to appreciate anything right now. After four days, the bruises on my body were a murky shade of green and an unnecessary reminder of my weekend indiscretions.

"It was *your* idea," I said. "Of course this is *your* fault."

Nick was busy unwrapping his sandwich and missed the glare I'd leveled in his direction.

"All you've said is that Rhode Island didn't go well," he said. "What exactly am I taking the blame for?"

Abandoning the salad, I stretched out on the bench and folded my hands under my head. If I was going to be salty, at least I could be salty with a tan. "I don't want to talk about it," I mumbled.

For all that we shared, there were a few areas where Nick, Cal, and I rarely dared to tread. One of those places was sex. There'd never been a conversation about how it was acceptable to talk about the people we were dating and allude to things getting serious, but that we weren't crossing the line into a live discussion of sex or articulating any sexual specifics. It was just how we operated.

Money was also in the no-go zone. Despite all of us living in the same apartment building at one point, it was implicitly known that we were at three starkly different points on the hospital's salary scale. Cal was at the high end, with more years of experience, an incredible gift for teaching interns and residents, and a reputation for treating celebrity patients. Nick was in the middle but definitely catching up to Cal. He was board-certified in two areas of neurosurgery —general and pediatric—and had the best bedside manner I'd ever encountered. That left me, still fresh off my residency and fellowship years, near the bottom.

"Then I can't take responsibility for it," Nick replied. "Where the fuck is Hartshorn? Can that guy be on time for anything?"

"No. It's not in his genetic code." I pushed up on an elbow and surveyed the food spread out on the table. "If he's not here in ten minutes, I'm stealing his pastrami sandwich."

Nick dragged the paper-wrapped sandwich out of my reach. "I told you to get a sandwich. In the three—almost four—years that I've known you, I've never seen you order *and* eat a salad."

"Can we save the food journaling for tomorrow? Please?" I asked.

I flopped back on the bench and stared at the cloudless sky. I never should've gone along with this silly plan to solve all of my problems with a make-believe boyfriend. Men were drama, and I didn't need any of their immature mind-game bullshit in my life. He played the part of the nice guy, but Riley was just like the rest of them.

"He's an asshole," I said eventually, my gaze still turned toward the sky.

"Walsh?" Nick asked. He crunched a chip and made an unconvinced sound. "Sometimes, yeah. But not when it *really* matters."

"I assure you," I said, popping up to meet his eyes, "it mattered and he was an asshole."

"I believe you. Next time I see him, I'll take him out back and throw rocks at him. Would that make you feel better?" Nick asked.

Before I could reply, the long line of a shadow fell over me. "Dude," I said, swatting Cal's leg. "You're blocking the sun."

"Sorry I'm late," he said. "I jumped into a bypass that had gone sideways."

I lifted my arm to peer at my watch. "Another two minutes and I was taking your sandwich," I said to Cal as he settled beside Nick on the opposite side of the picnic table.

Cal unwrapped the pastrami on rye and placed half of it in front of me. "Have it," he said. "I won't be able to finish this anyway. One of the pharmaceutical reps brought me a big-ass protein smoothie this morning."

That was bullshit. The not being able to finish the sand-wich part, not the steady stream of pharma reps lined up for an ounce of his attention part. Cal was the kind of guy who could clean out an all-you-can-eat buffet and then ask about dessert. But he was also the kind of guy who was generous to the core and never thought twice about giving everything —time, attention, money, pastrami sandwiches—to the people he cared about. And when he decided to give you something, he didn't take no for answer.

"Since I don't want to waste it," I said with a heavy note of faux reluctance as I sat up. "Thanks, Hartshorn."

He waved me off, uncomfortable and uninterested in acknowledgement. He wasn't great with appreciation or recognition or feelings of any sort.

"Your residents are in top form this week," he said. "I was listening in this morning while one of them caught an inflamed gallbladder that the ER attending was discharging as acid reflux. It was an interesting presentation and I can see how the attending missed it, but the best part was your resident wasn't a dick about the whole thing."

Now that was a blessing. Most surgical residents were under the impression they were contractually required to be dicks at all times.

"That's what I like about you," Nick said, wagging a chip at me. "Even when you're hooking up with an asshole and having a bad week, you keep your shit together and your residents on track. You don't take your problems out on people."

"I never said I was hooking up with him," I objected, but I couldn't force any sincerity into my words.

"I read between the pissed-off lines," Nick replied. "I know Riley, and I know he has some, ah, ongoing issues."

Like being an asshole.

Cal jerked his chin toward me. "What's going on?"

I picked up the sandwich and shook my head. "It's nothing. I went to Rhode Island with a guy. As it turns out, he's an asshole. End of story."

But that wasn't the end of the story. With every passing day, the sting of Riley's silence intensified. We'd become friends in the past two months, and even if getting in bed together had been the wrong turn, I deserved more than this. I was no expert, but I was certain he'd enjoyed himself in that bed. It wouldn't kill him to send more than some blasé texts with boilerplate apologies.

We hadn't agreed on any provisions for incredibly good sex followed by incredibly awkward tension when this started in August. But it wasn't about the arrangement anymore. We'd long since exceeded the terms, and we couldn't blame that construct for the events last weekend. No. *Hell no*.

If I was being honest with myself—really, *really* honest—I could admit that I was hurt, and it was more than some wounded pride. I'd thought there was something between us. Something significant. I'd allowed myself to believe that Riley had climbed over the wreckage left by previous relationships and found it in him to reach out for more…with me.

I could also admit that, just once, I wanted to be the one. Maybe not the *forever* one, but at least the *right now* one.

Cal studied me while he ate his half of the sandwich, his eyes narrowed and brow arched as if he was piecing together a response.

"At least you have the Chief off your back," he said. He wasn't quick to reply, much like Riley, but when he did, his words were meaningful. "Right?"

I lifted a shoulder. "Somewhat," I said. I wasn't in a glass-half-full mood. "He observed a laparotomy yesterday, and when he critiqued my surgical posture—again—he was kind enough to do it privately."

"That's an improvement," Nick said, his lips bending into a lopsided smile. "It's a game of inches, Emmerling."

"You're feeding into it if you let him bother you," Cal said. "He knows you're one of the best. He also knows you want to be *the* best. That's why he nudges you on every little thing. Don't you think he'd be the first one to say it if there was more to criticize about your work than your posture?"

"You make it sound like he's doling out tough love. He spends his evenings knitting a noose of rumors and dangles it in front of me every time the mood strikes," I argued.

Cal snickered as he balled up the sandwich wrappings. "He's got an old school Puritan streak, that I won't deny," he said. "But you can't give a shit about any of that. Know that you're good and don't give a fried fuck about anything else."

"Is that another Oregonian specialty? The fried fuck?" Nick asked. "Or is it one of those local treasures, like steamers and Fluffernutters? Maybe, if we're lucky, there'll be fried fuck on the menu Friday night. I hear the Four Seasons has an excellent preparation."

Oh, shit. *Shit.*

"This fucking gala," I said with an exaggerated sigh. "Since I brought the asshole to the Chief's party a few weeks ago, it's not like I can bribe the coffee cart guy to go with me. Not unless I want to play another round of *Ohh, She's a Whore.*"

Cal glared at Nick, ignoring me. "Is your wife traveling again?" he asked. "You get real punchy when she's out of town."

Nick tipped back his water bottle and drank deeply. "She's been in the Bay Area all week. She'll be back Friday afternoon," he said. "We might ditch the fundraiser. We have some marital business to catch up on, so y'all will need to report back about the fried fucks."

I gaped at Nick from across the table. "If you're not going, neither am I. The last thing I want to do is show up to this event alone."

Cal pointed at me with his water bottle. "The head of GI surgery is retiring in a year or two, and I'm teeing you up to replace him," he said. "You're going to this thing."

All of that was news to me. Everything from the retirement to the idea of staying at this hospital beyond the next few months.

"I just don't want to go alone," I grumbled.

"I'm going alone," Hartshorn retorted. "It'll be fine. We'll hang out together."

"It's fine for you," I said. "No one gives a shit about you being alone. When they see me alone, they start talking about the purity of interns and why I can't keep a guy without disemboweling him within a few weeks."

They offered grim smiles but staged no protest. They knew I was right, and it didn't matter whether several of my male colleagues had paired off with interns or residents. Those situations, they were expected. Acceptable, even. But with me, none of it was acceptable.

"One of y'all is gonna have to report back about those fried fucks," Nick said. "You've got my interests piqued."

Cal rubbed his forehead with an irritable groan. "How long until your wife gets home?"

Sparing a glance at his watch, Nick replied, "Twenty-seven hours, thirty-nine minutes."

What a splendid treat, being loved all the way down to the minute.

I WAS DRESSED and I was at the Four Seasons, and those were both significant accomplishments for me today. I'd even thrown on some makeup but that didn't include the most important accessory, according to my mother—a smile. It was bad enough that I was gala-ing tonight. I couldn't force cheerfulness, too.

I'd gone with a navy blue wool dress that wasn't quite fancy enough for this event but earned points for being simple and classic. Navy blue was my go-to shade. It always came through for me, unlike men.

Nick wasn't coming. That would make him a real bastard if he wasn't such a nice guy. It was no surprise that Hartshorn found a heart in need of his services, and wasn't arriving until later. Another nice guy right on the cusp of bastard.

Without them to entertain me, I was left wandering the ballroom. I'd stumbled into a discussion of exciting research on stem cell therapies for chronic GI illnesses. To me, that shit *was* exciting. That little chat would've met the minimum standards of socialization and given me a pass on leaving after the cocktail hour if the whole goddamn world wasn't asking after *my date*.

Doctors, they were a gossipy lot.

I nodded absently while a small group debated the merits of a new tool for minimally invasive procedures, and stared into my glass. It was mostly full. The wine was lovely but I wasn't interested in drinking. That was my position on most things right now—not interested.

Except when it came to food. I wasn't one of those people who lost her appetite in emotional or stressful times, and didn't my ass know it. Regardless of the situation, I was consistently hungry.

I was sure Riley would have a comment or two for that, and I washed down a bitter laugh with a gulp of wine.

Riley. Fucking Riley.

But then, as if he'd known I was thinking about him, he was here. Standing on the other side of the ballroom, his dark suit impeccable and his grin a little too knowing, watching me. The look on his face...it was like he was thinking about how his cock felt when it was inside me. Goosebumps broke out over my skin and the tiny hairs on the back of my neck stood up because I was thinking about it, too.

"I'm curious, Doctor Emmerling, where you stand on—"

I didn't listen to the rest of the question, instead turning away from my colleagues and moving toward Riley. He was doing the same, his strides long and purposeful, and within seconds we were face-to-face. The boring beige heels I was wearing—lengthen the leg—gave me some height, but I still had to crane my neck to meet his eyes.

And those eyes, they weren't caught in the headlights tonight.

"Get over here," he growled, lashing his arm around my waist.

"You came," I said. After some thought, it was clear that no, there was nothing more obvious to state in this moment.

"Of course I came," Riley replied, studying the crowd over my shoulder. His fingertips trailed down my bare arm like it was the most natural thing in the entire world. And it *was* natural. Touching me, growling at me, being here, everything. "I'd intended to pick you up. It seems I was too late, but I never considered breaking our agreement." He stopped touching my arm, stopped watching the well-dressed masses, and turned all of his attention to my lips. He stared, like he was trying to understand what they were, why they were there, what to do with them. "I fucked up everything last weekend. I'm sorry. I need another chance, Aly."

I bristled at that, and shook out of his arms. "Is that how it works?" I challenged. "I'm Aly at night but Alex in the morning?"

He speared me with a sharp, pained look before bringing his gaze back to my lips. He pulled me close and kissed me hard, and either everyone had stopped to watch or the world had slipped away but it really didn't matter at all because I was overcome with the feeling of possession. Good possession. Sexy possession. The kind of possession I secretly craved.

He edged back and stroked his thumb down the line of my throat, just like he had before pushing inside me last weekend. I didn't remember much, but that—that I couldn't forget.

"We're going to stop fucking around now, Honeybee," he

said. "I haven't the patience for it, and it's not what I want tonight."

"Then what do you want?" I asked, my words a breathy whisper. I couldn't have brought any fire to my tone if I tried. Not with that thumb on my throat.

He tipped his chin down at me. "I'm taking you home. I'm spending the night with you, and I'm not going to give you a single reason to regret any of it in the morning," he said. "Then I'm taking another night. And another. I'm taking it all, Aly. Everything you'll give me."

"You don't deserve another chance," I seethed.

"But I do and so do you," he said. "I remember how your nipples felt on my tongue. The taste of you. The way you looked when I'd fucked the words right out of you. Let me give that to you again."

Squeezing my eyes shut and shaking my head, I snapped, "Shut up."

"I haven't been able to think about anything but you this week," he said. "Your body—*you*, Honeybee, you—did something to me."

"It sounds like you're upset about that," I replied, an eyebrow arched. "Is that because you're so fucking busy pining for your college girlfriend?"

He held up a hand in protest, shook his head. "I'm not pining for—nevermind. It's not what you think. You let me worry about that."

"I don't recall giving you permission to dictate what I should worry about," I said.

Not waiting for a response, I turned on my heel and stormed out. I was certain that my colleagues were watching and whispering, and filing away nuggets of gossip that would evolve into Riley-sized boulders by

Monday, but I couldn't stop or slow down. I made my way through the ballroom and adjoining reception areas, dodging gala attendees and fast-moving waiters. I was blind to it all, even the car-hailing protocol at the sidewalk taxi stand.

"Ma'am. *Ma'am*," the attendee called from over my shoulder. "We'll do that for you." A young man dressed in the hotel's uniform motioned for me to lower my raised arm. "Step out of the driveway and we'll get a car for you. Where are you headed?"

"Beacon Hill," I said.

"Just one moment," he said, pointing at the curb. "Stay here, please."

I tapped my shoe against the pavement as I waited, needing any outlet for the furious energy building inside me. If only he'd dismissed the issues with his ex-girlfriend—more than *let me worry about that*—I would've been melting like butter right now. I didn't need extensive explanations or anything complicated, but I did need to believe that the ghosts of girlfriends past weren't in bed alongside us.

"Goddamn it, Alex," Riley yelled, breathless and harried when he burst through the doors behind me. He wrapped his hand around my elbow and pulled me to his side. "We're not finished."

"We're definitely finished," I replied. "You have other priorities right now."

"Ma'am," the attendant called, holding a taxi door open.

"Finished," I repeated, shaking out of his grip.

I slipped into the backseat and wrapped my arms around my torso as the chill of the night air prickled my skin. I turned my attention away from Riley and the hotel, opting instead for the ribbons of brake lights on Boylston Street.

From the corner of my eye I saw movement, and then the door slammed shut.

"I've already told you that I'm not fucking around," Riley said, "and how this night is going to end."

He leaned forward and spoke to the driver, rattling off my address and mentioning something about construction on one street and delays on another. The driver accepted these suggestions and shot out of the hotel's driveway, seemingly unconcerned with pedestrians or oncoming traffic.

"I don't know what you think you're doing," I started, "but I'm not playing along. You're not spending the night. You're not even coming up to my apartment."

"Hmm," Riley murmured, cocking his head to the side for a second. "As I recall, you did a much better job of following directions last weekend."

My breath caught in my throat and I squeezed my eyes shut. My thighs, too. His deep voice thrummed along my spine and sent a quiver through my shoulders. And those words, they called up the ones that had been swishing around my mind all week.

Hands on the headboard. Don't you dare move them.

Ass up, Honeybee.

You come when I let you. You understand me?

Take it, Aly. Fucking take it.

"Ah," Riley purred, the sound nothing more than a vibration against my ear. "There it is."

"This isn't real," I said through gritted teeth. "It's an arrangement because neither of us can deal with dating other people right now." I turned, meeting his gaze. "Can we forget about everything that happened in Rhode Island? Please?"

Riley's knuckles coasted down my cheek and over my

jaw, and he shook his head. "You don't want to forget," he whispered. He shifted beside me, forcing his elbow to my thigh as he reached into his back pocket. He pulled some bills from his wallet before tucking it away. "Stay where you are. I'll come around and get you."

"Go get your old girlfriend," I said.

It was the brattiest, most bitchy response at the ready, and it made me want to roll my eyes at myself. But it succeeded at chastening him a bit, and that was what I needed. Anything to gain some distance and think straight. I didn't know where to land, and I couldn't figure that out with him *right there*.

That face and those words. They were a lethal combination.

"I hope you don't plan on sitting much this week because I'm gonna spank the shit out of you tonight," he said under his breath.

The taxi lurched to a stop, and I peered out the window. We'd made it back to my apartment in no time at all. Riley thanked the driver and handed him the bills, and I took that as an opportunity to get the hell out of this car before saying something I'd regret.

Like *Yes, please.*

"Would you fuckin' wait?" Riley yelled as he met my eyes over the roof. "I open your goddamn doors."

"Why the hell do I need you opening my doors?" I slammed it shut behind me, and the taxi sped off. "See? Perfectly capable of doing it myself."

This was what I did. I pushed. Pushed away anyone who couldn't make me the top priority, and perhaps that was selfish or immature or something I should've outgrown by now, but it was my move. Most of the time, it was a silent move. I kept my distance. Stopped interacting.

But right now, it was loud. Snarky comments, door slamming, foot stomping.

"It's not that you need it," he said, striding toward the sidewalk. Again, he wrapped his hand around my elbow and held me close to his chest. "It's that you want it."

"I *don't* want it," I lied.

Of course it was a lie. I was in over my head with this man and diving deeper by the second, but I had to make some attempt at protecting myself, too. Drama was all over him. Distraction, too.

Riley sighed and rubbed his forehead as if this conversation was causing him great distress. "Upstairs," he growled. "*Now*."

The trouble was that I wasn't disciplined enough to resist those growls. He could be reading a grocery list and those growls would hit me all the same.

"Let go," I hissed as I dug my keys out of my clutch.

"No," he replied, shifting his hands to my waist. "I made that mistake on Sunday. I don't plan on making it again."

I didn't say anything while Riley followed me into the building and up the stairs to my floor. Didn't trust myself to find suitable conversation, not when the only things I wanted to say were *Go home, fuck boy* and *Will you do the thing that left thumbprint bruises on the back of my thighs again?*

My hand trembled as I brought the key to the lock, and his fingers circled my wrist. "Let me do that," he said, his breath whispering over my ear. "Let me come in, Aly. Please."

I took a deep breath, nodding as we inserted the key. Once I had the door unlocked, he bolted it behind us and plucked the clutch and keys from my grasp. He paced into the kitchen, the line of his shoulders tight and his head down, and he set my things on the countertop.

I brushed my hands down my skirt. "You have a situation," I said. "A situation with someone else. It's not wrong for me to keep my distance while you deal with that."

"Here's a question for you," he said. He folded one arm across his chest and tucked his fist under his chin, and I had to look away. Seriously. The man was trying to kill me with all of his scowly-growly-sexy. "Are you hung up on the douche waffle?"

"Steve?" I asked. "No. I'm really fucking annoyed that an intern with an unimpressive dick has left my professional reputation a hot mess, but that's the extent of it."

"And I'm not hung up on Dorrance," he replied.

"But you're—"

"No, Honeybee," Riley interrupted. "I promise, Dorrance is out of the picture. Just like you, I'm still working through some issues but there's no one else I'd rather be with right now. *No one*."

"That's it?" I asked. "Easy peasy?"

I wanted it to be that simple, and when I looked at it from the right angle, it was. We had our share of problems from past relationships, and we were handling them the best we could. I didn't understand how it was with Dorrance or why it was that way, but I didn't have to understand.

Riley nodded. "Lemon squeezy."

We stared at each other for a beat, and then we spoke at once.

"Do you want a drink?" I asked.

"That dress would look better on the floor," he said.

We laughed, but it was forced. Stiff but not awkward.

The air between us was charged, and I heard my breath coming in quick, shallow pants. Ragged, like I couldn't contain myself for even one more minute.

In two strides he was on me, flattening me against the wall with a hand to my chest. His thumb swept under the neckline of my dress, just over the rise of my breasts. He leaned into me, dragging his mouth up my neck and over my jaw until his lips were pressed to mine. He stayed there, kissing me like he was begging my forgiveness.

And he had it. He did.

He caught my bottom lip between his teeth, and nipped just enough to make me squeal.

"Don't move," he warned. He pulled an envelope from his breast pocket, and then tossed the coat aside. "This is one of several things I intend to give you."

Riley handed me the envelope and dropped to his knees. "What's this?" I asked, the words rushing out in a gasp. "What are you doing?"

Never taking his eyes off mine, he reached under my dress and tugged my panties down. They dropped to my ankles, and he took great care to help me step out of them.

"Good girl," he murmured, and it was possible that I'd never heard dirtier words in my life. Not spoken to me, not like that. He tipped his head toward the envelope clutched to my chest. "Open it. Read."

But I didn't. I watched as he pushed my dress up, over my hips. He stared at me for a long moment, and my cheeks heated as I felt a rush of wet between my legs. His fingers dipped between my legs, parting me, and the groan that rumbled up from his chest said all the things I'd wanted to hear. That he was as starved for me as I him, that he loved the way my body responded to him. That it was me he wanted to be with tonight. No one else.

"I didn't do this last weekend," he said, his words loaded with regret. "Probably because I knew that I'd lose my mind the minute I got my mouth on you." He glanced up at me as he pointed to his trousers. "If I come in my pants right now, it's your fault. Understand?"

Then he wrapped an arm around my thighs and leaned forward, mouth open and intent clear. His tongue slid over my skin, and everything inside me loosened and tightened, all at once. Two fingers pushed inside, filling me where I felt hollow. His lips and tongue worked a jerky spasm from my hips, and I started with the garbled plea-moans. I wanted to say something naughty, a little deviant, but words were lost to me when he worked my clit in concert with the fingers inside me.

My hand landed on his head and I fisted his dark strands while I murmured *Oh my god* and *Please, please, please* until they were nothing more than stuttered syllables against the sounds of skin and sex.

This wasn't a quick round of clit-licking foreplay. This was full-tilt pussy-eating, raw and primal and fucking amazing. It was almost too much to bear, and I was torn between wanting to feel my orgasm unravel right now and making this last forever.

"Riley," I said with a sigh.

"Read it," he growled. "I won't let you come until you read it."

I'd forgotten about the envelope. That, and the rest of the universe beyond those tender spots between my legs where Riley's tongue and fingers were replacing my ability to think rationally with lust-drunk desire.

"You're close. You're right there," he said as he stilled.

My center throbbed, wanting him to soothe the ache he'd created. I was uncomfortable like this, swollen and needy. I wanted more. Sucking, biting, stroking, something. Anything to ease this tension. I rocked against him, wanton, and forced a small spark of relief.

Riley laughed at my desperation. "Do as you're told and I'll give you what you want."

"This is just ridiculous," I muttered, tearing into the envelope. "I'm going to make you read a medical journal the next time I suck your—*oh*. Wait a second. What is this?" I flipped through the pages, blinking fast to gain my focus. "Why am I reading your lab report?"

"Because I don't have hepatitis," he replied. "Healthy as a horse and hung like one, too."

Riley's teeth closed around my slick skin, gentle but sharp enough for me to feel those sensations everywhere. Before this night, I never would've guessed that I wanted someone biting my pussy but I never would've guessed I wanted a man like Riley either. And it was a surprise. From the start, I'd believed he was all wrong for me. That we were wrong for each other.

But this…this wasn't wrong.

So I had to read the damn report. With a hand fisted in his hair, I pushed him away. Rather, I *tried* pushing him away. "Stop it," I chided. "I can't comprehend blood chemistries while you're doing that."

"If that's what you want," he replied. "But you were trying to fuck my face a second ago."

Riley eased away again, leaving tiny kisses and bites along my mound. As if that was any less distracting. "Acevedo ordered this workup," I remarked.

"Yeah, he also did the really fucking horrible thing with the long swab," Riley added. "I won't be speaking to him for several years."

I shook my head. "Thank him," I said. "Chlamydia's a bitch."

He tapped the papers. "You'll notice that I don't have that either. Now that I've confirmed I'm disease-free and the picture of good health, I'd like to get back to the task at hand." He dragged his gaze between my legs, then lifted my thigh and arranged it over his shoulder. "If you don't mind. Or do you need a background check? Maybe a bank statement? Hmm? How else can I apologize and make this greedy little cunt happy?"

A breath whooshed out as a fresh burst of heat sparked in my veins. I dragged him closer, forcing his face between my legs. It was rough and bossy, and he chuckled against my folds as he licked. The test results tumbled to the floor when his fingers curled inside me—just where I needed them— and his tongue lashed my clit with newfound purpose.

In my mind, I saw him over me, thrusting into me, taking me as he had last weekend. And I wanted all of that, even if a small voice kept telling me to proceed with caution.

My back bowed away from the wall and everything else fell away. I was spiraling down, falling and falling and falling, and I still hadn't hit bottom. Rocking against him without concern for how brazen it looked. Moaning and begging and crying out. His name was a slow but frantic chant on my lips as my orgasm spun out of control, twisting and rolling through my core like an avalanche of heat. He didn't stop, didn't let me hide from any of it.

"I can't, I can't," I whispered, slapping a hand against the wall as the fire burned through me.

"I know you can," Riley said through a groan.

He squeezed my ass—hard—and his fingertips walked down my crease. His touch was firm and certain, and those strange new sensations were enough to set off another round of explosions. I was coming again, grinding on him like it was the only thing I could do.

Time slowed as I dropped my head back against the wall and my eyes fluttered shut. Riley stood, bringing his arms around me and his mouth to mine. I tasted myself there. He leaned into me, his erection nudging my belly.

"How was that?" he asked, his words a little shy as he ducked to kiss my neck.

"You make me want everything," I admitted. "Things I don't even understand."

Riley's laugh vibrated against my skin. "Take me to the bedroom, Aly."

A cocktail of feel-good hormones tingled behind my breastbone. That nickname, it was powerful. It offered entry to a secret world, a place where only Riley and I existed, and we could be anything we wanted.

I crossed the small living room on wobbly feet, and Riley followed. He tugged my zipper down while we walked. The dress was off and flying over his shoulder when we stopped beside the bed. My bra followed and there I was, naked save for my boring beige heels while he gazed at me in his three-piece suit.

Those fucking vests were dangerous. They made me lusty and irrational. It was as though he required that extra layer to contain the beast that howled right below the surface.

"On the bed," he ordered, his fingertips coasting from my

clavicle down to my cleft. He circled my clit and then dragged his hand up, painting me with my arousal.

I kicked off my shoes and kneeled on the quilt, trying my damnedest to move with some semblance of grace. I patted the space beside me, needing to feel more than his heavy-lidded stare. "You, too," I said. "Or do you need some assistance?"

His brow arched and a smile broke across his lips. "I like it when you watch," he said, his hands popping the buttons on his vest. "Your eyes drive me wild. I look at you and I barely keep myself from ripping your clothes off."

My fingers covered my lips as he whipped his tie free from his collar. He cast it aside as if it had insulted his mother. His shirt was next, then his belt, though it all flashed at once like rapid-fire snaps until nothing was left.

His trousers and boxers hit the floor, and the movement sent his erection slapping against his belly. It made a heavy sound, like an apple breaking free from a grocery store display and hitting the linoleum tile with an ominous *thump*.

A gasp slipped from my lips when I caught sight of his cock. It was magnificent. I would know. It wasn't something I listed on my résumé, but I was a cock connoisseur.

Perhaps the proper term was erection elitist because limp dicks didn't interest me in the least. Though my pursuit was neither medical nor academic, I approached this work with the type of scholarly devotion only Tumblr and sketchy internet porn could offer. I had a well-fortified reserve of the hundreds —maybe thousands—of gorgeous bits and bobs I'd admired from the safety of faceless accounts and secret pin boards.

Such was the life of a cock-hungry girl on a man-free diet.

"You could do some damage with that thing," I said.

He dragged a fist down his length, twisting over the crown and then shuttling back to the root. The way he stroked himself was hypnotizing, and I imagined myself lurking in the shadows of his bedroom while he found his pleasure. I wanted that, and all the other hidden sides of him.

"Would you like a closer look?" Riley asked, a laugh rumbling in his voice.

I blinked, suddenly aware that I wasn't gazing at a life-less screen but this man, naked and hard and waiting for *me*. I'd remembered the feel of him from last weekend, but little else. It'd been dark and we'd been drunk, and this was the first moment I was really seeing him. And he truly was magnificent. Thick and long, and standing tall like a freaking flagpole.

"Or would you rather a taste?" he asked, stepping closer. He ran his finger along the line of my jaw and tipped my head back, sliding his cock against my lips. "The way you're looking at me, Honeybee, it's like you want something dirty."

This was the type of erection that demanded a scrap-book in its honor, and I might just be the woman to make it.

I gazed up at him, nodding. "Maybe I do."

He shook his head and laughed. "Show me," he said, dragging his cock over my bottom lip. "Show me what you want."

I took his hand, moved it to my breast. "There," I said, moaning as he clothespinned my nipple between his long fingers. I brought his other hand to the back of my neck, where my hair was gathered in a low knot. "And there."

His thumb found my pulse and he squeezed, lightly, and he said, "I'm giving you three minutes to play."

I ran my hands down his chest and abs, savoring the lines of his body before circling his cock. It throbbed under my touch, and seemed to harden with every stroke. I was wet and aching all over again, my hips already twitching as I thought about tasting him, taking him inside me, watching him shatter.

"What happens after three minutes?" I asked, staring up at him with the most coquettish eyes I could manage while I gave him a hard squeeze. "Is that when you plan on spanking me?"

"*Fuuuuck*," he groaned, low and long. "No, Aly, I'm going to fuck you and I'm going to make it so good that you'll think about it every day. For the rest of your life, you'll remember this night." He shook the pins from my hair and twisted it around his palm. "This cock. This bed and every-thing we do in it. You'll remember it all." His fingers clamped down on my nipple, and I moaned into his chest. "Then I'll spank you."

That was it. I couldn't wait any longer. I ducked my head and parted my lips, and hummed as the weight of him moved over my tongue. I couldn't take much, but what I did received the most voracious effort I could put forward. I kept my hand around the base, stroking as I sucked. He smelled amazing, and I wasn't saying that simply because I was sucking on his blue-ribbon cock. It was a light, natural scent that I'd forever associate with sex and need and man.

"Oh, fucking hell," he gasped. "Fuck, fuck, *fuck*."

He punctuated each muttered curse and growl with a pinch to my nipple, a tighter grip on my hair. I couldn't remember ever feeling this close to another person. This was about more than getting off. Much more. It was the connection we shared, one that spiraled down deep and gripped us in places we couldn't name.

"Look at you," he murmured, scraping loose wisps of hair from my face. "Just fucking look at you."

His hands moved to my jaw, his thumbs pressed to the hollows of my cheeks, and he held me in place while his length shuttled over my lips. He abandoned his control for a moment, thrusting with fast, jerky strokes. It was rough, rougher than I'd ever experienced or imagined wanting, but I didn't want anything different.

On a groan, Riley's hands shifted to my shoulders. He squeezed, easing me back, and I dragged my tongue down the underside of his cock before releasing him.

"Your time's up, Honeybee," he said, his voice hoarse. "Fuck, I need to be inside you again. Right fucking now. I've wanted you every fucking minute of this week." He pushed me down to the mattress and then climbed over me, caging me beneath him. "I can't go slow."

"I don't want slow," I replied. I dragged my fingers up his back and into his hair, pulled him closer. His cock nudged my belly as he stared down at me, and all those dark, angry thoughts I'd had about being his second choice evaporated. I wanted his body all over me, doing all the things I'd imagined, all the things I craved.

"You deserve it, Aly," Riley argued. He shifted and his cock was between my legs, rubbing up against my clit and making me see stars. "You deserve fucking *everything*."

"Then give me that instead," I said. "Give me everything."

He dipped down and kissed each corner of my mouth. "I want to fuck you from behind. I want to slap your ass and pull your hair while I'm giving it to you hard," he said casually, like we were discussing the weather. "But I also want to bite your nipples and see your face while you come." His lips brushed against mine and he hummed. "Yeah, that's it. I need to see you this time."

"And the next time?" I asked.

Riley sat back on his haunches and edged my legs apart. I was as open and exposed as I'd ever been, and his gaze was mapping every inch of me. I thought it would be uncomfortable but I found myself enjoying it. I wasn't worried about my pudgy belly or thick thighs, or even my most intimate places because the desire in his eyes canceled out my every doubt.

"You let me worry about that," he said for the second time tonight. His thumb found my clit and I was ready—so ready—for this. "Can we skip the condoms? I fucking hate them and you know I'm safe, but if you want them, I'll respect your wishes and—"

"Fuck me," I begged. I wrapped my leg around his waist, urging him closer. "Fuck me right now."

"Such a good girl," he murmured.

Then he was there, pushing inside me and damn near splitting me in half. We cried out together, and every little part of me surrendered to the overwhelming fullness. My hands were on his chest, his flanks. Pressing into his soft tissue, scratching, urging him deeper. Nails scraping over his nipples, his back. Leaving marks. Rising up to meet his thrusts. My mouth was on his lips, down his jaw and neck, kissing and biting and sucking until I was satisfied I'd drawn something out of him only for me.

"You were made for my cock," he rasped, his eyes snapping shut for a beat. "I can't wait to watch you riding me.

Those tits in my face. My hands on your ass, spreading you wide. That wet cunt bouncing on my cock."

Filthy didn't begin to describe his words, and I couldn't stop the hot blush coloring my cheeks. There was something about that word. *Cunt.* I hated it. I never used it. But it was so dirty and so, *so* right.

Riley slammed into me with enough force to rock the bed and trigger a landslide of lacy pillows over my head. I batted them away as his hands locked around my waist, his thumbs finding the fleshy spot beneath the jut of my hipbones and his fingers digging into my ass.

He stared between us, his breaths coming in broken grunts as he pulled out until only his thick crown teased at my folds. His hips continued rolling in a frantic, unpracticed staccato. "I want to make it good for you," he said, repeating his vow from earlier. "What do you need, Aly? Tell me how to be everything you need. I'm not stopping until you get it."

"You could start by getting your cock inside me," I said. The absence left me empty, squirming in discomfort. I rocked forward and reached for him, my hands sliding over his ribs and settling low on his back. "And I want to feel your hands on me."

Riley's fingers tightened around my throat, drawing a whimper from me. It wasn't pain or fear. It was the dizzying, stars-behind-my-eyes force of trusting him fully and completely. And that was what I needed. My breath caught as my release burst through my body, a rush of sated relief, a downpour to break the heat spell.

"That's it," he murmured. He growled, nodding as he watched the orgasm spiral through me. His hold loosened, his fingertips massaging my skin in small circles before sliding away from my neck. "Yes, Aly. That's fucking *it*."

I gazed up at him, my eyes halfway rolled back in my head and his chest hairs tickling my nipples in the worst-best way, and the only words I could manage were "I want to feel you come inside me right now."

If it was possible, he swelled and lengthened, and I was sure I'd be feeling echoes of his cock for days.

"Suck," he said, his fingers pressed to my lips. I opened my mouth and instantly tasted my arousal on him. "Hard. Bite me a little."

I did, and he brought his other hand between my hipbones. I moaned around his fingers, savoring the heavy drag of him over my swollen tissues and the pressure of his palm. It was so much. Too much. Like he was trying to claim a piece of me as much as I was claiming a piece of him.

At once, his body tightened. Every muscle was pulled taut, his jaw impossibly rigid and his hold on me almost painful. He pulled his fingers from my mouth and pitched forward, bracing himself on one arm.

"Oh, fuck. What are you doing to me, Aly? *Fuck*."

Riley stilled and our eyes met and I felt it then, the unmistakable throb and jerk that signaled his orgasm. He was humming and growling as he pulsed inside me, and I couldn't fill my hands with enough of him. I wanted to touch every inch, memorize his skin in this moment, absorb his scent, and stow it all away for the day when I wasn't the source of his pleasure anymore.

"I love fucking you," he whispered, ducking his head to drop kisses over my shoulders and neck.

For a moment, I thought he'd proclaimed something different. Something I didn't know how to hear, not yet. But then I replayed his words, understanding what he'd said when I put them in the intended order. Of course he wasn't professing his love for *me*. Just what we'd done.

I was relieved, and the tiniest bit wistful.

"It's mutual," I murmured.

Riley pulled out but instead of flopping down on the bed or heading to the bathroom, his eyes between my legs, a smug smile on his face. My entire body heated when I realized he was staring at his orgasm fresh on my folds.

"I'm going to jerk off to that for the rest of my fucking life," he said, rubbing his jaw as he gazed at me.

I layered my hands over my face, laughing. "You're still half hard and already making jerk-off plans?"

"Shut up," he said, slapping my thigh. "You start talking about lunch while you're eating breakfast."

"A girl's gotta eat."

Riley gestured to his cock. "So does he." Tucking himself beside me, he ran a gentle hand from my neck to my navel. "I mean it. I *love* fucking you. You're fun and dirty, and you make it hurt just like I need. My cock was made for you. I'm sure of it."

He smiled, and in my head, I heard *I fucking love you* again.

"Maybe it's the other way around," I said. His brows wrinkled as he considered this. "My pussy was made for you."

I brushed Riley's dark, wavy hair from his forehead, and pulled him down to meet my lips. He kissed me, and then pulled back only enough to say, "Maybe we're meant for each other."

And then I slid, all the way down that slope.

"I'M HUNGRY," Alex announced. I nodded; I was starved. A little dehydrated, too. "Let's get something to eat. Delivery, of course. I don't think I can walk right now."

I smiled over at her, still breathless and broken in the best —the fucking *best*—ways. "We'll order a pizza. I know a few places that deliver at"—I blinked at the alarm clock seated on the side table—"two in the morning."

"Yeah," she replied, nuzzling her face into the crook of my shoulder. "Let's do that."

But we didn't, not right away. Every time I'd shift to find my phone, the smooth slide of her skin overruled all other needs. Or she'd scrape her nails down my back and we'd tumble into each other again, hungry in new ways. Bent over the side of the bed. Straddling me. On all fours. Nothing quenched my desire for her. It multiplied, expanding in volume and density as I learned her body.

Hours passed and the sun rose before we climbed out of bed, bellies empty and limbs loose, and we raided her kitchen. We returned with an odd assortment of snacks—tortilla chips, several half-full pints of ice cream, string cheese—and ate naked, covered only by pastel sheets.

"This is going to come out wrong no matter how I say it," I said, brushing salt and bits of chip from her breasts. It was more than a lazy attempt at copping a feel. I was decent enough to keep crumbs out of the bed.

"Just say it," she said, laughing.

"Your apartment isn't what I'd expected," I replied with all the diplomacy I could manage. I fingered the ivy-and-violet-printed duvet, shot a glance to the matching curtains.

"Mmhmm." She nodded as she fished in the bag for another chip. "My mother decorates for me. It's her pet project. Whenever I move, she flies in and sets up my place. It used to drive me crazy because she only picks out things from the 1985 Laura Ashley catalog but I get it now. It's what she does. It's how she shows that she cares."

"Like the bracelets?" I asked, digging into a pint of salted caramel ice cream.

"Like what?"

I tapped my spoon against her wrist. "Bracelets," I repeated. "She sends you bracelets even though you don't wear them, and she decorates your apartment like *Little House on the Prairie*."

"You're thinking of Laura Ingalls Wilder," she said.

"Whoever it is. I went to art school. I know all about shabby chic." I scooped some ice cream and offered it to her, and that was a lazy attempt at seeing her suck on the spoon. "You probably have a lot of guilt about how much you hate all this frilly, flowery shit."

Her head bobbed as she dug for another chip. "You're right. I do."

"But you won't change a thing because you don't want to hurt your mom's feelings," I continued. "You rather be miserable than turn down the small ways she reaches out to you."

"I'm not miserable," Alex argued. "It's just some curtains." She glanced at the opposite wall, and a trio of framed prints featuring babies in flower pots. "And some weird photography that I don't think I'll appreciate until I have kids of my own." She shrugged and looked back at me. "But I can live with all of this. But you're right. It's her way of reaching out, of seeing me, even though there are constant nudges and reminders that I didn't turn out as she'd hoped."

I shook my head. "I see where they're coming from. You should try to get your act together, Alexandra. What makes you think being a surgeon is a real career?" I slapped my hand to my chest. "Drawing houses, that's a real career. That's making a difference. Saving lives? You should really stop with that shit."

She winged me with her elbow, laughing. "Hilarious," she muttered. "Seriously, there are times when I wonder whether things would've turned out differently if I was a boy as they'd expected. They always say that I'm their big surprise but it seems like they might've formed their vision for me before I was born and haven't been able to change that vision since."

"If we're comparing short ends of the stick," I started, "I'm pretty sure my father hated me long before I was born. That was the argument he relied on whenever he wanted to beat the shit out of me."

The bag of chips slipped from Alex's hand as she whirled toward me. "Riley," she gasped. "Oh, Riley—"

"You don't have to do that," I said quickly. "He was the worst of humanity. He was violent to no end. I can accurately say he terrorized us as kids. But that bastard has been dead for several years and I made sure he took his hate and anger to the grave with him. I don't worry about whether the vicious things he said held any truth or I deserved some of the hits I took. He's dead, and it's done."

Alex ran her fingers over my brow and through my hair, bobbing her head slowly, as if she could accept these revelations but didn't have to like them.

"It's not all dark stories and sadness. My siblings insult each other like it's an Olympic sport," I said, forcing some levity. "It's the only way we know how to praise each other. Every now and then, someone will say something nice or complimentary, and it's too fucking weird for life. We just stare at each other until someone comes out with, 'Shut the fuck up, shithead.'"

Alex smirked, and that was the best fucking response imaginable. Most people looked at the Walsh family penchant for beating up on each other as a sign of our depravity, but that wasn't the case. If we didn't have a fuck-ton of mutual respect, we wouldn't be able to run a business together. We didn't have to top it off with polite exchanges when our salty shorthand worked just as well.

"It's like that with Hartshorn and Acevedo," she replied. "We throw a lot of jabs at each other, and on the rare occasion that we offer real praise, it gets awkward as hell."

"That's precisely it," I said.

"At least you have a unified system with your family," Alex said. "My parents have different approaches with me and Adam. As far back as I can remember, they've always gushed over Adam's every little accomplishment but have never acknowledged anything I've done, not directly. My mother comes here and sets up my apartment, fills the fridge with food, unpacks and irons all of my clothes, but has never said, 'Nice job getting through medical school.'"

"Then allow me," I said, feeding her another bite of ice cream. "What you do is fucking amazing. I can't believe how smart and talented you are, and I'm impressed every time you talk about your work."

"You don't have to do that," she said, shaking off his words. "Please don't get the wrong idea. I'm not sitting around and thinking about how my brother is the favorite and my family doesn't appreciate me enough. That's just how things are in my family, and it's not a big deal. It could be far worse."

"I get that," I replied quietly. "Like I said, my father wasn't a good man. My mother died when I was four. She was pregnant and…something terrible happened. She bled to death. I was a little kid and I watched her die. So, I have that and one other memory of her."

"Oh, my god," Alex whispered, her fingers pressed to her lips.

"It was awful. I don't understand how I can store those images in my head without falling apart, but I do," I said. "You take all the horrible things and there are plenty of them, and set them aside. You let them be. They're not everyday issues. Not anymore."

"What are your everyday issues?" Alex asked.

I gathered up the ice cream containers and their lids, and set them on the side table with the spoon we'd shared. "Finding my favorite taco truck, helping clients who don't understand their preferences, spilling coffee on my trousers," I replied. "And making time with a hot, sexy surgeon."

Alex gave me a lopsided grin as her gaze pinged between me and the rumpled bed. "You're clumsy in the streets but you're a beast in the sheets."

"You're adorable," I said, matching her smile.

She pulled a sour face. "I don't want to be adorable. Kittens are adorable. Miniature roses are adorable." She pointed at the framed prints. "Babies are adorable."

"If it helps," I said, "you're adorable in that 'I want to bend you over and bang you like a screen door in a tornado' kind of way."

"Mmhmm. That does help," she said.

"What about adorable in the 'I'm gonna fuck you like your ex lives downstairs' kind of way? How do you like that?"

"I'm all for that *and* making my ex jealous," she said. "But Hartshorn lives downstairs, not Steve."

"I fucking hate that douche waffle," I said. "I hate the way he treated you."

"Me, too," she conceded. "But there's a silver lining, right? If it hadn't been for him wrecking my reputation, I wouldn't have needed a date to the cocktail party or gala."

"Grab your phone," I said, shifting to kneel between her legs. "Let's send him a picture and let him know exactly how much better your life is without him."

"Send him a picture of what?" she cried, pinning her knees together.

"Anything you want, Aly," I said, running my hands up her inner thighs. "But my tongue on your clit would send a pretty clear message, no? Or your face while I'm making you come?" Her eyes were unblinking and anxious, her head shaking from side to side in tiny jerks. "Or maybe we keep the pictures for our enjoyment, and send him a rotting bag of dicks. Then again, I don't mind posing for you if you'd like to give him a close-up of my balls."

A tremor moved through her body. "You—you want to take pictures? Naked pictures? Of *me*?" Her breath was coming in quick bursts, her chest rising and falling, and her lips parted with a sigh. "And do what with them? You're not going to share them, right? Or post them on—I don't know—some porn site, right? Tumblr's great but I don't want you publishing my unmentionables there, okay?"

"Of course," I replied. "Only for us. I don't want to share you with anyone. If you hate it, we'll delete them. We'll hop in the shower—where I'll fuck you until you have grout lines printed on your ass—and then I'll buy you brunch. I didn't get a chance to do that last weekend."

It was another attempt at apologizing. For everything.

"I can't feel my legs. I'm covered in hickeys and bite marks. My hair is a rat's nest, and I can barely see straight with how much I need your tongue on me right now," Alex said. "Brunch will have to wait."

"Should I," I started, wagging my phone at her, "take a picture or two while I'm licking?"

She glanced around the room, swallowing thickly. "Why?" she asked, her voice nothing more than a whisper. "Why would you want photos of me? Of us?"

"You, Honeybee, are perfect. I've touched every part of you. Bitten you. Sucked you. Why wouldn't I want to keep you this way, too?"

"I'm not perfect," she said, running her palms up her legs and over her belly.

"You're real," I challenged, "and to me, that's perfection."

"THIS IS FUN," I said, watching while Alex scrolled through the photos we'd taken in the past twenty-four hours. She stopped every so often, her thumb hovering over the screen while her breath burst out in heavy puffs and she rubbed her thighs together. "Sunday morning snuggles. Looking at dirty pictures. I like this shit. We're doing this every weekend."

"Good to hear it," she murmured, swiping past a blurry shot of something.

There were many out-of-focus, too-blurry-to-comprehend images, but I was committed to getting better at simultaneously fucking and photographing because seriously. *Seriously.* That was the hottest experience of my life.

We'd feasted on each other all day and all night, and photographed every filthy inch of it. We'd only stolen quick naps before the presence of naked skin stirred our need and we'd started all over again. I was tired and sore, and depleted in the most delicious ways, and so was Alex.

I wasn't sure whether this was exhibitionism or some kind of visual kink that we'd unearthed at the same time, but I liked it. I wasn't interested in sharing these images, not even the wholly anonymous ones composed of disaggregated anatomy, but I loved the rush of doing something scandalous and then reliving these moments with Alex. Despite her initial hesitation—we hadn't sent any to the douche waffle—she loved it, too. Hence the thigh rubbing.

"It's warm and cozy," I continued, nipping at her shoulder when a particularly filthy shot of her clit filled the screen. Now *that* was art. Straight up scandalous but art nonetheless. "Yeah, Sunday morning snugs are a grand time until someone gets an erection."

"You make it sound like I'm not going to help you with that situation," Alex scoffed. "Or have you already forgotten that I'm a big fan of the heat you're packing?"

I pulled her closer, ground my cock against her ass. My hand slipped between her legs, dipping into her arousal. "Can I have you like this? Slow and lazy while we look at photos of your fucking edible body?"

"You can," she said softly. "Of course you can."

She propped the phone against one of the thousand tiny pillows littering her bedroom and set the album to automatic shuffle. The first was one—my stiff cock on her belly—I'd taken while swearing that I'd guard these images with my life and everything else I could invoke. There was something magical and depraved about staring at that and remembering the way my skin had been stretched past pain when I'd pointed the lens at us.

Alex reached for me, tangling our legs together and positioning my length at her wet entrance. All I had to do was push forward and I'd slide into the place that was fast becoming my favorite.

"Riley," she whispered, rocking back. The undersides of her breasts flashed by, soon replaced by my cock on her folds, throbbing and shiny with her arousal. "Hurry the fuck up."

I eased in, twining my arms around Alex's torso. We groaned in unison when I bottomed out. "I want to take it easy and give you the sweet Sunday morning fucking you deserve," I said on a growl. "But I also want to tear you up. Spank you like the naughty girl you are. Make you beg. Tell you my cock was made for your pussy, and your mouth and ass and tits. Fuck you until you pass out. Fuck you again. Come all over you, everywhere."

My hips were rolling faster, the bedsprings creaking beneath us, and I couldn't tear my eyes from the screen. We were bodies, skin and muscle and bone, moving as one and searching for something rare. And we'd found it, whatever *it* was, in each other.

"Stop talking," she whispered as she clenched around me. "I can't—you say these filthy things and you're a fucking animal and I can't hold out."

"Don't," I said, my teeth on her shoulder. I brought a hand between her legs and circled her clit, grinning when it twitched under my touch. Fucking loved that. "Don't ever hold out on me."

It had only been minutes but I was there too, clinging to a motherfucking thread. I was astonished—and a little mortified—that she'd reduced me to this. But maybe that was the way of it when sex stopped being the simple act of penetration. It was more than in, out, done, goodbye. It was significant.

"Oh, *fuck*." It was spoken as a gasp. She reached for the phone and paused the slideshow on an image of my fist around my cock and my orgasm splashing across her thighs.

"Do you see how beautiful you are?" I rasped. "This is how I see you, Aly. Beautiful and filthy and *mine*."

"Mine," Alex whispered, layering her hand over mine.

We shattered then, crying out and convulsing around each other. When I regained the ability to move, I didn't go far, curling around her body and resting my head on her belly. Her hands were in my hair and I could taste sex on her skin, and there was nothing more I required in this life.

"That was," she started, pausing as she gathered the words, "that was intense."

In fleeting moments, I'd worried that I was demanding too much. Pushing too far. But then she'd scratch the shit out of my back or suck a mark into my chest, and I'd swept those worries away. Now, with my orgasm still warm between her legs and the late morning sun spreading over her well-fucked body, I wasn't sure about that decision.

Alex was strong and capable—she was my Shortstop for a reason—but she was also a woman. Tender and lovely, and deserving of some deference. I wanted to open the door for her, bring her flowers for no reason, kiss her in the middle of the grocery store, buy her soft and delicate things. And I still wanted to fuck her like a whore.

I didn't know how to arrange those desires into an order that made sense. "Too intense?" I asked.

"No. No, I don't have a problem with intense," she said. "But I think it's time for some modifications to the arrangement."

"What do you mean?" I asked, suddenly nervous. This could be the end. We'd made our peace and plenty of love, and now it was done.

"I don't want this to end after my parents visit next month," she said quietly. "I don't want it to be fake anymore."

"It was never fake," I replied. "Nothing has ever been fake with us, Alex."

"So…okay," she murmured, glancing away. "Are you saying—"

"I'm saying we'll work out new terms and conditions some other time." I pressed my lips to her tummy. "Today is for snuggles and snuggle-induced sex."

I stared up at her for a beat, gazing at her drowsy green eyes and kiss-swollen lips. She continued stroking my scalp and shoulders while my cheek rested on her tummy and when the fuck had this happened? When had I gathered up all the hard, cynical pieces of me, the ones long deeded to Lauren, and handed them to Alex?

Or was it happening right now? Was *this* what it meant to fall?

THERE WAS A NOISE, a blaring, bleating sound stuck on a continuous loop. I tugged the blankets up in an effort to tune it out but only succeeded in stirring a growl from the man wrapped around me.

"What is that?" I mumbled into his bare chest.

"Woodpeckers," Riley replied. He reached for my hand and steered it to his erection. "Speaking of wood, be a good girl and take care of this."

"Presumptuous much?" I shook my head but stroked, our hands moving together under the sheets.

"Not at all," he said. "You know how I feel about reciprocity."

The noise finally stopped as Riley's drowsy murmurs of appreciation and encouragement turned impatient, and his hips arched off the bed as I pumped his shaft.

It had only been a few days but I knew his body, his patterns. The way he'd bring his mouth to my skin, licking and biting when he needed to reel himself in. How he liked a flash of pain—fingernails, teeth—when he was about to detonate. His words, the ones that started dirty, found their way to filthy, and then turned depraved. And he made the best noises. Growls that grew in depth and intensity. Sighs and moans that I wanted to stow away for myself like secrets.

"Give it to me harder, Honeybee," he rasped.

I turned my head, brushing my lips over his nipple. I dropped tiny kisses there, and dragged my tongue over the dark circle, teasing him a bit. Then I sucked at his skin, sharp and deep like I was searching for the basis of his being. Then I found it.

"*Ohfuckyes*." Riley spilled onto his belly, uttering every deviant desire in his mind while he did it.

And then the noise started again.

"Seriously. What *is* that?" Levering up on an elbow, I scanned the room, bleary-eyed.

"If you don't come back here and snuggle me right now, we'll be having words about hand job protocol, Alexandra," Riley said, his voice still raw, rough. He trailed his fingers down my back, and I would've leaned into his touch if the sound wasn't scratching my brain stem.

"I think it's an alarm." I glanced to the side table, and spotted his phone flashing and vibrating. I held it up for him, but he was busy wiping the orgasm off his stomach and didn't notice. "That's your wake up call. I'm turning this bitch off before I stab it with nine scalpels."

"Oh, fuck," Riley mumbled, shooting a glimpse at the clock. "I have to go." He curled his arm around my shoulders, sighing into my hair as he held me close. "I have a meeting at seven thirty, but I also have to make a few stops before heading to the office. Can I take a quick shower?"

"Of course," I replied sleepily. Only a fraction of my brain was awake. A small fraction. "You can also take a longer shower if you'd like. Bathe as much as is appropriate."

Riley laughed and tightened his hold on me. It was like he was testing how hard he could squeeze me. Whether I'd bend or break, or squeeze him right back. Then he kissed my neck and rubbed my ass, and said, "Go back to sleep, Aly."

The mattress shifted, and soon I heard the water running. I debated joining Riley, but our time wasn't our own this morning. He had a meeting, I had rounds. I tucked the quilt around me and nestled into my pillow, and promptly dozed off.

"Honeybee," Riley whispered, kissing my forehead and jaw. "I'm leaving now."

He was dressed in the suit he'd worn to the gala, now creased from two days of abandonment on my bedroom floor.

"You're cute even when you're wrinkled," I said. I ran my hand down his chest, over his shirt's buttons, smiling. "Your vests make me cross-eyed."

Riley cupped my chin, his thumb stroking my cheek as his brow furrowed. "Is that good?"

"Yes," I replied. "I've wanted to rip it off you since that night in August, at the Seven Ales."

He blinked at me for a second, his jaw tight. "When I come back," he growled, his hand abandoning my face and traveling down, stopping when he was between my legs. I throbbed against his touch. "I want this bare."

"And when will that be?"

"Whenever you'll have me," Riley replied, exasperated. "When that time rolls around, I'm going to fuck you hard and call you princess. Do you understand?"

"I don't want to be a princess," I said with an undeniable pout in my voice.

He leaned in, nipped at my lips. "Why not?"

"Princesses need saving," I said, my mouth on his jaw and my hands sliding over his shoulders. "I don't need any of that shit."

"No, you don't, Honeybee," he replied.

Riley kissed me gently, like I was precious and delicate, and he hadn't made good on his promise to spank the shit out of me last night.

"I'M NOT READY FOR WINTER," Hartshorn muttered at we crossed the footbridge to the park. "It's too damn early."

I looked up at the sun-filled sky and breathed in the autumn air. It was crisp and cool, but that wasn't stopping us from enjoying a late lunch outside. Nick was waiting for us at our usual picnic table.

"This hardly qualifies as winter," I argued. A whimper squeaked in my throat when my backside hit the cold metal bench. It was yet another reminder of how thoroughly used every corner of my body was feeling today.

"No, but it's coming," Hartshorn said, scowling at the Charles River.

"I like October in this city," I said with a hint of hesitation. I hadn't stopped to note my previous Octobers, but I was enjoying this one.

"Dude, you gotta lighten the fuck up," Nick chided. "We can't have your storm cloud hanging over us on a fine day like today."

"You'll be saying that until your wife is off on another

research mission or business trip," Hartshorn replied. "At which point, you'll revert back to your irritable ways."

Ignoring their exchange, I pulled my phone from my pocket.

Alex: Do you want to know how busy my day has been?
Riley: As long as it doesn't involve discussing innards and entrails, yes.
Alex: I just sat down for the first time.
Riley: Seriously? It's almost 2:30.
Alex: Yep, and I'm telling you this because my ass is sore.

"AGREE WITH ME, EMMERLING," Nick said. "Tell Hartshorn he's lost his damn mind."

I glanced up from my phone, my gaze swiveling between them. "What happened?"

Nick motioned to Hartshorn. "He's met a lady."

"That's great," I said. "What's the problem?"

"Perhaps saying Hartshorn has *met* a lady is a stretch," Nick continued, "given that he hasn't spoken to her yet."

"Then talk to her," I said impatiently. "What's stopping you? Just go up to her and say, *Hey, I'm Cal. I'm disease-free and financially stable, and I think you're a cool chick. Can I buy you dinner?* That's it. That's all you need to say."

"Really? That's all women need to hear?" Hartshorn asked, squinting at me. "That seems remarkably simple."

"You won't know if it works until you talk to her," I said.

"The worst thing that can happen is she turns you down," Nick added.

"Says the guy who married his wife the same night he met her," Hartshorn muttered.

"That had nothing to do with me," Nick replied. "It was all Erin, and the boat and the planets and the lobsterman who officiated in his spare time."

Confused, I leaned forward and studied Hartshorn. "Do you not realize you're a decent catch?" I asked. "You have a lot going for you. Whoever she is, she'd be lucky to have dinner with you."

Hartshorn didn't reply, instead shrugging and rolling his eyes at his sandwich. I took that as an invitation to peek at the messages flashing across my screen.

Riley: Ah. Yeah. About that…sorry. For what it's worth, I've been there.
Riley: I feel it's my duty to tell you that spanking hurts but caning hurts substantially more.
Alex: Is this a dungeon story?
Riley: Yes.
Alex: I'm going to require more explanation of all that.
Riley: We'll see.
Alex: You have photos of my vagina on your phone.
Riley: I know. I'm looking at them right now.
Alex: You're going to tell me about this dungeon.
Riley: Nevertheless, she persisted.

"IF THE RUMOR mill is to be trusted," Nick started, drawing my attention away from my phone, "it sounds like you made peace with Walsh on Friday. Did y'all enjoy the gala?"

I ducked my head, chuckling to myself as I redistributed the slices of avocado between the bacon and tomato. "It was a lovely affair," I said as breezily as I could manage. "Riley and I enjoyed ourselves quite a bit."

"Uh huh," Nick murmured. "Sure you did."

"When did you leave?" Hartshorn asked. "I didn't see you there."

I continued fiddling with my sandwich, my tongue caught between my teeth. I wasn't a giggly girl but a small part of me was dying to share the wild details of my weekend. "We stayed through the cocktail hour," I said. "We had other plans."

"That's what you need, Hartshorn," Nick said, pointing at him. "*Other plans*. Your life will be much better when you have *other plans* on the regular."

My phone pinged with another message and I swung my leg over the bench. "I need to handle this."

Riley: So…what's a guy gotta do to get another date with you?

Alex: Not sure I'm free tonight.

Riley: That's unfortunate.

Alex: Yeah, some asshole told me to get waxed.

Riley: What a dickhead. Ignore him.

Alex: Totally, but he has some redeeming qualities.

Riley: Yeah? I'd like to hear about them.

Alex: Off the top of my head…he takes a damn good photo, makes me laugh like crazy, and he's an animal in bed.

Riley: That asshole can wait a day or two if he really wants you waxed.

Riley: I'm going out on a limb here, but I don't think he'd mind having you shaved instead. He'd probably enjoy doing it for you.

Alex: In that case, my evening is wide open.

Riley: Just like your legs.

Riley: I'm bringing my camera.

Alex: About that…

Riley: Yes?

Alex: It's a little weird, right? The photos? I don't understand why I like it.

Riley: Does it make you uncomfortable?

Alex: Somewhat.

Riley: Do you want to stop? We can stop at any time. I'll delete every single photo right now if that's what you want.

"EMMERLING," Nick called. "I'm stealin' the bacon out of this sandwich if you don't get back here."

"Touch it and I'll amputate your hand with a plastic knife," I shouted over my shoulder. "Then you'll need the moody new trauma guy to fix you up."

"I take my hands very seriously," he replied. "They're insured for millions of dollars."

"And I take my bacon very seriously," I said.

Alex: No. I don't want that.

Riley: Okay then. I'll see you tonight.

Riley: I'm bringing my markers, too.

Alex: What for?

Riley: The dungeon story.

I WAS busy rubbing the kinks out of my neck as I walked home, and didn't notice Riley waiting on the sidewalk until he asked, "What's wrong?"

"Long afternoon of surgery," I said. "A little strained, a little sore."

He came up behind me, swatted my hand away. He brought his palms to my shoulders and his thumbs to my neck, rubbing gently. "Can I help?"

"Mmhmm," I murmured, melting into him. "You can keep doing that."

"Upstairs," Riley whispered into my ear, nudging me toward the steps. "Much more of this, and the things I'll be doing to you will qualify as public indecency."

He followed me inside and up the stairs. We didn't stop to hang up our coats or stow our keys and bags once my apartment door snicked shut behind us, instead moving straight to the bedroom. Clothes hit the ground in heaps as we watched each other, unhurried. We were smirks and quick touches, quiet laughs and knowing glances.

"Can I draw on you?" Riley asked, trailing his fingertips down my torso.

"What?"

"Draw on you," he repeated. "Your skin is the most gorgeous canvas."

I found myself nodding. "Okay."

Riley tipped his head toward the bed. "On your belly," he said, fisting his hands on his hips.

He was still wearing black boxer briefs, the ones that made my blood feel fizzy, like I was an over-shaken bottle of champagne. I climbed onto the mattress, settling right in the middle. He knelt down and flipped open his messenger bag, and pulled out a sleeve of permanent pens and digital camera.

"Can we limit it to clothed areas?" I asked. "I don't want to have to explain anything to my residents tomorrow."

The mattress dipped as Riley crawled over me. His thigh was between my legs, his knee almost pressed to my center. "Of course, Honeybee."

His fingers traveled over my back in short, deliberate strokes, and I realized he was sketching his design. I waited, my teeth sawing over my bottom lip, for the first swipe of ink.

"I did this in Providence, too. I drew Rhode Island on your leg because I wanted to add to your collection of states. It wasn't my best work," Riley said as he reached for a marker. I shivered when the felt tip met my skin. "But I don't think you remember that."

I shook my head, dropped my face against the quilt with a groan. "Why did we drink so much? It was like spring break in Daytona multiplied by Cancun."

"You wanted us honest," he replied. "I think we got there. I know you did. When you were sucking on my thigh, you told me your favorite colors were cock and blue balls."

I burrowed deeper into the quilt, hiding the beet-red blush on my cheeks. "If you'll excuse me, I'm going to die of embarrassment now."

"Don't even think about it," he replied, laughing. "All right, listen. You're adorable and I love watching your ass jiggle, but you have to stop moving. I don't want this honeycomb pattern getting fucked up."

"I'll stop moving if you tell me about the dungeon," I said.

"I know this might surprise you," Riley started, "but I wasn't always this smooth."

I couldn't see his face but the slight distraction in his voice, the extended pauses between words told me he was busy with the task at hand. The one on my lower back. "If you tell me the dungeon rounded off your rough edges, I will laugh. Loudly."

"Like I said, I wasn't always this smooth. I used to have obnoxious pickup lines I'd lifted from *Maxim*. I sent cosmos and appletinis to women at bars. I kept flavored condoms in my wallet." He shifted, reaching for another marker. "One day, I met a woman in a deli. I dropped an obnoxious pickup line, and she laughed at me."

"Oh, you poor baby," I murmured.

Riley hummed in agreement. "She said she could tighten up my game and whip me into shape," he continued. "Turns out, she was a Domme and whipping actually meant whipping." He capped one marker, tossed it to the quilt, and then snagged another. "Now, I'm not going to bore you with the details because it was a lot of kneeling and boot-licking, and getting my ass beaten. But I learned a lot from the experience. I learned what I like and what I don't, and how to ask for those things openly."

"I'm deeply appreciative of all that you learned while you were with her," I said.

"It wasn't a relationship, though. I was never 'with' her," Riley said. "Mila and I, we were not dating. I was just another one of her slaves."

"Hmm." There was nothing strictly sensual about this, but the smooth drag of the tip was both electrifying and hypnotic. I was keyed up and aware of his every touch, breath, movement. But I was also floating along, relaxed to the point of drowsiness. "How long did that last? I can't imagine you enjoying the slave routine."

Riley shifted, moving to the other side of the bed, and turned his attention to my shoulder. "It was about three months," he replied. "There were a few things I didn't enjoy, but I couldn't handle all the rules." He laughed as he gathered my hair. "Sweet tiny Jesus. The rules and restrictions, and the planning. It was more of a process than anything else. Like, an oil change."

"Does that mean you don't miss it?"

Minutes passed before he responded, and in that time, I worried that the answer was yes. He missed it all. He wanted the boot-licking and the ass-whipping, and he was hoping I wanted those things, too.

"No, I don't miss it. I can see how some folks really enjoy it, but it wasn't my scene." He capped the marker and tossed it aside, then wrapped my hair around his hand. "This is the sexiest honeycomb I've ever seen," he murmured, leaning back on his haunches. "Don't move. I want some pictures of you just like this."

I shivered with those words and the rapid clicks of the camera. It was like someone was seeing me for the first time. Not my brother or my parents, my profession, my mistakes...me. Every photo was a reminder that he wanted to keep some piece off me too.

"You have a honeycomb and a honeybee," Riley said, trailing his finger over my back and shoulder, "and if I come all over you right now, it's definitely your fault." He gripped my ass, squeezing and separating my cheeks as he growled. "Can I have you here?"

I choked back a laugh-moan as he pressed his cock to my crease. "I've seen what happens when that doesn't go as planned," I said. "You forget what I do all day."

"I'll make it good for you," Riley promised. "I'll make everything good for you, Aly."

"I know you will," I replied.

And I knew he would.

Alex: Well, it happened.

Alex: I started rambling about Henry Bates and his journey through the Amazon during surgery today.

Riley: That movie was fucking epic.

Alex: So fucking epic.

Riley: We should go back to the Museum of Science and see it again.

Alex: I don't know that I can go again. I was in surgery for 6 hours today. My residents heard a lot about the Amazon. They'd revolt if they had to hear much more.

Riley: I can't do anything for 6 hours straight. I don't know how you do that. I'd never make it.

Alex: I'm sure there's something you can do for 6 hours.

Riley: Nice, Alexandra. Nice. Way to make it all about sex.

Alex: I was not referring to sex!

Riley: You were thinking it.

Riley: Hmm. It's cute how you don't deny it.

Alex: I was consulting on a case, thank you.

Riley: Sure. Whatever. I know how it is.

Riley: Let's go back to the Museum of Science tonight. I want to see that film again.

Alex: I have to pass on more Henry Bates and the Amazon. My residents actually requested that I put on "that oldies rap" that I usually play in the OR. I'm not sure when Biggie and Snoop crossed the line into oldies, but…

Riley: It sounds like they forgot about Dre.

Alex: Must've been all that gin and juice.

Riley: Things aren't the same for gangsters.

Alex: That's how it goes with surgeons. Once they get mo' money…

Riley: Mo' problems, huh?

Alex: They're coming straight outta residency. Like every single day.

Riley: Sometimes your words hypnotize me.

Alex: Play on, player.

Riley: Shake it, mama.

Alex: The skirts know what's up.

Riley: Well I do have a pocket full of rubbers…

Alex: I just snorted because we all know how you feel about rubbers.

Riley: I'm gonna board your ship and turn it on out.

Alex: I attract the honeys like a magnet.

Riley: I can do this all day, Alexandra.

Alex: You? I can throw the fuck down if you want to have a conversation composed entirely of song lyrics.

Alex: We can move onto movie quotes whenever you're ready.

Riley: Do we wear pink on Wednesdays?

Riley: When are your parents coming to town?

Alex: The second week of November, I think.

Alex: Not 100% on that. They haven't told me much about their foliage plans.

Riley: They're cutting it pretty close on the leaf peeping. Not much left to see come November.

Alex: I believe they're also exploring covered bridges and other quintessentially New England things.

Riley: Ah. Those bridges are something.

Alex: That's the rumor I hear. I'm sure they'd probably enjoy an official Riley Walsh tour of Boston.

Alex: Cannoli, too. From that bakery I love. I could eat that cream filling by the bowlful.

Riley: I could eat it off your skin.

Alex: I don't see a problem with that.

Riley: Well, it can be arranged.

Riley: Wear real shoes today.

Alex: As opposed to…?

Riley: Fancy lady shoes.

Alex: I'm not even going to explore those comments.

Riley: Right, so we'll be having a second breakfast this morning. Good to know.

Alex: Do we really have to do this? It seems a little too eighth-grade-class-trip for me.

Riley: You want to know something about eighth grade class trips? They're awesome. You'd be lucky to go on a mandatory educational visit to Boston.

Alex: Walking the Freedom Trail just doesn't sound that interesting.

Riley: Would it sound more interesting if we added a tour of the Samuel Adams Brewery to it?

Alex: Of course. You know how I feel about beer.

Riley: You like it more than you like most people.

Alex: Correct.

Riley: I admire that about you.

Alex: My fondness for beer?

Riley: Mostly the antisocial stick up your ass, but also the fondness for beer.

***

Alex: This is going to sound weird but stay with me.

Riley: Are organs and body parts involved?

Alex: Actually, yes but I think you'll like this.

Riley: That shit freaks me out, Honeybee.

Alex: A bunch of blood banks and organ and tissue transplant organizations in the area got together and they're hosting a spooky Halloween party.

Riley: Nothing terrifying about that.

Alex: They're running a blood drive and live donor screenings, but there's also a costume party with a band. It's this weekend.

Riley: Seems like a ripe opportunity for a visit from a sparkly family of vampires. They wouldn't even have to work that hard. Just roll up in their long cloaks, all pale and shit, and they'd fit right in.

Alex: It sounds like it's going to be a good time.

Riley: But blood. Lots and lots of blood.

Alex: We could have some fun with the costumes.

Riley: You've got a whole lot of Hermione going on but I can't pull off Ron. Sorry.

Alex: You could pull off Gale, and I might be able to whip up some Katniss.

Riley: You could be Agent Carter. I'm not convinced the world needs to see me in Captain America tights, but I'd be all over you in a spanky little uniform.

Alex: Superman and Wonder Woman. I could make that work.

Riley: Again with the tights.

Alex: The Joker and Harley Quinn.

Riley: Stop it right now.

Alex: You could go as Batman…

Riley: Ugh no.

Alex: Why not?

Riley: I'm always Batman. It's not even amusing anymore.

Alex: But have you been Batman while accompanied by Catwoman?

Riley: Full leather bodysuit? Bullwhip? Kitten ears?

Alex: Of course.

Riley: Ohhhhh fuck.

Riley: You've located my weakness but you should know I don't want to be anywhere near the blood suckers.

Riley: Or the vampires.

Riley: You haven't been to my place.

Alex: I know. Is that weird? It's not intentional. I'm not avoiding it. We just end up at my place all the time.

Alex: That's weird, right?

Riley: It's not weird. There are no teething babies at your place and I can fuck you in the kitchen without my brother bitching about the Must Wear Pants and the No Sex Outside Bedrooms rules.

Riley: I really hate the Must Wear Pants rule.

Alex: None of those rules at my apartment.

Riley: I know. I love it.

Alex: So…does that mean you're coming over and staying tonight?

Riley: Hmm. Let me think about that.

Riley: No pants, no crying infants, no one complaining about where I fuck you…

Riley: And then there's that amazing mouth of yours…

Riley: When can I move in?

Alex: Tonight if you pick up some of those egg rolls and dragon noodles we had a few weeks ago.

Riley: Done and done.

Alex: Are we still on for the basketball game tonight?

Riley: That depends.

Riley: Will you wear the appropriate quantity of Celtics green or will I have to go alone?

Alex: I can't believe you're serious about ditching me if I don't wear green.

Riley: I have standards. I enforce them ruthlessly. Your ass should know that by now.

Alex: What if I let you draw a shamrock on me?

Riley: What if you stop fucking around and you do as you're told?

Alex: You love when we fuck around. It's right up there with all your other favorite things, like sandwiches and front-clasp bras.

Riley: What if I pick up a t-shirt for you before the game?

Alex: What about a side boob shamrock?

Riley: Okay, that is a much better idea.

Alex: Something happened at the hospital today.

Riley: Do I want to hear this? Are there any guts involved?

Alex: A patient got aroused while I was examining him.

Riley: I have two very different reactions to this. Are you ready?

Alex: I expected nothing less.

Riley: First – you're gorgeous. Of course you have patients boning up when you walk in.

Riley: Second – how the fuck do you handle that?

Riley: Oh my fucking god. Please tell me you don't HANDLE it.

Alex: No, I usually give it a light whack with my reflex hammer.

Alex: But only if it's in the way.

Riley: Please don't ever hit my cock with a hammer.

Riley: We're going to need to write that into the marriage vows.

Riley: Something like, I, Alexandra, do promise to never raise a hammer to Riley's penis or scrotum as long as we both shall live.

Alex: That's charming.

Riley: Unique, right? People will be talking about it during the reception. They'll be like, Wow! Those two are a little wonky.

Riley: And we'll just laugh because they don't even know the half of it.

Alex: We're at the vow drafting stage?

Riley: You can never be too prepared.

Alex: Boy Scout much?

Riley: Not me. I was more interested in acting out Justice League reunions.

Alex: Makes sense.

Riley: But it's my duty to tell you that my siblings are known for fucking shit up at weddings. Someone is always sneaking off to have sex, someone else is boarding a boat, and there are shenanigans a plenty.

Alex: Did you type "a plenty" with a straight face?

Riley: Yes, but I said it with a pirate voice. Captain Jack Sparrow.

Alex: Sure…that's logical.

Riley: Shenanigans, Alexandra. So. Many. Shenanigans.

Alex: And you take issue with that because…?

Riley: I don't know.

Riley: I guess because I'm never the one having the shenanies.

Alex: If we get married, we'll have shenanies.

Riley: If.

Alex: I know, I know.

Riley: It's funny.

Alex: Is it?

Riley: Yeah. Like I'd ever let you go.

THE SUN WAS WARMER, the air crisper, the burritos tastier. All the love songs were written for me.

Life was good.

No, it was fucking *great*.

If you didn't count the rubber band winging off my forehead, of course.

"What the fuck?" I snapped, pressing my fingertips to my brow.

My gaze rounded the attic conference room table in search of the band-firing culprit. My siblings, they were smart enough to know when it was right to defend each other and when it was right to sell each other down the river, and they all pointed at Matt. I shot the band back at him, and was sure to direct it toward the fleshy part of his cheek.

"Motherfuck," he seethed, rubbing his face.

"Enjoy that welt," I said. He flipped me off, and I layered my hands over my heart with a wink. "Aww, fuck you very much."

I didn't want to beat the grin off my brother's face, and that was another reason why life was fucking great right now. I was snuggled up with an incredible woman nearly every night, restoring old homes every day, and I wasn't weighed down by anything else. Everything I'd been carrying around before Alex was gone. I hadn't forgotten any of it, but I couldn't wrap my hands around it to pick it up again.

There were moments when I still wanted to spike that goddamn iced coffee at Matt's head, but only because he was really fucking annoying with all that ice rattling.

"I've been talking to you for a couple of minutes, RISD," Patrick said, his lips folded in a scowl. "I'd love to carry on with this meeting at any time. Any time at all. Whenever it's convenient for you, of course."

"Let's start with Marlborough Street," I said, flipping open my notebook. "I have a few small details left to polish, but otherwise, it's done. Magnolia is wrapping up work this week, too."

Patrick tapped his pen against the table for a moment, his eyes narrowed. "Shannon and I walked that property on Friday," he said carefully. "The work on the roof deck, it was good. We should engage Magnolia's services more frequently."

I held my notebook up to my face and stifled a snort.

"Did he just say?" Sam started.

"I think he did," Matt replied.

"Is he delirious?" Tom asked.

"I couldn't believe it either," Andy murmured. "But I got a detailed report on his new love of roof gardens on Friday night."

"Perhaps we should make a note of this," Shannon said. "Mark this down as the day Patrick surrendered to roof gardens."

"The fight was long and valiant," I said, "but the resistance won out. It will henceforth be known that roof gardens are preferred throughout the land."

"Holy shit," Matt said with a chuckle. "I never thought I'd see the day."

"Would you all shut up?" Patrick snapped. "Goddamn it. I can acknowledge good work when I see it."

"You were dead set against seeing it for *years*," Sam argued.

"That's how long it takes to arrive at some decisions," Patrick replied.

"And that, friends," Shannon said, "is why he and Andy still haven't set a date."

Andy shot her a sharp stare. "Don't drag wedding dates into this."

Patrick released a heavy sigh. "Can we please get back to the agenda?" he asked. "It's almost nine o'clock. We're not even close to finished here, and I have to be in Newburyport at ten. Perhaps we could speed this the fuck along?"

I gestured to my notes. "Long story short: all of my projects are on or ahead of schedule."

"Budget?" Patrick asked, his attention turned back to his screen.

"On or below," I replied. "Except Berkeley Street, but we've already talked about the extra expenses associated with restoring the entry way and parlor crown moulding using that three-dimensional print shop in New Hampshire. It's fuck-all expensive but I think it's the right call."

Patrick shoved a hand through his hair and blew out a breath. "That shit still blows my mind."

"Thank god you're not running late, RISD," Shannon said. She ran a hand over the round of her belly and patted it twice. "Your schedule in January, February, and March is insane, and then you're booked straight through the summer, too."

"Sam isn't even booked that far out," Patrick added.

"Now *that* we should note," Matt said.

Part of me wanted to throw some confetti and pop the champagne because Sam had been the flavor of the week since flavor came to town. He'd been the darling of design— and in every worthy publication you could shake a T-square at—since the minute he'd joined the firm. He'd never struggled to define his style or find his place.

But the other part of me didn't believe this was real *and* my life. It wasn't long ago that I sat in these meetings wondering whether I'd made a terrible decision by joining the family firm because I didn't know what the hell I was doing. I'd bumbled through school and come out fat on wild stories and thin on practical skills. All of that had been immediately obvious to my siblings, and I'd labored under their reeducation program for a couple of tedious years.

But then Matt had trusted me to manage a project on my own. I didn't work the way my brothers did, and my thoughts followed different paths than theirs, but I'd discovered a niche alongside them nonetheless. I'd taken the long road to this point, but now I was here.

And life was fucking great.

"We just need to meet this girlfriend of yours," Shannon said. "Those Halloween pictures from last weekend were really cute. She seems like a lot of fun." She reached for her ever-present bottle of sparkling water. "I just wish we could get to know her outside of your Instagram feed."

"She's cute as hell and we have to meet her immediately," Andy agreed.

"It's almost like you're *trying* to keep her away from us," Matt said, his voice loaded with sarcasm. "I can't imagine why."

Sam shook his head and signaled for time out. "I fully support avoiding the tribe. There should be a three-month waiting period before introducing anyone to these hyenas," Sam said. "Sell her on *you* as long as you can. Don't let anyone pull her aside and unload the greatest hits of your ungentlemanly behavior."

"Stop," Andy chided with a glance to Patrick. "Some people find ungentlemanly behavior—"

"Save it, Asani," Patrick warned.

"There just hasn't been a good time," I said, keeping my eyes on my notebook. "Her schedule is crazy, and...I don't know." I ran my palm over my tie and shifted. "I like being with her more than I like being with any of you."

Sam whistled from the opposite side of the table. "Someone's not a baby bird anymore," he remarked. "But here's the real question: are your trousers zipped?"

A glance at my lap revealed that no, my trousers were not zipped. I knew my fly had been up when I'd left Alex's apartment this morning, but gravity wasn't always on my side. A quick maneuver had everything set to rights.

"Nothing to see here," I said.

"Nothing we haven't all seen many times," Matt said. "I think your dick is burned into the back of my eyelids. I see it every time I go to sleep."

"That's because you wish it was yours," I replied.

"When you're done with this sword fight, could we briefly touch base on Wellesley?" Tom asked.

The light, airy feelings of this morning burst like a bubble. Jovial expressions were fast replaced with scowls, and all the easy body language turned guarded.

"Certainly, Tom. I do like getting fucked in the ass early in the morning," Sam mused as he tugged his cuffs. "It keeps me on my toes."

Patrick growled in response.

Shannon rolled her hand in Tom's direction. "Get on with it," she said.

"I've scheduled an invitation-only showing for reporters and real estate agents," he said. "It's a small-scale showcase. You're getting calendar invites for the event later today. It's next Thursday. There's no obligation for any of you to attend but she"—Tom wagged a finger at Andy—"will be getting a lot of attention. We should celebrate her work."

"I'll be there," Patrick said. "Of course."

"We'll *all* be there," Shannon said, and her tone invited no dissent. "Andy deserves our support."

Sam dropped his head back and he moaned like an animal being mauled in the woods. "Please tell me there's going to be an open bar."

"Open bar with top-shelf liquors, and an assortment of vegan and gluten-free appetizers especially for you," Tom replied.

Matt slammed his laptop shut. "Lauren has a school thing that night," he said, a defiant jerk in his shoulder. "She won't be there until later."

"That's not a problem," Tom said easily. "We'll save her a plate of mini cupcakes."

Andy twisted the thin necklace at her throat. "Guys, you really don't have to—"

"They do," Patrick interrupted. "End of discussion."

"Since it's obvious we can't end on that sour note," Shannon said with an exaggerated page-turning gesture, "we should talk about the holidays."

Patrick tapped his watch. "You have three minutes before I'm walking out."

She guzzled her sparkling water and gave him an apathetic look. "You can walk out now if you'd like," she replied. "Leave, suck my dick, row a boat to Rome. I don't give a fuck."

"About the holidays," Matt prompted, ending Patrick and Shannon's glaring contest.

"Could we bullet point this? Maybe drop it in a distribution list email? How about a group text?" Tom asked. "This would be easier if we all got on Slack."

An immediate chorus of groans and protests went up.

"Stop trying to make Slack happen, Thomas," I yelled.

"The distro lists are for unimportant emails no one will ever read. The group texts are for lunch orders, emergencies, and photos from job sites," Matt said, ticking off each mode of communication on his fingers. "And Slack is for corporate windbags who don't work here."

"One more minute," Patrick said as he snapped his laptop shut.

"Let's do this real quick," Shannon said, holding up her hands. "Thanksgiving is at my house again this year. It's going to be a big crowd. Will's business partner Jordan is coming with his girlfriend April. Judy and the Commodore will be there. They arrive at the end of the week and they're staying— thank god for grandparents—until after this baby arrives." She patted her belly. "Will's brother Wes might even make an appearance."

"That's great," I said. "But what's on the menu?"

"Oh! You should bring Alexandra." Shannon slapped the table with each word.

Patrick pushed back from the table and swung his messenger bag across his chest. "Here's a suggestion. Think about wrapping up this conversation and getting some work done." He bent and dropped a kiss to Andy's forehead. To her, he said, "Text me if you need anything, kitten."

After Patrick left the attic, everyone else started filing out. Shannon tapped my forearm. "I want you to bring Alexandra."

"You've mentioned this," I said.

"Does that mean you will?"

Holidays with the family were, as Alex would say, a bridge crosser. It was a dive into the Walsh deep end, a front row seat to the circus. And what a circus it was.

I nodded. "It means I'll check with her."

Riley: Are we still good to go for the game tonight?

Alex: Ready and set. I've got a procedure this afternoon but it should be a quick in and out. What time am I seeing you?

Riley: Around 6? I'm working on finishing some designs this afternoon so I probably won't stop at home before picking you up.

Alex: I'll just meet you at your office.

Riley: Do you remember how to get here?

Alex: You know, I'm not completely helpless.

Riley: I never said you were. I only implied that you'd get lost going to work if it wasn't literally across the street from your apartment.

Alex: Thanks for that clarification.

Riley: No problem, Shortstop.

Alex: I'll meet you at your office. At 6.

Riley: Fantastic. That gives us an hour of flex time for when you get lost and text me to pick you up in Somerville.

Alex: Just you wait. I'll be early.

Riley: Yeah, I'll be waiting for something. Text me when you leave. Please.

Alex: Heading out in a minute.

Riley: Outstanding. I'll hang around outside, on Derne Street, at the off chance you don't get lost.

Alex: Sweetie, don't put yourself on the corner for me.

Riley: I'm going to spank you until my handprint is visible on both sides of your ass.

Alex: You and that big dick of yours make a lot of promises.

Riley: Are you challenging me?

Alex: Maybe.

"DIDN'T GET LOST," Alex teased, pushing up on her toes to wrap an arm around my shoulders.

"I'm proud of you," I said, backing her against the foyer wall on the main level of the office. I liked her here, the leverage it afforded. I could boost her up, wrap her legs around my waist, grind my cock against her belly. And she was at my mercy when she was pinned, a little helpless.

"If this is what I get for walking up the street and making a right turn," she said, moaning when my teeth scraped over the sensitive crook of her shoulder, "then I'll walk more often. Even if you do leave a handprint on my ass. Or two."

"Honeybee," I murmured, sighing into her skin. I loved the way she smelled right here. I didn't think I could drag myself away for anything. I didn't even want to spar with her. I just wanted to drown in the sweetness she offered me, and never come up for air.

I loved her. I knew it without qualification. More than that, I felt it inside me, heavy and expansive like a bottom-less lake.

"I want you right here," I admitted. "But I don't want to rub up all over you in the hallway. There are three security cameras recording this right now, and at least one guy in Virginia with eyes on us."

"The recording is fine," she said. "But the audience? That's not our thing."

"Nope. Not our thing," I agreed, releasing her from the wall. "Come on. Let's go to my office. The only cameras in there are the ones I control."

I nodded to the stairs, gesturing for her to take the lead. I followed her, my hands on her hips and my mouth close enough to her ass that I could lean forward and bite it.

I didn't. The security system Shannon's husband Will had installed last winter covered every door and window in the brownstone, and while it was probably contradictory that I enjoyed photographing her body in various states of pleasure, I had no interest in sharing.

"I brought something special," she said, waving a large envelope. We rounded the landing on the second floor, heading down the hall to my office. "It's special to me, that is."

"What do you have there?" I asked, leading the way past Shannon, Tom, and Matt's empty offices. Shannon worked from home on Wednesdays, and the other two put in early hours to leave by five each night. I held open the door, gesturing for Alex to enter.

"This month's issue of *The International Journal of Surgery*. I got an early copy."

I glanced down at the envelope, my eyebrows arched. "And you brought it along in case the game is a snoozer?"

"Of course not," she said. "If it's a snoozer, I'll drink more beer and send you off to find interesting snacks."

"That's my girl," I murmured. "Make yourself at home." I pointed at the sofa and the chairs in front of my desk. "I'm just wrapping up a few designs before shipping them to Matt for structural review."

"Don't you want to see what I brought?" she asked, drumming her fingers along the envelope's edge. I dropped into my desk chair, staring at the manila while I debated whether I had the strength for a magazine dedicated to guts.

"Show me," I said. "But warn me if any of this will cause emotional scarring."

She laughed at that while sliding the publication across my desk. Once it was in front of me, she flipped it open and tapped the text. I studied the page, eternally grateful to find words but no images, and then I saw it.

"This is you," I said, my fingertip circling her name. "You wrote this article?"

"I did," she replied, an irrepressible grin stretched across her face. "Don't read it. It's about bile duct surgeries, and the most effective methods given certain complicating factors, and you'll be horrified."

"No, I want to read it," I argued. I beckoned her closer, not wanting the barrier of my desk between us. She came to me and I tugged her into my lap, my arms laced around her body. "My girl is wicked smart."

"It's just a small thing," she said. "Nothing major. I was surprised they even accepted the article. I submitted it almost a year ago."

"It's completely major," I said as I skimmed the text. "I'm so proud of you."

"More than getting here by myself?"

"Different skill sets, different types of proud," I replied.

"You're the first person I showed," she said quietly, her head nestled under my chin. "Not Hartshorn or Acevedo, or anyone else."

"Thank you," I said, pushing back the urge to lay out my feelings like a summer picnic. I'd tell her. Soon. "I want to be the first person to hear your good news, and I want your bad news, too. All of it, Aly. I'll take it. Anything you want to give me."

"Do you mean that? Really?" She swallowed and glanced over her shoulder to catch my eye. "You're sure you want it all...with *me*?"

And there it was. The reason *I love you* didn't belong in this conversation. Alex was convinced I was carrying a torch for someone. She believed it was Dorrance, and I couldn't fathom a reason to correct her since I wasn't carrying a torch for anyone. Not anymore. The history didn't matter, and I couldn't see how divesting myself of those tales would help anything.

"Of course I mean that," I replied. My palm was flat against her backside and I rubbed in deep, deliberate circles. That type of pressure was our shorthand for *I want to fuck you right now and I want it to hurt a little.* "I want everything with you."

And then I was ready. To spank her until I'd chased the dark clouds of me wanting anyone but her away. To put my feelings for her out there. To rip off her jeans and bend her over my desk. I was ready for everything.

"If I fuck you right now," I started, trailing my fingers over her throat, "will we need to go home and get you some new panties before the game? Or will you wear the dirty ones all night?"

Alex laughed. "I think you know I want—"

"Knock, knock."

I lurched forward as Alex twisted away from me, and that resulted in her bent over my desk and my hands braced on either side of her. It looked like I was fucking her, and I was certain that was why Patrick was cursing at the ceiling and Andy's hand was pressed to her mouth. She was trying, failing to restrain a laugh.

"We weren't—it's not—we're not—shit, this isn't-isn't-isn't —*fuck,*" I stammered. I curled my arm around Alex's waist and scraped her off the desk. She was fighting the giggles, too. "Oh my fucking god. This isn't what it looks like."

"Regardless, we're sorry to interrupt," Patrick said, his eyes still aimed at the heavens. "We were leaving and saw your lights on. Obviously, we'll never make this mistake again."

"Hi, I'm Andy." She crossed my office, her hand extended. "That's Patrick." She pointed over her shoulder at him. He waved without looking. "We've heard so many wonderful things about you."

"Alex," she said. "This is really awkward."

"Less than you'd think," Andy replied. "Don't worry about it."

I cleared my throat and shot Patrick a *Get the fuck out of here* look. "We have Patriots tickets tonight," I said. "We're actually on our way out."

"Then we won't keep you," Patrick said, nodding to Alex.

"I'm sure we'll be seeing you again," Andy said. "You're coming to Thanksgiving, right?"

"Oh," Alex replied, sending me a confused glance over her shoulder. "I…I don't know. Maybe?"

"Good night," Patrick sang, smirking as he realized I hadn't discussed Shannon's invitation with Alex yet. I flipped him off over her head. "And good luck."

I dropped my chin to her shoulder and held my breath, listening for the clang of the front door. When I finally heard it, I exhaled and dropped back into my chair, taking Alex with me. "I'm sorry about all that," I said. "My sister wants me to invite you to Thanksgiving at her house. She's having about twenty people and small baby-children, and she'd like you to come."

Alex drew a finger over my brows and down my nose as she waded through my words. "Your sister?" she asked. "What about you? What do you want?"

"Of course I want you to come," I said, kissing her finger when it moved over my lips. "But my family is a complicated matter, and it's not just *my* family at this shindig. It's Matt and Shannon's in-laws, and Will's business partner and his girlfriend, and probably some other random people who wander in off the streets. It's a whole fucking lot for me, and I don't want to drag you into it if you're not ready."

It occurred to me then that—*of course*—Lauren would be there. And it didn't matter. Not like it used to matter. If anything, I was eager for her to meet Alex, and that was a welcome reaction.

Strange but welcome.

"It's fine if you don't want me to go," Alex said softly as she traced my jaw. "We don't have to rush anything."

I shook my head, frustrated that I'd swung hard in the wrong direction. "That's not what I'm saying. Not at all, Honeybee."

She hooked her finger in my tie, loosening the knot until the fabric was sliding free from my collar. "Have you ever brought a girlfriend home for the holidays?" she asked.

"No, I've never had anyone who meant that much to me," I replied quickly, and her face fell. It was a stab in the fucking gut. "Aly, no. Listen. I want you to come."

"You're saying that because of"—she gestured toward the doorway—"everything that happened with Andy and Patrick. It's okay to say no, Riley. It might hurt my feelings and I'll want to understand why, but I'd rather you be direct with me. I can handle it."

"I'm being direct. I'm just going about it in convoluted ways," I replied. "I meant what I said earlier about wanting anything you'd give me. I'd *love* it if you spent the holiday with me. I also feel it's necessary to warn you that my family is a big, noisy herd. They ask tons of personal questions and have no regard for boundaries. And they've been known to drink Boston dry." I slapped her backside, tearing a surprised yelp from her lips. "Think you can handle all that?"

"Easy peasy," Alex said, snaking her hand between us. She found my cock, stroked me over my trousers. "Lemon squeezy."

I growled and spanked her again, harder this time. "I hope you know what you're doing, Honeybee."

Alex shifted, pushing her breasts against my chest and her mouth to my neck as she rubbed between my legs. My cock was heavy, uncomfortably so, and I required more than fabric-covered friction.

"I do," she panted. "I know exactly what I'm doing."

That was the only confirmation I needed. I bolted up, lifting her from my lap and setting her on the edge of my desk. I shoved everything into a drawer before attacking her jeans, and then yanked them off.

"Shirt," I said with a pointed nod. "Off."

"Someone's in a bossy mood," Alex quipped.

"Someone was ready to fuck you twenty minutes ago," I replied, my words clipped and irritable. "And the bra. Let's go. I want some tits in my hands."

"Bossy, bossy, bossy," she murmured.

I pushed my trousers to my knees, boxers too, and watched while Alex's clothes hit the floor. My fist was on my cock, pumping and twisting to relieve some of the need I was feeling.

"How long have you been cultivating this fantasy?" Alex asked.

She was propped up on her outstretched arms, her legs

spread and dangling off my desk, and I didn't possess the language to describe the depth of my love for her in this moment.

"I thought I had a fantasy like this one," I started, reaching for my phone, "but that wasn't even close to what I really wanted." I stepped between her legs, dragging my cock through her folds. "I didn't know what I needed until I met you."

With the camera app open and the shutter speed set, I held my phone between us and pushed inside her. This angle was different, and she was impossibly tight.

I was growling into her shoulder after one thrust, sucking after the second, biting after the third. The echoes of *I love you, I love you, I love you* were powering every buck of my hips, and I wasn't going to last. That, combined with the odd pleasure of taking her in a semi-public place had me clinging to the edge.

"Oh, my god," she gasped, her body rocking up to meet me. "Every time you're inside me, it's the best I've ever had."

"You're the best I've ever had," I said. I drove into her, my arm wrapped around her waist for leverage as the photos clicked away, and I sensed the tension gathering at the base of my spine. "Get there, Aly. I'm not going to wait for you. I'm gonna finish and shoot all over you, and then I'll take you to the game and watch you squirm for hours."

"No, you fucking won't," she hissed. "I'm almost —almost—*ah.*"

Her fingers found her clit, and her inner muscles clamped down around me. I stilled, wanting to savor every one of those convulsions. "There you go, there it is," I whispered, growling against her neck as the sensations rolled through her body. "Keeping rubbing. I want to watch."

Alex reclined against the desk, her hand between her legs, and that was everything I needed. White-hot heat zipped through my nerves and I pulled out as my orgasm unfurled. I collapsed over her, my arms braced beside her shoulders and my release sticky on her belly.

She kissed my forehead, murmuring, "Can we fight about family gatherings more often?"

I nestled my head between her breasts and imagined all the filthy pictures I was taking before we cleaned up and left for the game. I didn't know what it was about my seed on her skin but it drove me fucking wild.

"Just be happy I didn't come inside you," I replied. "We don't have the time to go home for new panties, and I don't think I can survive driving down to Foxborough and back knowing you're wet from me."

She laughed, drawing her abdominal muscles in and perking her breasts up, and I seized that opportunity to start snapping photos.

Twenty–Three
RILEY

I WAS on my hands and knees in a narrow bedroom at my Berkeley Street project when Magnolia found me this morning. It seemed I was clocking a lot of time in this position.

"No one could ever accuse you of taking the easy route," she mused. She was leaning against the bedroom door frame, her arms folded over her chest and her dark pink wellies crossed at her ankles.

Paintbrush in hand, I nodded once. "I'm blending the original pieces," I said, pointing at the old hardwood floors, "with the new pieces."

"I can see that," she replied, tipping her chin toward the semi-circle of stains surrounding me. "I just don't understand why you aren't snatching pieces from a closet, or someplace where a uniformly stained floor isn't required."

I wrapped my brushes in a length of oil cloth and covered each can before reaching for my notebook and gaining my feet. An open can of anything was an invitation for me to knock it over.

"Because this house had a lot of fucked-to-shit flooring,

and I've already snatched everything I can," I said. "But thank you for questioning my methods before nine in the morning, Gigi. It really affirms my choices in life."

"Anything I can do to help," she said with a big smile.

"How are you? I never see you anymore," I said, lightly whacking Magnolia's arm with my notebook.

"I know, I know," Magnolia said. "This place is gorgeous. It was a wreck when you started, but I can't believe the transformation. Just gorgeous."

"Thanks," I said, lifting my shoulders in a shrug. "Shannon wants to get it listed and under contract before the baby comes, so I've been hustling."

She pushed away from the door frame and crossed the room. She studied the window casing, and paused to snap a photo of the fine millwork. It reminded me of the images hiding on my phone, the ones that were too hot for anything but complete privacy. There was something humbling about Alex trusting me enough to capture these moments.

Something I *loved*.

Shaking off those thoughts, I turned my attention back to Magnolia. "I take it you're watching football with someone else these days," I said. "What's going on with this Penthouse Peter character? You know, I can't decide if I like that name. Penthouse Peter. It seems to suggest he's a staff writer at *Penthouse*, and I don't love that idea. What about Peter Brady? Talk about some middle child syndrome. Of course, there is Peter the pumpkin-eater, but I don't know that story well enough to commit to the nickname. There was something about him not being able to keep his wife, right?" I scratched my chin, trying to recall the details. "Or maybe we go with Peter Parker. Yeah. That's probably the least offensive option."

She shot me an unimpressed look. "Peter is fine."

"Fine? That's not a resounding vote of confidence, Gigi," I said. "I'll remind you, Spider-Man wasn't always on the side of justice. He made some questionable choices. Also, he was a fucking creeper."

She shook her head and gave me *don't start with that* hands. "Peter is doing well. Work on his property is finished, and he's"—she paused, looking around the room as if the words she wanted would materialize—"he's got a lot on his plate right now."

"A lot on his plate," I repeated.

"Yes. He's going through a difficult time," she replied, her tone turning defensive. "I can't expect much from him at the moment, and that's okay. We all have rough patches, and we deserve some people who stick by us during those times."

There it was. The Magnolia Santillian Guide to Enabling Assholes.

"I'm gonna say this gently," I started, hoping I didn't botch everything. "You're too damn nice. You're good to people, and people are dickheads. Given that I gave up beating the shit out of dickheads as part of my New Year's resolutions, I can't kick this dude's ass if things go bad."

It didn't seem necessary to add that Gigi couldn't tell a douchebag from a donut.

She regarded me before replying. "What else did you resolve to give up?"

Decisions made in alleys; they never worked out favorably.

Sex on pool tables; felt burn is no joke.

Whiskey; everything about whiskey.

"That's pretty much it," I said, smiling to myself as I realized I was on the road to making good on all of those resolutions, whiskey aside. Assuming Peter with the Personal Issues didn't fuck everything up, of course.

"Peter isn't a dickhead," she said. "He's a really good guy. You'd like him if you got to know him."

I wanted to believe her more than anything.

"Except," she said, cutting her eyes to the side, "he's a Jaguars fan."

"Oh my fucking god, Gigi," I said, exasperated. "What have you gotten yourself involved with? A Jags fan? *Really*? Is someone blackmailing him?"

She lifted her hands and let them fall to her sides. "He's a big believer in rooting for underdogs," she said, but her tone made it clear she wasn't convinced. "Believe me, I'm working on it."

"Has he met your family?" I asked. "What do Ash and Linden think?"

"He hasn't met them yet, no," she replied. "But only because he's dealing with some major stuff and meeting my family isn't the most pressing concern."

Magnolia's family was an extension of her being. Her world was Sunday dinners and obscure Portuguese holidays and an endless cycle of birthdays, anniversaries, and no-reason-at-all celebrations. Anyone who mattered to her had a seat at the family table. That was why her brothers baffled me. If they understood how to look out for their sister, they did a piss-poor job at it.

I shook my head. "I want to be a friend right now, but I think I have to be an asshole instead. If he can't make you a pressing concern—which is bullshit, by the way—you need to step back and tell him to give you a call when he can. Don't let him take advantage of you any longer."

She flinched as my words moved through her like a blow.

She tugged her bottom lip between her teeth and stared at the protective covering over the newly restored plaster on the walls. Her lip was turning purple under the pressure of her teeth and her chin kept wobbling in a manner that suggested tears were coming my way. We stayed there, on opposite sides of the room, not saying a word.

In a certain light, it was wrong to say these things to Magnolia. She was an intelligent, capable woman and she didn't need me hanging a raincloud over her happiness because I'd witnessed years of her romantic disasters. In that light, I was the dickhead.

But what kind of friend would sit by while an undeniably shady situation got shadier? I knew Magnolia, and I knew these doubts were already putting down roots in every corner of her mind. I was still the dickhead, but I was the dickhead who didn't mind enduring an uncomfortable exchange and some awkward silence because my friend deserved honesty.

By that logic, Alex deserves to hear the truth about Lauren.

I swung my head from side to side, attempting to dislodge that thought. Things were good right now—*so good*—and I didn't want to fuck any of that up by bumbling my way through a retelling of ancient history. And it was just that: ancient.

It's over. It's gone. No sense telling Alex now.

Now that was a thought I could get behind. I had no interest in deceiving her, but I didn't see a reason to unburden myself of every bizarre truth. Did she really need to know that I learned Spanish by watching telenovelas—and *only* telenovelas—in high school? Or that I'd lied to the women I brought back to my college dorm about my roommate being a heavy sleeper? Or that I was painfully naïve once, and convinced myself Lauren would walk away from that fling with Matt and realize I was the one she wanted?

The world before Alex felt far away, and I couldn't comprehend the months and years spent pining for Lauren. I could call up those memories but I couldn't get inside them anymore. It was like paging through a high school yearbook and recognizing those moments as my own but struggling to understand why I believed that haircut to be in good taste.

Except that haircut was my sister-in-law and I couldn't write those years off as youthful indiscretion. I'd built my life around wanting Lauren. I'd dated women simply because they reminded me of her. I'd foreclosed the possibility of finding a love of my own until now. Until Alex put me back together.

Right on cue, Magnolia turned around and asked, "Still seeing the twin?"

"I am," I said. I wanted that *I am* to travel with more weight than two words, three letters. I wanted it to say *I am and I don't think I'll ever be able to let her go.* "Her name's Alexandra."

She tipped her head to the side and offered a watery smile. "Oh yeah. I remember her from the meetings," she joked. "I'm dying to know what her twin thinks of you. I mean, his approval is mandatory for your relationship. She can't possibly make decisions without her womb-mate weighing in. Right?"

I clapped a hand over my chest as she served me a dose of my own medicine. "Point taken," I said.

"Good, good," she said. "Now, let's go downstairs and talk about this courtyard. I'm thinking traditional. Ivy and wisteria, and creeping rosemary."

"I had no idea rosemary was such a pervert," I said. "All these years, I'd thought it was the chives."

I'D LOST track of my morning. The hours had slipped away from me while I hand-stained flooring all over the Berkeley Street project. Now I was running late for a meeting with Andy and Patrick and taking the office stairs two at a time. It didn't come without a price as the coffee I'd picked up on the way back—being late was preferable to going without my afternoon caffeine fix—was sloshing over the lid and vaporizing a layer of skin on my hand.

Skittering to a stop outside Patrick's door, I gestured to my watch. "I'm on time," I said, breathless.

"Andy ran into some delays at her Lexington property. She'll be here in five or ten minutes," he said as he shuffled through papers on his desk. "She wanted me to tell you that she ordered lunch for us, and she threatened the life of the delivery guy if your meatball sub wasn't in the bag. We'll meet you in your office when she gets here."

"I'll allow it," I said, my chest still heaving. I couldn't complain. Even if I'd hauled ass and burned my hand getting here on time, I was getting another lunch out of this. "I'll be waiting whenever Princess Jasmine is ready."

I headed toward my office, my legs carrying me in long strides as my body was still in *hurry-now-go* mode. I elbowed the door open and flipped the lights on with the back of my hand, and dumped everything on my desk. Coffee, paintbrush case, messenger bag, stainless steel water bottle.

Instead of organizing any of it, I reached for my phone, hoping to find a new message from Alex. We didn't get much time to talk during the day since her hands were full with, well, organs.

Alex: Hartshorn wanted to know whether we were redecorating last night.

Alex: I said yes and now he wants to see what we've done with the place.

Riley: He needs to get laid. Maybe he'll remember what it sounds like then.

Alex: He has a crush on a girl from the park where he jogs each morning.

Riley: There we go. Problem solved.

Alex: Not quite. He's never spoken to her. He just watches her.

Riley: And here I was, wondering whether it would be weird to crop this photo so I can have your belly button as the home screen on my phone. I don't need to see my dick or all that jizz, but your skin is gorgeous here.

PATRICK APPEARED OUTSIDE MY DOOR, his laptop tucked under his arm. I set my phone face down, mentally shutting off all thought of Alex's bare skin.

"We're meeting in Riley's office, Asani," he called down the hallway. "No rush. Whenever you're ready." He stepped inside and settled into one of the deep leather chairs on the other side of my desk. "This new project of yours on Charter Street is going to be a bitch."

Reaching for my water, I considered this. The North End was one of my favorite neighborhoods in the city, but similar to Beacon Hill and the Back Bay, it was a pain in the ass to run large-scale restoration projects there. The streets were impossibly narrow and parking was nonexistent, and all of this meant everything took longer than necessary. Add to that tedious restrictions that often required the approval of neighborhood preservation committees, and we were looking at a long-term relationship with this property.

"That's why I didn't want to take it on by myself," I said. "What do you think will come first? You and Andy getting married or me and Andy finishing work on Charter Street?"

Patrick rolled his eyes. "The two of you couldn't be more different in terms of design aesthetic and project management styles," he said. "I think you'll strangle each other first."

Andy poked her head inside. "How shall I interpret the dick pic you just sent me, RISD?" she asked, holding up her phone.

"What are you talking about? I didn't send you anything." I blinked at her, baffled, but my stomach was somewhere in the basement.

What did I do?

Shannon's voice echoed in the hallway. "Why is your penis in my phone, Riley?"

Patrick rubbed his temples. "What the fuck just happened?"

Matt crowded the doorway, a step behind Andy. "Hey, dude. Quick question. Did you mean to text me your dick just now?"

And then everyone was in my office. Shannon, Matt, Tom, Patrick, Andy, Sam…all talking at once and looking to me for some explanation. Instead of messaging Alex, I'd sent that picture of her belly button—the one in need of cropping because my cock was in there too—to my All Walsh group chat.

Of fucking course.

"I'm assuming this is Alexandra," Shannon said.

"Oh my fucking god," I whispered, dropping my head into my hands.

Some people made lots of small mistakes. A symphony of screw ups. I, on the other hand, preferred big fucking disasters. Flooding basements. Cutting live electrical lines. Texting a picture of my cock lazing in a puddle of jizz on my girlfriend's belly to my entire family.

"I have to say," Tom said, his deep voice carrying over the low rumble, "the composition of this image is beautiful. You could frame this and it would make for some striking artwork."

"That is appreciated," I started, "although I think Alex would die of mortification and I'm not sure I need to see pictures of my dick around the house."

"Why the hell not?" Matt asked. "Your dick's out often enough."

"Not to belabor the point, but this picture was taken *here*," Andy said. She pointed at her screen, and Shannon nodded in agreement. "That's his desk. When you zoom in, you'll see those two knots in the wood—"

"Andy, for fuck's sake, don't *zoom in*," Patrick cried.

"The ones that look like the Bat Signal?" Sam asked. "Goddamn. I didn't build that desk for you to rub your sac all over it."

"Everyone's had sex in the office," I argued.

As if it made a difference in this situation. It did not.

"False," Shannon said.

"Not me," Matt said.

"Then you've come pretty damn close," I snapped.

Patrick plucked Andy's phone from her hands. "Stop looking at that," Patrick said to her.

"Why?" Shannon asked. "Are you worried she'll notice a family resemblance?"

"There is," Andy murmured. "A bit."

"Oh my fucking god," I repeated. "Just delete it. Please. It's my mistake, not Alex's."

"Oh, no," Sam said. "No. We're going to enjoy this. You've walked in on all of us. Now it's your turn."

"This is not the same," I roared. "It's not the same at all."

"It's exactly the same," Patrick replied.

"Now I really want to meet her," Shannon said. "But with less of your junk involved."

"Everyone has to stop talking right now," I roared, snatching my phone up. "Shut up. Just shut up."

I had to tell Alex. It was awful and embarrassing and entirely my fault, but I had to tell her.

Riley: Honeybee. Precious. Darling. Beautiful. Angel. Love.
Alex: What did you do?
Riley: I was trying to send you my favorite image from last night.
Alex: …and?
Riley: I accidentally sent it to my family.
Alex: Oh shit.
Riley: Yeah that was my reaction.
Alex: I'm afraid to ask but, which image was it?
Riley: It's my favorite one. I'd send it to you but I'm worried I'll somehow forward it to all of my clients.
Riley: And none of them need to see my dick in a cum bath on your belly.
Alex: Oh shit.

Alex: This is one way to meet your family…not the one I would've chosen, but it could've been worse.

Alex: At least I look good. My waist looked skinny in that picture, right?

Riley: You are so fucking hot that I can't look at this without wanting your ass on my desk again.

Alex: I can't read your texts in public. I have to shield my screen if anyone else is around.

Alex: Cross my legs, too.

Riley: I'm putting that on the board as a point for me.

Alex: You do that.

Alex: So…did I mention about tonight? Erin's taking me to pedicure night with your sisters-in-law.

Riley: Oh my fucking god.

Riley: You don't have to go.

Riley: Come home and beat me with your tiny hands instead.

Alex: Excuse me? Tiny hands?

Riley: Yes, Honeybee. They're child-sized.

Riley: I love you and your little hands. They make my cock look enormous.

OH SHIT. *I've never said that before.*

"Riley!"

My head snapped up at the chorus of siblings shouting my name, and my phone slipped from my grasp like a greased pig. I shot out of my chair to grab it, but knocked my water bottle over in the process. The phone landed on the ground as I surged forward to save my laptop and notebook from the flood. Cups of markers and pencils fell victim to my hasty rescue efforts, spilling and rolling off my desk. I froze in place, desperate to end the chain reaction.

"I'll get the paper towels," Andy called.

"That was quite the trick," Tom said from the doorway.

I was holding my notebook and laptop—both blessedly dry—aloft, and asked, "Has anyone seen my phone?"

"Yeah, we've seen it," Matt murmured, scowling at the floor. Sam, Patrick, and Shannon stood beside him, all making faces as they looked down.

"I'd rather not be seeing it," Shannon added.

"What, exactly, am I seeing?" Patrick asked, cocking his head to the side.

Sam reached into his pocket and whipped out a handkerchief. "And all along, everyone thought I was the pervert," he said. Using the cloth as a shield, he plucked the device from where it had landed on the rug. He handed it to me, pinched between two fingers like it was a pair of pungent old gym socks. "Please disinfect this."

I dropped my things on the chair behind me and murmured my thanks when the phone was back in my hands. One glance at the screen explained their reactions. It was filled with thumbnail images from last night. Close-up shots of me pushing inside Alex. My cock, shiny with her arousal. Her clit. The underside of her breast. A nipple.

Everything. They'd seen all the things that belonged to me, and I couldn't get any of it back.

The air rushed out of me like I'd been punched in the gut. I pitched forward, bringing my hands to my knees as I struggled to breathe.

"All right, okay," Shannon said as she came to my side. She patted my shoulder and murmured quiet words that my brain was too frantic to hear.

All those times that I'd found myself a party to my siblings' private moments, was this what it was like for them? Because I wanted to simultaneously hide under my desk and beat the shit out of them until they promised to wipe out any memory of those pictures.

Alex is going to slice my balls right off when she finds out about this.

"I know I shouldn't be enjoying this," I heard Sam say, "but I definitely am."

"Am I the only one taking issue with him scrolling through those photos *in the office*?" Patrick asked.

"Shut up. You've had sex in the office," I growled, my head still between my legs. "Repeatedly."

He didn't bother denying it.

"RISD," Matt called. "You need to lock that shit up. Encryption. Thumbprint password. Retina scan. All of it. You cannot walk around with sex photos on your phone." Without dragging my gaze from the hardwood floor, I flipped him off. "I'm not trying to be an asshole, man. Just being honest. If you're not careful, you'll accidentally forward an entire album to a contractor, or post it to Facebook."

"He's right," Sam added. "And you have lost five phones in the past four years."

"Fuck you all very much," I snapped.

"Everyone, that's enough," Shannon said with a snap of her fingers. "Get out of here."

"Those two can go, but I'm staying. Riley, Andy and I are meeting to discuss an upcoming project," Patrick said. Matt and Sam ignored this, and stayed right where they were. "Actually, we're about fifteen minutes past our scheduled time. And we're waiting on lunch."

I wouldn't turn a meatball sub away but I groaned at the thought of carrying on a business conversation right now.

My head was pounding and my stomach churning, and I sank down to the floor. Within a matter of minutes, I'd sent an unwelcome dick pic to my siblings, thrown the mistimed *I love you* curveball, and flashed all of Alex's unmentionables despite promising to keep her safe.

The fucker who was in charge of making sure I wasn't fucking things up was really fucking fired.

"You can reschedule," Shannon said. "Back to your offices. *Now*."

Instead of leaving, they stayed right where they were, chattering about all the ways I could accidentally share naked photos of my girlfriend. I wasn't sure which part of me was collapsing right now, but the only things holding me together were the floor and Shannon's hand on my shoulder.

I didn't care whether they'd gotten a good look at me. I had enough trouble keeping the snake in the cage, and I didn't give a good shit about that. But Alex wasn't available for public consumption. She was mine, and those images were for us.

That I'd accidentally sent them to my family left me feeling possessive to a degree I didn't understand. It wasn't the same old sense of not wanting to share Alex. It was a desire to protect her, to wage war for her, to sacrifice for her. I wanted to pull myself together and be the man she needed me to be.

"If I get down there, you're going to have to help me get back up," Shannon said as she maneuvered herself to the floor beside me. "Now, listen. Those images were mostly indecipherable. I mean, it was obvious they were—*ahem*—personal, but I couldn't tell you exactly who or what was on that screen. So, put that out of your mind."

"Yeah, sure. Let me just forget the events of this afternoon," I replied, brushing my hands off. "All set."

She rolled her eyes. "There's no need to be snippy," she said. "I'm pregnant as fuck and sitting on the goddamn floor with you."

I wagged a finger at her, not falling for her delicate daisy routine. "Alex is supposed to go out with you and the rest of Pussy Riot tonight. But"—I held up my phone—"this happened and I'm freaking the fuck out because-because-because—"

"Calm down," she said. "First of all, Lauren will be there and she's physically incapable of being rude to people who aren't her husband."

"And second," Shannon continued, "Andy won't put up with any shit. If it gets weird, she'll shut it right down."

"It better not get weird," I said. "If it does, you won't get another taco from me."

"Paper towels to the rescue," Andy announced. From my sheltered view, I watched her booted feet move across my office and stop in front of my desk. "Don't stand there watching me, boys. Pick up those pens and pencils. Come on. No one is paying you to have a tea party this afternoon."

Grumbling, Matt, Sam, and Patrick set to collecting the spilled items from the floor. Patrick wanted to separate out the Chartpak from the Prismacolor markers, Matt wanted to get rid of the cheap mechanical pencils I preferred to his fancy ones, and Sam wanted to run antibacterial wipes over everything. I heard the perforated rip of the paper towels, soon followed by the soggy *thunk* as they landed in my wastebasket. Then my siblings decided to reorganize my desk.

Despite this commotion, Shannon was still beside me. "What's her nickname?" she asked.

"What?" I asked, my voice still raspy and raw.

"Her nickname," Shannon said. "You always find the perfect nicknames for the people you care about, so I'm just wondering what you chose for her."

Gastro Girl. Shortstop. Honeybee.

But that wasn't it. I couldn't force Alex into the narrow mold of a comic book heroine or fairy tale princess. She wasn't a handful of conveniently aligned characteristics. She was my Elektra, my Mystique, my Leia, my Katniss, my Daenerys, my Agent Carter, my Elizabeth Swann, my Arwen Evenstar, my Buffy, my Beatrice, my Catwoman, my Dorothy Gale, my everything, my...

"Aly," I said. "She's my Aly."

Twenty–Four
ALEXANDRA

I GLANCED at Erin again as we crossed the street. "Are you sure about this?" I asked.

She gave me a confident nod and mouthed "Definitely" as we darted around a throng of people headed for the Boylston Street T Station.

"You're supposed to say that," I continued when we fell in step together on the sidewalk. "They're your family."

She chuckled as she paused behind me, yielding to a woman pushing a double stroller. "I've never said what I was supposed to when it comes to my family," she said. "And believe me when I tell you that I'm more surprised than anyone to be getting a damn pedicure with Shannon and my sisters-in-law tonight."

Erin shot me a look, her gaze sharp and eyebrows lifted, that said *this is a big deal*. I knew from Nick that she'd had a fractured relationship with her siblings, and spent many years living overseas where she worked in field-based climate change research. He'd never shared the specifics, and my friendship with her was in its infancy, so I couldn't offer a response.

"Trust me," she continued. "I would be the first one to tell you if this was going to end badly. It won't."

There was something direct and unaffected about the way Erin spoke that made me believe her. "In other words, that text—"

"That text will get five minutes of intense discussion before something more interesting pops up," Erin said. "These girls get squirrely when the tequila starts flowing." She turned down a side street and gestured for me to follow. "Usually. Sometimes they talk about one ridiculous thing for two full hours, and that's why I keep a book and some science journals in my bag."

The spa was light and bright with white walls and sparkling chandeliers, and unlike the mani-pedi spots my mother favored back home, there was no cloud of chemicals hanging in the air. It smelled like…

"It's citrus," Erin said, grinning at me over her shoulder. "Nice, right?"

"Yeah," I said, surprised that I didn't hate everything. That was my approach to most things. "Listen, lady. I'm counting on you here. Don't let me go down in a 'So you guys take dirty pics?' fire. I'm not embarrassed but I'm not the kind of person who has detailed discussions of my sex life with people I just met. Or anyone for that matter. Okay?"

"Trust me," she repeated. "That isn't even the weirdest thing that will come up tonight. I heard they once debated the best lubes over lunch."

Erin explained to the receptionist that we were meeting up with a group, then snatched a bottle of polish from the display and marched into the spa. I grabbed the first red to catch my eye, and followed her.

"Shut up, they're here," someone whisper-yelled as we rounded a low wall. Seated there were four women with their leggings and trousers rolled up to their knees, and a pile of shoes and purses abandoned between them.

"It sounds like they hit the margaritas without us," Erin said under her breath.

After everything that had gone down with Steve, I was familiar with the feel of walking into rooms where people had been talking about me. This had none of the hostility of those moments, but it was still peculiar.

"Hi," I said. "I'm Alex." I offered a quick wrist-and-hand wave and a pointed grin toward Andy, the one with the miles of dark, curly, enviable hair and the shiny engagement ring. I could ice skate on that diamond.

The peculiarity only intensified when they stared at me, not saying a damn word, for the longest minute in recorded history.

Oh, my god. These people have seen me naked. Or part of me. And a whole lot of Riley.

Then the blonde spoke.

"One time, my husband forgot to give me the courtesy tap until it was too late," she said. "I mean, I'm a married woman. I only swallow on special occasions or when I'm too drunk to know better." She glanced to the pregnant redhead at her side, but she was busy shaking her head and rubbing her temples to notice. "By the time I understood what was happening and backed off, the situation had gotten away from me. I got a face full of spunk that night, and I had to walk around with an irritated eye for three days." She held out her hand in my direction. "I'm Lauren, by the way. I'm married to Matt."

I shuffled to her side and accepted her hand. Why not? I was certain she'd washed her hands since that episode and she was clearly trying to put me at ease.

"This is Shannon," Lauren said, gesturing to the redhead.

"I can't believe you told the whole eye splooge story before introducing yourself," Shannon—she looked just like Erin—said. "Honestly, Lo. You go around with your twee little dresses and creamsicle toes, and you pretend you're such a *nice* girl but you're a dirty, dirty bird."

Lauren replied with an angelic smile. "I believe you've mentioned this before."

Shannon turned a pointed glare toward Lauren's empty glass. "You're cut off. I wouldn't want you getting another splooge-related injury tonight."

Then she opened her arms in my direction and motioned for me to hug her. I went in for it, careful to steer clear of her belly. I knew better than to ask about the number of babies she was incubating in there or whether she was going to make it through the evening without giving birth, but I thought it. I also thought about smacking Riley with one of my tiny hands for not mentioning that I might be called upon to supervise a delivery tonight because she was extremely pregnant.

"I'm so happy you could come out with us tonight, but you shouldn't pay any attention to these girls," Shannon said into my ear. "They get mouthy when they're drunk."

"I'm only trying to illustrate that the text Riley sent wasn't that bad," Lauren argued. "We've all been there, or somewhere near there."

Erin tugged her socks off and pushed her glasses up her nose. "If y'all don't stop being weird, we're leaving."

"Isn't it adorable how she sounds more and more like Nick?" Lauren asked. "I love that *y'all*."

"I'm Tiel and I'm married to Sam. Riley lives at the firehouse with us," the woman on the far end said. "And you should know that Riley has seen all of us in some state of undress at one point or another." She roundly gestured at the group with her yellow margarita glass. "And he's walked in on us having sex so many times, we've lost count."

"Every single one of us," Andy said. "He's got a gift for it."

"Will broke Riley's nose when he walked in on us," Shannon said. "It hasn't happened since. Just saying."

"I love the kid, but he does not know how to knock," Tiel said.

"It's like there's a Bat Signal only Riley can see," Andy mused. "But instead of Gotham needing a hero, his siblings are having sex and he needs to interrupt."

"Right. That's great, and incredibly strange. To recap," Erin said, pointing at the women, "that's Lauren, Shannon, Andy, and Tiel." She steered me toward the pedicure chairs waiting for us. "This is Alex, and we're going to stop with the campfire stories until after she's had a few drinks. Riley will spill all the secrets he has on us if we're not nice to her."

"Nice to her?" Lauren repeated. "*Of course* we're going to be nice. You're the first woman Riley's ever introduced to us, and I don't take that lightly."

Shannon leaned forward to catch my eye. "I have just one question for you."

I ran my fingers through my hair and twisted it into a loose knot at the base of my neck. A technician was busy examining my toes, and there was a margarita waiting for me on the small side table. "Sure," I said, reaching for the beverage. It was delicious, and *strong*. "I won't even stop you at one. Go ahead and ask two, even three questions."

"Who's your Batman?" Shannon asked.

I set the glass down and rubbed my palms together as I considered this. "Well, that depends," I started, "Adam West and Michael Keaton when I need nostalgia. Clooney and Kilmer when I want the nineties and overacting. Affleck when I want to hate something. But for all other purposes, Bale."

The group was silent save for a giggle that slipped from Tiel's lips, and she slapped her hand over her mouth in response. Confused, I glanced back at Shannon and found her eyes glistening with tears.

"Satan suck a dick, I love you already," Shannon said through a laugh. "You should know we're loud and we swear a lot. And we're nosy, too. We're up in each other's business and we probably spend too much time together, but it's hard to find friends who can hold their tequila." She cocked her head, smiling despite the tears spilling down her cheeks. "I get the sense that you can. You're here, aren't you? After everything that happened today, I figure it takes a whole lot of balls to come out tonight and meet all of us."

"My balls *are* pretty big," I started, "but it's fine. I only had a minor role in that text message."

"Yep," Lauren said, holding her palm up to me for a high five. "You're one of us. Welcome to the tribe, sister."

"Oh my god," Shannon said to herself. "When did he grow up? Where was I when that happened?" She curled an arm around her belly and exhaled. The tears were still flowing. "Really. This is too much for a pregnant lady to handle on a Thursday evening."

"Are you all right?" I asked. I couldn't remember the last time I'd delivered a baby, and I didn't want to put those skills to the test tonight. "I apologize if this is too forward but are you experiencing regular contractions?"

"No contractions." Shannon waved me off. "I'm perfectly fine," she said. "I look twelve months pregnant but this kid isn't going anywhere for several weeks."

Small miracles.

Collecting my drink from the table, I lifted it to my lips and drank deeply.

"Alex, you should come to the farmers' market with us this weekend," Tiel called from the far end of the row.

Erin held up her hands for silence. "What did I say about letting her have a few drinks first?" she asked. "We're going to talk about something else now."

"*Yes*, the farmers' market," Shannon said with a hearty groan. "I could go for some Jam Man in my life. I don't know what it is about those red plaid flannel shirts and how he rolls the sleeves up. *Fuck*. Don't even get me started on those jeans."

"*Mrs. Halsted*," Erin chided, staring at her sister. "You are married *and* pregnant. You have to stop ogling strange men."

"I'm with Shannon when it comes to the Jam Man. This guy was put on earth to be ogled," Tiel said. "I'll offer neither shame nor apologies."

"Yeah, *Mrs. Acevedo*," Shannon said to Erin. "Maybe if you came to lunch once in a while, you'd be able to appreciate the Jam Man, too."

Erin leaned back in her seat and folded her hands in her

lap. "I'd rather appreciate my husband on Saturday mornings, thank you."

"Ignore her. My sister is still basking in semi-newlywed bliss," Shannon said to me. "There's a new guy at the farmers' market and he's—"

"So fucking hot that it hurts," Andy interrupted.

"And growly-sweet," Tiel added. "You'll get a cavity from talking to him, and then you'll go home and attack your husband."

"If you're not busy orgasming on the spot from his smile," Lauren said. "To be quite honest, I think I could ovulate just from looking at him."

"True story," Shannon said. "He owns a berry farm in"— she swiveled her head from side to side, her brows crinkled —"somewhere or other. He sells fruit, but his homemade jams are life-altering. I have a few jars in my office. Sometimes, when I've had a difficult day, I'll close the door and turn off the lights, and then daydream about red plaid flannel shirts while eating jam straight from the jar."

Erin groaned and turned her eyes toward the ceiling. "That makes Lauren's story about jizz in the eye sound nearly normal," she said.

"We don't have normal stories," Tiel replied. She elbowed Andy. "Tell them about the shower."

"I had a legitimate fight with Patrick about shower sex last weekend," Andy said.

"Like, legit how?" Lauren asked.

Andy held up her hands, gesturing toward her aggressively curly hair. "He thinks it's glorious and I think it's a pain in the ass because I don't wash my hair every day," she said. "I have a system, and it fucks up the system. So, we tried it where I leaned away from the water and out of the shower a bit, but I lost my balance and smacked my head against the wall. I was *so* irritable about the whole thing. I told him he was being selfish, and he pouted over that for an hour."

"Once upon a time, I got a black eye from shower sex," Erin said, but quickly shook her head as if remembering her vow to keep the conversation clean. "No, forget that. We're not comparing our weird sex stories tonight." She turned to me. "I'm sorry about this." ·

"You've already seen my weird sex story. *All* of you," I said, fighting a grin. "But I also removed forty-seven goldfish from a guy's stomach today. That was pretty weird, too."

Once again, all conversation stopped and the women turned curious stares in my direction. After a long moment of brow furrowing and lopsided frowning, Shannon said, "We're keeping you. Regardless of whether everything works out with Riley, you belong with us."

IT WAS LATE when Riley knocked on my door. He'd been beating himself up about that text message for hours, and it didn't seem to matter that I wasn't freaking out over the incident. Sure, it wasn't how I'd intended to introduce myself to his entire family or that I'd desperately hoped to keep our bedroom activities private, but they didn't seem to take any of it too seriously.

And we had bigger issues at hand. The matter of the *I love you* he dropped into a text came to mind.

I took him by the hand and led him straight to the bedroom. He undressed down to his boxers and curled his big body around mine, but didn't speak.

"Your sisters and sisters-in-law," I started after a long silence, "they're all so nice. They invited me to join them for brunch."

He shook his head against my back. "Don't let them fool you," he said. "They're little devil women. They do yoga and eat berries and cast crazy spells on their husbands."

"What are you talking about?" I asked, my body shaking with laughter.

"It's too late. They've already gotten to you," he said, sliding one hand under my shirt and the other into my panties. "They must've poisoned you with that potion of theirs."

His fingers were working my clit and nipple simultaneously, and I was certain an electric current connected the two because I was careening toward a hard, fast orgasm. "You mean the margaritas?"

"Yes, that's the one," he replied, kissing my neck. "Very dangerous."

"Are you drunk?" I asked, wiggling my ass against his erection.

"No, not at all," he replied softly. "What else did they say?"

"They mentioned you've walked in on all of them having sex," I said.

Riley blew out an enormous breath, as if his entire existence was deflating. "That is true," he said. "Unfortunate and psychologically devastating, but true." He hooked a thumb around my waistband and pulled my panties down. "Not that I've ever gone looking, mind you. These people have sex all over the damn place."

I slipped out of my t-shirt and tossed it to the floor. "They seemed to take the photo in stride," I said. "In fact, they offered up their own awkward and painful stories."

"I don't want to hear those," Riley said.

He levered up to kick his boxers off, and I reached for his cock the minute it was free. "I want you on top of me," I said, dragging my fist down his length. "I love the way you hold me down."

"That's the least I can I do," he murmured, climbing over me. "I love how you feel underneath me."

Kneeling between my legs with his erection jutting out from his body, he gazed at me, his lips parted as if he wanted to say something but couldn't get the words out.

Ah, there it is.

I sensed it all around us. The *I love you*. It was a living, breathing creature, doubling in size the longer we ignored it.

"No photos," Riley said, tapping the head of his cock against my clit.

"Not tonight," I agreed. I hooked my legs around his waist, urging him forward. He followed, filling me in one slow thrust. "But some other night."

"Fuck yes," Riley said through a growl. "Those pictures of you drive me fucking wild. I love everything about them. About *you*."

"I love them, too," I said, grasping for the headboard as he pumped faster. He leaned down, gathering my wrists in his hand, and pinned me in place. Everything else drifted away, and all that remained was the heat between us and the slow road we were taking to those three little words.

His free hand angled my legs wider and then slipped down to tease my folds. "I love your clit," he whispered. "It's my favorite place on your body."

"I love your cock," I said, scraping my nails down his back as I felt myself walking the edge of my orgasm.

"You should. There's a lot to love," he replied.

Then I was coming and laughing and clinging to him because "I love you," I murmured. "I *love* you, Riley."

"I love you, Aly," he replied, his voice heavy with laughter.

And that was it. That was our new arrangement.

Alex: My nips are sore.

Riley: Oh no. I'm sorry, Honeybee.

Alex: You know the expression "all bark and no bite"?

Riley: Yeah…

Alex: Your bark and bite are both remarkable.

Riley: Oh my fucking god. I'm so sorry.

Alex: You don't have to apologize. It was good. I'm just sore today. I feel like I need tiny ice packs in my bra.

Alex: Maybe cucumber slices or a little bag of frozen peas.

Riley: Would you like me to bring some to you?

Alex: I'm at the hospital.

Riley: I know.

Alex: You'd come here? With frozen peas?

Riley: Of course I would. I was the one biting your nipples. If you're going to be in pain as a result of something I did, I'm going to do whatever I fucking can to make you feel better.

Alex: But you hate hospitals.

Riley: I do but I love you.

Riley: Any chance you're free Thursday night?

Alex: What kind of "free" are we talking?

Riley: For some of our noteworthy properties, we have showcase events where trade publications, real estate agents, and vendors are invited to see the finished product. We have one coming up on Thursday.

Alex: Sounds like you're adding another date to our agreement.

Riley: Then you'll have to add one so it's fair.

Alex: Maybe we could go back to Rhode Island sometime. That inn, too. Do it all over. Without the whiskey.

Riley: Yes. Pick the weekend.

Alex: I'll do that.

Riley: But not that inn. I don't think they want to see us again.

Alex: Why not? We're delightful.

Riley: We are delightful, but when I was settling up, the owner mentioned that we'd been a little loud.

Alex: That's entirely possible.

Riley: The Dean Hotel would work. We'll drink at Magdalenae and then only have to drag ourselves up a few flights of stairs when you want to rip my clothes off.

Alex: I'll look at my schedule.

Riley: About Thursday…

Alex: Yeah. I'm on call but I can swap with someone if you want me to.

Riley: If it's not asking too much, yes. This event is…ugh. I'm dreading it, but you would make it tolerable.

Alex: Why is it ugh?

Riley: Long story short, it's our childhood home. We don't have great memories of the place but we do need to show up for this fire drill.

Alex: I see.

Riley: Yeah, so, I'd appreciate it if you could wear something distracting. Something that would make me drool over your ass.

Alex: I'll see what I can find.

ALEX NUDGED me with her elbow. "Are we fighting?"

"What?" I asked, glancing down at her as we bustled up the circular driveway at Wellesley. "What was that?"

I was in a shitty mood. Really shitty. And I didn't have a good reason for it, other than being marched at gunpoint to this event. I wanted to be anywhere but here, and that attitude was rolling off me in waves.

"I asked if we're fighting," she said. "You haven't grabbed my ass once tonight, and lately we're to the point where I think something's wrong if you're not fondling me."

I chuckled and slid my hand down her back. Her coat prevented me from getting in a good squeeze but the sentiment was there.

"Nothing's wrong," I said, shaking my head. "It's just this—this place." My gaze pinged around the roofline. "It's fucking haunted."

"What kind of haunted?" she asked. "There's the intriguing-charming variety—"

"Not that kind," I said under my breath.

"Then there's the creepy-nightmarish variety."

"Less creepy, more nightmare," I said, steering her away from the front steps and toward the side entrance. We weren't here for the bells and whistles tour, and hanging out in the kitchen—away from anyone who wanted to prattle on about the wonders of this house—was a suitable way to kill time. We arrived at the door and I paused there, my hand on the knob, and forced a smile. "Actually, it's not that bad. I just don't like being here."

A frown tugged at her lips. "Can I make it any better?"

There was no reason for us to be standing outside in this weather. It was too fucking cold for November, with a deep freeze expected overnight. But I leaned into her anyway, kissing her like she held my salvation.

"Just that," I said against her jaw. "That's all I need."

I pushed the door open, ushering her inside. Unsurprisingly, I wasn't the only one interested in hiding out. The majority of my siblings and their spouses were gathered around the kitchen table, picking at a tray of canapés and staring at their phones. The door banged shut behind us, and all eyes turned in our direction.

"Hey," I said, raising a hand in greeting. "Everyone, this is Alex. Alex, these are some hooligans."

Shannon bustled forward, arms outstretched, while I helped Alex out of her coat.

"Good to see you again," she said, pulling Alex into a hug. "Sit down. We have snacks over here. Will just went to get a round of drinks, too. There's a bar in the front living room if you want something else."

"Hi, Alex," Tiel called from the far end of the table. Sam, Matt, Nick, and Erin flanked her. "Have a seat. We need new —and less bitter—people to talk to."

We engaged in a round of greetings and nestled between Tiel and Shannon. I kept Alex close, almost in my lap.

"Lauren is joining us a little later," Shannon continued,

ignoring Tiel's comment. But it wasn't a snub. It was clear Shannon was doing everything in her power to keep this tribe in order. "Andy and Patrick are talking to real estate agents and reporters, and Tom's giving tours. He'll bring them through here soon enough so don't get too comfortable."

I rolled my eyes. "Great."

"We should've camped out in the pool house," Matt groused.

Or skipped this entirely.

Sam pointed at him, nodding. "You're absolutely right. No one's dragging their ass out back in this weather."

"By that line of reasoning, y'all shouldn't be trekking out there either." Nick tipped back his beer bottle and muttered to himself, "But I don't think y'all are working with reason tonight."

"It's getting really chilly out there. I bet we get some snow soon," Tiel said brightly, and that alone was enough to tear an unexpected chuckle from my throat. Tiel was a lot of rainbows and sunshine, but she wasn't one to invite herself into our dramas or take the lead on dragging us out of that drama. "Magnolia told me she was running around to all of her properties this afternoon and covering up delicate plants."

. "I can't believe you two are practically best friends now," Sam muttered. "Just add that to the list of unbelievable things I'm dealing with today."

"We're settled here now," Shannon said firmly. "Let's not make it more complicated than it already is."

"I don't think it's complicated, Shannon," Sam replied. "I think it's very simple. We picked the wrong spot to congregate."

"The Red Hat would've reserved a table for us," I offered. "At least then we would've been able to catch the game."

Erin leaned back in her chair, her arms crossed over her chest and a scowl on her face. "Can we go yet?" she asked. "What is the point of us being here right now?"

"What she said," Matt added.

"We're here for Andy," Tiel said gently.

"Right," Shannon said. "And we're meeting after the real estate agents give Tom some feedback."

"I fucking hate meetings," Sam grumbled, patting his chest. "I feel unwell in this house. I think I'm contracting some type of virus that sucks the joy out of my soul. If I stay here much longer, I'll never be cheerful again."

"You were never cheerful to begin with," Erin said.

I shifted away from the stress-bickering, toward Alex, and pressed my lips to her cheek. Her eyes closed and she smiled, fumbling under the table for my hand. When she found it, she squeezed.

"What can I get you, Honeybee?" I whispered to her skin.

She brought her palm to my chest, resting it on my tie as she said, "Vodka cranberry, but I like these shoes. I don't want to see them wet and sticky, okay?"

"I can't imagine what you're referring to," I said. She laughed, and that sound lightened the weight in my chest. "Do you want to come with me to the bar or are you brave enough to hang out with this crew?"

"They don't scare me," she whispered, her eyes sparkling with amusement. "If all else fails, I can show them pictures of some really gnarly gallstones."

"Careful with the pictures," I warned. "These people, they'll swipe right and they'll swipe left. They don't respect unspoken photo album laws."

The warm burst of her laugh hit my neck, and I kissed her temple. "You say that as if they haven't already seen a few from our private stock."

"Yeah. Thanks for reminding me," I said. "Maybe you should just come along. You can hold your own damn drink, and then I'll show you the secret passageways."

Alex tugged her bottom lip between her teeth. "I wouldn't mind that either."

I glanced back at the table, ready to make a run for it, and found everyone staring at us. "What?"

"*Ohhh*. I'm just so happy," Shannon said. She blinked, and though I couldn't be certain, it looked like there were tears in her eyes. Actual fucking tears. "This is great."

"Seeing you," Tiel clarified with a sappy smile. "Both of you. Here. Together."

"I didn't interpret this as an optional event," I said.

"That's because it's not fucking optional," Sam snapped.

"I believe she's trying to say that it's nice to see this," Nick said, drawing an invisible circle around me and Alex. "You're welcome, by the way."

Alex ducked her head as she stifled a laugh. "Acevedo is right more often than he's not."

"Don't say that," Erin protested. "I'll never hear the end of it."

I stood, holding my hand out to Alex. "We're going to take advantage of the free liquor," I announced. "Good luck with the rest of your bitching and moaning."

I couldn't stay in here with the doom and gloom squad. The tension was already pulling my neck and shoulders tight, and I didn't trust myself to bite my tongue much longer. I hated this as much as they did but I didn't have the capacity to discuss it. I rarely talked about my father or any of the fucking awful things he did to us, and that approach worked for me. I didn't need to commiserate or vent or anything. I just needed to get the fuck out of here.

I pulled Alex out of the kitchen and backed her against the wall, crushing my lips to hers the moment we were out of my siblings' line of sight.

"I feel like," I started, my kisses quick and biting, "like I'm coming apart at the seams."

"What do you want?" she whispered. "Just tell me. Whatever it is, we'll do it."

"I don't know," I admitted, resting my forehead against hers.

"Are there actually secret passageways in this house?" she asked. I nodded, my lips busy mapping her cheeks and jaw. "I want to see. Maybe we can find a fun spot for some naughty photos."

"No," I hissed. "Not here. I can't touch you here and feel right about it."

Alex's hands smoothed down my chest and she edged me back. "Okay. We'll get a drink and then see a secret passageway. It'll be an adventure." She wiggled her tiny purse, the one she wore around her wrist, at me. "If an early exit is needed, I can always get an emergency call from the hospital."

"I'd love an emergency call from the hospital," I said, hooking my arm around her shoulders as we walked down the hallway. "Something gory. Liver stones or enlarged intestines or something like that."

"None of those things are happening tonight," she laughed. "Post-op complications are more likely, and they're also real."

Will rounded the corner, his hands filled with drinks and

his smile genuine. "RISD," he called. "How's it going, my man?"

"Can't complain too much," I replied. "Alex, this is Will Halsted. He jumped on the grenade and married Shannon. Will, this is Alex Emmerling."

"Someone had to do it," he said, laughing. "And look—Alex is jumping on the grenade for you tonight."

"Isn't that the truth," I mumbled.

Will smiled at her, and asked, "What's your call sign, Alex?"

"My what?" she asked, her brows knitting.

"Your nickname," I replied. "It's Shortstop. That's one of them."

"I like it," Will said, grinning at her. "If you'll excuse me, I have to deliver these beverages."

"You never did explain that one to me," she murmured as Will headed back to the kitchen. "Shortstop. I assume it's at least somewhat complimentary but I don't understand the dynamics of baseball enough to really make sense of it."

"Hang on a second," I said, leaving Alex by the main staircase while I approached the bar. Making eye contact with the bartender, I dropped a twenty behind the ice bucket and grabbed two uncorked bottles of wine. "Have a good night, man."

"Same to you, sir," he replied.

When I returned to Alex, I gestured with the bottle for her to follow me upstairs. "Basically, the shortstop covers second base on the third base side, and often sticks close to third because right-handed batters tend to drive the ball down that line. But they're also responsible for covering second in double play situations, and when a runner is stealing the bases in left-handed batting situations."

"Yeah," Alex said when we reached the landing. "Of course. That clears it all up."

"The shortstop is the most skilled, agile defensive player on the field," I continued. "It's a difficult position to play and play *well*. They aren't usually strong hitters so they don't make headlines and they rarely get any credit for the wins, but they're still responsible for covering the most ground and knowing all the moves before anyone else."

"Hmm. Okay, then."

Alex followed me down the hall and around the corner without further comment, which meant she'd probably missed my point. I firmly believed that understanding something meant being able to explain it, and I'd fucked that up.

"In here," I said, stepping into the last doorway on this floor.

I handed her the wine and then went to work on the window seat. The house was loaded with picture-perfect furnishings for this event, and that meant removing a pile of cushions and pillows before I could access the levers.

"Old homes often have oddities like this," I said. "Hidden staircases, secret rooms, false doors. All kinds of strange things. But they also have typical things that seem strange because they're uncommon these days. Dumbwaiters, laundry chutes, little pass-through spaces between the interior and exterior for delivery of bottled milk, coal, firewood." The window seat popped open, revealing a ladder that led down to a dark corridor. It also brought a blast of cold, stale air and a cloud of dust. "This house has all of the above, and this"—I beckoned Alex closer—"is a passageway to the attic."

She stared inside, her brows arched. "You go down to get up? Is this a 'lift to lower' situation?"

"I never claimed it was logical," I said, peering at her

shoes. Those fancy heels weren't right for wooden rungs. "I've climbed down this ladder, around the chimney, and up the stairs to the attic more times than I can count, but I don't think you're dressed for that, Honeybee. The attic's great but I think we'll skip it."

"What makes it so special?" she asked.

"No one else went up there. I was free to do whatever the fuck I wanted and no one was the wiser. Or, instead of going to the attic, I'd follow the other passages into the basement. I could sneak in and out of the house from down there. I did that a lot," I mused. "Altogether, I probably spent more time *pretending* to be holed up in here than anything else."

Alex swung her gaze from side to side, swallowing up the room in one quick glance. "This was your room?"

With a firm shove, the window seat snapped shut. I tossed the decorative pillows back but didn't bother to arrange them. They were going to be boxed up and shipped off to a warehouse within a matter of days, and I refused to believe that the positioning of a pillow was critical to selling this house.

"It was," I said, my eyes trained on the floor.

"I'm trying to imagine you as a kid but I can't get there. I don't know how to shrink all this"—she circled her hand at me—"into a small, innocent package."

"Not sure I was ever innocent," I said, chuckling.

"Maybe you weren't." Alex walked the length of the room, trailing her fingers over the restored plaster. "Did you have a lot of girlfriends in high school? Is that why you snuck out all the time?"

"Not really," I said, scratching my neck. I had an idea where this was going, and I didn't like it. Growing up in the Walsh home was a lot like Fight Club. You didn't talk about it unless you wanted things to get ugly. "I was pretty fucked up back then. I liked weed, sandwiches, comic books, and football. In that order. I didn't have a lot of leftover brain space for the high school dating scene."

She glanced at me, smirking. "Really? You're trying to tell me *you*"—her gaze ran up and down my body—"were celibate?"

I stood, shoving my hands in my pockets, and shrugged. "I didn't say that."

"Didn't think so." Alex stared out the window for a long moment. "What about college?" she asked, not looking back at me. "What about Dorrance?"

"What about her?" I snapped, all the stress and frustration of this ridiculous night combining in three angry words.

"I'm curious," she said easily, like I didn't just bite off her head. "It seemed like things were serious with her. I'm just wondering what happened."

"Alex. Honeybee. I love you but this has to stop," I said, my hands shaking with agitation. "I don't poke and prod at you about the douche waffle all damn day, now do I?"

She reared back as my words hit her like a physical blow. "No, but—"

"That's right, I don't," I said darkly. "I know he screwed you over and left you doubting every-fucking-thing when it comes to relationships but I don't bring it up. It's you and me, Alex. Not you, me, and fucking Steve."

She shook her head as she stepped toward me, her lips parted. "Riley, I was just asking—"

"I know what you're asking and here's your answer," I hissed. "I'm not in love with Dorrance. I don't have any residual feelings for her, nothing more than basic nostalgia. It's over, I'm happy it's over, and I don't think about her. I want the best for her, of course, but I don't love her. I *never* loved her."

"Then why…" Alex's voice trailed off and she tipped her head to the side, confused. "Why did you need me to go to RISD Weekend with you?"

"Because she refuses to recognize that I ended things with her," I shouted. "And because I'm a dumb fool and I can't help but get caught up in her crazy art schemes and pumpkin patch hops, I needed a fake girlfriend to play some offense for me."

"You're…you don't have feelings for her?" Alex asked.

"Not at all," I yelled. "She was a million fucking years ago. I don't even know who I was back then, and I'm sure as shit not that guy now." I strode toward Alex but she held up her hands, warning me off. "I'm not even the same guy I was four months ago."

She shook her head, staring at the floor as she backed away from me. "I don't understand," she whispered. Her eyes were hooded and her hands were quivering, and I didn't know how to stop what I'd started. I shouldn't have said anything. "I don't understand. You've been… there was *someone*. I know it. If it's not Dorrance, who is it?"

"Alex. Let it go." I pressed the heels of my palms to my eyes and paced to the opposite side of the room. "You have nothing to worry about."

"Hey, Riley," Lauren drawled from the doorway. My entire body swiveled toward her, and I gazed, pleading for something. Anything. I couldn't decide whether to forcefully escort her from the room or beg her to stay and create a diversion. "Just the man I was looking for. Can I get a minute with you while everyone else is occupied?" Lauren stepped into the room and caught sight of Alex. "Hi, Alex. Didn't see you over there."

"Not a good t-t-t-t-time, Miss Honey."

She glanced between me and Alex, and then nodded to herself as she recognized she'd walked into a heavy conversation. To her credit, her bright smile never faltered. "I'll text you later," she said, pulling the door shut behind her.

I stared after her, digging deep to find a solution. I couldn't fuck this problem away and I probably couldn't feed it either. That left me with words, and I'd never been good with those.

Alex's eyes swung from the closed door to me, her lips parted. "It's her," she said. "It's always been her, hasn't it?"

I tried to deny it but my tongue wouldn't betray the old, hardened scars on my heart by forming the words. "Yes."

Twenty–Six

ALEXANDRA

I'D ALMOST MISSED IT. The tender, needy way Riley's eyes drank her in. The imperceptible lean in her direction. The smile that was more than familiar. And I'd almost missed it.

But instead of swerving to avoid hitting a stalled car, I plowed right into it.

It wasn't Dorrance. Of course it wasn't Dorrance. But he'd been wading through something, something that seemed impossible to him. But nothing was impossible for Riley. He was brilliantly creative, attractive and funny, and had a family who adored him. And yet there'd been *something*.

"Hi, Alex," she said, all smiles and joy. "Didn't see you over there."

Riley shook his head, his eyes still glued to her. "Not a good t-t-t-t-time, Miss Honey."

"I'll text you later," she said.

Riley watched her go, gazing after her like she was—the one. It was her. Lauren. The one with the awkwardly comforting stories of blow jobs gone bad. The one with the husband.

"It's her," I said. "It's always been her, hasn't it?"

"Yes."

And she wanted time *alone* with him.

And he had a *nickname* for her.

And I was silly and stupid, and too desperate for affection to know better. It was her. It had always been her. The one Riley had been pining over all these months.

Oh. Oh Jesus, oh fuck. I had to leave. Collect the tattered edges of my dignity and go. *I should've known. I should've known.*

There was something wrong with me. Something really fucking wrong. A blind spot in my consciousness, an error in my intuition, a weak link in the evolutionary chain. There was no other explanation for repeatedly being the woman men used for ladder-climbing and appearances. The perennial second choice.

"But-but-but-but," Riley stuttered.

His face twisted in frustration and his hands fisted, and I resented that my first instinct was to soothe him. Sweep my fingers over his cheeks and erase the blush blooming there. Needing distance, I paced away from him, to the other side of the room. "So, what then? When is she leaving her husband?"

He loosened his tie and wrenched his collar open. "That's not how it is, Alex," he snapped. "She doesn't even know."

It wasn't hard to imagine Riley and Lauren together. She was peach pie, the best parts of sweetness and summer and serenity in one curvy package. She'd indulge his need for fun and adventure, and he'd build an altar to worship her. They'd have adorable children with her sunny blonde hair and his easy smile, and they'd wrap those babies up with love like satin ribbons.

My hands flailed at my sides as that ribbon slipped away from me. Was it ever mine? Probably not. I wasn't peach pie, and I wasn't the kind of woman who anyone worshipped.

"Great. Awesome. I love it when people have long-running affairs. How long has it been now?"

"That's not what I meant," he roared, whipping the tie from his collar. The silk snapped, feeding the electricity between us. "She doesn't know anything. She doesn't know that I have feelings for her. *Had*. Motherfuck. *Had* feelings for her."

I turned around, forcing his words to meet my back rather than allowing him to see my trembling lips. I was not crying tonight.

He had feelings—*fucking feelings*—for her. Without question, there wasn't room in my heart to love Riley *and* another man. I knew it to be a fundamental truth, and one he obviously didn't share. And I knew that I deserved more than scraps. I'd never considered his affection to be anything less than complete but I'd also missed the part about him wanting another woman. My emotions weren't to be trusted here.

But…I *had* known. I'd known right away. He was a player man-child, and he wanted someone else. She'd been there all along.

"Alex, please," Riley said. He was right behind me, his body warm and calling to mine. It required real effort to lean away from him. "I'm fucking this all up. I need to start over. Please let me explain."

There was nothing wrong with my intuition. My judgment was the issue here. I'd known the facts, at their most basic, from the start. I'd simply chosen to overlook them. And wasn't that my way? Ignoring the obvious until it was kicking me out of my own bed?

"There's nothing to explain," I said, stepping away to put space between us. I ran my fingers over the bed's crisp white coverlet. "If you'd like to do something helpful, you could take me home now. If you're not angling for time with Lauren, that is."

"God*damn* it, Alexandra," he snapped. "Would you fucking listen to me?"

"I will not," I said, reaching for a small pillow. I held it to my belly, an inadequate shield against this assault. "We had an arrangement, and I believe the terms have been fulfilled. I'll just order a car service. Good luck breaking up your brother's marriage."

It was harsh, but so was watching your boyfriend's heart leap out of his chest and chase after a pretty blonde lollipop. I set the pillow back on the bed and turned to leave, but Riley came up behind me. He flattened his hand on the door, effectively locking us in.

"Let's get a couple things straight," he said, pressing his chest to my back. "First, you're not going anywhere until you hear the truth, not the cocked-up version you've decided on." I rolled my eyes, but with my back to him, it went unnoticed. "Second, you're the only one I want. You know that, Aly. I know you do."

"Say what you need to say." I crossed my arms, needing any layer of protection I could find, but it only pushed me back, into the cocoon of Riley's body. "But spare me the gory parts. I don't show you the inflamed bowels, and I'd appreciate it if you didn't mention your deep and infinite love for Lauren."

"I don't love her," he said. I almost believed it, too. But then he added, "Not anymore."

I'd never been in love before. There'd been plenty of love-like lust in college but Riley was my first. My only. And I knew that it couldn't be turned on and off. It was a presence; one I couldn't cast away even when I wanted it gone.

Like, right now.

"When did you arrive at that conclusion?" I asked.

He exhaled, and his breath danced over the nape of my neck. He was *right there*, and if I leaned back just a bit, I'd be in his arms. I could take my place as his second choice, the consolation prize, and ignore every glimmer of doubt. A shiver rippled through my body like a warning shot.

Don't do it. Don't be the alternative.

"Honestly, I don't know," he said. "Maybe I've always known. It was never...I was never going to act on it. Fuck, *no*. I'd thought about it plenty of times—"

"Gory details," I warned.

"I thought I loved her. I'd spent all this time feeling that way, but then—then, there was you. And the love I have with you, it's everything. It's big and messy and real." He roped one arm around my waist—the other still holding the door shut—and dropped his forehead to my shoulder. "You changed everything, Aly. You're the only one I want. I swear to you. On my mother's grave—on my life—I swear you're the only one. "

"You're not ready," I said, almost to myself. "I'm not going to be the runner-up. I've done that my entire life, and I'm not doing it with you."

"Aly, please believe me," he begged. "You're my first and only choice."

"You're not ready," I repeated, my chest aching with every

word. The only thing separating us from a night of promises and make-up sex was the wobbly knowledge that I wasn't the first choice. That even if Riley had no intention of pursuing Lauren, he'd long ago carved out a special place for her. Who could compete with that? And why would I choose to compete?

"I saw it for myself. She's the one you wanted to be the one, and you're not ready to let her go."

"Alex," he protested. "You're wrong about that."

"I know you believe I'm wrong, but I can't stick around while you fall out of love with her," I said.

Oh *fuck*, those words hurt.

"Fucking hell, Alex. Don't say that," he said. "Just don't say that. Everything that happened before us is just that— before. None of it matters."

Even an hour ago, that declaration would've closed the deal. Riley could've put the story of his last-season love for her on the table, and I would've believed him when he said it was a thing of the past. An affection now gathering dust on the shelf alongside youth soccer trophies and the Brothers of Sigma Alpha Epsilon Founder's Day Celebration mug.

More than that, I would've understood. I would've accepted it as a chapter of his life before we'd met, and set it aside along with thoughts of the women who'd shared his bed before me. But stumbling across the truth like this upended everything.

"I'm leaving now," I said, prying his fingers from my waist.

"Not without me you're not," Riley said, his words loaded with heat. "We're not finished with this conversation."

I'd held my emotions in check for too long. I didn't have

the strength to argue with Riley about whether there was more to say *and* walk out of this house without bursting into tears. So, I replied with a jerky shrug and brought my hand to the knob. A heavy moment passed before he released his hold on the door.

The house was a maze of doors and staircases—I was on the short road to distraught—and couldn't remember where I was going when we exited the bedroom. Riley reached out, grabbing my elbow, and steered me to the main hallway. When we reached the foyer, he hooked a thumb over his shoulder, toward the back of the house.

"I need to let everyone know we're heading out," he said. "Come on."

I hated the slow, deliberate way he was forming each word. I hated that he was as devastated as I was right now and working just as hard to keep it together.

Riley didn't wait for me to agree, instead leading me through the first floor and into the kitchen. His siblings and Andy were gathered there, seated around the table. In the adjoining family room, their significant others were scattered on sofas. All eyes snapped to us as we appeared.

"Finally," Shannon said, waving Riley to the table. "We're reviewing the feedback we received from the agents who came through, and deciding what we want to—"

"Burn it down?" he interrupted. "Leave the doors and windows open all winter and hope nature does its worst?"

"No and no," Andy said, her arms outstretched as if she was holding brawlers at bay. "The options are sell it or keep it."

"We're selling," Riley snapped. "There's never been a question about that, so why do we keep asking?"

"It's a big decision," Sam said grudgingly. "It deserves a thorough discussion."

"Sam's right," Matt said, his head braced between his hands.

"Are you sure? Because none of us want to be here right now," Riley argued. "And the worst part is that we might be able to go home tonight, but we can never leave this place." His gaze traveled over each of his siblings. "You think some paint changes that? Maybe refinished floors, new pipes, a few solar panels? Clean up the landscaping and chase away the evil living in the walls?"

"Let's not do this, Riley," Shannon said softly. She brought her hands to her belly, rubbing. "We're not digging up the dead tonight."

"I'd really like this to be over," Erin said.

"You know what's amazing?" Riley continued. "That we lived. That we can walk the fuck away from this house and never look back." He leaned forward and tapped the papers on the table. "It's time to walk the fuck away and stay away."

The table fell silent, and I was immediately aware that I didn't belong here. This was a family meeting. At the minimum, I belonged on the other side of the room with Tiel, Will, Nick, and...*her*. Lauren. She was cooing over baby pictures on Tiel's phone, and as much as I tried, I couldn't find it in me to resent her.

I saw it. I saw all the things Riley loved about her. Everything about her was feminine and pretty, and sweet and adorable. She'd baby him and he'd love it. I wasn't maternal and I couldn't pull off sweet with ten pounds of sugar, and I wasn't about to be any of that. And he didn't *want* that. Not really.

And I couldn't be the backup. I had to draw the line

somewhere, and if it wasn't at the hospital or with my family, it was going to be with here, with Riley.

Eventually, Patrick said, "Riley's right. It's time to end this discussion." He reached for a packet and flipped through the pages, stopping periodically to scribble his signature. Looking up, he held the packet out to Shannon. "You know he's right."

From the corner of my eye, I saw Will approaching. He stopped behind Shannon's chair, his hands resting on her shoulders.

"It's okay, peanut," he said. "You don't have to make any decisions tonight. Let's get you home. It can wait until tomorrow."

"It's fine," she replied, accepting the papers. She took care to check the details on each page before moving onto the next, and she held her pen above the signature line for a long moment. She shifted her gaze from the document to Matt, pointing her pen at him. "Is this what you want? Selling? Or do you want to keep the house in the family? It's all we have left."

"The thing is," Riley started, "you'll wake up one day and you'll realize that whatever you were clinging to is gone. The nice parts of our history, the happy memories…you'll keep those. But everything you've wanted to believe about this place, all the impossibilities and awfulness that you have to set aside, it will be gone. And that's when you'll realize you didn't truly want it. You wanted to believe it could be yours in a way that it never truly was, and it will be okay. You'll realize that everything you have isn't what you thought you wanted, but it's what you need. This house isn't what we need."

He glanced at me, a not-so-subtle hint that this speech

wasn't just about the house, but everything we'd discussed tonight.

"Somehow, that makes complete sense." Matt held out his palm and then slapped it on the table. "I have no interest in living here. It's difficult to imagine anyone else living here, but I don't even want to be here right now. There's no way in hell I could move in."

Shannon stabbed her pen toward Sam. "You. What's your vote?"

Sam tugged at his cuffs and twisted his wedding ring before meeting her gaze. "There's nothing in this house for me," he said. "The good times, the memories of Mom...I don't need to be here to hold onto them."

Shannon shifted in her seat to face Erin. "I know how you're leaning," she said. "But I need to hear you say it."

"Sell," Erin replied. "Accept the first offer you get."

"Then we're in agreement," Shannon said. With a heavy exhale, she brought her pen to the page.

"And we're leaving," Riley announced as he retreated from the kitchen.

His hand was still wrapped around my elbow, but I didn't shake him off. It seemed that he needed something to keep him grounded, and nothing I'd heard tonight killed my feelings for him. I was hurt and angry, and stinging with betrayal, but I still loved him.

We walked to his SUV in silence. Riley held the passenger door open for me, and waited until I was seated to round the vehicle. The roads were clear and the drive back to the city was quick, leaving no room for another round of discussion. And that was a blessing. Perhaps there was more to be said, but giving voice to those thoughts wasn't closing the gaps between us tonight. Our positions hadn't shifted since leaving that bedroom, even with everything he'd said about the house—and by extension, himself.

When Riley pulled up in front of my building, I paused, my fingers curled around the handle. "Riley—"

"Alex," he said, dragging his gaze from the street to me.

I nodded as my heart caught hold of this simple sentiment. "I know," I said, willing the sob out of my words. "But I think it would be best if we spend some time apart."

I pushed the door open and stepped out, and then risked everything by glancing back at Riley. He made no attempt to follow me onto the curb, and I imagined that was a good thing. I couldn't say no when he was close and touching me.

I climbed the steps and then glanced back at him once more. He was shattered, but if it was possible, I didn't think anything he was experiencing hurt more than the pain of walking away.

"I know you don't think I'm ready now, but the next time you see me, Alexandra," he called, his words anchoring me at the front door, "I will be."

The knob was cold under my fingers and I stared at it for a moment. Going upstairs alone would be difficult. Stripping off my dress and falling asleep without him close in my bed would be even harder. But I didn't see any other way. I required space to sort this out, and I couldn't have it with Riley right there, insisting he didn't want her anymore.

Pushing the door open, I called over my shoulder, "Be sure."

Twenty—Seven

ALEXANDRA

Riley: I know you don't want to hear from me right now but if you need anything, I'll be there for you.
Riley: Tacos, dragon noodles, cannoli, anything.
Riley: I walked by your building and your lights are on. Can I come up? Can we talk?
Riley: I just want to know if you're okay.
Riley: I know you're seeing this.
Riley: Aly…please.

"THIS SUCKS," Cal grumbled as I unpacked the take-out containers. "Really fucking sucks."

I glanced around the lounge, looking for the source of his annoyance. Not finding one and not capable of thinking beyond basic tasks, I went back to sorting the food. I wasn't sure whether this meal qualified as lunch, dinner, or an early breakfast. The clock was pushing two in the morning, and we'd been in and out of surgeries since the morning. *Yesterday* morning. I was exhausted, certain I was about to waste away from starvation, and in desperate need of a shower.

Oh, and I couldn't forget the part about being a heart-broken wreck. There was no escaping that reality, and I'd tried. I'd spent the weekend picking up shifts in the Emergency Department and assisting on any surgery where an experienced pair of hands had been helpful. The weekend had turned into a new week, and I still hadn't left the hospital.

Why should I? Everything I required was here. An unending supply of clean scrubs. Suitably distracting work. Decent on-call rooms. Interns willing to pick up food at any hour of the night.

There was one more perk: a complete shortage of men by the name of Walsh.

I couldn't walk away from my memories of him, but at least the hospital didn't make those memories more vivid. My apartment, on the other hand, was nothing but Riley. If things didn't improve, I was going to have to abandon the place and everything in it.

"I take it you're not talking about these sandwiches," I said, pushing one in his direction.

He rubbed his brows and heaved out a sigh. Earlier in the day, before a string of traumas and critical patient transfers upended our schedules, he'd mentioned problems with his silent pursuit of the woman at the park. The one he adored but hadn't yet approached.

"She was walking with someone this morning," he said. "A guy."

"Why is that a problem? They could be friends," I said,

gesturing with the aid of a limp french fry. "We're having dinner together but we're not *together*."

"They looked *together*." He popped the plastic container open and reached for his sandwich. "She touched him a few times, too. A hand on his arm. Bumping her shoulder into his. That kind of thing."

"Still don't think it means all is lost," I said.

I couldn't decide whether I was instilling hope in Hartshorn because I wanted things to work out with his friend at the park or because I wanted to believe *anything* could work out.

I yanked the toothpicks from my turkey club and dove in. This was the perfect meal after nineteen hours of surgery. That extra layer of bread in the middle did it, and the bacon always came to my rescue. Everything worked out when bacon was involved.

"He's totally wrong for her," Cal continued. "And will someone please tell me when grown men started resembling fourteen-year-old boys? With their flippy hair and slim-fit chinos?"

I tipped my head to the side and stared at my sandwich as I considered this. "I've never heard anyone other than my father call them chinos," I said.

Oh, right. My parents were still coming to town this weekend. I'd dodged their calls and replied to their texts with vague promises to see them but the last—the actual last —thing I needed was an evening filled with stories about my amazing twin brother. I doubted the reverse was true for Adam, but my parents only talked about him in my presence.

His beautiful home, the one he'd built with his bare

hands. He'd even pried rocks straight out of the river—or some nonsense like that—for that fireplace.

His amazing work at the dealership, and the record number of cars sold every single fucking month.

His lovely wife and her lovely book club, her lovely cooking, her lovely knitting, her lovely garden. Even her bleached asshole was lovely. Or so I assumed.

How they were *trying* for a baby. Trying, trying, trying. All that trying, and all the mess that went with it. Just because I was a doctor didn't mean I wanted to hear about my sister-in-law's cervical mucus or my brother's sperm count.

And if all of that wasn't bad enough, I'd repeatedly promised they'd meet Riley. I'd told them all about my architect boyfriend and our adventures in Boston, and I'd told them how much they'd love him. Just like I did.

"You're a real help, Emmerling," he snapped. "Thanks for calling me old."

"Not suggesting anything of the sort," I replied. "Just saying that most people don't call them *chinos*."

"She needs a real man. None of those flimsy boys who can't grow a beard without making a Pinterest board first." He grumbled something indecipherable at his sandwich. "Someone who can take her over the knee and teach her—"

"All right," I interrupted. "Let's just simmer down there. I'm not ready to travel *that* road with you, Hartshorn. The 'take her over the knee' road. Okay?"

"Fair enough," he murmured. "But she does need a real man. I know it."

"Then you should act like a real man and get your ass back to that park," I said, plucking a flavorless tomato out from under the bread. "And for fuck's sake, *talk to her*."

Cal nodded, and *we* ate in silence for several minutes. "If I talk to her, you should talk to Riley," he said eventually.

Motherfuck. He wouldn't leave it alone. I'd dumped the whole sordid story of Riley and his sister-in-law on Cal's lap Sunday night. He'd been surprised by it all, but struggled to see it the same way I did. Something about not understanding why I would've wanted Riley to confess his feelings for Lauren earlier in the game. That I would've used that information to immediately disqualify him and break things off.

Cal was right about the last point, but I didn't trouble him with that information. He'd also been dropping not-so-subtle suggestions about me answering one of Riley's texts. I wasn't doing that either.

I wiped my hands on my thighs and loosened my tied-and-retied bun. My hair was tangled and in desperate need of washing, and I devoted entire minutes to dragging my fingers through the slightly oily strands.

"You talking to the girl at the park is considerably easier than things with me and Riley."

"What if I introduce myself and we hit it off, and everything is marvelous until I find out she has an old crush on the other guy? The one with the flippy hair," he clarified. "What do I do then? Do I put her out like yesterday's news? Or do I accept that her life didn't start when she met me, and therefore she has experiences and relationships that have absolutely no bearing on me or *us*?"

After all these years of living in this skin, I knew my soft spots. I knew that I *always* wanted to be the best, the first, the favorite, the most. Whatever it was, I wanted to be it. It came from never being *it* when I was a kid, and then never being able to claw my way into the top spot as I grew up. College, med school, residency—I was always a few steps short of where I wanted to be. I woke up and fought harder every day because I was going to get there eventually, but I couldn't do the same with my heart. Not again.

I scooped my hair into a ponytail before responding. "I guess it all depends on whether you believe she's ready to move on from that crush or she'll hold out hope—even a tiny glimmer—that the flippy hair guy—who turns out to be her brother-in-law—will want her someday." I held up my hands and let them fall. "Could you live with that? Wondering whether you're her first choice every time she looks at him over the sweet potato casserole at family gatherings?"

"I don't think so," Cal said. "I don't think I could do that."

"Neither can I," I replied. I forced a smile. "But you should still talk to her. Maybe she doesn't like chinos or flippy hair that much, but you'll never know if you never ask."

Cal scoffed, nodding. "And maybe Riley's really done with the sister-in-law," he countered. "You'll never know if you don't listen."

"Maybe you're right," I said, rubbing my fingers over my brows. And it was possible. But I was too exhausted and broken to see from that perspective.

The one thing I knew to be true was that I needed to be loved all the way through. I wasn't accepting anything less.

Twenty-Eight

RILEY

PATRICK KNOCKED on my open office door and poked his head inside. "We're talking through the North End project, right?"

I glanced up from the laptop screen I'd been staring at without seeing. "Yeah. Sure," I replied. "Whatever you want."

He nodded to himself. "I'll grab Andy, and we'll get started in a few," he said. "Hey, one more thing. Can you tell me about that RISD student, Trevor?"

"Huh-who?" I asked, rubbing my temples. This fucking headache had been trailing me for days. Nothing seemed to chase it off, and I was damn close to asking Nick to examine my head. That would be some comedy.

"Trevor," Patrick repeated. "I don't remember his last name, but the email you forwarded said you'd met him when you were down in Providence for RISD Weekend."

"Yeah," I muttered. "What about him?"

"I like him," Patrick replied. "I think we'll invite him up for an interview. Presuming he's half as good as his portfolio suggests, you might have an apprentice this summer."

"Delightful," I replied. "Talk to me when it's done. Until then, *vaya con dios*."

I turned back to the screen, not trusting myself to look at anything else without devolving into a drooling pile of useless skin and bone. I thought I'd known shambles but this, this was true and total disaster. I couldn't breathe around it, couldn't find up or down. I wasn't sure I remembered how to put one foot in front of the other.

Eight days. That was how long it had been since Alex walked into her apartment and out of my life. Every one of those days felt like cold, screeching eternities. Forevers enclosed within colorless mornings and darker nights. There was no reprieve. Nothing eased the ache of this, of knowing I'd hurt Alex and ruined everything we'd created.

I'd put one thousand miles on my car this past weekend, aimlessly driving highways and back roads until I couldn't focus any longer. I'd gone in search of anything—distraction, nostalgia, an antidote to my self-inflicted agony. But none of it materialized.

My usual haunts offered no solace. The sports bars, Rhode Island, comic book stores. Everywhere I went had been tinted with Alex, even if we'd never been there together. She was my first thought and my last, and alive in all the thoughts in between. I couldn't go more than a few hours without wanting to share an observation with her, or ask her opinion.

And it wasn't the same as when Lauren lived in all corners of my life. That was like the burn of a brutal paper cut. This was like sawing off my own hand, inch by inch.

It was no better when the work week had rolled around. I was empty and angry, and Tom's announcement during the Monday morning meeting that he was holding four offers on the Eastern Pond property had served as an unnecessary reminder of the catastrophe I'd set in motion.

It should've been a strange moment when my siblings and I grappled with gaining closure on our childhood and the loss of our parents. A finality of sorts. And it would've been the right moment for all of that if I hadn't walked out of the meeting. Not because I couldn't handle talk of the house but because I was long overdue to hammer the shit out of something.

That, or punch myself in the fucking face. Anything to bleed out the complete horror of losing the woman I loved to my own stupidity.

The rest of the week had been a blur of hard, sweaty work—any bit of demolition I could find in our collective portfolio of properties—and when there wasn't any of that left, there were batting cages. I was shit when it came to hitting the fucking balls—there was certainly a metaphor for my life somewhere in there—but it felt good to direct all of my energy into the swing. Like every slice through the air served as a kinetic offering to the gods.

Take everything I have, every ounce of me, and make it right with her.

But the absolution, it never came. I still didn't know what to do, where to start, how to find the words.

"Are we all set?" Patrick asked.

I blinked up at him, and then startled when I found Andy seated to his left.

"Is this still a good time?" he asked. He was tucked into one of the chairs in front of my desk, his laptop open on his knees and his tie loose. "Is everything okay?"

"Yeah," I said. "You start. I'll jump in."

I reached for my notebook, the one that was filled with

drawings of Gastro Girl. There was nowhere I could go without Alex right beside me. Flipping through the pages, I gazed at the sketches of her crime-fighting alter ego. The earliest attempts were disaggregated bits of the woman I'd thought she was, a shallow rendering of her features and carriage. But the more recent ones, they gazed straight into her soul. As always, there was the razor-sharp wit and snappy exterior, but there was also the softness, the sweetness. The vulnerability. Love.

And those images left me flattened on the floor of despair, gazing up at the sky and the clouds with neither methods nor means to climb my way out. It was like The Pit, the ancient prison from which Bruce Wayne escaped. But the harsh reality was that I was no Batman, no Dark Knight. I wasn't the hero Gotham—or Gastro Girl—deserved.

"No," I whispered. "Not all set. Not okay."

Patrick and Andy exchanged a glance.

"What's wrong?" she asked as she tucked her designs away.

At the same time, Patrick said, "I know that look. Yeah, I know all about that look."

"What are you talking about?" Andy asked, shifting to face him.

"When was the last time you spoke to Alex?" Patrick pointed at me. "The last time you saw her *and* she wasn't avoiding you like cracks in the sidewalk?"

Andy turned back to me. "This is about Alex?" She shook her head and waved off the question. "You didn't say anything, and everyone's been in snarly moods because of Wellesley so I figured that was it. I'm sorry, I had no idea." She edged her chair closer and folded her arms on the corner of my desk. "What's going on? What happened?"

Patrick flipped open the buttons at his throat and yanked the tie from his collar. "How long?" he repeated. "This is important. Timing matters. There's a critical window, and if you've missed it, you're shit out of luck."

I dropped my head to my hands. "Last Thursday," I mumbled. "After we left Wellesley."

"And she doesn't want to hear from you?" Andy asked. I shook my head. "What happened?"

I shrugged. "I...I fucked things up. I don't know how to fix any of it but I need her. I *need* her back."

"Okay, but *what* did you fuck up?" Andy asked.

Patrick snapped his laptop shut. "Irrelevant," he said to her. "Unless he's also dating her mother or running an underground toddler fight club or something reprehensible, whatever's fucked up just needs fixing. Let's talk containment and clean up. Have you contacted her since last Thursday?"

"A few texts," I said, jerking a shoulder. "She didn't respond."

"That's inadequate and eight days is too fucking long to let this linger. She's going to have a profile on eHarmony or Bumble by now, and résumés out to every hospital west of the Mississippi," he replied, shooting a pointed look at Andy. I didn't want to know what that shit was about. "You need to mount a full-scale attack. Use every weapon in the arsenal. Lucky for you, I've got a multistep plan ready."

I glanced up, not certain I'd heard him correctly. The only advice Patrick ever doled out was of the *Get your shit together* variety. "What?"

"I'm going to step out," Andy said, gathering her things.

"We'll reschedule this meeting," Patrick said. "Again."

"Am I that bad off?" I asked when the door whispered

shut behind her. "That we have to cancel meetings? You never cancel meetings. You love meetings and agendas and shit."

"No, you're not that bad off," Patrick scoffed, shaking his head. "We've all been there."

Sam and Matt barreled into my office, Sam holding baby Dave and Matt chomping on an apple.

"What's going on?" Sam asked, pacing and rocking while he spoke. "Andy sent us in. Said you needed some help."

He and Tiel were still searching for that perfect unicorn nanny. Until they found that person, she was with the baby each morning and Sam was with him each afternoon. Dave had a small crib in Sam's office and a tiny hardhat, but they didn't visit many construction sites.

"Gentlemen, it's happened," Patrick said with a nod toward me. "Young Master RISD has found himself a woman worth keeping. Naturally, he's wrecked the whole thing."

"Did you leak more photos? Is that what happened?" Sam teased.

"Shut up, Sam," Patrick replied.

"What's the root issue?" Matt asked. "Walk us through it."

I stared at Matt and the shiny red apple between his fingers, and I thought about asking him to leave. I couldn't discuss *the issue* with him here. Not unless I wanted to experience some first-hand defenestration.

But then again, I couldn't discuss *the issue* with any of them.

Shambles.

"She says I'm not ready," I replied.

"Why?" Patrick asked. "What precipitated that?"

"Um, I, uh, haven't, I mean," I stammered. "She's worried that I still have feelings for—for someone else."

Matt's head popped up at that, his brows arched as he met my eyes. He didn't say anything, but he didn't look away.

"Who?" Sam asked incredulously. "Sure, you've got your slutty history like the rest of us—"

"Excuse me," Patrick snapped. "*Slutty history*?"

Sam waved him off between pats to Dave's back. "Please," he said. "You whored it up like the rest of us. You're just too domesticated now to remember your tomcat days." He speared me with a glance over his shoulder, but the burp cloth draped there softened the effect. "How could you have feelings for anyone else when you can't remember their names?"

"Doesn't matter," Patrick said. "Alex believes it. You have to deal with that head on."

"Or deal with the other woman head on," Sam offered. "Call her up. Unburden yourself."

I could talk to her. Lauren. Maybe it would help. The prospect was terrifying and it was more likely to result in a level of destruction I'd never before achieved, but wasn't that the only way? Wasn't an armload of real fear the only thing that could give me the strength to rise from this rubble?

That had worked for Bruce Wayne and Talia al Ghul. I had a fifty-fifty shot of saving the city and wreaking havoc. As per usual.

I blinked back at Matt, and his eyebrows climbed higher. Like he could hear my damn thoughts.

What the fuck is that about?

"You could also put your head down and cry," Sam continued. "I'm fairly certain each of us has done that at some point."

"Your advice is terrible." Patrick rolled his eyes. "Can we

finish this conversation over some beers? It's after four on a Friday, and this fucking week just needs to end."

"Amen to that," Sam muttered. "But it has to be a restaurant or something. No bars. It's too noisy, and I can't bring the baby to a bar and expect that my wife will let me sleep with her tonight. Oh, and I need to grab the diaper bag."

"So many damn issues," Patrick muttered. "There used to be a time when we could go out for a drink without alerting a half dozen people and packing luggage for small children."

Matt tossed his apple core in the waste basket, snickering. "You say that as if your balls aren't dangling from Andy's key chain."

Patrick tossed up his hands. "They're all hers. She can keep 'em."

"You bitch and whine now," Sam said. "But wait until you have one of your own. You'll adapt."

I leaned back in my chair and folded my arms over my chest, squinting at my brothers as they sniped at each other. "Should I call Will instead? Maybe Tom? Or literally anyone else because you can't talk about anything but your own assholes? My life is in actual shambles here."

"Now that you mention it, Will could be helpful. I'll text him. He's got a lot of negotiation skills. Not from the Navy SEALs, but, you know, from living with Shannon." Patrick stood and herded the others into the hallway. "Let's get out of here. We need to talk containment and clean up," he said. "And beer."

I SENSED her before looking up from my coffee and meeting her smiling eyes. I couldn't fight the sensation, but it was different now. Muted. As if the volume had been turned down but the vibrating bass still remained.

She dropped into the chair across from me and spoke, but I was too busy finding my words to hear hers.

"Thank you for meeting me. I know it's really early." Gesturing feebly at the plate loaded with pastries on the table between us, I said, "I thought you might like these."

"I do love croissants," she said, reaching for one and tearing it into thirds. "Even if they're consumed before eight on a Saturday morning."

She licked the buttery crumbs from her fingers and I braced myself for the pulse of inevitable heat to course through my body.

It didn't come.

Like an ill-mannered masochist, I kept watching while she ate. I didn't look away when she brushed some crumbs from her shirt or tongued a dollop of apricot jam from the corner of her lips.

I watched it all, digging inside for—for anything. But it was as though I'd stared at the sky too long and now I couldn't see anything but bright blankness.

"Are we talking birthdays?" Lauren asked, snapping me out of this internal inventory. "Because I think we need to talk birthdays. I know Matt, Patrick, and Shannon usually pick one day because they're all within a week or so of each other, but they also blow off the entire affair and never allow proper celebrations. I'd like to change that. "

"Birthdays," I said slowly. I reached for my coffee and gulped, choking down the words I'd intended to say.

"Isn't that what you wanted to discuss?" she asked, her brows quirking up in question. "That's why you wanted me to ditch Matt, right?"

"Where is he?" I asked, glancing around. "Right now, where is he?"

"Gym," she replied, her hand over her mouth as she spoke around the croissant.

"Yeah, right," I said, squeezing my eyes shut.

It'd been *years* that I'd been carrying feelings for Lauren. It was a familiar weight, one that left me stumbling, off balance, now that it was gone.

"Was there something else?" she asked. "Something you wanted to discuss this morning?"

Her eyes were patient, warm. So damn warm. Like I could tell her any outrageous thing and she wouldn't think any less of me.

Any outrageous thing.

"It's been a—a strange couple of months," I started. "It seems like everything has changed. Like I'm not the same person I used to be." I glanced at her. "Does that make sense?"

She nodded as she wiped her hands on a paper napkin. "Tons of sense. I went through something similar a couple of years ago." She paused, dropping her gaze. "Around the time I met Matthew, actually."

That caught my attention. I leaned forward, laced my hands around my cup, and waited for her to continue.

"In a matter of months, the life I'd once known was upended," she continued. "I went from being a classroom teacher to a school principal, my college friends faded away, and then there was Matthew." She reached into her bag for her phone and glanced at the screen, then placed it on the table. "By themselves, one of those things would've qualified as a big life change, but altogether?"

Her wide eyes and open palms said it all.

"Shambles?" I offered.

Lauren laughed. "Something like that, yeah."

She tucked her hair over her ears, and my mind went straight to Alex. Her hair, and the way it curled after being tied up in a bun under her scrub cap all day. How it felt between my fingers or tickling my torso, or fanned out on her flowery pillows.

"I saw my college girlfriend last month," I said. "I had to force myself to remember what I'd liked about her."

Lauren bobbed her head eagerly. "Same with my roommates. We'd been so tight through college and then moving to the city, but then we grew apart. Almost overnight. We just weren't the same people anymore, and we couldn't find our way back to the people we'd once been."

"It's unsettling," I said. "There are moments when I'm lost in my own life."

She gave me a *Yeah, tell me about it* smirk.

"The biggest adjustment for me was going from teaching to opening a school. I was convinced that I was going to fuck it all up. That the people who'd put me in charge would realize I wasn't qualified, and it would be over."

"Every damn day," I murmured.

"And Matthew, he rearranged everything. Invited himself in, made room for himself, got cozy, and announced he'd be staying a while." She blinked at that, shaking her head just a bit, like my brother had been a crafty little wrecking ball with his unbelievable charm. "It didn't take long to realize he was—*is*—it for me. It took longer to get a grip on everything else, and I couldn't see what was right in front of me because I'd been in survival mode." She shrugged. "I had to get past all of that other stuff before I could focus on anything—or any*one*—else."

Lauren tore the corner off another croissant and popped it in her mouth, all while shooting me expectant glances. She didn't have to announce that she was waiting on some details about my shambles.

"Lauren," I started, feeling the pressure build in my chest, "I have to tell you something."

"Anything."

The words were right there on my tongue, but I practiced one last time. I wasn't sure whether I was trying to get them straight or confirm I actually wanted to say them. Then I blinked at the whitewashed bakery and the passing foot traffic outside, and the reality of what I was doing— professing my once-rampant love for my brother's wife— brought everything to a breathless halt. I expected to find pieces of me scattered about, cups and jars filled with every twisted urge I'd ever felt because I couldn't say I owned them any longer.

They didn't own me either.

And then—*oh, motherfucking hell, what am I doing?*—I couldn't tell her anything. Holy fuck, no. Not as it pertained to my feelings for her. Those feelings, they hadn't been real. Not real in the way my feelings for Alex were real.

I gulped. But there was one thing I needed to say. Something she needed to know. "Do you remember the night my father died?"

She dropped her hands to her lap and sat back. "Uh, yeah. Of course."

"I never—" I stopped, blinking away the vision of him in that hospital bed. Plugged full of tubes, machines living for him, dead by most definitions.

But that night, he'd been more alive to me than he'd ever been. Or, more *human*. He'd been frail. Not the tempest of grief-hate and misplaced rage and liquor that he'd been as far back as my memories could reach. On the night he'd died, he hadn't been a monster but a man.

One who had to account for his good and his evil the same as everyone else.

One who'd fought like hell to leave the world a little worse off.

One who'd seriously underestimated our ability to recover from his abuse, with spite as our primary motivation.

"I never thanked you," I said, gazing into her eyes. I was finding I could do that now without fear—or hope?—that she'd see every one of my secrets, right there treading water. "For helping all of us say goodbye. For staying with him while he died."

She lifted her shoulders and let them fall like she shep-herded fucked-up families through taking their fathers off life support every day.

"Of course," she said gently. "That night put a lot of things in perspective for me. It forced me to see that all of my issues were bullshit."

I barked out a laugh. "Does that make my issues bullshit, too?"

She hummed as she went for more croissant. "Maybe. Do they feel like bullshit?"

"I've put a lot of fucking energy into these issues," I argued. "If they are bullshit, I've wasted a fuck-ton of time."

"Just know that it's tough to kick your own ass, so you'll have to get over it instead."

"Noted," I said, laughing. "But seriously, Lauren. What you did that night—" I swallowed around a throb of emotion.

She'd stood in that room with me, surrounded by the hospital awfulness, and she'd held my hand while I'd listed everything terrible my father had ever done to me. All the times he'd taken a belt to me because I couldn't speak prop-erly. The times he'd told me I was stupid, worthless, nothing. That my mother had never wanted me, and he certainly hadn't either. The fists he'd raised until I'd outsized him and started hitting right back.

Then I'd told him that shit was going with him to the grave because those charges were on his tab, not mine.

Part of me had expected the miserable bastard to claw his way out of that brain-dead coma to call me a useless turnip one last time. It hadn't happened. The steady hiss and beep of the machines keeping his blood warm had been the only response. I'd promptly lost all of my shit once I'd known the shackles of my father's hateful resentment were gone. Lauren had been there, holding me while I'd cried on her shoulder.

"What you did that night, it was important," I said. "Thank you."

"You're welcome."

We stared at each other, and I sensed the physical presence of my affection for her taking on a new shape, one that was colored with good moments and bad moments, care and concern, and a love that knew nothing of lust or romance.

I heard a throat clearing nearby, but didn't look away.

"Are we all right here?"

Lauren's smile bloomed into a heated smirk as she tore her gaze from mine.

To Matt. The throat clearer. He was standing beside us, his hair damp and his gym bag hooked over his shoulder.

"We're great," she said as she stood. "You sit. I'll be right back, and I'll grab you a snack."

She kissed him quickly and headed through the café, toward the restrooms. I felt nothing. No stir of jealousy, no resentment. *Nothing.*

Matt took her seat, again asking, "Are we all right here?"

I didn't know how to answer, not when I was still attempting to understand the emotional shape-shifting I'd experienced this morning. This morning, and the past few months, too. This didn't start today, but it did end.

Matt leaned forward, his arms folded on the table. "I trust you," he said solemnly. "You know that, right? That I trust you to handle yourself."

I had a quip ready about great power and great responsibility, but then I caught the serious glint in his eyes. It didn't make any sense and I had no evidence beyond an ominous statement and a *glint* but—he knew.

He *knew.*

"I trust you to do the right thing," he continued.

It wasn't a warning. Just a statement. A confirmation of facts we both understood, objective and passionless.

I'd imagined moments like this a million times. When I'd lay it all out there for Matt, and then walk away with the victor's spoils. But this was not that moment, and there was no victor because there'd been no fight. I wasn't waging a holy war for Lauren anymore—had I ever, really?—and I wasn't leading with my confused brand of heartsickness either.

"I trust you enough to let my wife come here alone," he said. "And I trust her more than anyone. Including you."

I could manage only a spastic nod in response.

Lauren emerged from the restrooms and paused in front of the café's display case, and we both shifted to track her movements. That yielded another throat clearing.

And then the words were sliding out before I could think better of them. "How long have you known?"

"Long enough. You can only joke about her leaving me so many times before I start looking a little closer," Matt replied. He was still calm and even, and studying me as if the entire world hadn't been thrown off its axis for the second time today. "But she doesn't know." He knocked his knuckles against the table. "Can we keep it that way?"

Those words, they detonated a series of tiny explosions inside me.

"There's nothing—Alex—no, but I—I mean, Alex, and I— I never, I was never going to do anything, you know? And I wouldn't—holy fuck, did you think I'd?—We'd? Have you? Did you? Does anyone else? But-but-but-but-but—*Alex*—"

Then I knocked the coffee cup from its saucer, sending lukewarm liquid into my lap. In my attempt to right the cup, the pastries flew from the plate. I tried to catch one midair but that only resulted in me tripping out of my chair. I looked up at Matt from the floor, coffee and bread all over me.

I hadn't completely shaken off the shambles.

"No," he said quietly. "This is between you and me. No one else knows." He tipped his head, watching Lauren at the counter. "And I don't want to make you dig your own grave before I kill you, but I'll do it if the situation warrants it."

If Hartshorn had been lusting over Alex and biding his time until I was out of the picture, I didn't think I could've managed Matt's cool. I wouldn't have been able to hold this conversation without also wrapping my hands around his throat and watching him struggle for oxygen.

But Matt was one of the best people. So good that he'd stand by while I painted myself into a complicated fairy tale with no hope of a happy ending. So good he could confront me—and put the foundations of our relationship right there on the table—with only one threat of mortal violence. He was the best people, and I deserved to be sitting in a mess of pastry.

"I love Alex," I said, breathless. "She's the only one I want. I *swear* to you."

Lauren loomed over me, iced coffee and a yogurt cup in her hands, and a worried expression on her face. "I leave you two for five minutes and you get into a food fight."

Matt pointed at me. "He started it."

I glanced down at my stained clothes, shaking my head. Alex would've had something to say about this.

"I have to go," I said, gaining my feet. "Lauren, thank you for talking. Matt, yes, to answer your question. Yes, definitely. Absolutely. We're going to keep it that way." I checked the time on my phone. "I have to go. I need to see Alex. I'm ready. I'm really ready now."

Lauren took the seat I'd gracelessly vacated, and set the coffee and yogurt in front of Matt. "I'll text you about that other thing," she said. "We'll make some plans."

Matt, to his credit, focused on stirring his coffee.

"Andy, too," I replied. "Start a group chat. You and Andy, and me. We'll figure out something good, and then loop in the others."

I didn't wait for a response, instead hauling my ass out of there as fast I could manage without inciting another catastrophe.

I **WAS** on the hunt for surgeries. Anything to keep my mind —and hands—busy. I didn't care whether it was interesting. I'd take a procedure as simple as a hot appendix or some basic suturing in the ER. Whatever it took to avoid my empty, joyless apartment and push off dinner with my parents.

Of course, I was already committed to dinner tonight and all day tomorrow so I wasn't blowing them off for obstructed bowels. Just delaying the inevitable questions about my boyfriend's vanishing act and when I'd be finding a *nice* guy and settling down.

Except I didn't want a nice guy. I wanted the man who was kind and loving, quirky as all hell, and an absolute fucking beast.

Too bad that beast wanted someone else.

Staring at the surgical schedule, I spied three different cases where my residents were slated to assist. They could live without biopsying a gallbladder or patching up an ulcerated stomach today. I'd motioned to the nurse who ran the board—the only one permitted to change a damn thing —when a hand landed on my head.

"Are you robbing your residents of procedures again?" Hartshorn asked.

I pivoted under his hold and glanced up at him. "It won't kill them to run labs or catch up on charting today," I replied. "I spoil them. You know it's true. I never keep the good surgeries for myself when teachable moments are involved. They owe me a day or two of hoarding."

He offered a vague murmur and shook his head. "How many appies have you pulled this week?"

I jerked a shoulder up. "A few," I said.

Seven. I'd removed seven inflamed appendixes.

"But you were the one who taught me that it's essential to take routine cases to keep your skills sharp," I added. "You used a metaphor about chefs who forget how to dice carrots when they spend their days running the kitchen and imagining new dishes."

He folded his arms across his chest. "You haven't forgotten how to dice the carrots, Emmerling."

"I haven't," I admitted, softening under his stare.

"Then go home," he said. "Your residents know how to page you."

"But I need to stay busy right now." I held up my hands and let them fall to my hips. "I get the sense you understand that phenomenon because it's Saturday morning and you're lurking around the surgical wing, too."

Nodding, Hartshorn turned his attention to the board. It seemed like he'd dropped the topic for a minute, but then he said, "Riley's at your apartment."

I turned, gaping at him as if he'd said the Pope was

preaching in Copley Square. "What do you mean, he's *at my apartment*?"

He didn't respond right away, instead touching his index finger to each surgery listed, one after another. I understood many of his methods but none of his madness, and stood silently while he studied the scribbled details. Patient name, procedure, anesthesia type, attending physician, surgeon, scrub nurse.

But my greater concern was whether Riley was loitering around my building. Hartshorn had a key to my place, and it was possible that he'd let Riley hang out on my couch. Not likely, but possible nonetheless. None of that was good news for me. At some point today, I'd have to stop at home to change into clothing appropriate for an evening out with my parents because scrubs wouldn't cut it. I didn't want to also dodge Riley while coming and going.

Hartshorn finally tore his gaze from the board and glanced at his watch. "He's been there since nine."

I leaned back as the velocity of that information hit me. "I'm going to need more specific details, please."

He ran his knuckles down his chin. "I was in the kitchen making breakfast. Then I saw Riley was on the fire escape," he said. "I think he was attempting some kind of Spider-Man move."

"Batman," I murmured.

There were only a few reasons Riley would be there. Either he was coming in search of the stray items he'd left at my place because it was down, out, and over, or he wanted to fix the things he'd broken.

Like my snappy, snarly little heart.

"Since I didn't want to watch him fall off the fire escape—

or put him back together when he hit the ground—I invited him in," Hartshorn continued.

I stared at him, incredulous. I could feel the steam coming out of my ears. "You fed him, didn't you?"

He shrugged but didn't bother looking remorseful. He was a real-life Mother Goose. "It was no trouble to make some more scrambled eggs," he said. "He's a fascinating guy."

And there it was. The indomitable charm of Riley Walsh. People couldn't help but be taken with him, what with his odd, artsy ways and occasional stutters and unzipped pants. No one was immune, not even Hartshorn, the great king of stoicism.

"Oh, would you shut up?" I snapped.

"He invited me to watch the Patriots play the Broncos with him next month." Hartshorn's eyebrows popped up as a smile crossed his face. "Do you think you could go talk to him? Sort things out? I'd really like to see the Broncos."

"And here I was, thinking you were on my side, Hartshorn."

"I am on your side," he replied, affronted. "I didn't let him into your apartment. I told him he could wait in the stairwell."

I pressed my palms to my eyes and sucked in a breath, willing myself to keep the tears at bay. I shouldn't have been upset about the football game. So what if Riley and I'd planned to go to that game together and now he was buddying up with Hartshorn instead? I didn't even like football that much.

Stray items it is.

"I'm not saying he's right," Hartshorn continued. "I'm simply saying he has a perspective and it's worth hearing.

He also had some interesting thoughts on my friend at the park."

"Of course he did," I said, groaning.

Hartshorn plucked the scrub cap from my head and held it out to me. "Go home, Emmerling. Consider it an order," he said. "Batman's waiting."

FOR THE FIRST time in my life, I left the hospital without changing out of my scrubs. Pens and instruments rattled around the pockets of my white coat and my stethoscope was hanging from my neck, and I had every intention of escorting Riley out of the building and then going right back to work.

I stomped up the stairs to my apartment, my red clogs squeaking against the polished floorboards. When I reached the landing, I had to dig deep for the same fortification that I used to sidestep emotions while delivering bad news to patients.

I knew he was perched on the flight of stairs leading to the top floor apartment, but I didn't bother with a glance in his direction. Instead, I unlocked the door and breezed inside. If he wanted to follow, the invitation was clear.

Unfortunately, there was no tidy box to hand him. It'd never crossed my mind to gather his things until now. Grabbing a reusable grocery bag from under the sink, I flew through the rooms. I tossed t-shirts and hoodies, markers and neckties into the bag while he stood near the door.

Watching me.

I held the bag out to him but instead of accepting it and

getting the fuck out of my home, he set it on the couch, never once taking his eyes off me.

After an unbearable silence, I said, "You can go now."

"I'd rather not," he replied.

"What are you doing here?"

He looked around, confused. "Of course I'm here," he said. "Your parents are visiting. We have a deal."

I crossed my arms over my chest, my shoulders tight. "That's it? You're here because of our *agreement*?"

"No," he said. "I'm here because I fucked a million things up. But a couple of months ago I promised I'd be by your side when your parents came to town. Even if you hate me right now, I'm not going back on anything I've promised you."

"You're taking Hartshorn to that football game," I said. "The one next month. What happened to that promise?"

Riley shook his head and brought his fingers to his temples. "That fucking guy," he murmured to himself. "I told Hartshorn that *the four of us* could go to the game." He pointed at me. "You, me, Hartshorn, the woman he's stalking. I have to say, I find that whole situation a little unsettling. I told him to make a move or get a new hobby before he's going to be slapped with a restraining order."

"Why?" I asked. I couldn't keep up with any of this. "Why would you want to do something like that?"

"Because I love you," he said. "And I'll keep fucking things up"—he cut a glance to the side, grimacing—"but I'm hoping those instances will be smaller and less fucking awful because these past nine days have been the worst of my life and I can't go through this again."

He held out a hand to me. I glanced down at it, wanting

to take it but terrified I was his backup plan. I couldn't do it. I didn't have the strength to take second place in his heart.

"Come here, Honeybee," he whispered. "You're so far away and I've missed you so much."

I shook my head. No. I couldn't. Not yet. "What about Lauren? Your one true love?"

Those words were sharp, but as I watched them slice through Riley, I wasn't sure who they hurt more.

"I loved the idea of her," he said. "And I loved the idea of being loved by—by someone who understood *me*." He glanced around the apartment, looking at the walls and furniture as if they'd changed since his last visit. "And I think I wanted someone to love the way Matt loves Lauren. Completely and loyally, and without any restrictions or limits. I wanted that, but I never wanted to come between them."

"Are you sure about that?" I snapped, shoving my hands in my coat pockets. "How do you know you won't feel differently the next time you see her?"

"I saw her this morning," he replied. "I spilled coffee all over my crotch and literally fell out of my chair when I realized how fucking delusional I've been." I glanced at his jeans but found no stains. "I went home and changed. I wasn't begging for your forgiveness with wet pants, and there were crumbs everywhere, too."

"Crumbs?" I asked, the word tumbling into a hysterical giggle.

Riley sighed and ran his fingers through his hair. "From the plate of croissants I knocked over before I hit the fucking floor. How's that for you, Aly? I was in a puddle of coffee and croissants, and wishing you were there to laugh at me." He stared at me, his eyes sharp and certain. "I don't want her. Not now, probably not ever. I wanted the *idea* of her, and you have to know that the reality of you is far better than any idea I've ever had."

He reached for his belt, yanked his zipper down, and pushed his jeans to his knees. His boxers were goldenrod and printed with a pattern I couldn't identify from this distance. Then he pivoted, giving me his backside.

"What are you—*oh*," I mumbled. *Follow the yellow brick road* was embroidered across his ass in shiny red thread. "Oh."

"I've had these for a few weeks. I seem to have developed a thing for *The Wizard of Oz*," he said, shifting back to face me. "I know that some boxer shorts don't prove anything but I also have a notebook full of drawings of you. Of Gastro Girl. You're the only woman I've ever drawn. No one else. Not Lauren. Only you." He pointed to the backpack he'd abandoned by the front door. "And I've been drawing you since that night at Nick and Erin's house. "

"Is that it?" I asked.

I was aiming for flippant but my words came out closer to thin and fragile. And that was exactly how I felt. I'd barely slept in the days we'd been apart, and I'd worked so hard at distracting myself from the pain of being second best once again that I'd only exacerbated it. And now...I couldn't breathe or blink without a reminder of how much I missed him. How much I needed him. How, despite all the firm decisions I'd made and lines I'd drawn in the sand, I was wavering.

"There's a dozen cannoli in there, too. I figured it couldn't hurt." He scratched his chin. "I thought about hiding a ring in one of them, but then I realized you'd be too busy scarfing down the cannoli to notice. And then that would be a giant disaster, you know, with a goddamn diamond in your stomach." He gestured to my coat and scrubs. "Knowing you, you'd want to perform your own ring retrieval surgery. At the very least, you'd want to be awake during the whole thing so you could tell everyone they're doing it wrong. I have to be honest here, Aly, I don't think I could deal with that after the week I've had. I can't handle the idea of you going under the knife and being away from me again. I'd be a fucking wreck. More than I am right now, if you can believe it."

"It would be endoscopic," I said, because that was the only thing I could manage. "No scalpels involved."

Riley waved his hands in a *Like that matters* gesture. "So, I brought cannoli," he continued. "And because my better judgment won out, there's no ring in there. But know that I want you—and only you—for the rest of my days." He offered a lopsided smile and held out his hand to me again. "If I haven't sufficiently apologized or met the criteria for redemption, I'll keep trying. I'll wait." A smirk pulled at his lips. "I'm really good at waiting."

I gripped the ends of my stethoscope, needing something to hold onto while my heart thumped straight out of my chest. "Be sure," I whispered. "Be really fucking sure because I won't survive this again."

"I'm not good at too many things," he said.

"Don't say that—"

He waved me off. "Let me finish. It's true. I can't speak eloquently and I knock shit over all the fucking time. I have a narrow subset of skills that mostly involves reciting song lyrics, knowing which sandwiches are best with chips in the middle, redesigning old homes, and giving people nicknames." He took a step closer, right into my space, and the absence of that distance crushed the last of my resolve. "I'm not good at many things. But I'll always be good to you."

And that was *it*. Like those prize fighters who circled each other for ages before throwing the one punch that ended it all, I was *done*.

"COME *HERE*," I said, my voice rough and desperate. "Please. Just come over here and—"

And she did. She flew into my arms and held me with a fierce grip, and all the relief in the world washed over me. I buried my face in her hair and sucked in a breath.

"My hair smells like cheese," she said. "I haven't been home in a couple of days. I used some random shampoo that someone had left in the locker room. You can tell me. It's cheesy, isn't it?"

"You're perfect." There was a slight cheddary quality. "Do you need to go back to the hospital?" I asked, my lips on her neck.

Alex shook her head. "No, I wasn't scheduled," she said. She glanced up at me, her eyes sheepish and her cheeks coloring pink. "Or on call. I was lurking around, looking for surgeries. I just didn't want to be here."

"Oh, Honeybee." She was clinging to me, her hands curled around my shirt. I sighed because I was doing the same. My fingers were digging into her hips like I was hoping to leave a mark on her bones, some proof that she belonged to me. "Come on. Let's get you a hot shower."

"Are you coming with me?"

"Of course," I said, towing her into the bedroom. I ran my hands over her shoulders and arms, and tugged her coat's lapels. "It might not be the proper time for this observation but you are fuck-all hot in your doctor clothes."

"That's a bit of a stretch," Alex said, stowing the stethoscope in her pocket and shrugging out of the coat. She kicked off her shoes—ah, I'd missed her red shoes something fierce—and yanked off her socks.

"It's not," I said, a proud smile stretching across my face as I studied the embroidery on the breast of her scrubs. It consisted of her name and a bunch of letters, and it reminded me that my girl was amazing. "I love that you're talented and capable. It's impressive, and it's really fucking sexy."

Alex pulled her shirt over her head and let it fall to the floor. "That look of yours," she said, wagging her finger at me. "It's trouble."

I stepped into the adjoining bathroom and flipped on the taps. "Which look is that?"

"The one where you narrow your eyes and stare as if your cock is already inside me," she said.

I leaned against the doorframe, crossing one ankle over the other and folding my arms across my torso. "That's good," I said with a shrug. "It's exactly what I'm thinking."

"But yet you're still dressed," she said as her pants joined the pile of discarded clothing.

"Right again, Doctor Emmerling," I replied. "I'm going to

order some food, and give you a few minutes to rinse off without me. I don't want you hungry or worrying about whether your hair smells like cheese while I fuck you." I hooked my thumb over my shoulder. "Let's go. Wash up. Get that ass nice and clean so I can make it *very* dirty."

As she approached, I noticed the dark circles under her eyes and dull tone to her skin. Her shoulders were rounded, her steps unsteady. My heart lurched, knowing that she'd suffered these past days and I was responsible for it. It was one thing to put myself through hell, but it was something entirely different to do it to Alex.

"Honeybee," I whispered. I reached for her, sliding my hands from her waist to her breasts. "I'm so sorry."

She dropped her head to my chest, nodding. "I know and I am, too," she said. "I jump to the worst conclusions and then I don't give anyone a chance to share their side of the story. I hold onto things for way too long, and I'm going to get better at letting go of the old shit." She looked up at me, her teeth sawing over her bottom lip. "But I think we should stop apologizing. It's been a really tough week and we've said so many things, and I just want to love you now. Okay?"

Tears spilled down her cheeks. "I'm good with that," I replied, sucking in a breath as I struggled against the same rush of emotion she was experiencing. "But I want to love you, too. I want a new arrangement. Something a little more permanent. Okay?"

She sniffled. "Yeah," she said. "Meet me in the shower and we'll discuss the terms and conditions."

I escorted Alex into the steamy bathroom and closed the shower door behind her, then quickly called the best local pizzeria. It was a hole-in-the-wall place, the kind that didn't have a website or punny hashtags on Instagram. The lady who worked the phones was known for yelling at every customer who called, but their pies were made to order and there was something addictive about their red sauce.

I needed that small task to gain control of the hammering in my chest. My brain and body were gradually processing the news that I'd survived this disaster and I didn't require any additional bursts of adrenaline to fight through the day.

Following Alex's lead, I discarded my clothes and shoes as I made my way to the bathroom. There was a time for tidiness with laundry, and it was known as not right now.

When I returned to the bathroom, the steam was thick and I was half hard at the thought of Alex naked, soapy, mine. My cock twitched when I stopped in front of the shower to admire her form through the frosted glass.

"Mind if I join you?" I asked, stepping under the spray.

"I was starting to think you'd gone to fetch the pizza yourself," Alex replied. She folded her arms across her chest as the water poured over me.

"You can't get rid of me that easily," I said, wiping the water from my face. I stared at her, and at once, my entire body breathed a sigh of relief. "Get over here, Honeybee."

She came to me, and I wrapped my arms around her. Her lips were on my chest and neck, kissing every inch of skin, humming and murmuring as she branded me. "I love the way your skin tastes," she said. "I've tried to figure out what it is but all I know is that it's you, and I love it."

I tipped her chin up and bent to kiss her. "I love everything about you. Just fucking everything, Aly. The way you smell like a color and taste like a sin. Your brain, your moods, your desire." I dragged my hands down her sides, squeezing the globes of her ass before sliding back up to cup her breasts. "Hello, my lovelies," I said, swiping my thumbs over her nipples. "It's been far too long."

I pinched them both, and her breath caught, breaking into a cry. She dug her nails into my back as I pinched harder, a fine shot of pain. Every touch went straight to my cock, and all the relief I'd felt was now replaced with stiff need. My cock was heavy between my legs, my skin pulled taut.

"Hands on the wall," I whispered, spinning her around. "Don't you dare move them." I leaned forward, catching her eye. "Do you understand me?"

Alex stared at me, nodding, and I knew she heard all the things that lived inside that question.

Do you recognize that I'm in charge but you have all the power?

Do you see that I want to worship you in every way possible?

Do you trust me to take your most fragile pieces and keep them safe?

"Yes," she replied. "I know."

"I was going to wait," I said, trailing my finger down Alex's spine. I traced the line of her ass, teasing her a bit because it made her squirm. "Get you clean and then take you to bed and get you dirty all over again."

"Has the plan changed?" she asked.

I crowded her against the wall, fitting my length between her cheeks. I could feel my pulse pounding in the head of my cock, and I slid against her back channel to relieve some of that pressure. "There's no reason to wait for the bed when I can fuck you right here," I said as she moaned.

"Mmm. I like that plan," she said.

"I'd get on my knees and lick your pussy until the water ran cold," I said, edging her legs apart. "But this shower was not designed for that kind of action. I'll fix that. I'll build you a decent bathroom with plenty of space and a big-ass shower. Or we'll find a new place. Anything you want, you can have it, Aly."

"Yeah," Alex said, her voice cracking as I pushed into her. "*Yes*."

There'd be foreplay with the next round, and many of the rounds after that. We had the next sixty years to play and tease and bring each other to the edge. We had only this moment to start over.

"What do you need?" I asked, my words rushing out in a gasp as I moved in her. I was doing everything in my power to take it slow, savor the suck and drag of her flesh as it wrapped around my cock, memorize her moans. But after nine days without the dizzying clench of her body, that power was limited. "Aly, I need you to tell me because I can't—"

"Fuck me the way you need to, Riley," she cried, slapping the tiles. "That's all I want. You, exactly the way you are."

She was flattened against the wall before the last word left her lips. I had one hand curled around her throat, the other on her hip, and I was thrusting into her like I intended to prove a point. Maybe I did. Maybe I wanted her to believe that we were the same, even after all the heartache and distance, and that we'd always be the same.

"You need me like this?" I asked, digging my fingers into her waist. She was trembling under me, my name an echoed plea. "Out of my goddamn mind with how much I want you? Wild for you?"

Alex's head dropped to my shoulder, and that angle had her pulse hammering under my thumb. Her moans vibrated through my fingers and straight down to my dick. "I want you to feel this," she whispered. Then her hand slipped away from the wall and she reached for me, lacing our fingers together and bringing my palm to her pelvis. "Feel this with me. Feel how I was made for you, and you were made for me."

Instinct ordered me to close my eyes. My mouth was on her shoulder, my balls were about to burst, sex and purple were in the air, and her words and moans were hitting me like a million pin pricks. My senses were overloaded, and I couldn't look at my grip on her throat or the way my thrusts shook her entire body.

"I fucking love you," I whispered, my voice hoarse.

I exploded inside her like a knockout punch. The force of it left me staggering, slow and woozy as I struggled to blink. I wanted to curl up with my woman and not wake for six or seven days.

We stayed there, gasping and shaking and clinging to each other. The water was cool and goosebumps rippled down Alex's arms, and a shiver moved through her shoulders. "Should we get out?" I asked. "Are you all right?"

She shook her head. "I'm wonderful," she said, turning off the water. "I'm an incapacitated bowl of orgasmic bliss and I don't think I'll be walking right this week, but I'm *wonderful*."

"That was good for you?" I asked, rubbing my hands along her arms. I knew she orgasmed but my head was still ringing with white noise. The specifics of the past few minutes were lost to me.

"It was spectacular," she said, laughing.

The buzzer sounded and I dropped my head to her shoulder. "Oh my fucking god. How the fuck did the food get here that fast?" I asked, stepping out of the shower. "I'll be right back. Where did I leave my jeans?"

"I don't know. The bedroom?" Alex offered. "But you have some pajama pants in the closet."

I rubbed a towel over my head and down my chest. "That's great, considering I won't be leaving here for at least thirty-six hours. But it doesn't get me any closer to locating my wallet."

"Why do you need your wallet?" she asked.

"Is pizza free where you're from, Alexandra?"

"Of course not, but I haven't paid cash for delivery in years. GrubHub, Seamless, Foodler, Peapod, Venmo. Why would I need cash when everything is online?" she asked.

"My only goal was getting food and getting you naked," I called from the bedroom. "Sometimes you have to go old school. I'll be more savvy on the next go-round."

My jeans were on the floor beside her scrubs and sparkly red shoes, and I snatched my wallet from the back pocket. I wrapped the towel around my waist and headed into the living room, cash in hand.

A knock sounded at the door, and I called, "Coming."

"Yeah, you were," Alex murmured from the bedroom.

"Someone pulled on her sassy pants," I said as I opened the door.

"Someone isn't wearing any pants," she yelled.

"Surprise!"

I blinked, glancing from the man clutching a pastel pink teddy bear to the woman with her arm curled around a basket of violets. They were nicely dressed, in their fifties or sixties, and their body language suggested they were either married or well acquainted.

They did not, however, appear to be delivering a pizza.

"Hi," I said slowly, suddenly aware that I was dripping wet and clad in an ill-fitting bit of terrycloth. One wrong move, and my dick was popping out to say hello. "Can I help you?"

"Does Alex live here?" the man asked, squinting at me.

"Yeah," I replied. I gave that teddy bear the side eye. "This is her apartment."

The woman frowned at him. "Oren, we should come back later. I told you we should've called ahead."

From the bedroom I heard a flurry of commotion followed by "Oh, shit," and then I understood. These were Alex's parents and—*oh my fucking god*—I was practically naked and still panting from fucking their daughter in the shower.

"Because you thought she'd be at work, not"—he glared at my chest—"*entertaining*."

Alex scrambled around the corner and pressed her hands to my back. She peeked out from behind me. "Mom. Dad. Hi," she said breathlessly. "You're *here* and you're *so* early."

"Your father thought it would be fun to surprise you like you're always surprising us," her mother said. "It seems we've caught you at a bad time."

"Not at all," I replied with every ounce of enthusiasm I could muster. It wasn't much considering my plans for sex and sleep just evaporated. "We were just discussing our favorite spots in town, and now we can get a jumpstart on the tour." I shot a look at Alex and her hastily tied robe. Under my breath, I said, "As soon as we find some clothes."

Alex's mother glanced at my towel and Alex's wet hair.

Her cheeks reddened the same way her daughter's did when I said *cunt*. "In the shower?" she asked.

"That's where I do all my best thinking," Alex said.

Alex's father stared at me, his gaze hard. Maybe a little furious. "And who are you?"

"Riley Walsh." I held out my hand. "I'm going to marry your daughter."

FIVE MONTHS *later*

"OH, YES," I said as I adjusted the cap on her head. "Yes, this is *perfect*."

She threaded her ponytail through the opening at the back. A small smile tugged at the corner of her lips, like she had a secret that she couldn't help but spill. "This is it? This does it for you?"

"Are you kidding me?" I asked, waving at her jeans, Red Sox t-shirt and matching hat. The dark lines of new ink peeked out from her sleeve on the right side, and I swept my knuckles down the jagged edge of Cape Cod. "We're going to opening day at Fenway Park and you're decked out in Boston gear. And you're beautiful and amazing *and* you let me do very rude things to you. This, right here—*you*—you're better than any fantasy." I ran a hand through my hair, considering this. "Let's be real. It's not like you don't enjoy the rude things."

She dropped her hands to her waist, but instead of assuming that fuck-hot hands-on-the-hips pose, she loosened the buttons there. "Are you sure? There's nothing that could make this day better? Nothing at all?"

I cut my eyes to the side and scanned the apartment, in search of some clue to explain this line of questioning. It wasn't like Alex to hopscotch around the point, but nothing caught my attention. She still lived around the corner from the hospital, with Cal downstairs and the new trauma surgeon upstairs. I'd seen the guy—Stremmel—in the hall many times since his arrival last October, and I didn't like him. Ego the size of Australia. Always stomping around up there like a damn ogre.

Alex didn't mind the ego or the stomping. She was too busy being awesome. She was still at the hospital and kicking ass, and now she was in line to take over the gastrointestinal surgery department later this year. She'd insisted she wanted to continue on at this hospital, despite all the shit she'd endured, because it would give her a chance to prevent it from happening in the future. Now, she was finally getting some of the recognition she'd long deserved, and the Three Musketeers of Surgery—her, Cal, and Nick— got to stay together.

Yay for nonstop surgery talk.

I crossed my arms over my chest. "That sounds like a trick question."

She shrugged and tugged her zipper. "What about this?" she asked, wiggling as she edged her jeans down her hips. "Hmm?"

My first thought was that we were kicking off opening day with a bang. Aside from missing the first pitch because *quick* wasn't part of our lifestyle, there was nothing wrong with this approach. We were late to nearly every family gathering, dinner party, and event because we didn't know the first thing about quick. And it wasn't because we didn't know how to get down to business. There'd never been any issues there. But we didn't know how to bounce right out of bed and shake off the intimacy. There was love to make and photos to take, and none of that could be rushed.

We'd been the last to arrive the day Shannon and Will's new baby Annabelle was born, and even four months later, my siblings were still joking about how nothing got us out of bed. And it wasn't about to change. I was certain we'd be late to meet Matt and Lauren's baby come that kiddo's arrival in July. We'd probably hold up the rehearsal dinner before Patrick and Andy's wedding—whenever that happened—and stumble into some shenanigans on the big day.

And I was well on my way to excusing our opening day tardiness when I saw what she was hiding under those jeans.

Batman panties. Fuck me. Fuck *me.*

The Bat Signal was shining on my favorite spot on this planet. And I thought the t-shirt and hat and Massachusetts tattoo were perfect. This was…this was my brain winding up for an explosion if I didn't do something right now.

I pointed at her. "Don't move," I said, pinning her with a heavy stare.

Darting into the bedroom, I made for the closet and the box on the top shelf. It was a spot Alex couldn't reach, not even with the step ladder. Technically speaking, we didn't live together. My name wasn't on the mailbox but I did spend most nights here, and the majority of my clothes had made their way to the closet. We'd talked about making it official here or finding a new place together plenty of times, but then we always found something more interesting to do. The living arrangement discussion bore many similarities to the marriage discussion.

For now, this arrangement was one that worked for us.

"Running away from a woman with her pants down is rather insulting," she called. "Did I blaspheme Batman?"

I returned to the living room, where my woman was exactly as I left her.

"Just tell me if you don't like it," she said, hooking a finger around the waistband. "It's not—"

"You're perfect," I said. "Don't change anything. Ever." I knelt before her and wrapped my arms around her thighs, bringing the Bat Signal to my cheek.

Goddamn, I love this girl.

"What's the deal, Riley? Why are you freaking out and running around the apartment? You freaking out is making me freak out."

"I was going to wait. Do something really nice, like take you on a harbor cruise or to the butterfly landing at Franklin Park, or something special for your birthday. I wanted the right moment."

"We're really bad at the right moments," Alex said, laughing. "We're much better at the wrong ones."

She ran her fingers through my hair, and I looked up, catching a glance at the crooked smile on her face. I shook my head, wishing the words would fall in line.

"Aly," I started, "I—I want, I mean, I love—"

"So you're saying the Batman panties are a hit?" she asked, her eyes sparkling with humor. She dragged her fingers over my scalp again and then brought her palm to the back of my neck.

"You're the most amazing woman in the world. You're

fuck-hot gorgeous when you come home after seventy-two hours on-call. But these panties. Motherfuck. They make me want to bend you over and bang you like a drum. And then watch *The Dark Knight Rises* while eating your cunt." I shook my head once and pressed my forehead to her belly. "Do you even understand how much I love you? Do you have any idea?"

"I have a good idea," she replied. "Do *you* even understand how much I love you?"

I needed her to see how *much* this was. How much we had here, together. How it was everywhere, all around us. How she was the only one, the *only one* I'd ever love with all of me. "Tell me."

"On a scale of elementary school cafeteria hamburgers to In-N-Out Double-Doubles, I'd have to say I love you bacon cheeseburgers from Harry's in Providence."

"That's not on the scale," I replied.

"No," she said. "It's not. It's way, *way* off the chart."

Alex smiled at me, one of those desert-in-bloom, worth-the-fucking-wait smiles that made me want to touch every inch of her and then follow those touches with my tongue, my teeth, my cock. I pushed her shirt up and nipped at the soft rise of her belly. She was going to be the one beside me for decades to come, the one who opened up my wild and gave it space to roam free, the mother of my children.

She was the love of my life, and she was the only one.

"You're wearing Batman underwear and coming to Fenway's opening day with me and I fucking *adore* you," I said, as if that could sum up all of the *everything*. I opened my palm, revealing the necklace I'd hidden in the closet. Thin chain, thick diamond, approved by both Shannon and Erin. "I need you to marry me."

"Wait a minute," she said, holding up a hand. "Are you really doing this right now?"

"I think I am," I said, trying not to choke on my own saliva. I cleared my throat and ran my thumb over the diamond suspended from the platinum chain. "It's not a ring. I know how you feel about rings, but if you want that instead—or both—you can have it. You can have anything you want. I walked around the jewelry store for a few hours last month and saw—"

"Last *month*? This has been in your head since last month?"

"It's been in my head since I climbed your fire escape. Before then, actually," I said. "But I decided it was time to get it out of my head last month. We've been talking about it too long. I want to stop talking and start being married to you."

"Oh," Alex said. The hand she had on the back of my neck trembled.

"And I'd wanted to find the right time and say all the right things, but the only right for us is *right now*," I said. "Promise to keep me for always, and I'll give you everything I have to give, and then I'll find a way to give you more. I love you, and I want you and I need you."

"Riley." She sucked in a breath as she said my name, her chest rising and her eyes bright.

"Aly," I said.

She pressed her fingertips to her lips as she sighed. "Oh, my god. I'm going to marry you."

"Yeah, you are," I said. "Consider it an arrangement of mutual benefit."

. . .

THANK YOU FOR READING! *I hope you loved Alex and Riley's journey. Cal Hartshorn eventually talks to the woman he's adored at the park. He also—accidentally—knocks her down and falls on top of her. Keep reading for a snippet from* Before Girl, *now available.*

IF YOU'RE *ready for a big serving of the Walsh family,* Thresholds *is now available! Keep reading for an excerpt!*

JOIN *my newsletter for new release alerts, exclusive extended epilogues and bonus scenes, and more.*

IF NEWSLETTERS AREN'T *your thing, follow me on BookBub for preorder and new release alerts.*

VISIT MY PRIVATE READER GROUP, *Kate Canterbary's Tales, for exclusive giveaways, sneak previews of upcoming releases, and book talk.*

Vital Signs

Before Girl — Cal and Stella
The Worst Guy — Sebastian Stremmel and Sara Shapiro

The Walsh Series

Underneath It All – Matt and Lauren
The Space Between – Patrick and Andy
Necessary Restorations – Sam and Tiel
The Cornerstone – Shannon and Will
Restored — Sam and Tiel
The Spire — Erin and Nick
Preservation — Riley and Alexandra
Thresholds — The Walsh Family
Foundations — Matt and Lauren

The Santillian Triplets

The Magnolia Chronicles — Magnolia
Boss in the Bedsheets — Ash and Zelda
The Belle and the Beard — Linden and Jasper-Anne

Talbott's Cove

Fresh Catch — Owen and Cole
Hard Pressed — Jackson and Annette
Far Cry — Brooke and JJ
Rough Sketch — Gus and Neera

Benchmarks Series

Professional Development — Drew and Tara
Orientation — Jory and Max

Brothers In Arms

Missing In Action — Wes and Tom
Coastal Elite — Jordan and April

Get exclusive sneak previews of upcoming releases through Kate's newsletter and private reader group, The Canterbary Tales, on Facebook.

about Kate

USA Today Bestseller Kate Canterbary writes smart, steamy contemporary romances loaded with heat, heart, and happy ever afters. Kate lives on the New England coast with her husband and daughter.

You can find Kate at www.katecanterbary.com

facebook.com/kcanterbary

twitter.com/kcanterbary

instagram.com/katecanterbary

amazon.com/Kate-Canterbary

bookbub.com/authors/kate-canterbary

goodreads.com/Kate_Canterbary

pinterest.com/katecanterbary

tiktok.com/@katecanterbary

Acknowledgments

My husband…who knows he's lucky to have me.

Julia…the most professional, constructive, deliberative editor in the business. My writing would be a sloppy bowl of word-spaghetti without her.

Amanda and Robyn…who tirelessly cheer on my journey through each book and don't seem to mind me wondering out loud whether I'm allergic to oatmeal.

The Walshlovers…those with one calm tit and one party tit, those sitting on their grabby hands, and those who've been reading since way back when.

The book community…those bloggers, authors, and readers who've embraced my books and characters, and introduced new readers to them.

My immediate family, and the cousins, aunts and uncles, and others who've been around long enough to be called family…those who read my books and hound others to read them too, those who think they're going to get the spoilers before anyone else, those who joke about my new career writing *porn*, and those who say they can't look at me the same way anymore. (Actually, I am sorry about that last part. I'm sure Riley didn't help matters.)

This is the one instance when my words don't carry the weight I want them to, and I find myself wanting to shower every sentence with all the bold, italicized emphasis.

Thank you. Truly.

And to those wondering if this is the end…there's something terribly unsettled about a prime number.